Also by John Campbell Rees
Winter Squad

SUMMERTIME BLUE

JOHN CAMPBELL REES

THE TIMELESS PRESS

SOUTH WALES

First published in the United Kingdom in 2016 by
The TIMELESS Press, 15, Stuart Street, Treherbert, Rhondda, CF42 5PR.

ISBN-13: 978-0-9576444-6-5

ISBN-10: 0-9576444-6-9

FOR MY FAMILY.

History

*C*ascades of titian ringlets framed and emphasised the palidness of her skin. Isabelle Louise Cartwright was a sickly child, born in an age when so many children failed to reach their fifth birthday. Her parents should have rejoiced when she passed that landmark. Sadly to her family her late appearance, gender and continued survival was an embarrassment.

She loved apples, constantly trying to get the seeds within to germinate and grow, so she would have an apple tree all of her own. She never quite succeeded until one morning in the autumn of 1827 she was presented with a beautiful red apple by her Uncle Francis.

'There you go my dear, what do you make of that?'

'Oh Uncle, it is the most beautiful apple I have ever seen, it seems such a shame to eat it.'

'But Izzy, if you do not eat it, then it will shrivel and go to waste, and you would not want that to happen.'

'No Uncle, I would not.'

Her uncle took a pen-knife from his pocket and cut a sliver from the fruit and handed it to her.

'There you go my dear. Enjoy.'

Her uncle was the only adult who paid Isabelle any attention. He was so unlike her absent Pappa. Many years younger to start, with a pleasant smile always on his face. His hair was ginger like Isabelle's. In fact he was the only other redhead in the normally blonde family. Isabelle looked forward to his *visits. He always brought such interesting gifts and told her such enjoyable stories.*

She thoroughly enjoyed the bright red fruit. It was the most apple-y apple she had ever tasted. She so wanted to grow a tree that would produce identical fruit and was delighted, some time later, when one of the seeds germinated. She poured more love into that tiny scrap of life than anything she had ever known.

There are many alternate realities in the infinite Cosmos. In one alternate reality, Earth is called Arbouron.

Arbouron is many times larger than Earth, as are its trees. These amazing biomechanical constructs, part grown and part manufactured, tower above the planet, extracting life from the thin and chilly atmosphere of the world. Each giant tree starts its life as a seed, a tiny scrap of life.

The Seed planted by Isabelle Cartwright on Earth had its match on Arbouron. Dispatched by its parent tree surrounded by the soft fleshy padding of an apple, it alone had found a safe place to germinate. Its first root went down into the darkness of the soil and began to extract water from the earth around it. This doubled the size of the seed and its Life-force awoke for the first time. Inside the seed, a team of eight Simple Anthrobiotic work units, or Sprites from the parent tree, laboured to build the first components to augment the swelling seed.

The Life-force of the seed knew the internal designation code of each of the Sprites. It regarded them as more than mere tools. He saw each one as an individual to be nurtured, just as they nurtured him. The Sprites did not care about the Life-force, for them only their job mattered.

As the seed became a young plant, so more Sprites were required. These were grown from the body of the plant inside brand new Sprite-pods. The Life-force lavished care on these

Sprites and when they finally noticed the Life-force, the Sprites began to worship him as a god they called "The Spirit of the Tree".

Even within the safety of the soil, there were dangers. The Life-force had access to the combined knowledge of all the trees that had gone before him. He knew how to augment the Sprites that had come from the parent tree. He made them taller, faster and cleverer according to the blueprint for Advanced Anthrobiotic Defence Units. The Life-force hated this name, so called them Anthers. He organised them with ranks and chains of command so they could defend him more efficiently. They were his officers, all blond hair and blue eyes, how handsome they all looked.

*A*rthur Jenkins had worked for the Cartwright family for years. *He had started as an Apprentice Gardener during the reign of Mad King George and had risen to the post of Head Gardener. His skin was almost as brown as the earth the plants he tended grew in. He rarely had much contact with the master and his family, so he had been surprised, one cold Spring morning, to see the daughter of the house walk into his greenhouse carrying a sickly looking twig in a pot.*

'Good morning Mr. Jenkins,' said the girl. That was unusual, the family had never called him Mr. Jenkins before, it had always been either Jenkins or "Gardener".

'A very good morning to you Miss, how may I help?'

'I want to plant my apple tree in the garden, so that it can grow big and strong. Will you help me please?'

Arthur looked at the sad looking stick. It did not have a hope of growing any further. He could see that it did not have the rootstock that would help it thrive.

'I'm happy to help, Miss, but I'm afraid that you may be disappointed,' he replied.

'I have been reading a book in my father's library Mr. Jenkins. It says that it must be grafted onto a stronger rootstock to have any chance.'

'Why yes Miss, we could try that.' The girl was clever, Arthur could see that. He could also see that despite being rich, the girl was poor in so many ways. Her Father constantly away on duty with the Army, she was ignored by her Mother and with her Brothers away at school she was alone in the world.

'I will have to get a suitable root-stock from a local orchard, Miss. This is not the sort of thing I have regularly to hand.'

'Then do it Mr. Jenkins. Young Isabelle here must have her apple tree.'

'Uncle Francis, thank you.' Neither girl nor gardener had noticed the other man approach.

'Leave your plant here, Miss, I will tend to it.' Then turning to the other man. 'The orchard will require payment.

'Don't worry, Mr. Jenkins,' Said Uncle Francis.

It had seemed like an ordinary day to the Life-force. An ordinary day of struggle. No matter how he tried, he could not get its roots to grow in an efficient manner.

From nowhere disaster struck. An alien force split the young plant in two. The stalk and leaves were sent spinning into the great void in one direction, the roots in another. Only twenty-eight Officers and four hundred Sprites survived this catastrophe.

With eighty percent of his workforce lost forever, the Life-force knew it would have to start again. If it could start again, with limited water, heat and building materials.

Then when he thought all hope was lost the stem and leaves came to rest in what remained of another tree. The Life-force had found a new Root-stock, one superior in every way to its old one. The Life-Force could inhabit these roots, control the Sprites he found there and communicate with their officers.

To its utter joy, the plant these roots had originally belonged to had modelled its officers on female humans from one of the nearby realities. The Life-force didn't care for what female humans called themselves, "wimminz" or something equally silly. He had pretty blonde haired blue eyed Root Style Officers to play with now that it was growing again. The inhabitants found their own words to describe the two genders. The males officers remained as Anthers, the female Root Style Officers became Styles.

*M*iss Mary Sarah Hathaway had been appointed by Isabelle's distant Mamma, to be Isabelle's governess.

Three years had passed since the seed had been planted. Isabelle had also grown and Miss Hathaway was entranced by her young charge. How could Isabelle's family ignore a now healthy and strong child with a thirst for knowledge.

The sad little twig had grown into a healthy young tree under the care of Mr. Jenkins. Isabelle never failed to find an excuse to visit the tree every day.

'Isabelle, did you have to drag me all the way out here?' asked the governess.

'I wanted to show you mybeautiful tree in full blossom.'

'I know you love this tree, but it's not as if I have not seen it many times.'

'But look how skilfully Mr. Jenkins and his son have cared for it. When it is fully grown, it will make a pleasant place to sit and enjoy the beauties of this garden.'

'Indeed it will,' replied Miss Hathaway.

'And the way Mr. Jenkins is training the branches will make it so much easier to pick its fruit.'

'Again, you tell me something I already know,' continued Miss Hathaway, with a sigh.

'You should include some of its first fruit in your bridal bouquet when you become my Aunt Mary,' said Isabelle.

Oh good Lord, thought Mary Hathaway, the child is so clever. How had the girl known?. She had worked so hard hiding the growing love between herself and darling Francis. No, Mrs. Cartwright, the girl's mother, disliked her enough already. If she were to find out about the friendship with Francis, she would be sent away, far from the two people she loved the most, Francis and this child.

'Bridal bouquet. Don't be ridiculous my dear. I am not getting married to your Uncle Francis.

'He is your employer now, wouldn't you prefer it if he were your husband?' asked Isabelle.

'Exactly, since your father passed away he has been your guardian. I could not marry him, it would not be proper,' the Governess replied.

'Only until next month, when my brother Alfred celebrates his twenty first birthday and inherits the estate.' Isabelle was smiling. 'I know how much you and Uncle Francis love each other. There will be nothing to stop you then.'

'Oh Isabelle, my dear, you have found our secret. I thought we were hiding it so well.'

'So it is true. I knew it.'

'Yes my dear, it is true. However, you must tell no one."

'It will be my secret also, Aunt Mary. Although I will not call you that until after your big day.'

Lonely, so very lonely. Where were the young Tree's orchard-mates? Why was it growing so far from any other tree? Was the Life-force that inhabited this apple tree to go mad?

The Life-force could only answer one of those questions, and the answer was "no". To that end he had taken the officers, his Anthers and Styles, and given them all names. He had found a way of making each of them different. He delighted in the way they had created rules on what a young cadet officer could call itself. They were such creative little creatures.

The Seed had held an encyclopedic source of information which the Spirit of the Tree had spent many hours reading. He noticed that all his people had the same light blue eye-balls and lash-less eyelids, other part of their appearance depended on where the officer lived in as a Sprite. Each area was given the Human Culture most resembled the appearance of its inhabitants.

The Canopy officers with red hair, green irises and pale skins became Scots/Irish. The inhabitants of the top quarter of the Trunk became Afro-Caribbean in outlook. Mid-Trunk, the next quarter down had officers with a faux Chinese culture. He gave the officers in Lower-Trunk, the third quadrant a South Asian flavour. Those living in the Base, the final quarter, became generic Mediterranean in appearance and outlook. The inhabitants of the Roots and solid mass of wood below ground, that anchored the Tree remained blond haired and blue eyed and so became very Scandinavian in their world view.

The Spirit of the Tree regarded the Canopy Styles as the prettiest of his creations. Far prettier than the ones from the Roots. He had no idea what the long term consequences of his favouritism would be. The Life-force, or the Spirit of the Tree, as his toys called him, was a child. With a child's indifference he did not care that the Officers from the Roots resented the affection he lavished on the Officers from the Canopy. In the years to come, when the Spirit of the Tree's attention moved from his creations, the Root Officers would become dominant and repay every slight they had received by a factor of five to the Canopy Officers, making them second class citizens.

O n Isabelle's tenth birthday, tragedy struck when her distant Mamma died whilst returning from London. Nobody seemed to know what to do with the child. As the months passed she turned in on herself, spending more and more time in the garden of the family estate, sitting beneath her precious apple tree.

'Your governess thought you would be here,' said Aunt Mary. She had a very low opinion of the latest woman to try and fill her shoes. There was still no reply from the child when her husband arrived at the tree.

'Don't you have even a kiss for your Aunt? You used to be so close,' asked her Uncle Francis.

The couple had recently been blessed with their first child, a healthy young boy called George. They had come from their home in Herefordshire to show him off to his relatives.

'Izzy my dear, what is the matter?' asked her Uncle Francis.

'Go away, you don't care for me, nobody does.'

'Izzy, that is not true,' said her Aunt Mary.

'You abandoned me. Just as everyone else has abandoned me.'

'But your Aunt Mary and I love you, when he is older George will love you too. For without you, he would not be here, as we would never have met.'

'All you care about is your new home and your new baby. You are just like Alfred.' The girl was crying now. Her brother had recently married, and just like Uncle Francis, he had become a father. The years of pent up anger turned to tears.

'That silly young fellow has just received a piece of my mind,' said Francis, 'he knows exactly how displeased your Aunt and I are with him.'

Isabelle looked longingly at the two adults. They had been closer to real mother and father than her biological parents. Many times she had wished that they could be her parents.

'All words and no actions,' said Isabelle, 'you shall return home, I shall be forgotten once more and nothing will change.'

'Izzy my dear, your Uncle Francis and I have decided that this is not a good place for you to grow up. Especially if you are to be ignored so thoroughly by Alfred and his silly young wife. We are making arrangements for you to come and live with us in Herefordshire. Would you like that?'

Isabelle was suddenly torn. To be with her beloved Aunt and Uncle again would be wonderful, she had felt so alone when they had moved last Christmas. However, Hereford would be so far away from her tree.

'I can see what you are thinking,' said her Uncle Francis. 'You would be parted from this tree. What a fine specimen it has become.'

This brought a smile to the child's face.

'Do you know Izzy, in Herefordshire we have an orchard? Forty fine cider apple trees and twenty desert apple trees.'

'Sixty trees, that's nearly a forest,' said the child, now excited by the prospect of moving to a new home.

'Also, my lovely, your Uncle knows some powerful men called lawyers.' Aunt Mary was smiling at her, 'we love you like a daughter, and these lawyers can grant a special paper called an adoption, which would make you our daughter in the eyes of the Law, isn't that so Francis?'

'It is indeed,' replied her husband. 'Just to think, at a stroke of a pen, young George would become your real brother.'

'And you and Aunt Mary would be my Pappa and Mamma?' asked Isabelle. 'Really?'

'Yes darling, really.' Aunt Mary smiled. 'So what is it to be my lovely?'

Isabelle thought she could hear a singing. No, that was not possible, The babies George and Henrietta were asleep in the house, and they were too young to sing anyway. Could it be coming from the apple tree? At that moment she felt so much love and happiness, she was almost bowled off her *feet. Her Aunt and Uncle, they loved her so much, of course she would go with them.*

'I shall come with you to Herefordshire, Mamma and Pappa!' The young girl hugged the two overjoyed adults. Her world was now such a better place.

'Oi! Apple Tree, can you hear me?'

Was that a voice from another tree? No it couldn't be, there were no other trees within shouting distance. Since the girl in the Human's Universe had gone, he had nobody to sing to. Only the once he had managed to get through to her, and she left immediately after that. Was his voice that bad?

'Yes, you! Apple Tree! Are you deaf or something?' asked the other voice stridently.

'I don't think so,' replied the Spirit of the Tree.

'Good, so we have managed to repair your connection to the Network,' said an older, calmer voice.

'Looks like it, doesn't it,' said the first voice.

'My connection, the Network? I don't understand.' The Spirit of the Tree was terrified and excited in equal measures.

'We would not expect you to, young tree,' continued the older voice. 'The important thing is you are no longer alone. For some reason you didn't have any singers in your toolkit. I have solved that problem for you.'

'Thank you,' said the Spirit of the Tree.

'Don't mention it,' the older voice replied.

The older tree had made changes without considering the effect on the creatures that lived within the Tree's body. The Singers needed to devote so much of their time to their songs that they could no longer play an active part in normal society.

The Spirit of the Tree had become intrigued by Monasticism. He made the homes for his singers resemble the Abbeys and

Convents of the Middle Ages, filled with Monks and Nuns singing their Gregorian Chants. Establishing religions proved to be a mixed blessing. Having so many highly trained and heavily armed people arguing about religion in such a small space was far from ideal. The Spirit intervened and created a single religion, dedicated to worshipping him.

Years passed, and the now happy child soon became a beautiful young lady. Isabelle eventually married Gilbert Spenser and had children of her own. Like her children, the apple tree prospered. In the summer, she often returned to visit this distant child, it was almost as if the Tree knew she was there, as it grew stronger during her visits. They continued until her brother Alfred gambled the family estate away, in the 1850's. Forty years later the Estate changed hands again. This time a property developer purchased the land. He recognised its potential, being a few miles from Cardiff and close to the increasingly prosperous town of Penarth. He built houses on the site. He reserved the best house with the biggest garden for himself. That garden contained Isabelle's apple tree.

Three generations of the developer's family had cared for the tree before the house had been bought by Harold and Esme Spenser and their young family. Harold Spenser had no idea that he was a descendant of Isabelle Spenser, née Cartwright, a connection between him and the venerable old plant in his new garden. Becoming the owner of a fine tree like this had been the main factor in deciding to buy the house. He loved the appletree as much as his ancestor had. It was the pride and joy of a man with no horticultural talents.

One hundred and eighty five years had passed since the seed had first been planted by a lonely little girl. On our world, the date was 15th March, 2012. Harold Spenser took his daily walk to examine the Tree. The nights were noticeably shorter and the days noticeably warmer. He could see the trees and bushes in the street were covered with swollen buds which would soon burst into flower or leaf. The precious apple tree was undoubtedly the finest plant in the street. It too sat on the cusp of new life. The experts from the local University had done wonders pruning and overhauling it the previous year. If only the upcoming Spring and Summer would be warm and dry then everything would be perfect.

PART ONE
GEOGRAPHY

CHAPTER ONE
ENDS AND BEGINNINGS

Harold Spenser had no idea that his apple tree, just like every tree on Earth, is merely the tip of a multi-dimensional iceberg. That sideways in time and space, in a reality where the Earth is known as Arbouron, his tree existed on a much grander scale. On Earth, the solid trunk measured five foot from ground level to the Crown where it separated into the branches of the canopy. The highest twig is ten feet above the ground. Every inch of the Tree in our World equalled one mile on Arbouron. So the Trunk towered sixty miles over the surface of Arbouron before splitting into a maze of branches. The highest tip of the highest twig was a further sixty miles above the surface, giving the Tree of Life a total height of one hundred and twenty miles.

Within this colossus there is a complex ecosystem that supports an advanced civilisation. For the inhabitants of the Tree the date 15th March, 2012 was meaningless. In their calender, it was Sunday Camma of Rydtemp, 184 Years After the Graft. Today was the last day of the last week of the third month in a year that started the day after the Winter Solstice.

After the Equinox Holiday, the Canopy's population would all have returned home ending their Winter exile. The branches, twigs and leaves at the top of the Tree would once more be a huge industrial hub.

The Tree's apparent return to life actually began about a month after the Solstice, when the first batch of Leaf Builders and Flower Fabricators arrived in the Canopy, to work within the Bud Chambers on the branches of the Tree.

They had been delayed this year. A month long war against an invading virus that called itself the Glory prevented any travel through the ten miles of solid wood that separated the Trunk from the Canopy. The Winter Squad, the branch of the Maintenance Regiment that cleaned up after the previous Spring and Summer and prepared for the next year had fought the invader. They had prevailed, but at a terrible cost. Three of the Squad's forty two members had been killed and two had received life threatening injuries. With the crystalline alien defeated, the already exhausted Winter Squad had begun to repair the damage done by the virus.

When the Leaf Builders reported back to the Roots the ruling High Council knew that the Winter Squad should receive all the praise they so valiantly deserved. A special ceremony had been arranged to honour the dead of the Winter Squad and award the survivors a medal for gallantry. The Tree Marshall, the most senior officer in the Tree would be there, as would the whole Council. For many of these high ranking officials it would be their first visit to the Canopy. Power rested in the Roots, and the High Council usually stayed where the power was.

'Well, this makes a nice change,' said Ensign Tabbernant, 'usually the Squad slink back to base in the Roots tired and hungry.'

Tabbernant was the oldest member of the Squad, an anther, a male mature Tree Person. Today he was due to retire. Although age had turned his hair grey, it was due to his infamous disciplinary record, he remained an Ensign. By becoming a Pensioner overnight he would go from being the lowest of the low to the highest of the high. This seemed to magnify the twinkle in his deep blue eyes.

'They think they can buy us off with this cheap Dog and Pony Show,' said Commander Sharlensya, 'a few minutes of theatre with nothing to follow,' she was a Style, a female mature Tree Person. Her height was the first thing most people noticed, as she was taller than average, with a head turning figure and beautiful face to match. Despite looking like a super-model, she was a Mentor, a school teacher who taught Officer Cadets during their frighteningly rapid sixteen week adolescence.

'It's not going to work though. Old Myghcomant has got them by the short and curlies this time. He's a war hero, a celebrity. We all are. The ordinary Officer Corps members will listen to what he has to say and support him.' Tabbernant grinned.

'So what difference does that make?' asked Sharlensya 'why does the Winter Squad's Commanding Officer suddenly have all the cards?'

'The Bean Counters could only ever get away with stuffing us because Squad business is usually printed at the bottom of page nine of any newspaper, beneath the story of a skateboarding cat. This year, we saved the Tree. Winter Squad business will be front page news.'

Sharlensya had to agree. The accountants in the Roots would not dare query any request the Commanding Officer of the Winter Squad submitted this year.

'He wants to double the size of the Winter Squad as well. Which means I will be busy as there will be eight cadets in my class next year instead of the usual four,' said Sharlensya.

'But you will be one of "Them" next Winter. When you are confirmed as the Matriarch of Family Fangkart, you will have your family's seat on the Council and a full-time job down in the Roots,' said Tabbernant ruefully.

Colonel and Matriarch Sylmransya, the seventh head of Family Fangkart, had died quietly on the morning of the Treequake. Tragically it also cut short the life of her heir, Captain Sannarlsya Fangkart, so the title passed to the next in line, the Captain's daughter, Sharlensya. The new Matriarch-Elect would gladly have exchanged this unwanted title for the life of her beloved mother.

'A time consuming job, yes, a full time one, no. The Council only meets for twenty weeks a year I'll be able to do both jobs. Anyway, Cousin Sendarnsya is more than happy to continue as Matriarch's Voting Deputy whilst I'm posted up here. After all, she has been Matriarch in all but name for years,' said Sharlensya, with a touch of sadness. 'It is only because of a technicality she is not the Matriarch-Elect now, instead of me.'

'She's no spring chicken herself, is she Shaz?' asked Tabbernant, slipping into the informal use of the shorter and punchier names he used instead of the official gobstoppers.

'No Bernie, but she knows the job and does it well. I know my job, and have been told I do it well. This arrangement suits us both perfectly.'

Both officers laughed and went their separate ways. Tabbernant continued on to the main parade ground. Sharlensya had to make a detour.

Two Weeks Earlier:

'There we go,' said Captain Jomlirdant, 'the last flower node plumbed into the matrix.'

'The instruments show it has been primed and is ready, Sir,' said Sprite NR251/07 as it packed away its tools and laughed. 'You can now return to base, whilst I return to the Roots.'

'Are you excited, NR251/07?' asked the Officer.

'Yes, Sir. I am excited. Sorry, the Sprite is excited.'

'It's alright NR251/07, you don't have to worry about speaking in the third person any more.'

Technically sprites are the immature form of the Tree People who could be trained to do one job well. If like NR251/07 they were one of the ten percent capable of more, they became fully formed Tree People. In the Trunk and Canopy all sprites are regularly tested to see if they have this potential.

'Thank you, Sir,' replied NR251/07. Unusually, it wanted to remain as a Sprite, it was good at its job and liked the officers it worked with and had discovered it could now lie to keep them happy.

'You're nervous about the change, aren't you NR251/07?' Captain Jomlirdant and his wife Captain Raddconsya had been working together for years and they had come to rely on this Sprite because it was so efficient. They had not been a surprise when NR251/07 had passed the regular test for Officer Training. 'Change is good, but it doesn't have to be too big. When you have finished your Officer Training, you will have to choose a career.'

'Career, Sir?'

'Yes, it's the job you want to do after you get your commission.'

'Are you saying I could come back here and work with you and Captain Raddconsya?'

'I don't want to put pressure on you, but yes, you could become an apprentice Leaf and Flower Builder, you already have a good grounding.'

'Oh thank you, Sir,' said the Sprite.

'So have you chosen a name yet?' The officer asked.

'Yes, Sir. My rootname shall be Nostrom,' it replied. 'The new version of the test says I will be a style, so I will be Nostromsya.'

'Well Nostromsya, let's head back to base.'

'Yes, Sir.'

All Sprites, regardless of what some Rootborn Tree-people might say are created identical. Their bodies all have the same genetic pattern. They are all the same height, have the same basic facial features and the same voice. The only way to tell them apart is by the registration code tattooed above their right ear, which fades on activation.

A creature called a Key changes the lucky Sprite's body. The process that releases the Sprite's potential adds a series of random factors to the genetic pattern, giving Tree-people a variety of body shapess. It also activates the part of the pattern unused in Sprites, thus separating males from females Environmental factors would also alter the Sprite's genetic pattern.

Early in its history, the controlling Spirit of the Tree saw that a further set of modifications was needed to the body of a Tree-person when they reached the age of eighteen months. It salvaged the method for creating fully formed Tree-people that had been used by the Root-stock prior to the graft, for this purpose. A style underwent a pseudo-pregnancy, hosting the development of a creature called a Lock within her body for nine weeks. In the Rootstock, when the Lock was "born", it would attach itself to a Sprite, turning it into an adult, now it attached itself to and upgrade an unmodified adolescent tree-person. Not surprisingly this created a strong emotional bond between the "mother" and "child". It also passed on the unique signature whether male or female. In subsequent generations this signature was passed on by all the "daughters", when they became "mothers" to their "children". Thus creating the twenty-eight Families.

Two Weeks Later:
There is nothing remotely masculine about me,' said Subaltern Nevamarsya 331/29 as she sprayed the lower half of her body with a thick foam. 'No, nothing masculine at all.'

Immediately the mild depilatory in the spray dissolved any hair on her legs. Most cloth in the Tree is made of Emprintable Fabric. Consisting of millions of microscopic Brethinite spheres held together by an electrostatic charge. The Fabric Emprinter built into the full length mirror took an electrostatic hold off the tiny Brethinite sphere in the foam, turning it first to raw emprintable fabric and then into a pair of opaque grey tights.

From the perspective of the Human world, Nevamarsya appeared to be a seventeen year old young woman, but within this tree on Arbouron, the truth was very different. Six months earlier she had been an interchangeable cloned Sprites, a leaf operator on one of the high branches of the Tree. Over the past six months she had transformed into the young style admiring her reflection. Nevamarsya had only been female for three months, the process of gender assignment, which should have occurred the day she began to grow had been delayed by illness. A wrong-headed belief that she was destined to be an anther meant she was still catching up with her contemporaries, who had started being female from day one.

'Not even remotely masculine,' she repeated as she slipped on a light green blouse. Buttoning it concealed her bra, but not the swell of her breasts. 'My, how you two have grown,' she said with a giggle.

However, her claim she was not remotely masculine was not completely true. Few styles were taller than five point seven height units [five foot eight and a half inches]. At five point eight four height units [five foot ten inches], Nevamarsya was as tall as an average anther.

Nevamarsya turned from the mirror and surveyed her dressing table. Sitting there was her tiara. Even though it was only protein glass and cheap wire, Nevamarsya loved it. She picked it up and slid it into her hair, which the day's dress code demanded be worn up in a large sock bun on the crown of her head. Memories of the party at New Year's Eve, when she had finally accepted she was female flooded in. The tiara had been borrowed from a lost property box, where it had sat unloved for many years. Her darling boyfriend Pemisegant had bought it for her soon afterwards. She loved him so much.

'And, I look so good in a skirt, even a green regulation uniform skirt like this one,' she said to no-one in particular, as she removed the tiara.

The jacket came next. It looked as new and highly pressed as the skirt, because like every other piece of clothing Nevamarsya possessed it was created from scratch every time it was worn. Tiny pulses from the emprinter made minute adjustments to the garment, so it would fit perfectly.

'Oh bother,' Nevamarsya said to no one in particular. Her dyspraxic fingers were having problems with the four small buttons on the inside of her jacket. They invisibly held the front of the jacket in place so the remaining flap of material could be buttoned into place on her right hand side. The six shiny external metal buttons were just as hard for her to close. She had poppers and velcro fasteners to adapt her civilian clothes. Uniforms still had buttons and never formed fully fastened. The Quartermaster Stores, who had made then scanned the original uniform this one had been copied from, allowed no adaptations. They still refused to accept Dyspraxia even existed.

The external metal buttons looked like they were polished each day until they shone. This was not the case as buttons, clasps Velcro fasteners and zips, in fact all non-fabric components of clothing were made of emprintable resin. Shoes were made of a mixture of fabric and resin. The Formal Dress Uniform with oodles of golden resin brocade looked pretty spectacular.

'You know, you cannot spend all day looking at yourself in that mirror Neva, no matter how much you want to,' Serynazsya said. She would Nevamarsya's older sister after the formal adoption. 'This stupid ceremony is starting in thirty minutes.'

The transfusion of hormone rich blood that had saved Nevamarsya's life, and kick-started her transformation had come from Serynazsya's mother Sharlensya. This was why, with every passing day, Nevamarsya looked more and more like the other girl. In the Tree adoption was biological as well as legal.

'OK, Serah,' Nevamarsya turned away from the mirror and left her room. 'I'm sure this ceremony won't be that long. Then we are on holiday for two weeks.'

'Lush, Oniswanant Resort in the Trunk, including a huge Equal Day fireworks display. Then finally I get to study in the Sacred Sisterhood Hospital's School of Nursing.' It had always been Serynazsya's ambition to become a nurse, she had begun her studies in the Winter Squad's tiny Medical Centre, so she was looking forward to proper training in the most prestigious hospital in the Roots.

'Do you have to spoil it all by mentioning work?' This would be Nevamarsya's first proper holiday, and she was determined to enjoy every second of it.

'I suppose that was a bit full on. Yes, the holiday, I am so going to enjoy it.'

The sound of the front door slamming must mean someone else was now in the apartment.

'Are you girls ready, I want to be at the Parade Ground early?' This confirmed the inquisitive newcomer was their mother.

'Yes Mam, the girls replied in unison.

Nevamarsya did not think she would ever tire of calling the older style her mother. That she would never tire of having a family, even though she was yet to be formally adopted.

'And indeed you are,' said Sharlensya as her ordinary uniform began transforming into the garish Formal Dress Uniform as soon as she was in range of the fabric emprinter. 'I wish I was. I haven't done my hair yet.'

Sharlensya carefully pulled the trichoplast hair-styler out from its tank, with programming tongs. It was one of the many bio-mechanical devices found in the Tree. An augmented crustacean with a metal carapace with flashing LEDs and sockets for its computer components. The tongs interfaced the creature and it was hard to believe it was natural. Placed on Sharlensya's head, the trichoplast's computer augmented brain drove naturally occurring pincers, more sensitive than anything built, to undo the long fishtail plait Sharlensya was currently wearing. Within minutes that task was completed and it began a complicated dance tieing and pinning Sharlensya's hair into a bun that matched her two daughters. Once it was finished Sharlensya returned it to its home. She dropped a snack in the water to feed the creature. The trichoplast reverted back to animal as the biological components retook control. As skilfully as it had manipulated Sharlensya's hair, it stalked its prey, pouncing on the shrimp and devouring it.

'I hate that thing,' said 'Serynazsya, and I would hate to meet its larger unaugmented cousins that live wild in the Central Channels.'

'There is little chance of that dear,' said Sharlensya. 'To flush those brutes out would require a massive flood somewhere in the Tree.'

'Good,' said Serynazsya.

'You still use it though, don't you dear?' asked Sharlensya.

'Unlike you two, I have learned to do my hair myself.'

'Are you sure you're not training with the Hairdressers Regiment?' asked Nevamarsya, 'You have a real flair.'

The sound of laughter filled the room.

Before there had been officers, there had been Sprites, before there had been Sprites there were the Sprite-pods. The twenty six Sprite-pods were specially adapted buds from the Tree, making all Tree-People the Children of the Tree.

The core of a Sprite-pod lasts for roughly a quarter of a century. Then the Sprite-pod receives a new core primed with material taken from the other Sprite-pods, keeping the population of the Tree rich and diverse. However, two of the Sprite-pods are primed only with genetic material predating the Graft. A year previously the core of Sprite-Pod "D" had been replaced with a cutting of its previous core and it continues to produce Anthers identical to those from the original Sapling. The core of the other special pod, designated Sprite-pod "S", was primed with material that came from the Root-stock before the Graft, it only produced styles. These special Sprite-pods were two of the six Officer Only pods of the Root. Unlike the Canopy and Trunk, only the sprites grown specifically to become officers reached their full potentionial.

The current core of Sprite-pod "S" was coming to the end of its useful life after only seven years. The previous core had lasted for ten years. It was believed that the source material was worn out and a two thirds infusion of new genetic material was required. Enough new material to give the core longevity, but retaining enough of the existing genetic material to keep it exclusively female. A small minority, born from Sprite-pod "S" found this notion abhorent.

We've had another miscarriage in Sprite-Pod "S", Ma'am,' said Subaltern Synzbarsya, a worried looking young style medical technician. 'It looked fine this morning, but the Sprite-sack has died and is being ejected from the pod.'

Is there a mosquito in here, thought Symbzamsya, as she noticed a low whining buzz. I will have to run through the hygiene protocol. I had a cup of that muck this morning, that is never a good sign. Well, at least I don't have to drink it every day like my friend Kilkennsya, whose enzyme deficiency is really bad.

'That's three duds in as many weeks! No new sacks forming?' asked Chief Inspector Sylvkohsya, the recently appointed Head of Security at the Sprite Production Centre.

'Yes Ma'am.' replied Symbzamsya, 'I'm afraid this might be the end for that Sprite-pod and the end of an era.'

'Indeed it might be Subaltern. Unless we act quickly. We must take a full core sample and use it to grow the Primer for the new Sprite-pod "S".'

'What, you really want me to do it?' asked the horrified med-tech.

'Of course, we have discussed it many times,' said the Chief Inspector.

'As an academic exercise yes. We can't actually do it Ma'am. I thought you wanted to know more about your new posting. I didn't realise you actually planned on going against the High Council. They want the new Sprite-pod "S" to be as cosmopolitan as a normal Sprite-pod. They did agree it would be female only, so they aren't completely breaking with tradition.'

'I was merely probing to see which of the medtechs here could do the job. You said you knew what had been done wrong last time. That you would not repeat those mistakes.'

'Sure, I can do it. I could do a better job in my sleep. But that didn't mean I would do it.'

The volume of the buzzing had increased. Was she imagining it, the old witch seemed to be totally unaware of the noise.

'Do you have any loyalty to the Pure-stock, girl? Or is

that just for show?' The older style pointed towards the medtech's hair. 'You wear your blonde hair as defined by the Pure-stock Code.'

'Yes Ma'am,' replied Subaltern Symbzamsya. 'Wearing my hair like this is usually useful camouflage for avoiding people like you.'

'Regardless of what you think, we cannot allow the last link with the World before the Graft to be broken,' said the Chief Inspector. 'So, to hell with the Council, I am making it a direct order.'

Every job in the Tree had a military structure, where one officer could order a subordinate and expect instant obedience. Subaltern Symzbarsya knew the order was illegal, it was her duty to refuse.

'The Council outranks you, Ma'am,' replied Symzbarsya.

All of the Root born officers from Sprite-Pods "D" and "S" belonged to the Pure-stock Caste. Many ignored this fact. However, a large minority took it very seriously. They lived their lives according to a strict Code of Conduct that stated through their connection to the World before the Graft, they were the natural leaders of the Tree.

'Through our heritage we take our rightful place at the head of the Officer Corps, maintaining the supremacy of the Roots. Without us, there would be anarchy.'

'You do realise this is the Nineteenth Decade, and nobody outside of your crazy cadre gives two stuffs about that sort of thing,' said the younger style as she left the lab.

Symbzamsya had arranged to take this afternoon off weeks ago, when Sprite-pod "S" started its terminal decline. She was the only medical technician capable of saving an unadulterated Sprite-pod "S", so did not want to be in the lab at when it happened. Each passing minute was taking her further from her lab. By the time she came back to work in the morning there would be no problem following the High Council's order, only forty percent would be salvagable. Material from other pods would be necessary for the replacement pod.

Rats, she had left her glasses. She would have to go back.

'Changed your mind,' said the Chief Inspector. 'I knew you would.'

'Only for my glasses,' Symbzamsya replied.

'So not for the Code?'

'You know what they say about Root Styles like us, that we're stupid. Well that's only true about Pure-stock Styles,' she laughed. 'You lot live by your Code because you're too thick to think for yourself,' she laughed again. 'I activated shortly after Sandampsya's aborted coup. When the Pure-stock Academies were closed. I had no problem in rejecting your silly Pure-stock Code.' Symbzamsya snorted contemptuously. 'I'm amazed the Council ever let the Pure-stock Academies re-open.'

There was something odd about the Chief Inspector's voice, it had a strange metallic undertone. The older style had picked up a black metal box. Subaltern Symbzamsya now recognised it as an illegal Psycho-Modulator. She also knew her medical history made her one of the few people in the Tree it would have no affect on.

'So, back to old fashioned methods of persuasion.' The Chief Inspector was pointing a gun at her. 'Now make the cutting.'

'No!' said Symbzamsya. 'And you won't shoot me because I am the only person who can do the job properly.'

The weapon discharged. 'No, but I can injure you, so you can't run,' said the older style. 'Don't worry, its only a flesh wound, but now you know I'm serious.'

With a pain-killer patch on her leg, Symbzamsya set to work. Why me, she thought miserably. Why did I have to be on duty today. More importantly, why didn't I just keep on walking, I have a spare pair of glasses at home.

Symbzamsya had no doubt she was a good as dead. What was happening today must be part of something larger and far more sinister. She had made it perfectly clear she was not a willing conspirator. The Chief Inspector's Psycho-Modulator could not brainwash her. The only way that bitch could guarantee her silence was by killing her when she was no longer useful to the conspirators.

There was a level of activity in the Crown that had been missing for six months. For the upcoming festival, everything was awash with pastel Summertime Blue, the colour of the sky on a sunny day, and of happiness within the Tree. In addition to the first wave of returning Summer residents, came the cavalcade of officials and flunkies that accompanied the High Council wherever it went. The most high profile being the Enforcers Regiment's Special Protection Service, whose job it was to protect the Tree Marshall and the High Council from anyone with a grievance and a weapon. Guns might be plentiful but it also stored securely.

Unfortunately for Tree Marshall Pentwynsya, one of the SPS had a grievance and a weapon. Given his job, Inspector Dayvaiyant had unique access to the Tree Marshall and was quite prepared to die for his cause.

Deep down Inspector Dayvaiyant felt nothing but contempt for the Tree Marshall. He followed a new and radical political theory developed by an anther called Misogynant, who said Anthers were in all ways superior to Styles, who should adopt their natural second class status. Dayvaiyant hid his belief in Misogyny, believing a silent majority of anthers did the same. Soon there would be a revolution that would sweep away gender equality and put anthers in charge.

CHAPTER TWO

ASSASSINATION

Dear sweet Tree preserve me, thought Nevamarsya, this is duller than dull. How was it possible to make something so terrifying to live through seem so tedious?

Her friend Natalicsya's heroism, losing her left leg and having a new one grafted sounded so run of the mill here. Natalicsya had insisted on attending the ceremony, standing throughout. She radiated her pain like a beacon, and was becoming uncomfortable for Nevamarsya who had the Gift of Empathy.

Nevamarsya could see beyond the mask and feel another person's true emotions. People opened up to her and told her things they would normally never dream of telling another. Many Tree-People saw it more as a curse than a blessing and were uncomfortable in an empath's presence at the best of times. Someone was whipping up fear of Empaths, so Nevamarsya kept her gift well hidden.

'Finally,' intoned the Tree-Marshall, 'we remember Subaltern Roseteesya 407/35 Floom, who has been under the care of neurologists in the Roots.' The Tree-Marshall paused for effect. 'She survived an encounter with the enemy but has paid a terrible price. The specialist treatments she has received, have restored as many of her memories as possible. She has chosen to start a new life as a Tree-Nun, having been accepted as a novice by the Sisterhood.'

Tell us something we don't know, though Nevamarsya. Rosie had been wearing a purple and blue Aspirant's armband as long as she had known her.

The Tree-Marshall closed the book she was reading from. 'I call upon the Winter Squad's Pastor, Brigadier Rumsfelant to lead us in a prayer of remembrance for the members of the Squad who had lost their lives in the conflict.

Then the Tree-Marshall pinned a campaign medal onto the chests of a very proud Winter Squad. Was that the end of the Ceremony? No such luck.

The Tree-Marshall moved into yet another long speech, but General Myghcomant 200/01 Islaw didn't care. He had written most of it. All the long overdue upgrades and improvements the Winter Squad he had been requesting for years. He knew this year they would not be blocked by the Rootbound.

'After the sacrifices of the past, we must move onto the future,' intoned the Tree-Marshall. 'This viral incursion has shown us all the true value of the work done by the First Battalion of the Maintenance Regiment, and therefore as of today, its size will be doubled and its budget substantially increased. For too long it has been called upon to make savings. We now see the error...'

'Tree-Marshall, Ma'am. Look out!' he shouted. He had spotted something out of the corner of his eye. A light flashing on in an empty building. A silhouette of an anther with a rifle. Was he imagining things? He didn't care if he looked foolish afterwards, now he was running with his instincts. The General broke rank and pushed the Tree-Marshall from the dais.

The retort of a high powered rifle filled the parade square. The Tree-Marshall was bundled to safety, but the General remained on the ground.

'Quick, bring me my bag,' shouted Colonel Keltonnant, the Squad's doctor, who had been standing next to the General. His niece and nephew, Commanders Voynvarant and Voynvalsya, the twin nurses, were already loosening the General's blood stained uniform and making him comfortable. Their own pristine dress uniforms were now also smattered with red.

'He has been hit in his abdomen,' said the Colonel, as he removed a portable scanner from his bag. 'Fortunately, the bullet has missed all the major organs.'

'An ambulance is on its way, Sir,' said one of the bodyguards.

'What the hell are you still doing here, shouldn't you be out catching the maniac that did this?' asked Colonel Keltonnant.

'This area needs to be made secure. Please Colonel, I don't question your medical judgements,' said the Lieutenant.

'I'm sorry, Lieutenant. I thought I had seen all the mayhem imaginable for this year,' regreting his outburst.

'Sir.' said the bemused Lieutenant.

The bleeding had stopped but the General was still deathly pale. Colonel Keltonnant could hardly hear his patient's ragged breathing. An ambulance was on its way, the sound of its rotors drowning out everything else.

Nostrom cursed its luck. It had taken a wrong turn about twenty minutes earlier. It knew it must have come up from the warren of service tunnels under the Central Officer's Residential Centre into one of the buildings surrounding the Central Parade Ground, but it had no idea which one. This building was a worse maze than the one it had emerged from. Nostrom was desperate to get out and onto the Parade Ground so that it could take its place at the ceremony. Once the ceremony was over, it would travel down to an Academy, becoming a female Officer Cadet en route.

First, however, Nostrom had to get to the Ceremony. Why did this building have no lighting? Was it ever going to get to a stairwell and out into the fresh air and light?

At last, an unlocked door. Sure enough, a window overlooking the parade ground, and a light switch. The room filled with light, it spotted the Enquirer officer with a very large rifle at his shoulder. It was Inspector Dayvaiyant a minor celebrity and major heart-throb throughout the Tree. What was he doing here? It heard the Officer swear, and then fire the gun. A warning bell sounded in Nostrom's head and it started running. Desperately stumbling around identical corridors in the dark, hoping to find somewhere to hide.

'Is it done?' asked Chief Inspector Sylvkohsya.

'Yes Ma'am,' Subalternamsya said blandly. 'The core cutting I was forced to make has been accepted by the matrix of the Nursery. Within a week it will be ready for use as the new core for Sprite-pod "S". A Sprite-pod producing Officer Only Sprites with the same genetic pattern as the old Sprite Pod S. Blonde, beautiful and 100% female.'

'Excellent,' said Chief Inspector Sylvkohsya. 'A new generation of Pure-stock Sprites for the Roots' Officer Crèche.'

'Yes Ma'am,' agreed Symbzamsya, keeping a straight face.

'Our place as the superior power-bloc within the Officer Corps is preserved. No contamination of this priming material will take place. But unlike you, they will be pure in thought and deed as well as pure in body.'

It was no good. This triggered a hoot of laughter from the medtech, as she pressed the send button on her comconsole.

'Did you really emerge from Sprite-pod "S"?' asked the Chief Inspector.

'Yes, unfortunately.'

'Well, when the new Tree-wide order is established, your sisters in the lost generation will be re-educated,' said Chief Inspector Sylvkohsya.

'Oh dream on. You lot are so pathetic. My best friend Kilkennsya is from the Canopy, she's a great style and I don't see myself as superior to her in any way, shape or form. My boyfriend Kylvorvant is from the Trunk.'

'You disgust me, girl.'

'And you disgust me, Chief Inspector,' said the young style.

The Chief Inspector's comlink chimed.

'This is our Agent of Change, the Tree-Marshall is dead. Now is the time we make our move, and return the Tree to sanity and order.'

As the conversation continued the Chief Inspector became angrier, and the muffled voice at the other end of the com-link grew more concerned.

'Oh. That makes things so much simpler.' The irony was dripping from the Chief Inspector's every word. 'OK. Go and cover your tracks. I have the details of NR251/07 here. It's one of the backlog of activations. I will deal with the sprite. It will never get the chance to report to an academy. Arranging a tragic accident before its activation will be a piece of cake.'

'Still with us then?' asked the Chief Inspector once she had cut the comlink.

'You deadlocked the door, I tried but couldn't get out.'

'So, too stupid to think for myself am I?' Chief Inspector Sylvkohsya said, quoting Symbzamsya's barb. 'At least I would have run away, when I had the chance.'

'You'll have to run. For how long though? Your little coup attempt has gone tits up now, hasn't it? Instead of the

Tree-Marshall, you have shot one of the Heroes of the Winter Squad. They are going to be after you.' It had not been a great feat of detection to work out what had happened.

'No dear, we learnt from Brigadier Sandampsya's mistake. Only I know who all the plotters are and there is no way to link me to the conspiracy. I'm as clean as a whistle.'

No you're not, Ssymbzamsya thought. As well as working on the cutting, she had produced a package of evidence about today's events. She had just sent it to her family and friends, they would take it too the authorities.

'Sorry dear, you know that message you have just tried to send from here,' the Chief Inspector said as the weapon also spoke. Symbzamsya fell to the floor. 'It has just been completely scrambled. Beyond recovery!' Sylvkohsya planted her heavy brown leather boot into the dying girl's belly. 'Contrary to what you said, I am not more stupid than average. You on the other hand were. In life you were a traitor to your kind, but your death will be useful. You will become the only conspirator the authorities can trace.' The Chief Inspector began to expertly decorate the scene. 'When they interview me, I will tell them I discovered you making an illegal cutting, something you constantly talked about. We struggled and your weapon accidentally discharged and you shot yourself. How very like a Root Style,' the Chief Inspector callously kicked again, just to make sure Symbzamsya's body was beyond repair. 'You might have lived a traitor, but thank the Tree you did not die one,' she laughed. In a few weeks it will start producing Sprites, and will by default become the new Sprite-pod "S".

Symbzamsya heard laughter as the cold darkness claimed her.

N ostom had found a crawl space behind a wall, and had been able to see Lieutenant Dayvaiyant walk into the room. It had hoped that he would walk back out again if he thought the room was empty.

No such luck, the anther had sat down at a desk and called his accomplice. It was all it could do to stopitself gasping as it listened to the conversation.

'I missed,' he said.

'What do you mean you missed? You never miss!' said the distorted voice of his conspirator.

'General Myghcomant, he must have spotted something. Put himself in between the bullet and the Tree-Marshall.

'You idiot. He's a war hero. They are going to redouble their efforts to find you.'

'A stray sprite wandered into where I had set up. Switched a light on. That must have been what Myghcomant saw.

'It gets worse. There was a witness, you say?'

'Yes a stray sprite. It ran off as I was firing. Its vanished.'

'A sprite. You do realise that there are over two point five million of them in the Tree. Its like looking for a needle in a haystack.'

'But only a handful of those sprites are wearing a girls Officer Cadet's uniforms. I managed to take down part of its IndesnCode. It was NP215'

'Oh. That makes things a lot simpler.' The irony was dripping from every word. 'OK. Go and cover your tracks. I have the details of NR251/07 here. It's one of the backlog of activations. I will deal with the sprite. It will never get the chance to report to an academy. Arranging a tragic accident before its activation will be a piece of cake.'

To Nostrom's relief, Lieutenant Dayvaiyant left the room. It heard his receding footsteps and was satisfied that the officer had left the building. Nostrom emerged from hiding.

It was now experiencing regular pulsing waves of nausea.

Shortly after passing the test for Officer Training, she had been fitted with a neckband that monitored its health whilst it waited for the Activation. Almost as soon as it had been fitted it had chafed Nostrom's skin so badly Captain Jomlirdant placed it on a loser lanyard which had stopped the chafing. It could feel it warming up. and threw it as far as it could. While in mid-air, the neckband emitted a spark of blue light then laid lifeless after landing on the floor.

Over the past two weeks, the couple had treated her like a child, their child. She no longer slept in the Sprite cupboard, but in her own bed. She had dresses and a little red wig to wear off duty. They called her Nostromsya. She wanted to go back to them, but she knew that would put them in danger.

No-one would listen to the story of a sprite. No-one ever did. Right thought Nostrom, getting to somewhere safe was its first priority. Somewhere the anther Dayvaiyant would never think of looking for it. Somewhere down in the Roots, where sprites without function and those looking for a new assignment were ten a penny. That was where it would go.

Nevamarsya was in shock. If the General were to die now, having survived the carnage of the Viral Invasion it would be a sick joke. The presence of Lieutenant Dayvaiyant was not helping. There was something about him that she did not like. Nevamarsya supposed that he was only doing his job. It was a shame, she thought, he could not have done it better an hour earlier.

'So, you did not see anything untoward at the ceremony this afternoon?' he asked.

'No, nothing at all, I was standing to attention, looking forward, showing off all the training I have been receiving in the past six months, Sir.'

'Have you any idea what tipped off the General.'

'None whatsoever, Sir.' Now she really didn't like this anther. 'It is fortunate for everyone he noticed, otherwise the situation could have been so much worse,' she could feel herself filling up with tears. The General had been one of the few constants, in her short life. He had ordered that she should undergo the test she had passed with flying colours. Because of him Nevamarsya was now an Officer. General Myghcomant was a rock that everything else in her life was built upon.

'Don't worry. He is as tough as old boots, he will pull through this.' The Lieutenant offered her his handkerchief, but it meant nothing to him. In his next breath he said, 'I think that is all for the moment.' Then got up and left the room.

Inspector Dayvaiyant was still on edge. He had never missed in his life, his kills had always been clean. He was cursing himself that Tree-Marshall Pentwynsya was still alive. At least all the fuss about General Myghcomant had allowed him to cover his tracks, and now taking witness statements meant that he could clean up any loose ends.

'Thank you for your consideration Inspector,' said Commander Sharlensya. 'It has been a tough time for my daughter, she has been through so much and she is still so young.'

'I have yet to speak to Subaltern Serynazsya 120/06, Ma'am. Subaltern Nevamarsya 331/29 is listed as unattached,' said Inspector Dayvaiyant.

'No, I do mean young Nevamarsya,' she was smiling. 'I received confirmation from the Family Planning Bureau this morning. My application to adopt young Neva has been ratified. Since 0600 today, Nevamarsya 331/29 is legally a Child of Family Fangkart and my Half-Daughter,' Sharlensya explained. 'Thirteen months from now, Nevamarsya will become my full biological daughter when a Lock will carry a copy of the Fangkart's Genetic Signiture from me to her. Until then its the strange legal status of half-this, half-that and half-the-other with every member of my family. It is a very silly system.'

Inspector Dayvaiant already knew the system, but as a Mentor, Commander Sharlensya couldn't help but explain it.

'I'm sorry,' replied Lieutenant Dayvaiyant, 'my records need updating.'

He looked at the style. All he could see was a female Pure-stock, so therefore she must be stupid. Soon to be a Matriarch, a title that in his opinion should only be ceremonial. Soon her stupidity would be at government level.

'I can see why the girl is so unnerved by today's events, she has my sympathies,' he lied. But that silly bitch didn't know that. 'I shall get back to you if I need any more information.'

'Goodbye Inspector, and thank you.'

'Ma'am,' he said politely, then saluted and left the apartment.

His thoughts were racing. The missing sprite was an unwanted loose end, one he would now have to tie up himself Although with the added bonus that in killing the sprite before it activated as a style, there would be one less inferior female Officers to keep in check.

When they were complete, the new Eltravators, rocket powered elevators running along four shafts the length of the Trunk, would massively cut the journey times from Roots to Canopy. The ageing shuttle fleet, that travelled up and down the Grand Central Channels of the Trunk would not be able to compete in the vital passenger market. Not surprisingly, the owners and operators of these Shuttles had delayed the Eltravator's construction for years. With the last of their objections blown away, there had been nothing to stop this exciting new project getting under way.

However, the biggest headache facing the builders of the Eltravator shafts came from the Recidivists. This small group of malcontents believed any technological development not spoonfed to His children by the Spirit of the Tree was a blasphemy. They had been so totally ineffective in their protests, so they had began performing minor acts of sabotage. Somehow the Saboteurs had never been caught in the act.

The progress on the project had led to a false sense of bravado amongst those working on the project. In a few hours, a whole world of complications would be loaded on their shoulders For now they were enjoying being so far ahead of schedule, the third shaft nearing completion and the fourth recently started.

'Oh great green apples, what was that?' Major Vyslorrsya asked as the drill ground to a halt.

'The Sprite wishes to report, Ma'am,' said XZ904/15, who operated the drill.

'Report then Sprite. What is the problem?' Vyslorrsya might have developed this project, but she knew its construction depended entirely on skilled sprites. If there was a problem, a sprite would find the solution far faster than a computer.

'Ma'am, the Sprite reports that the drill has hit an uncharted fistula. The drill will not be able to continue cutting the shaft until this fistula is charted.'

'Thank you XZ904/15.'

'The Sprite does not require thanks.'

'Thank you anyway.' Major Vyslorrsya knew that this was going to cause a delay. Fortunately the project was ahead of schedule, but who knew how long that would last.

Pensioner Tabbernant 089/99 Islaw was not a happy anther. His pet project had hit a snag. He was looking at the first report the engineers had produced.

A naturally occurring break in the structure of the Trunk meant there would be less drilling needed to create the lift shaft for his company's new Eltravator. However, this section of the shaft would need to be reinforced and that would cancel out the savings from drilling.

'Well Lorsa, do you think the Recidivists knew about this fistula?' he asked the project's chief architect.

'I doubt it Bernie,' she replied. 'Those nutters have only reduced their protests because they'll be celebrating the Equal Day, like everyone else.'

'So after the festival, they will be back again?'

'Worse than ever, I'm afraid Bernie,' said the engineer.

'How come?' he asked.

'Because they'll argue that our blasphemy is weakening the integrity of the Tree itself.'

'You know that's a pile of horse-feathers?' he asked, as the image of the engineer on the screen began breaking up.

'What was that Bernie?' she asked a few seconds later.

'I said their protests are a load of old horse-feathers.'

'Yes, Bernie. If anything, sending a reinforced hollow tube through the fistula will add tensile strength to that section of the Tree.' Once again the picture began to break up.

'We could've done with something like that during last year's Tree-quake,' said Tabbernant.

'You can say that again, Bernie,' she said, as the screen flickered again. 'Communication up and down the Tree has been rubbish since the Tree-quake.'

'Yes, well that is a problem for another day. How long do you think you will be delayed for, down there?'

'Hard to tell Bernie. I'll let you know when I've more data.'

Lieutenant Kilkennsya 180/41 Plussume sat as elegantly as possible, in her uniform's regulation green pencil skirt, on the last free stool at the diner counter. Since the consumption of food and drink had been prohibited at her workplace, this place was doing a roaring trade at lunchtime.

Kilkennsya hated the diner with a fiery passion. She desperately hoped overnight someone had shot the chef and there was now something edible on the menu. No such luck, it was the same selection as ever.

Kilkennsya was short and comfortably curvacious. Like all styles, she worried about her weight, but knew there was nothing she could really do about it. Despite being from the Canopy, her long loosely curled hair was a very dark brown, almost black, only the red highlights gave any clue to her region of origin.

Recently promoted, Kilkennsya worked in the Hydrology Department of Central Command and Control. It was her job to monitor the amount of water entering and leaving the Tree. A thoroughly lousy Spring, as wet as the Winter that had preceded it, had been forecast. Kilkennsya had watched with dismay the number of inundations, when the Roots had been unable to cope with downpours from beyond the Tree, grow alarmingly. It looked very much as if the Summer would be the same. Steps should have been taken to prepare the population of the Hub for possible floods. None had been.

Immediately before lunch, Kilkennsya had another pointless daily meeting with her new and deliberately obstructive boss Commander Dyscolnant.

'But Sir, the amount of water entering the Tree has been higher for the past three months than at any time in the last decade,' she had said.

'Are the sensors working properly? Is that log correct?' he had asked with an incredulous sneer.

'Yes Sir. We must act now,' Kilkennsya said with growing impatience, 'all of the Roots and the Hub should move to an amber alert.'

'Nonsense, Lieutenant.'

'Unlike me, you're from the Roots, Sir. You know the importance of Flood Awareness instinctively. It's something Canopy people like me have to learn.'

'That will do Lieutenant. I do know all about Flood Awareness. I know a move to Amber Alert would only cause unnecessary panic. I do not want you or anyone in this Department spreading rumours and feeding gossip. Do you understand?'

'Sir, yes, Sir,' Lieutenant Kilkennsya knew it was pointless trying to argue any further. She would just have to gather her evidence and send it to someone who outranked that idiot.

Things would have been so much easier if Captain Xandropant had been here. The old anther had never been the healthiest of people, and now he was on long term sick-leave. This left the obnoxious Press Officer, Commander Dyscolnant, as the acting Section Head.

'Afternoon Kelsha, and how's life treating you?' asked Lieutenant Hyetalkant, an Academy classmate and good friend.

'All the logs point to the fact that we need to be taking more precautions against flooding throughout the whole of the Roots and the Hub, not less.'

'Talking shop, is that all you ever do?'

'This is important Hazzo.'

'I know it is, that is what brings me to this part of the Tree. My editor wants a story on why the annual flood awareness exercises haven't started yet.'

'Is this a business meeting then?' asked Kilkennsya.

'Only to the extent that I can now claim this meal on

expenses. Run that stuff about the logs past me again.'

Oh great green apples! she thought to herself remembering Hyltalkant was not one of her colleagues. He was a journalist. Commander Dyscolnant would be furious if he found out she had spoken to the Press.

'Please forget what I just said, and if you must use it, keep my name out of your story, my boss will have kittens if he finds out.'

'Don't worry Kelsha, I have my facts from another source.'

'What Commander Dyscolnant's new Press Unit actually talked to you?' asked an incredulous Kilkennsya.

'Hell no, they refused to comment. As I expected.' The anther smiled. 'As we are such good friends, this conversation is strctly off the record.'

'But you're a journalist Hazzo, you would sell your aunt for a good story.'

'Very true, but she deserves it. You don't. So Kelsha, what do you recommend for lunch?'

Tabbernant's old friend, former superior officer and nephew, General Myghcomant 200/01 Islaw, was clinging to life in the Sacred Sisterhood Hospital, down in the Roots.

'How is he, Kelly?' he asked as Colonel Keltonnant's face appeared on the comlink screen.

'As well as can be expected, Bernie. The surgeons are the top in their field, they managed to get the bullet out and stabilise his condition. Nine hours in an express shuttle down from the Canopy didn't help. We just have to hope that he is strong enough to make a recovery.'

'Since his mother recycled, I am his oldest living relative. I will have to go and visit him.'

'I'm afraid not, the SPS has set up a Level Red security ring around him. They want to make sure whoever took that pot-shot at the Tree-Marshall doesn't try to finish off the anther who saved her. Even I can't get in.'

'I'll wait until they change their minds,' said Tabbernant.

'That's not going to happen anytime soon. Go on and enjoy your holiday. If he could, Myke would tell you the same.'

'I suppose you are right Kelly,' said the old anther. 'How soon will you be joining the rest of us?'

'More of a case of you joining me,' replied the medic. 'I'm closer to the resort now. Three hours in an express shuttle for me, six for you.'

'It's two days actually, Kelly. This business has messed up the schedule. No places left on any express down shuttles for a week. We will have to take it slow.'

CHAPTER THREE

THAT SINKING FEELING

All her previous journeys aboard a shuttle had been as a Sprite, in cramped cargo containers down in the hold. With only the brief cold blast of a cryogenic chamber and another cramped journey to look forward to.

Nevamarsya's jaw dropped to the floor when she had entered the central atrium of the passenger section. Three decks of shops, bars and restaurants surrounded this impossible empty space.

'Pick your jaw up dear, you are making the place untidy,' said her half-sister Serynazsya.

'If the ladies would like to follow the Sprite, it will show them to their cabin,' said a high pitched voice. 'The standard charge is ten credits per person.

How much, thought Nevamarsya as a Sprite tried to load their carry-on luggage onto its trolley.

'Thank you, Sprite,' she said, picking up her bag. 'I think we will find our own way.'

'Have a nice day,' said the departing Sprite.

The family's cabin was comfortable, but not somewhere anyone would want to spend time in. Not surprising really, the owners of the Shuttle wanted passengers to spend as much time and money as possible in the public rooms.

'Well, we might as well go out and enjoy what this shuttle has to offer,' said Sharlensya. 'We will be on board for two days.

They were sorely disappointed. It took no more than half an hour to navigate the vessel. This was supposed to be one of the top class shuttles that plied its way up and down the Central Channels of the Trunk.

'Mother Sun, this is grotty,' said Sharlensya.

'Isn't it just.' A familiar voice cut in.

'Bernie, you're the main investor in Eltravator's project. I thought you were banned from every shuttle in the Tree?'

'I still need to travel by the old method, so I bought this hulk. Who in their right minds would try to ban themselves from their own property?'

'You own this tub?' asked Serynazsya.

'Yes, the one and only shuttle I will ever own.' The old anther sighed. 'Soon I won't need it.'

'What will happen to it then?' she asked.

'I'll recuperate some of my losses from its scrap value. There is just no money in it. Especially after I stripped out the crooked casino that was draining travellers' money into the Syndicates' pockets.'

'And they just let you do that?'

'They did. The Five Syndicates might not like me, but they do tolerate me. Over the years I have built up a bank of information that could destroy each and every one of them. Insurance against anything untoward happening to me.'

'Why don't you bring them down? They are evil,' asked Sharlensya.

'Because, if I did, within a few years new Syndicates would have sprung up in their place, ones I had no leverage over. My life wouldn't be worth a fig and their evil would continue.'

'Oh, I hadn't thought of that,' said Sharlensya.

'As much as I hate the Syndicates, I suppose Bernie is right, having them is better than the anarchy of not having them,' said Galeroysya, a Chief Inspector with the Enquirers and one of the representatives of the Police Service on the Winter Squad. She and her husband Untrugyant were in the process of adopting Natalicsya. When the sisters noticed the arrival of their friend, there was an explosion of squeals, hugs and kisses.

'However, there must be something that now has no value to you, come on can tell us,' said Galeroysya, eventually continuing the conversation. 'If only so that we can close some cases.'

'You aren't going to get all official on me, are you Gale?'

'No Bernie. But spill some of the beans. What happened to Drwgdynant?'

'Gale! Just don't go there,' said Untrugyant, trying to avoid a scene, but it was already too late. Tabbernant had gone an unpleasant shade of red and his anger could melt an ice cube.

'I have no idea what happened to that bastard,' he said in a low whisper. 'If you wish to remain my friend, madam, you will never mention that name in my presence ever again.' With that the old anther turned and left.

'Oops, looks as if Mum pushed one button too many,' said Natalicsya.

Twenty Six Years Earlier

The term Organised Crime had never caught on in the Tree. All major crime, argued the Tree-people has to be planned and executed. In other words, organised. The mafia-like criminal organisations were called Syndicates and their activities refered to as Syndicated Crime.

For all their unpleasantness, the one area of misery that the Syndicates refused to touch was illegal money lending. Loan Sharking was beneath their dignity.

When he first met Captain Drwgdynant, in the summer of Year 158, Tabbernant had no reason to regard him as a criminal. Drwgdynant appeared to be a respectable business-person whose company could be found working on many medium scale building and civil engineering projects in the Trunk. Only a handful of people knew he was responsible for all the unlicenced money lending in the Trunk. Many of his clients, or should that be victims regarded him and his minions as evil. At that time Loan Sharking was not classed as criminal. The Syndicates ignored him and the Police were powerless to stop him.

The young hotshot Captain Tabbernant was in the dark about Captain Drwgdynant's plans to expand his illegitimate business operations up into the Canopy along with his legitimate ones.

Tabbernant's dealings with the Tax Authorities were spot-less, which more than made up for Tabbernant's reputation with other branches of the authorities. This made him an ideal partner for Drwgdynant, a lilly white screen to hide the older anther's midnight black activities.

It was the hottest day of the year so far Duosday Delta of Sextemp, Year 158 (30th June, 1986). Tabbernant and his Legal Executive, Lieutenant Annaprysya, had arrived in one of his many businesses here in the Crown, a shaded café for an extended semi-working lunch.

'This is too much of a risk Bernie,' said Lieutenant Annaprysya to her boss.

'Why?' he asked.

'Because Drwgdynant is a shady character,' she replied.

'Admit it Annie, you don't like Captain Drwgdynant, because he gives you the creeps,' said Lieutenant Yajimalsya, the gifted software engineer they had come to the Canopy to meet.

'Yes, Yaji, he gives me the creeps,' replied Annaprysya, 'there is something inherently wrong about him.'

In front of them was the majestic sweep of the Great Lake of the Crown. The more relaxed atmosphere of the Canopy suited the software business, and it definitely suited Tabbernant was a little annoyed that they were still talking shop now their meal had arrived. The office was now closed for lunch.

'I am a shareholder in a civil engineering project. Captain Drwygdynant is a successful Civil Engineer in the Trunk, who has bought his way into the same consortium, to extend his business into the Canopy. I have a number of successful businesses up here. In the Trunk my only business is a small haulage and warehousing company my Father owned. It's losing money hand over fist.'

'I know,' she said after taking a sip of her Kuffa. 'I know, forming a joint company to run your shared interests in the Trolley-bus Consortium will give you both more clout down there and him leverage up here.'

'Which is good for both of us,' Tabbernant said, 'which in the end is good for you too.'

'But he must be fiddling his taxes,' Annaprysya said draining her cup. 'He's employing my brother as his tax accountant. Isn't that warning enough?'

'So he's fiddling his taxes. More fool him. Bernie here doesn't, so he's fine,' said Yajimalant.

'So, Bernie, you're determined to sign this contract, aren't you?'

'Yes, Annie, I am. How many other crooks do I do business with?'

'Too many,' she smiled. 'As a lawyer, I can find nothing to fault this deal. As a friend, I am asking you not to touch it.'

Tabbernant regarded his legal executive with wry amusement. She was a fine one to talk about morals and dodgy characters. A child prodigy, who jumped straight to Lieutenant at the age of five, with a great future in the Advocate's Regiment. However, he knew for a fact that she was the most skilled hacker in the Tree. If she wanted to get into your private computer records, you could have firewalls and security systems from the Canopy to the furthest tip of the Roots, she would get in.

'I suppose you are still enjoying your dangerous hobby?' asked Yajimalsya, who also knew about Annaprysya secret.

'Yes, it's starting to get interesting,' she laughed 'It is about time some light was shone on the Sisterhood. That much power concentrated into such an unaccountable body just isn't healthy.'

'Well you be careful,' warned Tabbernant.

'They aren't the Syndicates you know,' she laughed.

'No,' he said, 'they're worse. The economy of the Tree would grind to a halt if it were not for the wealth of the House of Clergy.'

'There, don't you think that is a bit suspicious, that two organisations that claim to be living a life of poverty having so much spare cash they can loan the Officer Corps the deficit between tax income and government outgoings every year?'

'It's the way the system works dear,' said Yajimalsya.

'And it stinks,' replied Annaprysya.

'Like I said, be careful,' said Tabbernant.

'Oh Bernie, you're starting to sound like Gaemlovant. What are they going to do. Trespassers don't get prosecuted.'

'No, they get recruited,' said Yajimalsya darkly. 'Do you fancy losing all that lovely blonde hair? I'd hate to lose my ebony tresses.'

'Well Yajay, I'm getting tired of looking after it, and wouldn't we both look good in wimples?' For a moment she looked serious, before breaking into giggles. 'They wouldn't take us, we haven't got a religious bone in our bodies.'

'You gave me some friendly advice,' said her boss, 'let me return the compliment. Please find some other organisation to practice your dark arts on.'

'OK, Bernie. I'll think about it.'

Tabbernant sat watching his fellow passengers as they milled around the shuttle. If only I had listened to her advice he thought. If only she had listened to mine. How different our lives might be today. At the time they had both been young and arrogant. As she dug into the Convent's secrets, by a strange osmosis Annaprysya became more religious, more spiritual; otherworldly, less and less concerned with the day to day. It had come as no surprise to Tabbernant, when as the old saying ran, "Her Sisters came to take her home." Replacing her had been a nightmare, as it came without warning. It had taken years to break all her security measures, as the Tree Nuns refused to let her out for long enough to hand everything over to her successor. 'Novice Annaprysya is now beyond such mundane matters,' they had said.

The truth about Drwgdynant had become apparent in the middle of Year 160. Tabbernant had finally decided to call time on the loss making haulage business in the Trunk. Habitats in the Trunk are as varied as the people who live in them. The Haulage Business was based in a series of interconnected chambers in a wide band of solid wood, close to the top of the Trunk.

Tabbernant planned a surprise inspection to catch the light-fingered red handed. Then he would close the old business and relocate the handful of trustworthy employees to one of his other business, so they could start again.

The worst offender was Commander Queltheant, the Depot Manager. For years he had been a loyal employee and friend. Tabbernant had been so disappointed to discover he was responsible for most of the low grade theft going on at the depot.

The plan had been to sack Commander Queltheant and hand him over to the Enforcers. That plan had fallen apart when Queltheant's body had been found hanging from a beam in one of the warehouses. The closure plan would be delayed until after Queltheant's funeral. Tabbernant hated funerals and Queltheant's the was worst ever. The mourners all looked far more dowdy than the circumstances dictated.

'Is everyone in this town broke, Clippa?' Tabbernant asked Subaltern Clipaudsya, the dead anther's secretary. It was shortly after the funeral and nobody had stayed for the wake.

'Not everyone Bernie, I'm still holding my own,' she replied, 'but I'm young and haven't got the financial responsibilities that are weighing down the people around here. Also, I don't have a loan with Mr. D.'

'Mr. D. what sort of silly name is that?' asked Tabbernant.

'I wish it was silly, but for many people around here Mr. D. the Money Lender is deadly serious.'

'I despise loan sharks. The lowest form of parasitic scum.'

'All fine words Bernie, but I saw what fear of Mr. D. did to one of your most loyal employees. First it drove him to steal from you, and then to killing himself when he got caught.'

'But I pay everyone who works here better than a living wage.'

'Yes, Bernie, but the actions of one good employer can easily get cancelled out if a family has only one decent wage coming in.'

'And the rest of your family?'

'Well, Mum and Dad both work for you. Jella is working for a magazine down in the Roots. We all miss her. You really should invest in a better way of getting around the Tree.'

'Maybe I will Clippa, one day maybe I will.'

He knew that Clipaudsya was telling the truth, her family was one of the few not struggling.

'I've got some good news. I'm streamlining my Dad's three haulage businesses into one. Moving everything to this habitat because of its location. A big investment for up here. Lots of new and well paid jobs. You're going to be running it, Lieutenant Clipaudsya. With this promotion, you'll be able to afford more trips down to visit your Sister.'

At first, turning his resructuring plans on their head had seemed like an over generous guilt trip. However, the more he worked on the changes, the more sense it made. This Habitat was perfectly placed, but Mother Sun and Father Earth, it needed inward investment badly.

After a week in the habitat, Tabbernant was more than angry with this Mr. D. character. Anger alone never achieved anything. He was going to destroy the waste of skin. Draining these good people dry was evil. Tabbernant knew he employed just the right person to do the job.

'You know it's going to be dangerous,' Annaprysya said when he called her into the office on his return to the Canopy.

'I won't send you alone, Waldo and Benny from accounts will be travelling with you.' Waldo and Benny, or to give them their full names Gwalduvant and Belliniant, were Bernie's hired muscle. 'And as far as the Tree is concerned, you will be investigating the unacceptable levels of petty pilfering going on in the depot.'

'OK boss, when do I start?'

It had been four months since he had asked Annaprysya to investigate the problems in the Trunk. The dark half of the year was rapidly approaching and the project that his company was working up in the Canopy had been put on hold for Autumn and Winter. At first, he had asked for regular progress reports, and received contradictory snippets of information. So Tabbernant left Annaprysya to carry on quietly with her task. After months of silence Annaprysya contacted him. She said she had finally cracked the case, arranging a meeting for the following morning.

He was surprised to see Annaprysya pushing her older brother into his office. It was half an hour before the office opened, and there was nobody else in the building.

'So you monstrous little shit, tell my Superior Officer what you have told me.'

Tabbernant could not remember when he had last seen Annaprysya so angry. 'That's a nice way to talk to your brother, isn't it?' said the anther she was shouting at.

'Morning Annie, Gezz. What's happening, why so cross?' asked Tabbernant. The normal friendly banter between the siblings had disappeared.

'Look Gezz, I haven't got time for niceties. Sometimes I am embarrassed to have you as a brother. One of those sometimes is now.'

'For the record, I warned you about going into business with Captain Drwgdynant,' said Annaprysya, 'or should I say Mr. D.'

'What, run that past me again?' It was too early in the morning for Tabbernant to take this in.

'Tell him, Gezz.'

'As I explained to my sister, my former client, the building contractor, Captain Drwgdynant of the Civil Engineering Regiment has been running a profitable little side-line in loan sharking in the Trunk for the past five years.'

'Former client?'

'Yeah, I may be morally questionable, but I don't deal with crooks.'

'Oh pull the other one Gezz, you are working for all the Syndicates in the Tree at one level or another,' said Tabbernant.

'That's not true, I only help legitimate business escape the punitive taxes imposed by people who don't want hard working tree-people to prosper.'

'Stick to the facts, Gezz,' she shouted at her brother.

'Sorry, Annie!'

The style picked up a folder stuffed with documents. 'I hacked into Gezz's records. Which, by the way, was really easy. If you think you don't deal with any front organisations for the Syndicates, then you really are stupid.'

'Anyway, through Gezz, I got into Drwgdynant's system and did some nosing. The fact that he uses my embarrassing sibling made me suspicious. I found Drwgdynant's accounts. Not the work of fiction that Gaemlovant is given, which he then copy edits into an even bigger fairy story for the tax authorities. I got to the real thing. The ones that record details of his loan sharking. It made unpleasant reading.'

'Then she brought these figures to me,' said Gaemlovant, 'I was able to cross reference them with the figures he had given me. They are genuine. So that is when I resigned as his accountant.'

'So, how did Captain Drwgdynant react to that?' asked Tabbernant.

'Not well. I have never seen anyone lose their temper so completely. I decided to run for it,' said Gaemlovant. 'I got on the same express shuttle from the Upper Trunk to the Canopy as Annie. Drwgdynant's influence doesn't reach very far.'

'These figures show that a large portion of your employees have at one time or another taken out questionable loans with Captain Drwgdynant, aka Mr. D.'

Tabbernant mulled this over. 'So why don't they borrow from proper banks?' he asked.

'They go to Mr. D. because Roots based banks just won't lend money to anywhere more than a quarter of the Trunk above ground, whilst the Trunk based banks really don't have enough capital to invest in anything other than sure fire winners.'

'So our Mr. D. offers loans to the desperate, who can't get credit anywhere else. Charging exorbitant rates of interest, and using brute force to get money from late payers.'

'What evidence have you got for strong arm tactics?' asked Tabbernant.

'Once I had proof of what Drwgdynant was up to,' said Annaprysya, continuing her explanation, 'I was able to access the medical records of people who owed Drwgdynant money. It is remarkable how many of them have had unfortunate accidents when they missed payments.'

Tabbernant picked up the dossier and began reading.

'This is terrible,' he said after finishing the dossier, 'but as evidence goes, it's all circumstantial. Unless you can get some of these victims to give evidence against that bastard, it is just a pile of paper.'

'Don't worry, I'm working on that. In a day or two I will have this dossier and a disc full of recorded witness statements to hand over to the Enquirers.'

'Who will do little or nothing. Maybe a few assault charges against Drwgdynant's thugs isn't going to harm him.'

'Last year the High Council passed a new law,' said Gaemlovant, 'it made all forms of unlicenced money lending illegal. They wanted to stamp this sort of thing out.'

'Sadly,' continued Annaprysya 'that law has been useless, because nobody wanted to investigate. Many of the local Enforcers are in Drwgdynant's pocket and beyond the Regional Command, nobody cares.'

'In a few days they will care and something will be done. Congratulations Annie. A job well done.'

'There is a problem though.'

'Go on Annie, I'm all ears.'

'When the Enquirer's get hold of this dossier, they are going to want to double check all the facts.'

'As they should, it is after all their job.'

'And they are going to be paying particular attention to any business partners Drwgdynant may have.'

'So?' asked a confused Tabbernant.

'Think about it Bernie, guilt by association. No smoke without fire. Plus half a dozen other clichés.'

Tabbernant got the picture, anyone who had done business with Drwgdynant was going to be closely investigated. He knew he had done nothing wrong, but in a few months, when Drwgdynant's evil empire collapsed the rubble would flatten him. Tabbernant had a very colourful reputation and a shed load of people just waiting for him to fall flat on his face. This was not going to help at all. What a wonderful New Year's Present this would be for his enemies.

The fact that Drwgdynant had been given bail had come as no surprise to Tabbernant. His former partner's first day in court was the last day of the year. Nobody was going to be sent to prison on the eve of the HolyDay.

The Syndicates carry out their own special brand of Justice for those foolish enough to commit a crime on the HolyDay. It was to be assumed that like the High Council, they had finally decided they had to do something about loan-sharking. It was giving criminals a terrible reputation. Drwgdynant never turned up for his day in court. Never turned up for anything ever again. Nobody knew where his body went, nobody cared much either.

Annaprysya's dire warning about being associated with such a shady character came true. All of Drwgdynant's assets were confiscated by the High Council and sold to compensate his victims. This affected Tabbernant because it included all the assets of the partnership in the Canopy Autobus Consortium. Being demoted back to Lieutenant hurt his standing in the business community. This wasn't the first time he would be demoted and it was not the last time, but it hurt the most, as he had been instrumental in bringing down Drwgdynant.

'I'm sorry about this afternoon Bernie,' said Galeroysya after tempers had cooled.

'And I am sorry I exploded.' The old anther took a sip of red wyn, 'it was a long time ago.'

'Before I was born.'

'Precisely. My unwise dealings with Drwgdynant have been a millstone around my neck for years.'

'You completely regenerated the economy of the Upper-Trunk, which made you a hero to so many people.'

'I suppose so Gale,' he replied modestly.

'And unless his body turns up, it is in the past, and there it will remain,' said her husband.

'You mean neither of you have heard?' asked Tabbernant.

'Heard what?' asked Untrugyant.

'A body was found in my Eltravator shaft. It's been positively identified as Captain Drwgdynant 075/76 Raarkart. That stone cold case is now an active murder enquiry again. Hotter than a Lower Trunk Curry.'

'No wonder you exploded, Bernie,' said Galeroysya.

'Don't worry my dear. I have nothing to hide. I have no idea what happened to Drwgdynant two decades ago. Naturally, I will be investigated, but your colleagues will have to look elsewhere for their killer.'

CHAPTER FOUR
WHERE THE HEART IS

Sharlensya had spotted some familiar faces in the crowd. They had trained as Mentors together.

'Kepkalmant, Cariyonsya! Fancy meeting you here. How in the Tree are you?' asked Sharlensya.

'I'm fine, except this thing has put a damper on all my fun,' said Cariyonsya 232/05. 'I had a miscarriage six weeks into the first attempt.'

'I can certainly sympathise,' Sharlensya said to her old friend, who was unmistakably pregnant.

'The Medics advised I took the second punt at a pseudo-pregnancy as soon as possible. So I'm here, like this.' The poor love, she sounded as worn out as she looked.

'Couldn't you have changed your holiday booking?' asked Nevamarsya.

'Kepkalmant, couldn't alter his leave,' said Cariyonsya.

'What a shame.'

This holiday was meant to be a way to unwind for both mother and son after the rigours of pseudo-pregnancy and rebirth. Sharlensya had been Guard of Honour for Cariyonsya at the couples Pair-Bonding Ceremony, and knew how upset her friend was about her meticulous planning going so spectacularly wrong.

'How much longer have you got?' asked Sharlensya.

'Six weeks after we get home,' Cariyonsya replied.

'Really! You're only three weeks, your bump is twice the size mine was at three weeks.'

'Medics say it varies from style to style. Of course, still being so full of the hormones from the failed pseudo-pregnancy is filling me out. Great green apples, I'll soon reach a stage where walking is something other people do. I've had to abandon the planned mud skiing tomorrow.'

Mud Skiing was a bit of a misnomer, mud sledging would have been more accurate. It involved sitting on a large metal board and using movements of the body to negotiate your way down a thin film of liquid mud oozing down a steep slope. Staying clean was not an option, falling down a lot was obligatory.

'I'll just be passing comments from the side-lines. I don't suppose you know anyone who would like to use my ticket?'

Nevamarsya's ears pricked up as soon as her half-mother's friend mentioned Mud Skiing.

'Can I Mam?' she asked.

'What, really, getting dirty and wet,' said Pemisegant. 'When there is an awesome water park here, where you can get as wet as you like and stay clean.'

'But it'll be fun,' Nevamarsya said to her boyfriend. And then she turned to her half-mother. 'Can I Mammy?'

'If Cariyonsya and Kepalomant are in agreement, I don't see why not.'

'Thanks Mam.'

There had been a time when any youthful prank might have cost hundreds of lives. As the years passed and the Tree became secure, the luxury of being juvenile was invented.

Sharlensya sometimes worried that Nevamarsya was a little too grown-up for her own good. That the Virus Invasion had robbed her daughter-to-be of being a child and learning from the mistakes of childhood. Of course Sharlensya agreed. Mud skiing was one of the most juvenile and messy things available at the resort. Maybe Nevamarsya wasn't that grown up after all.

Everything within the Tree requires light to live. The sunlight the basic ingredient of all things within the Tree. A similar amount of light falls on the Trunk. This is collected by the bark and travels along naturally occurring protein glass fibre cables to giant power storage facilities of the Lower Trunk. Originally the fibres illuminated the interior, but as the Tree grew, they became less and less efficient. So the Tree taught his Officers how to build Daylighters, which imitate Mother Sun, bringing light to the inhabited parts of the Tree.

The greatest concentration of Daylighters is in the Agricultural Region of the Central Trunk, which resembles a stack of pancakes. Museum Farms with live animals occupy the top layers. They provide the priming cells for the Protein Vats beneath them.

Next come deck after deck of market gardens growing potatoes and other root vegetable along with hectare after hectare of brassica. Next come decks of arable farms growing cereals. Around the Heartswood, the main overflow valve for the Grand Central Channels, where water is plentiful are vast mechanised rice farms.

At the bottom of the Agricultural Region fruit and vegetables are grown in hydroponic farms in the flooded chambers called the Hydropone. Alongside the Hydropone are the gigantic vats where cell samples from cows, pigs poultry and fish are fed raw syrup and produce all the meat the inhabitants of the Tree require. Banks of ovulators produce millions of "hen's eggs" a day and Lactator Tanks produce all the milk the occupants of the Tree needed.

Lieutenant Popisedsya 100/97 Siylm sat back in the deckchair on the porch of her family's rice farm. She had first arrived here as a Sprite. Returned to its once tight knit community after her Officer Training, then finally joined the farm owner's family, when his elder daughter adopted her. Petite, pretty and unmistakably Mid-Trunk/Oriental she had fitted right in.

Her grandfather, Pensioner Remixerant still owned the property, but retired as the farm's manager shortly after her adoption. Her cousin, Commander Rolinalant had taken over the management of the farm. After a few short months of doing things Rolinalant's way, the community of the farm, which had taken years to build was destroyed. Like many of the adult family members, her parents had moved to new jobs elsewhere in the Trunk. It had been decided that it was better if Popisedsya remained in the stable environment of the farm, in the care of the cousin she knew as Aunty Mae.

On her fifth birthday, Commander Rolinalant had made it clear there was no job for her or Aunty Mae at the farm. So Popisedsya volunteered for the Winter Squad. This was when Popisedsya first met Crysgoxant. It seemed everything Popisedsya touched was destined to be taken away from her. In the middle of her second tour with the Winter Squad, the Virus invaded. Crysgoxant had been one of the casualties of war. Unable to say a proper goodbye, because her poor fiancé's body was never recovered after the Virus had been defeated, she found herself unable to face the enforced joviality of the other members of the Winter Squad at the Holiday Resort. She had travelled to her parents' home. Although she loved them dearly, where they lived had no special tie. Her grandfather had invited her to return to the farm and she had gladly accepted the invitation.

Popisedsya was contemplating how sad and unloved the garden had become, when she heard somebody coming up the stairs from the living quarters beneath.

'It pains me to see you so sad, Little Flower,' said the familiar voice of her grandfather. Everyone on the farm called the old anther Rex, only a select few still called him Grandad Rex.

'It pains me to be so sad,' she said to Grandad Rex.

'He was such a nice boy your Crysgoxant. Such a terrible thing to happen to him.'

Her grandfather pulled up a chair. Over the years his hair had turned from jet black to white and since his retirement his once well trimmed beard had become long and whispy. Decades of hard work and accumulated wisdom were apparent from the lines on his face.

'Grief is like an illness, Little Flower.' The old anther stopped when he saw his granddaughter's face. 'I'm so sorry, my words of comfort were ill thought out.'

'Don't worry Grandad Rex, I know you meant well. Please continue. I thought I wanted solitude, to be alone with my memories. It hasn't helped,' she said quietly.

'As I was saying, grief is like an illness, Little Flower,' he had used this homily many times in the past, he felt it was an effective form of comfort, as it so accurately described the stages of bereavement. 'First there is the infection, the death of a loved one. Like a disease poisons the body, grief poisons the mind, filling it with sadness and remorse,' he turned and smiled at Popisedsya. 'The antibodies of happy memories destroy the illness. Then, the antiseptic of time washes the pain away. Sometimes something will trigger a secondary infection of sadness, but the body now recognises the source and is able to fight it off.'

'Still spouting that old pseudo-philosophical clap-trap, are you?' said Commander Rolinalant as he arrived back at the house after a day in the fields. 'You really are an old fraud, as well as an old fool.'

'The only foolish thing I ever did was appointing you as manager of my farm,' said Rex.

'You'd not dare replace me now. The farm's reputation would be damaged, and you would lose too much face.'

'What more possible damage could be inflicted upon this farm, it has lost its soul because you have dispersed the family. Also, what do I care, I am forty one years old. My life is almost over. When it ends, your contract is automatically terminated and my heir will have a clean slate.'

'Your designated heir died, so the inheritance skips a generation. You have never made a new Will, as your oldest grandchild, the farm will automatically fall to me when you do go,' replied Rolinalant haughtily.

'Do not be so sure you are my oldest grandchild.' The old anther grinned enigmatically.

'Well she certainly isn't. I'm ten, she's six.

'Commander Rolinalant, this is neither the time nor the place. Your cousin here is in mourning, I will be grateful if you respect her wish for quiet and solitude, by making yourself scarce.'

'She's been here for two weeks now. This is a working farm, not a hotel. I told you, we have no place for freeloaders, especially not a weak and feeble one like her.'

'Weak and feeble am I?' said Popisedsya with a snort. 'I could split you in half without breaking sweat.'

'Is that a threat? If it is, I have legitimate grounds to have you removed from the farm.'

'No, simply a statement of fact, you accused me of being weak because I am small, but I have studied the Iron Dance to the Tenth Level, there is more to me than meets the eye.' Popisedsya was angry now. Nobody treated her grandfather with such little respect.

'Oh, please. You and your silly martial arts, you're as big a fraud as he is. I have had enough. You will leave this farm immediately.'

Rolinalant had punctuated every word of the final sentence with a prodding hand like an arrowhead of fingers against her chest. Popisedsya grabbed hold of Rolinalant's outstretched thumb. Then using it as a key, turned the entire arm through ninety degrees. Rolinalant's eyes began to water, and the rest of his over-extended body followed the arm, crashing on to the porch.

'Thank you, that camera will show you assaulting me. More grounds to have you evicted from this property.'

'From that angle,' said Popisedsya, 'it will show you repeatedly trying to fondle my breast. I had to defend my honour,' replied Popisedsya with lightning speed.

'It would take a hell of an advocate to convince a court of that. One hell of an advocate.' Popisedsya asked.

'If you do,' said Remixerant, who had been watching this exchange quietly, 'then even the suggestion of you sexually harassing your cousin, whilst she is a guest on my farm, will be grounds for instant termination of your contract.'

'You might have won this battle, but in the long run, I will win the war.' With that, Rolinalant disappeared down the entrance stairwell into the house below.

'Well Little Flower,' said Remixerant, 'I see that the fire hasn't gone out completely.'

'For some reason, I feel invigorated, Granddad Rex.'

'An adrenaline rush. Be careful not to crash back down into depression afterwards.'

Popisedsya thought about this. The scuffle with her cousin

had lightened her mood considerably. 'I knew Rolinalant had ordered his cronies to ignore me. I didn't realise he hated me that much.'

'Whilst I live and own this farm, you will always be welcome, regardless of what Roley says.'

'Thank you, Grandad Rex,' she said.

The conversation was paused by the sound of a car landing.

'Cousin Peripalsya, do you want to see her? I can always send her away?' her grandfather asked.

'No, Grandad Rex, Aunty Mae is like another mother to me. It is not surprising she wants to see me.'

'I never did understand why you call her Aunty Mae, she is not your Mother's Sister, and her name is not Mae.'

'Because when that Little Flower first became my ward, she kept asking "aunty, may I do this" or "aunty, may I do that",' said the style who had arrived in the car, 'so I said to her that she didn't have to keep asking my permission for everything, but I quite liked being called Aunty Mae.'

The two styles hugged. They were polar opposites. Popisedsya was petite, Peripalsya was built like a Sumo Wrestler.

'Well, you are a lot happier today than you were last week. Though I know you are still sad inside.'

'Crysgoxant would not want me to be permanently sad, would he Aunty Mae?' asked Popisedsya.

'No, Little Flower,' Grandad Rex cut in, 'he would not.'

'Good, you and Granddad Rex there are coming with me,' said Aunty Mae.

'A party?' Remixerant asked his cousin.

'No Granddad Rex, I would not go that far. A meal at the Singing Frog. I shall call Poppy's parents, tell them to meet us there.' Peripalsya said as she walked with Popisedsya towards the porch and the stairway down to the living quarters.

CHAPTER FIVE
BAD HAIR DAY

That was fun, thought Nevamarsya as she arrived back at the apartment slightly earlier than she had expected. Very messy too. Her scalp had started itching in the car. The showers at the mud slope had broken down so they had been unable to clean up there.

'Thank you for a wonderful day, Carry,' said Nevamarsya as she clambered out of the autocab. The little vehicle was designed to ferry people to and from the slopes. It was hosed down each night. At the moment it was as dirty as its passengers.

'Think nothing of it, Neva dear. It was nice having your company, wasn't it Kall?' said the heavily pregnant style sat on the other side of the vehicle.

'I think the boys enjoyed having you along,' said her husband.

'Sure, it was great having Neva with us,' said one of the boys. 'See you at the farewell disco tonight?'

'You might Mal, you might.'

This elicited a grin from Mallownant, 'Last chance for me to practice my moves before the adoption process reduces me to a dribbing wreck.'

'But he's a dribbling wreck already, so there is no change there,' said his cousin Needvisant.

'You're still wearing the nappies, Nedis, so you are a fine one to talk.'

'You get better, it's only temporary,' Nevamarsya said, feeling Mallownant's deep seated nerves. However, neither boy seemed to be listening. They were roughly the same age as Serynazsya, who had already gone through the debilitating process that all Tree-People needed to continue their healthy growth. Although both acted like newly sprouted cadets. Worse sometimes. By dropping down to their level she had so much fun. Nevamarsya supposed her half-mother was right, sometimes she did forget how to be a child.

Not today, you just could not get more pointlessly stupid than careering down a mud slope at high speed. Nevamarsya had fitted perfectly into the group. The parents had been almost as juvenile as the children. She supposed the day would not have been half as enjoyable if Keepcalant and Cariyonsya had been po-faced. In fact, Cariyonsya's barbed comments from the sidelines had been the highlight of the day.

Boy, did she need a shower now. That damn mud got everywhere. She was itching like crazy. Nobody else back yet. Good, that meant she would have the bathroom to herself.

Sharlensya arrived back at the chalet as her friend's cab was taking off. As she walked through the door she heard the sound of the shower being turned on.

Then the screaming started. Long ululating cries of pain followed by an ominous silence. When Sharlensya reached the bathroom she saw Nevamarsya lying on the floor convulsing. Most of the shampoo had been washed away, but not all. Where it touched Nevamarsya's skin large red welts were forming. The most damage had been inflicted on Nevamarsya's head, stripped of all hair, her scalp looked like a battlefield.

Sharlensya heard the door behind her open. She thought for a moment it was an attacker back for a second bite at the cherry. She was about to spin and punch the newcomer when she heard a familiar voice.

'Quick,' said Serynazsya, 'get her back into the shower, she is still covered in whatever is causing the allergic reaction. We need to wash it off.'

Great Tree protect us, what wonderful timing her daughter had.

'Isn't the shower tray contaminated?' Sharlensya asked.

'We will both have to hold her to make sure her skin doesn't touch any contaminated surfaces.'

Easier said that done as Nevamarsya was taller than both of them. Once Nevamarsya had been thoroughly washed and toweled dry, she was put into bed to keep her warm.

'I'm going to check Uncle Kelly's war chest,' said Serynazsya. 'He packs for all sorts of medical emergencies.'

On a shelf in the corner of the room sat the huge first aid box her uncle insisted on packing for every holiday. Although I bet the only anti-toxin serum he didn't pack is the one we need Sharlensya thought morosely. No, thank Mother Sun, it was there, and Serynazsya inserted the podule into the hypospray and pressed it against Nevamarsya's arm. A light was flashing on the hypospray. She knew that the built in transmitter in the device was informing the authorities of when, where and why it had been used and that paramedics would soon be on their way.

The strangest thing was she immediately heard sirens. No she must be imagining that sound, the signal had only just been sent. No there was an ambulance parking outside the chalet.

'This is starting to become a bit of a bad habit,' said Nevamarsya as she opened her eyes, 'waking up in a hospital bed again.'

'Its not your fault my dear,' said her Half-Mother. 'The Paramedics insisted.'

'You were very lucky, to have an ambulance on patrol in your district,' said the Medic standing on the other side of the bed, 'it acted on the telemetry from the hypospray even before it had reached us here at the hospital. This, in tandem with your half-sister's swift actions should guarantee a swift recovery.'

The Medic was not her great-uncle Kelly. Nevamarsya began to panic, she had never been treated by a different Medic. This anther was far younger than Uncle Kelly. She wondered how long he has been qualified? Would it make any difference to her treatment? Pull yourself together girl. Colonel Keltonnant is not the only medic in the Tree. Just because this one looks young, it doesn't mean he is not good at his job.

'It appears the shampoo reacted with the Shambling salts in the mud you were caked in. Given your past medical history, once the Paramedics had treated the toxins, they pumped you full of Oestrol and rushed you to this hospital.'

'Why, what's wrong with my medical history?' Nevamarsya asked. She could guess the reason, her late blooming last year.

'Did you nearly suffer a terminal differentiation crisis a few months ago?' explained the Medic in a lecturing tone.

'Yes, but isn't that all in the past now?'

'That was a result of you being a Passive Hermaphrodite at the time,' said the Medic, reading from his notes.

'A what?' Nevamarsya asked.

'All Sprites have both sets of gender organs,' continued the Medic. 'Normally one switches on at Activation and the others get absorbed. You should have only had your female organs, but the presence of undeveloped male organs, nearly prevented your emergence as a Style.'

'So?' asked Nevamarsya.

'Have you ever heard of Gender Regression?' he replied with a question.

'A gender what?' she parried.

'You must have noticed some weedy anthers or flat chested styles?'

'Yes, what about them?' asked Nevamarsya. Was nobody going to give an answer in this conversation.

'They are Passive Hermaphrodites who have reverted back to neuter, a Gender Regression,' said the medic, at last giving an answer. 'The opposite gender specific organs have only atrophied. The correct ones do the same They keep living male or female lives though.'

A horrible thought crossed her mind and she went white. 'It didn't happen today but, is there any chance of Gender Regression happening to me in the future?'

'Further examination today showed no sign of any vestigial male organs. The Oestrol finished them off.'

'So, all my girly-bits are now fully formed. And any boy-bits have been reabsorbed,' Nevamarsya laughed. 'That's a relief.'

'Yes, you are very feminine now,' replied the medic.

Indeed, thought Nevamarsya and you are now looking with a less than professional eye at my curves. Please stop. The medic must have realised what he was doing, because he went a few shades pinker, and turned to read a medical chart.

'On a more mundane level, Am I going to be staying here tonight?' Nevamarsya asked.

'I shall be discharging you from this facility tomorrow morning, it's too late tonight. Don't worry, you won't miss your Shuttle tomorrow. So, if you will excuse me, I have other patients to visit.'

'Thank you,' said Sharlensya to the departing Medic. She then turned her attention to her daughter-to-be. 'Neva dear, don't worry about packing your things, Serah has already done that.' Not that anyone in the Tree travelled with suitcases full of clothes. Emprintable Fabric made that unneccessary.

'Did she remember to pack my favourite brush?'

'Were you trying to be ironic there Neva?'

'No Mammy, I will still need it, to keep the wig you are holding tidy.'

'Ah yes, the wig.'

Sharlensya slipped it onto her half-daughter's head. It was designed to look as realistic as possible. Nevamarsya knew it was fake, and hated its artificiality. On the other hand it was better than being completely bald.

'I'm actually looking forward to tomorrow more than I was looking forwards to the holiday,' she said, changing the subject.

'Are you dear?' asked a confused Sharlensya.

'Yes, seeing all the sights and hearing all the sounds of the Roots for the first time. Going further than the Sprite Storage Centre or the Convent.'

'You'll soon get bored of the place, counting down the days until we return to the Canopy with the Winter Squad.'

'I thought you were permanently posted down in the Roots now? Being a Matriarch and everything.'

'No dear. Cheap, fast and efficient transport throughout the Trunk, all year round with Bernie's Eltravator is going to change the way everyone works.'

'That's OK then,' said a yawning Nevamarsya.

'I'll leave you to sleep now. Big day tomorrow.'

PART TWO
HOME ECONOMICS

CHAPTER SIX

MOVING IN

The Arrivals Lounge at the Hub's Shuttle-port was the most cosmopolitan place in the Tree. Sharlensya knew that young Nevamarsya was expecting something as drabbly functional as the other Shuttle-ports in the Tree. She could see the girl was bowled over by the riot of sounds, colours and smells.

She thought she could hear someone calling her name through the hubbub. Yes, there he was, holding a sign saying Matriarch-Elect Fangkart. The three styles said their goodbyes to the rest of the party and began weaving their way to him.

'Matriarch-Elect Sharlensya 120/15 Fangkart,' said a neatly turned out young anther from the Canopy. 'I'm Lieutenant Vordautant 265/49 Fangkart, I've been assigned as your chauffeur by the High Council'

Chauffeur my eye! You're my bodyguard. thought Sharlensya, It would explain the mix of Sergeant's rings from the Police Service on a military green uniform of a chauffeur. The SPS sent you, not the High Council, to provide discreet security.

'Thank you Lieutenant. I wasn't expecting this,' said Sharlensya, trying not to sound too shocked.

'Did you not receive the email, Ma'am?'

'No Lieutenant, I haven't checked my inbox for days. I've been on holiday with my daughters.'

'Oh, I see. Well Ma'am, as a Family Matriarch you are entitled to an official car and driver whilst you are in the Roots,' the anther said, letting nothing interfere with his plans.

'But I'm not Matriarch yet,' she told the Lieutenant.

'No Ma'am, but you will be, so the Protocol Division have assigned me to you anyway. If you would like to follow me.'

The family followed the chauffeur through the throng of people. What other surprises were in store for today.

Then she saw the car. It was more like a barge, big and black and shiny, with darkened windows all around. Where the wheels would be on an Earth car, there were short arms that sloped to the base of the large circular antigrav generators, each as tall as the car.

Sharlensya watched as Vordautant open the door of the passenger compartment for her. Once inside, her senses were assailed by the faded opulence of the vehicle. Acres of leather and wood with enough space for seven people to sit comfortably. Once all three styles were aboard, Vordautant climbed into the separate driver's compartment.

Sharlensya had no way of knowing when the transition from taxiing castors to flight occurred, only that the ground had dropped away as the car joined the stream of flying vehicles. It might look like a barge, but it did not fly like one. Despite its speed Sharlensya barely felt as if she was moving. She could get used to this.

'Well girls, this is a turn up, isn't it?' she said as she made herself comfortable.

'I thought you said our house in Root Gamma?' asked Serynazsya a few minutes later.

'It is,' Sharlensya replied.

'Well, we are heading onto the Root Alpha Expressway.'

'Matriarch-Elect, we will be arriving at Fangkart House in five minutes,' Vordautant's pleasant voice chimed over the car's intercom. 'The staff have been alerted and the house has been prepared for your arrival.'

'Thank you Lieutenant,' Sharlensya said. Nevamarsya could feel the growing waves of panic emanating from Sharlensya, who was activating the car's workstation and hurridly logging into her email.

'Look at this girls. This message has been flagged as most urgent, it came from the Protocol Office of the High Council. I should have read it several days ago. As it directly affects you two, you had better read it too.'

'It looks as if we are moving up in the World girls, Sharlensya said as she closed the email. She could see her daughters were excited.

```
From:     General Easthamant 050/02 Islaw, Protocol
          Division, Administration Regiment.
To:       Matriarch-Elect Commander Sharlensya
          120/05 Fangkart
Subject:  Arrival & Fangkart House
Body:     Welcome to the Roots. You will be met at
          the shuttle port by your Chauffer, Lieutenant
          Vordautant 265/49 Fangkart.
          As Matriarch-Elect, yourself and your
          family will be taking up residences at
          Fangkart House, in the Executive Centre on
          Alpha Root.
          Fangkart House is one of the smaller
          residences. It has a domestic staff of
          five officers and twenty Sprites. I hope
          you find it satisfactory.
          If there are any problems, please contact
          me immediately.
```

'Wow, look at those houses. I thought only the Crown had actual buildings?' said Nevamarsya.

'There are a lot of similarities between the Hub of the Roots and the Crown dear,' Sharlensya a little overawed by the architecture, once a mentor always a mentor.

The car hovered over a landing pad on the flat roof of an impressive mansion.

'Neva dear, you'd better put your wig back on dear,' she said.

'Yes Mammy. I only took it off to adjust it.' Nevamarsya replaced the wig on her head. Sensors in it detected body heat as soon as it touched Nevamarsya's scalp, reactivating the nano-motors that drove each strand, making it look like real hair.

'But she hates it,' said Serynazsya. 'Why does she have to wear it all the time,' she ran a hand through her own long copper tresses. 'Why can't she just wander around with cropped hair like she used to?'

'We've been through this before dear.' Sharlensya sighed gently. Why was Serynazsya, a student nurse who should know better, being so silly about this? It's not as if she is the one wearing the wig.

'Because that was before I became a style. I'm a girl now,' said Nevamarsya cutting in. 'It would look odd.'

'Excuse me ladies,' said the Chauffer. Thankfully this ended the discussion but not the problem. It was not the petulant Serynazsya who was the cause for concern. There should have been a childish tiff. The way Nevamarsya had dealt with her half-sister's petulance, in such a mature and reasonable manner was just wrong for someone only six months old. Her worries about giving Nevamarsya and her classmates that field promotion surfaced again. Had it been a mistake? Was missing out on the childhood rank causing them to miss out on a childhood completely.

'On our arrival at Fangkart House. Please wait for the antigrav field to fade before exiting the vehicle, thank you,' continued Lieutenant Vordaunant.

'Thank you, we enjoyed the ride,' said Nevamarsya.

'You're welcome, Subaltern Nevamarsya.'

'The Sprites will be ready to take any hand luggage and unpack it, Ma'am,' said the Chaufer.

'Really. I could get used to this.'

'I'm sure Major Ernnwolant, the Butler, is hoping you do. I beleive he has lined the staff up outside the garage on the roof for you to meet them.'

'I'm overwhelmed. I truly am.'

So this is my home now, thought Natalicsya as she looked around the tiny box room in the apartment her adoptive parents rented on Root Gamma. Three decks down from the Roadway, it was deeper than she had ever been in her life.

'How am I supposed to keep my bike in here?' she asked.

'I'm sorry dear, we had to return it to the Maintainance Regiment. You were only ever borrowing it.'

'But I loved that bike. It was retro and cool.'

'It was big and cumbersome. Are you sure you wouldn't like a nice foldable gee-Bike instead?' asked Galeroysya.

'I suppose so.' Natalicsya was deeply disappointed. Peddling a gee-Bike to generate enough of an antigrav field to lift the bike and produce forward momentum was as much of an exercise as her old bicycle. She felt safe on that clunky old thing. Other roadway users had to respect its bulk, if not its petite rider. Whilst on the subject of bulk she had to ask her half-mother something, 'Why does the door have such a thick seal Mum?'

'Because this room also doubles as the apartment's Flood Room,' replied her Half-Mother.

'Flood Room?' asked the bemused Natalicsya.

'Yes dear, every dwelling, office or workshop below soil level has to have one. It is where we would come in the unlikely event that the seals break and there is a flood in the

Roots. The door is airtight, and there is an oxygen recycling unit that will keep us going for a week.'

'All three of us and a chemical toilet, in a room designed for the safety of one person,' she peered out into the living room. 'This is a single person apartment. One of you moved in with the other when you pair-bonded. That explains everything, doesn't it?'

Her father-to-be put a comforting arm on her shoulder. 'This isn't going to work, is it? This was a roomy Batchelor pad,' Untrugyant said to his wife and half-daughter. It was just about alright when it was just me and your Half-Mother, but now we have you, this place is too tiny.'

'So tomorrow we go home hunting?' asked Natalicsya.

'Yes, we start. I have no idea how far we will get. It's a seller's market. Property down here is at a premium, as it rarely comes on the market.'

'Which is why we will be renting again,' said Galeroysya, with a resigned air.

'Aunty Sharlee has a nice place. It's a shame that it's not available.' Natalicsya had seen pictures of where she thought Nevamarsya was going to be living. Compared to this pokey little hole, it was a palace. Little did she know that her friend was currently moving into a small palace in the Executive Centre.

'She doesn't rent it either. Her mother owned it outright, and her place in the Canopy. Her branch of the Fangkarts are a family of Medics. You never see a poor Medic. Or in the case of her late mother a poor plumber. She can afford a place like that. As could Popisedsya. The rest Winter Squad members aren't that rich, they're ordinary, like us.'

This meant nothing to Natalicsya, who was still a child, with a child's grasp of economics. 'Neva is taking a long time to get here,' said the girl.

'I suppose that flash chauffer has got himself lost. Not used to coming down the gamma Root,' said Untruguyant.

This made Natalicsya laugh. 'That barge couldn't negotiate some of the roadways. Even in the posh parts.'

'It's huge, I didn't think that sort of thing was still in service.' Her Half-Father shared her love of all things automotive. 'All that armour plating must kill its battery.'

'Didn't you see, it had a double battery pod. Might even have been a treble pod,' added Galeroysya.

'Excessively increasing the width.' An idea flashed through Natalicsya's head. 'Perhaps I should call Neva, see what's happening?'

'I wouldn't Lisha dear,' said her half-mother, 'she'll be as tired from the journey as you are.'

'I'm not tired,' she replied with a huge yawn.

'You were saying.' Her half-mother smiled. 'Take a nap now, while you have the chance. When you start training you will be wishing you still had the opportunity.'

However, Natalicsya was already fast asleep.

Major Ernnwolant 179/44 Fangkart looked at his staff, lined up to meet the new boss. What would she think. They had remained unchanged during the incumbencies of the two previous Matriarchs. What a sorry lot they were. He was no spring chicken. His wife, Captain Farnwelsya, the Cook, was as old as he was. Their daughter, the recently promoted Lieutenant Ensfibsya, the Housekeeper and Sprite Manager, was the only youngster, but having spent the five years as an Ensign and the past three as a Subaltern here, she was as set in her ways as any of the other staff.

As for the rest, Captain Osterixant, the handyman, didn't actually do any work. He was an invalid nearing retirement. Lieutenant Singlowsya, a former nurse, officially the

Matriarch's Lady's Maid was another older officer cruising towards retirement. He doubted that the new young and healthy Matriarch-Elect would want the kind of specialist care Singlowsya provided her predecessor. In fact, he doubted she would want a Lady's Maid at all.

The hatch of the official car popped open and three girls emerged. Strange, thought the Major, where is the Matriarch-Elect? She only had two very young children, so who was the third youngster. And wasn't she from the Roots anyway, a Pure-stock, just like all the previous Matriarchs. These three were all from the Canopy.

'Major Ernnwolant, Sir. May I present the Matriarch-Elect, Commander Sharlensya 120/05 Fangkart,' said Lieutenant Vordaunant.

'Matriarch-Elect?' The Major refused to let his shock show. He knew she was young, but didn't realise the new boss was this young. I should have read that briefing sheet again, last night, he thought to himself.

'It's a pleasure to meet you, and your sisters. Are your daughters travelling separately?'

'It's a pleasure to meet you too Major. Don't worry, you're not the first person and won't be the last to make that mistake. This is my daughter Subaltern Serynazsya 170/26 and half-daughter Subaltern Nevamarsya 331/29.'

With three attractive young styles in the house, things were going to be interesting for the foreseeable future.

Althallant was so glad that he and Pemisegant were not heading for the Central trolleybus station in any of the packed trolley buses that had passed while they were waiting for theirs. The short and stocky Mid-Trunk anther looked as if nothing frightened him. However, he had been a Sprite in the sparsely populated Agricultural Zone, then an Officer Cadet in the

Canopy which was deserted for Winter. In truth he was terrified of being crushed in a crowd.

'So, you are certain we will be billeted in the same dorm?' asked his friend Pemisegant.

'Yes, Pezzi your residency chit says Dorm 7D13, Juvenile Barracks 157. Just like mine. We attended the same Academy as Cadets, officialdom refuses to split us up. What if we hated each other?'

'What I hate the fact that I have to share my room, even with you. We were so lucky with the Winter Squad, we had rooms exclusively to ourselves. I don't know how I will cope with the lack of privacy.'

'Oh stop moaning Pezzi, it wasn't a problem during the Boot Camp, why should it be a problem now.

'Because, Alth, me old mate, that was just for a month, this is indefinite.'

'At least a year. Until we find parents. Or have them found for us.'

'That's bad enough.'

'Who knows, we might get lucky and find families straight away. The girls have,' said Althallant cheerfully.

'I very much doubt that.'

'Glass half empty again, Pezzi?'

'Whatever,' replied Pemisegant, lost in thought.

'And its "we had rooms exclusively" or "we had rooms to ourselves",' said Althallant, 'one or the other.'

'What?'

'Nevermind. At least you won't stick out in this dorm. The other boys are like you, Canopy born.'

Their trolleybus arrived, which cut their conversation short. Both boys spent the journey looking out the window as they travelled to their new home.

'This place is huge,' said Serynazsya, in hushed tones. 'Are we expected to fill all of it?'

Nevamarsya was thinking the same, as the family and Major Ernnwolant made their way down from the Matriarch's private garage in the attic to a grand entrance hall on the ground floor.

'No dear, it's called the Matriarch's Residence, but most of the building is a government office complex,' replied Sharlensya. Most members of Family Fangkart, until now herself included, only ever see the offices, so she had no idea what to expect from the rest of the building.

'Indeed, Matriarch-Elect. Although I think you will find you have more than enough space in your new home.' The Major opened the door and lead them into a large hallway. 'The Matriarch's actual residence within Fangkart House is called the Lilac Suite, which is accessible from this hallway via the Lilac staircase.'

'Thank you Major.'

'Normally you would have access to it from the garage, but I've had to bring you the long way whilst the Security System updates its biometric profile of you and your daughters. Other family and friends will also need to have a profile logged here at the Main Entrance on their first visit.'

On the first floor, the staircase split in two, one with green carpet, the other with lilac. The Buttler stopped at a comconsole display by the foot of the Lilac Staircase.

'Ah, you have your first visitor, Commander Sendarnsya is waiting for you in the Drawing Room.'

Behind his bland façade, Nevamarsya could tell the Major hated Commander Sendarnsya.

The three Styles followed the Major up the lilac carpeted staircase, through a door into another hallway, then into the luxurious drawing room. Standing in the middle of the room was a blonde style in full dress uniform. She was middle aged and looked as if she had not eaten for the past decade. Everything about her was pinched and thin.

'Commander Sendarnsya,' said Major Ernnwolant, 'this is the Matriarch-Elect Sharlensya, and her daughters Serynazsya and Nevamarsya. Ladies, this is Commander Sendarnsya.'

'Thank you Major,' she said, without a smile. It would have been hard to smile and look so horrified at the same time.

'If you would excuse me, I will be in my office.' With that, the butler was gone. The room seemed to become a few degrees colder.

Calling Juvenile Barracks 157 an ugly building would be an insult to ugly buildings everywhere. Its horrendous institutionalised architecture and its cheap and nasty building materials formed a harmony of hideousness that took it beyond ugly. Its location next to one of the drainage canals from the Central Channels could have been pretty, if the entire bank had not been concreted over with parade grounds and seventeen identical barracks.

'So this is home?' asked Althallant as they walked into the entrance.

'Not a lot I can say,' replied Pemisegant.

'Then say nothing, Ensign.' The voice belonged to the anther sitting at a desk in the entrance hall. 'I'm Subaltern Grispelant, one of the Dorm Wardens for this barracks, also its Drill Sergeant.'

'Drill Sergeant?' asked Pemisegant.

'Yes, Ensign. Do you think all the parade grounds are for decoration? You will adress me as Sir and do everything I tell you first time, every time. Is that understood?'

'Perfectly, Subaltern,' replied the two friends.

'I don't think you heard me, Ensigns, I said you address me as Sir.'

'Well, I would, if I were an Ensign. As we're all Subalterns, I don't see the need.' Pemisegant immediately disliked the Dorm Warden, who was almost as ugly as the building he was in charge off.

'Ah, a joker,' said the warden. 'Impersonating a superior officer is a serious offence.'

'I know, I wouldn't dream of doing it.' Pemisegant placed his IndesnCard on the reader and turned to the other anther. 'I believe I'm to be billeted here for the forseeable, as is my friend Subaltern Althallant.'

'That doesn't mean a thing. Chronologically you're years younger than me, still kids and as so you do what I tell you.'

'Chronologically, but not legally,' said Althallant, who also didn't like the Warden's attitude. 'We might be young, but we have had forty two days of terror. Not knowing if our next meal would be our last. Forty two day of real combat experience. You will respect that! How much combat experience have you got?'

'And what do you think you are, an Enquirer?'

'Eventually. I start my Enforcer training this week.'

'None.' Subaltern Grispelant took this news in his stride. 'I have, the Tree be praised, had a very quiet life.' The warden looked at the screen of his wristcom, obviously checking up on his two new charges. 'However, you have been assigned to my Building. So you will also treat me with respect, you understand! Now follow me.'

Dorm 7D13 had four beds in its main room. It shared a central lobby and toilet facilities with the other three dorms on the fourth floor of the barracks. This floor was under the supervision of Subaltern Grispelant and was a joyless as a prison cell.

'Damn, it was bad enough when I thought I would only be sharing with you,' said Pemisegant. 'Now I find I will be sharing with two others.'

'I did tell you Pezzi, but as usual you were more interested in messing around with something mechanical,' said Althallant. 'Currently it is one other. The name plate on the door only has three names on it.'

'A mild improvement,' said Pemisegant.

'The fourth bunk will soon be filled, Subaltern. The other resident is out, you'll meet him soon enough.' Subaltern Grispelant laughed. 'You will probably get to know him quite well. He wants to be an Enquirer as well.'

'Thank you for showing us to our quarters, Subaltern. I don't doubt you are busy,' said Althallant as he closed the door on the objectionable anther.

'What a jerk, any intel on him Alth?' asked Pemisegant.

'Here we go,' replied Althallant who was looking at the BioProfile of the Warden on his comlink. 'Subaltern Grispelant 207/04 Burke. Aged thirteen and never been higher Subaltern, Second Grade.'

'That my friend, takes a special type of stupid,' Pemisegant said, 'most people have been at least Lieutenant, Fifth Grade by the time they're ten. Thirteen years old and still only a Subaltern, Second Grade.'

'It explains why he is still working in this dump,' said Althallant. 'I wonder how the girls are getting on?'

Great green apples, all the rumours are true thought, Commander Sendarnsya. She believed in traditions, so she followed the Pure Stock Code to the letter. She instinctively knew the Roots were superior to anywhere else in the Tree. The new Matriarch had gone native after spending so much time in the Canopy. The elder daughter had also turned her back on the Roots. The half-daughter was a hick anyway, natural red hair, the girl was naturally inferior.

Before she had gone gag-ga, old Symraltsya had been a moderate. So steering the Family Fangkart back to the Traditionalist group on the High Council had been easy as the toothless Family Forum had shown no particular political persuasion. The new Matriarch would change all that. She would encourage the Radicals in the Forum, alter the balance of power back in the Radicals' favour.

'Matriarch-Elect, what a pleasure to meet you at last,' she said, every word dripping with false sincerity.

'Cousin Sendarnsya, it is a pleasure to finally meet you as well. Please call me Sharlee. This is my daughter Serynazsya and my half-daughter Nevamarsya.'

'Charmed, I'm sure. And thank you for permission to use your familiar name. You may call me Darsah.' The older style walked over to a mirror, and the uniform changed into a civilian suit. 'Now, I understand that you wish to discuss the continuation of my arrangement with the late Matriarch. For me to act as your voting deputy when duty calls you to uncivilised parts of the Tree?'

'That is right. I will be unable to attend every meeting of the Council's Winter Sessions, someone will have to sit for me in Council and on any committees I am assigned to.'

'I can see no problems with that.' Father Earth, she is even starting to talk with that dreadful accent. The Matriarch could stay up there all year if she liked. Sendarnsya would continue to vote with the Traditionalists and any stupid idea the new Tree Marshall floated would quickly sink.

'Although I will be more reflective of the Family, which appears to be more radical than the previous Matriarch. As a Radical myself, I am more than happy to follow that mandate.'

'That won't be a problem,' Sendarnsya replied, her false smile pinned firmly in place. 'After all, I am only a deputy, I do what I am told.'

Lying cow was all that Sharlensya could think. There was something deeply disturbing about the way that the older style smiled. It gave away the fact that she would rather drink poison than vote the way she was instructed. Still, surely it would not be that difficult to find a new Voting Deputy.

'Well, I won't disturb you any longer.' Sendarnsya was heading towards the door, 'I'm sure you and your lovely daughters have a lots to do.'

'It was good to meet you. Do call again soon,' Sharlensya said. Upon the occasion of Hell freezing over, she thought.

'What an unpleasant piece of work,' she said when she was sure the older style was gone, she turned to her daughters. I'm starting to think old Symraltsya wasn't the dyed in the wool reactionary her voting record in her latter years made her out to be.'

'Excuse me Ma'am,' said a style, old enough to be Sharlensya's grandmother, who had been sitting quietly in the background, 'that poisonous old witch has misrepresented us Fangkarts for far too many years, it is nice to see that there will be someone with a bit of reformist zeal fighting our Family's corner in the High Council for a change, either you, or who ever you select as your Deputy.'

'What has the Family Forum had to say about that?' asked Sharlensya.

'She has the Moderators in her in her pocket. They do what she tells them, not the other way around. If a Thread gets out of line, they get shut down. But as soon as you are installed, you'll be able to sack them all, hold elections for a new set of Moderators. With luck, one that accurately represents the will of the Family.'

'You must be Lieutenant Singlowsya,' said Nevamarsya.

'That's right miss. I am the Matriarch-Elect's Lady's Maid.'

'Lady's Maid. I don't think I need a Lady's Maid. I am used to looking after myself.'

'These days, it is merely a job title. I was Ralla's carer and best friend towards the end. The only one she would trust. That perfumed princess tried to get rid of me on more than one occasion, but the only person who could fire me was Ralla herself, may the Tree give her rest.'

So much information for Sharlensya to take in during a single session. She was getting a headache.

'As I said, I don't think I need a Lady's Maid, even one with a job title only.'

'Then Ma'am, may I suggest the job of Social Secretary, you will need one now, someone to deal with your Appointments Diary. That is another job I used to do for old Ralla, not that she ever went out much towards the end.'

'Thank you Lieutenant, that is very helpful.'

'You will certainly need a local guide to help you survive in this pool of piranhas,' said Nevamarsya.

'I thought piranhas were fruit eating pysgod,' said Serynazsya.

'Mostly, but under certain circumstances they can strip the flesh from an anther's bones in under thirty seconds.' The Lieutenant smiled. 'You must be Miss Serynazsya, the Matriarch-Elect's heiress.'

'That's right, but I have never been called Miss before.'

'It is your official title now, Miss Serynazsya, or Subaltern Miss Serynazsya 178/20 Fangkart.'

'Oh, I think I can get used to that,' said Serynazsya.

'And so the other young lady must be Subaltern Nevamarsya 331/29.'

'Don't I have an official title?' asked Nevamarsya.

'Not yet. When you become the Matriarch-Elect's full daughter, you will also gain the honorific "Miss" on all your documentation and you will be addressed as Miss Nevamarsya, even when not on duty.'

Mother Sun thought Sharlensya, what an archaic situation.

'I can see that you don't approve of titles and all that goes with your new possition, Ma'am.'

'Yes Lieutenant, it all seems so old fashioned,' she said.

'It is Matriarch-Elect, but a lot of people find it charming in a strange sort of way, which is why it persists.'

'I can see I am going to be relying heavily on your services over the next few weeks.'

'I aim to please,' said the old lady.

There was the sound of giggling from the stairway.

'That will be the Sprites with your luggage. Do you want to supervise them as they unpack.'

With that, some sort of normality returned to the situation and Sharlensya felt she could relax. She heard her comlink ping, as did Nevamarsya's and Serynazsya's

'Oh great green apples!' said Nevamarsya, 'Bernie has been arrested and charged with murder.'

Sharlensya consulted her comlink. It was true, her old friend was currently in the guard house, charged with a twenty year old crime. So much for a sense of normality.

HAPPY FAMILIES

Kanonypsya Rust looked at the photograph that had just arrived in the post. A picture of a young Tree-Nun from the Upper-Trunk. Great green apples, it was a picture of herself. Somebody must have been clearing out the Convent's Hall of Records and sent her one of the many photographs it contained. Somebody deeply dedicated volunteering for such a Herckulantian task. Then she thought it was more likely to be some deeply disobedient individual doing the job as a penance. There was something scribbled on the back, "Remember. We didn't just have Sisters. AP.", what in the Tree was that supposed to mean.

The photograph had been taken on the day she had professed her final vows and received the Sacred Rosette, the gold and silver representation of the Tree on a chain around her neck. Like a noose forcing her into a life she had not chosen to lead.

Years earlier, the only copy of The Book of Song, the Tree-Nun's sacred text had been lost in a flood. The Book of Song had been written by the Spirit of the Tree. Its replacement had been written by a committee of Tree-Nuns with imperfect memories. It contained many mistakes.

One Sunday morning at Temple Parade when she had heard the Spirit of the Tree singing along with her, Kanonypsya knew her future had been decided for her by the biggest mistake in the Book of New Songs.

Kanonypsya's pose left no doubt she was not happy. Her left arm resting on her hip, right hand pointing accusingly, her face full of anger. She remembered that the other three reluctant novices that day had already accepted their fate and their photograph would have been bland in comparison.

Then the years of bored disinterest ended. The Spirit of the Tree began paying attention again to the world He had create. When He discovered styles had been forced to join the Sisterhood, He was angry. He appeared as a beam of multicoloured light at Evening Prayers in the Convent to admonish the Abbess and her assistants. This triggered the Great Return, releasing the reluctant sisters from the vows taken under duress. Now a young style would take her vows only if she chose to.

For Kanonypsya, the Great Return came and went. She believed that her beloved Keltonnant must have found a new love and pair-bonded with another. She knew if she could not be with him, there was no life for her beyond the cloister. Life within the Sisterhood became unbearable as she really was not suited to be one of the Tree's Blessed Handmaidens. Eight long and miserable years after retaking her vows, she had been marooned in the Canopy. At first it had been torture. She discovered that Keltonnant had remained single, her foolish choices made him as inaccessible as ever. Then at the height of the war with the Virus, the Spirit of the Tree himself spoke to her again. He would release her from his service as her reward for helping to defeat the Virus Invasion. She and Keltonnant had both grabbed the chance to be together at last.

Today she was going with young Nevamarsya and Natalicsya in search of a wedding dress. A proper wedding dress this time, not the perpetual wedding dress of a Tree-Nun. Kanonypsya wanted a bride's white dress but not a bride's white veil.

She had worn veils for long enough, thank you very much.

With the sound of happy laughter in the hallway, Kanonypsya knew she would have to decide what to do with the photograph, and whether to read the accompanying note later. She had a pair of visitors.

'Hello Aunty Kandy, are you ready?' asked Nevamarsya.

'Neva dear and Natalicsa, you're both early,' Kanonypsya replied from the bedroom.

'Are we? I thought you said 1345.'

'Great green apples, is that the time?' Kanonypsya glanced at the clock on the wall. 'You're on time, I'm running late. There's a bottle of pop in the fridge. Do you want a drink?'

"Aunty Kandy," being called that by Neva was still a pleasant experience. She had long given up hope of being anyone's aunt, only their sister.

She could see, through the doorway, the two girls were both wearing the short clinging dresses with hoods loved by the young at the moment. Just for fun she typed a code into her emprinter and the mirror showed an image of herself in a similar dress, then her clothes rearranged themselves to match, whilst a mesage asking to confirm the purchase flashed on screen.

'I bet Uncle Kelly would love it if you wore a dress like that,' said Nevamarsya.

Kanonypsya was horrified. She had thought she was alone in her room and the girls were busy in the kitchen.

'No, he'd hate it. It would remind him of how much he has aged in the past twenty years, whilst I have remained almost the same,' said Kanonypsya, cancelling the sale and changed her outfit again.

The Tree-people live shorter lives than the Human on whom they were modelled. The Tree needed the more advanced officers in a hurry, so it had dispensed with the childhood and shortened the teenage years to sixteen weeks.

At twenty eight years old, Kanonypsya should have been the equivalent of a 56 year old woman on Earth. However, she had spent twenty years in the Convent, which is built in a place where the Tree's life force is far stronger than usual. Exposure to this energy slows the metabolism of Tree-Nuns so they stay younger for longer. This ironic situation is wasted on a group of styles who have no interest in their appearance.

'Oh Neva, it is starting to come between us.' Kanonypsya was crying now, 'the gossip about him being my sugar daddy is beginning to annoy him. Because that is exactly how it looks to people who don't know us. They think he is a lecherous old anther with his young trophy wife.'

'Has he actually said anything about this to you?' asked Nevamarsya.

'No, I can see it in the way he acts towards me, the way he talks to me.'

'Which is why you have been dressing like a granny since we arrived in the Roots?'

'Exactly. Trying to undo the damage. The last couple of months up in the Canopy were amazing. We had twenty years of fun to catch up on. I think Kelts has been shocked.'

'Nothing wrong with having fun.'

'There is if you're a staid old anther like your Great Uncle.'

Nevamarsya was surprised that her friend and soon to be great Aunt, upset about something so trivial. She thought a person's character was more important than their appearance.

'Anyway,' said Nevamarsya, 'it's really got nothing to do with him, or anyone else how you dress in your downtime. We all dress the same on duty, so everyone dresses to please them-selves off duty. The Golden Rule.'

'It's not that easy when you are in a relationship,' said the older style.

'Yes it is. If Pezzi doesn't like what I am wearing, it's his problem.'

Nevamarsya knew exactly how old the apparently youthful Kanonypsya was. Two years older than Uncle Keltonnant, so definitely not a younger "Trophy Wife". She also knew how much happier he had been since Kanonypsya had returned to his life.

'Don't worry Aunty Kandy, it's just pre-bonding nerves,' she said to the older style.

'I hope you're right dear.'

'I'm sure of it. Mammy says she has never seen Uncle Kelly looking so alive, it's like he has a whole new lease on life.'

'Really? He seems to be more miserable to me.'

'You mean you haven't noticed the spring in his step?'

'No, I haven't.' Kanonypsya started crying again. 'Whenever he sees me he clams up. Oh Neva, it's all going wrong!'

Nevamarsya could feel the panic that Kanonypsya was broadcasting. Groundless panic with no basis in reality.

'Don't worry. Mammy says Uncle Kelly has never been the most demonstrative of people.'

'That didn't use to be the case. He used to be full of random acts of love.' Kanonypsya paused, remembering the happy days when she had first met Keltonnant. 'He has changed so much and I have stayed the same. It is so unfair.'

'I think you should both have a chat with my half-mother. She'll soon show you how silly this all is.'

Nevamarsya hugged Kanonypsya The course of true love never ran smoothly. Her relationship with Pemisegant was going through a rough patch.

'Thank you Neva, I'll try that,' said Kanonypsya.

'Try what?' asked Natalicsya as they walked back into the living room.

'Oh nothing,' replied Nevamarsya.

'And you're not wearing that are you?' There was a note of horror in Natalicsya's voice.

Kanonypsya was still wearing the very prim outfit, with high collared blouse and floor skimming skirt, she had changed into a few minutes earlier.

'I know you are old enough to be the bride's granny, and not the bride herself,' said the "ever tactful" Natalicsya. 'And you don't want anything too flashy, but come on Kanonypsya, at least try.'

'Come now, Natalicsya, I know you are only ever trying to be helpful, but we all have the right to be wrong. So it's up to me how I dress whilst off duty.'

'I'm sorry, I'll never get used to this Golden Rule thing.'

Nevamarsya could hear her Aunty Kandy begin to laugh. 'Hang on, I'll be right back,' said the older style, who quickly returned once again in a dress similar to the two girls, but as a top with jeans and boots.

'You think I'm being silly now?' asked the older style. 'I suppose I am, but being able to dress like a youngster when I am at the end of my third decade pleases me. To hell with what the narrow minded think.'

'If I look that good in my third decade, I'd be pleased to,' replied Natalicsya. There was a buzz from a portable emprinter, and Kanonypsya's jeans became tights. 'If you want to look like a younger style, do it properly.'

'And please, call me Kandy, we're off on an informal shopping trip, let's keep it informal.'

'Thank you Kandy.'

'You're welcome,' she replied as Kanonypsya locked her front door behind them.

'Are you leaving us so soon Little Flower?' the old Anther asked.

'Yes Grandad Rex,' replied Lieutenant Popisedsya.

'I have a posting at Heartswood, to journey there each day is wasteful.'

The unmanned Trolley-cab she had been waiting for was landing, and it would be five minutes before it would be ready for her.

'I think I have stretched Cousin Rolinalant's patience as much as I dare,' she said with a hind of sorrow.

'That fool does as he is told. I still curse the day my son chose to pair-bond with his mother.' The old anther sat down on the chair next to Popisedsya.

'His late father was my designated heir. As myoldest grandchild. When I recycle, the laws of the Tree mean he will inherit this farm.' The old anther smiled. 'But it's not his yet.'

'And long may it remain so.'

A sad look crossed Grandad Rex's face. 'You know those days are numbered, Little Flower. It's no use pretending otherwise.'

Popisedsya wanted to deny the inevitability of things. If nothing terminal happened earlier in their lives, Tree-people lived for exactly forty-two years from activation to recycling, and Grandad Rex was forty-two next birthday.

'Are you still travelling up to the Corps' Regional Offices next week?' asked Popisedsya.

'Yes, there is life in this old dog yet. I'll be up in the Heartswood for a week.'

'You have called a Thread Meeting of the Family Forum, here at the farm, for as soon as you return home.'

Each Family Matriarch was answerable to her relatives through the Family Forum. This was made up of many smaller units called threads, which held regular meetings.

Each thread elected a representative who took its opinion to the District Meta-Thread. In turn this selected the Regional Sub-Fourum which mandated the Moderators who briefed the Matriarch, or her Deputy, in the High Council.

'Yes, it has been a season since the last one. We have to keep Matriarch Siylm and the rest of the Family Forum informed about what this Thread of the Family wants.'

'We are such a small Thread on the Family Forum, do you think the Matriarch even cares?' asked Popisedsya.

'A small Thread we may be. But there are enough neutral threads to stop our illustrious Matriarch from voting for the latest crazy idea to come from either the Radicals or the Traditionalists.'

'Finally, one thing we disagree on. You know I'm a Radical, Grandfather. I would like the Matriarch to be more radical in her voting.'

'Yes, well, nobody is perfect. However, you will be there won't you?'

Popisedsya knew that her grandfather didn't have to plead like this. It was all for show.

'Of course, it is my democratic duty to be there.'

'Good, very good.'

She recognised that look in his eyes. 'Tell me, what are you planning you wily old anther?'

'Me, I'm not planning anything. Just doing my duty to the Family, just as you will on the night of the meeting.'

'Ooh look, a flying pig!'

'Don't be silly girl, only horses fly.'

They both dissolved into laughter.

For nearly two decades, whenever he was stationed down in the Roots, Colonel Keltonnant had used the same barber. These days it only took his friend Major Harpowlant a few minutes to run a trimmer over what remained of his once thick dark locks. It was more of a social visit to an old friend than a necessity to keep his hair the regulation length. Harpowlant's Barber Shop had been old-fashioned when he had first visited there. It had not changed and deep down Keltonnant didn't want it to change.

'Married life is suiting you, Kelly' said Harpowlant.

'I'm not actually married yet Harpo, the Pair-bonding Ceremony is in a month,' replied Keltonnant.

'Still in the Settling, then?'

'Yes, Harpo. We are.' During the Settling Period prior to the ceremony, couples moved in together, to see if they could live as a Pair-bond. 'but I know what you mean. I've been happier in the last few months than I have been for years.'

'You're a very lucky anther. Finding an attractive young style who will put up with all the bad habits you picked up as a bachelor. How old is she, early in her second decade?' This was roughly in her thirties in human terms.

'Kanonypsya is two years older than me.'

'Really, you wouldn't think so to look at her.'

'Ex-Tree-Nun, I think they must pickle themselves in that Convent. They live so much longer than us mere mortals.'

'That explains your hair then,' said the barber. 'You are using up the last of her supply of Rohotel.'

'Certainly not. The use of Rohotel by anthers as a hair restorer is prohibited, far too many side effects.'

'Sorry, no need to bite my head off, Kelly.'

'Harpo, old friend, you should know I never joke about things medicinal.'

'So if its not Rohotel, what is making you so hirsute all of a sudden,' asked the barber.

'Married life must really suit me,' said Keltonnant, perfectly mimicking his friend's earlier comment.

'I always found it odd that Rohotel destroys hair for styles, but actively encourages it in anthers. Biologically we are almost identical, only a variation in the plumbing,' said the barber.

'Variations in plumbing. Is that the technical term, Harpo?'

'Yes Kelly, it is.'

'There are variations in chemistry to consider as well.'

'Oestrol and Testerol,' said Harpowlant helpfully.

'That's right Harpo. I wish I could tell you more, but I have to be getting on.'

'Don't worry, I can look it up on Wikipedant's,' said Harpowlant, smiling because he knew about his friend's outdated dislike for the online encyclopedia. 'So how do you explain why you are suddenly so hirsute.'

'It must be the Power of Love,' said Keltonnant glumly.

'Something wrong, old friend?' asked Harpowlant.

'Yes Harpo, there is.' Keltonnant sounded even more upset. 'Kandy is becoming a bit irrational about the apparent age difference.'

'How's that?' asked the old friend.

'I don't know. You would think that she would be delighted that she still looked like a teenager in her at the end of her third decade, wouldn't you?'

'Who knows how styles really think. They did after all come from a different plant.'

'Two Sources, one Tree, served equally by two equal types of Officer,' said Keltonnant who was reciting one of the basic principles of the Officer Corps. 'I suppose it must be pre-bonding nerves. Every time she hears someone making a comment like yours about a pretty young style and an older anther, she gets really worried. Or rather, thinks I get upset, which makes her worried.'

'And do you get upset Kelly?'

'Of course not,' replied Keltonnant, 'why should I? There is nothing to be worried about.'

'You've told Kandy that?'

'No, there is nothing to be worried about.'

'There is the root of the problem,' replied Harpowlant, 'she thinks there is a problem, even though there isn't. You have to reassure her that there is nothing to worry about. That's all.'

'I'm afraid of saying the wrong thing. I have been a bachelor for so long.'

'Believe me Kelly, saying nothing is far worse than saying something wrong. She might act all upset for a few hours, but it shows you care. In the long term she will be glad you noticed.'

'I suppose so,' said Keltonnant, still worried.

'Well, that's you done for another three weeks.' The barber had finished trimming Keltonnant's beard

'Just in time for the ceremony,' said Keltonnant. As he was putting his uniform jacket back on,

Keltonnant heard the tinkle of the bell as he left the barber shop. He had not noticed it for years. So he opened the door again and asked, 'Have you had a new bell installed?'

'No Kelly, it is the same as it ever was,' replied the barber.

'It just sounded different,' he waved. 'See you in three weeks.'

Although the singing of the little bell was not the only thing he had heard for the first time in years. And his eyesight was slightly better than it had been. Was being with his darling Kanonypsya really having such a positive effect on him?

All other clothing in the Tree was made from emprintable fabric Pair-bonding dresses were special. Each dress is unique, made to measure from mycelium silk, for the one and only time it would be worn.

Kanonypsya was feeling extremely nervous. She had found the pattern for the dress she had planned to wear two decades earlier, before fate had intervened.

'I'm sure you will find this horribly old fashioned Lisha dear,' she said as she showed the cover picture to Natalicsya and Nevamarsya.

'Old fashioned my eye,' said Natalicsya.

It was a surprise to her that young Natalicsya, the slave to fashion had loved the old dress pattern.

'It's a proper Pair-bonding Dress,' Natalicsya continued.

'Really? You do surprise me,' said Kanonypsya.

'Oh yes,' the youngster said. Brides today look as if they only have half their dress on. All bare shoulders and backs.'

'Remember the Golden Rule,' said Kanonypsya. 'No-one has the right to critisise what anyone else choses to wear. Especially on someone's Pair-bonding Day.'

I know, but there should be some sense of decorum shown towards what is supposed to be a sacred ceremony.'

'Will this shop make someone else's design Lisha?' asked Nevamarsya, tactfully changing the subject. 'I thought it was run by one of your designer friends?'

'Look in the window Neva, all these dresses are very retro, Veladrosya is always on the lookout for old pair-bonding dresses for inspiration,' replied Natalicsya. 'She'll love this.'

True enough, the hologram projected in the window of the shop had full white meringue skirts, high collars and lacy bodices. After the model had done a twirl the image updated, the next dress again had acres of white silk and lace.

A successful day, with the dresses for the Bride-to-Be and her bridesmaids purchased, the three returned to base.

'And this, Lisha dear, is the last time I got married,' said Kanonypsya as she showed her the old photograph.

Natalicsya spotted the writing on the back of the photograph and read it. "Remember. We didn't just have Sisters. AP." What in the Tree does that mean?'

'Of course, why didn't I think of it before?' said Kanonypsya, with a sudden bolt of inspiration.

'Think of what Aunt Kandy?' asked Nevamarsya.

'Abbess Annaprysya.'

'What about her?' asked Natalicsya.

'Don't you see girls. She took her vows the same day I did. Her brother, Commander Gaemlovant, was a friend of Tabbernant. He was with him the night Drwgdynant went missing. He could verify Bernie's alibi.'

'That's great, where is he?' asked Nevamarsya.

'The Tree only knows. He had made a lot of enemies. He found a way of vanishing into thin air.'

'So he's dead then,' said Natalicsya, her professional stoicism shining through.

'No, his name is not on the Great Wall. Everyone knew Drwgdynant was dead when the Spirit of the Tree inscribed his name there.'

Kanonypsya was talking about the exact spot where the Graft occurred. It was a shining marble wall a mile high circumnavigating the Tree. When a Tree-person dies, their full name, rank and InDesn code is engraved on it by an invisible hand. Whenever a row is completed, the engraving moves upwards. Even after nineteen decades, the list of names is less that a hundred height units tall.

'So,' said Nevamarsya 'the hunt is on. We have to find out where Gaemlovant is hiding himself.'

CHAPTER EIGHT
THE TRAP

Monesday afternoon. First day of the working week, and Pemisegant was bored already. This posting was so tedious. It had not taken him long to realise that being a Patent Office Clerk was the most mind numbingly dull thing in the Tree. After three weeks, he was losing the will to live.

Pemisegant and his three friends were now classed as attending lectures, seminars and workshops and their afternoons working to pay their tuition fees.

After all the cool things he was learning during his morning classes, the afternoons just dragged. He never dreamed being based in the Research and Development Regimental Headquarters would be so deadly dull. Waiting for someone, no make that anyone, to come looking for a particular Patent Certificate. Nobody wanted to see hard-copy these days. Spending the time studying or doing class homework was frowned upon. On the first day he had been told that they call it homework for a reason by at least six different officers. Not that the homework was a challenge to Pemisegant. Usually it took him a few minutes when he returned to the barracks. So he was left with nothing to do but wait.

Pemisegant knew any doodling which led to a practical product, created whilst he was being paid by the Regiment would legally and morally belong to the Regiment.

'Fancy a fresh cup of Instaht then Pezzi?' asked Lieutenant Fordtesant, one of the old hands from the Patent Office, who had taken pity on Pemisegant.

'Not at the moment thanks, I have brought a flask of Calla with me,' replied Pemisegant.

'Yuck, cold, sweet and fizzy,' said the Lieutenant. 'It can't be good for you.'

'I'll go and get you your drink,' said Pemisegant. 'Its not as if I am rushed off my feet.'

'Thanks Pezzi, you're a gent.'

The main door opened for the first time in hours. The person had three choices, left to the lift down to the Prototypes Collection, right for Pemisegant in the Patent Office or straight on for the Reception of Regimental Headquarters.

'Heads up, looks like you have a customer,' Lieutenant Fordtesant said as someone walked through the inner doors and up to the desk.

'Subaltern, you look like somebody who needs some hard physical work.' It was Commander Yestarnsya, from the Prototypes Collection. Pemisegant had never seen such a tall style. At 6.2 units tall, the Commander was as tall as Pemisegant and towered over most female Officers, including his girlfriend. Commander Yestarnsya's most striking features were her large almond shaped eyes typical of officers from the middle of the Trunk, who from an Earth perspective resembled the Chinese. Everything else about her pointed to her being from the Canopy, just like Pemisegant.

She was smiling and in the short time he had been working here, he had learnt that the Commander, a miserable old witch, normally had to have a smile plucked from her with pliers.

'Hard physical work, Ma'am, in this place,' Pemisegant laughed. 'What's hard physical work in this place?' He had failed to notice the sweat dripping from her brow.

'You really shouldn't have said that youngster,' said Lieutenant Fordtesant under his breath.

'Subaltern, follow me,' she ordered.

'Yes, Ma'am.'

Pemisegant followed the miserable witch into a service elevator down to a sub basement. This was a part of the building everyone knew about, but few had ever visited.

'As you know, Subaltern, it is impossible to patent an idea. You have to have designs, reams of research to back up your designs and eventually a working prototype.'

'Yes, Ma'am,' said Pemisegant.

She lead him through an air-lock.

'This is where we keep the prototypes,' she made an expressive hand gesture. 'Not just the prototypes for successful inventions, but prototypes for everything.'

Pemisegant looked beyond the gantry he was standing in. All he could see was miles and miles of shelving in the cavernous room below. A room that must stretch beneath not just the R&D Regimental Headquarters, but the headquarters of several other regiments. It was like he had been let into the biggest toyshop in the Tree.

'Yes Subaltern, this is a naturally occurring structure that stretches far beyond our Regimental HQ. It is completely water tight, accessible only from the single entrance. We have installed a microclimate generator, should the Hub ever flood again, this collection would be completely protected, as would anyone trapped in it.'

'Over the past year I've tried sorting out the paperwork in this place. I've come to the conclusion that it needs to be cleaned out and properly catalogued. Lieutenant Ryzinasant, the new Chief of Headquarters Security has requested a full inventory. So I am killing two avians with one stone. Do you understand?'

'Yes Ma'am,' replied Pemisegant.

'I'm supposed to have an assistant. So far I've not been successful in finding one.' Nobody wanted to work with the imfamous Yestarnsya the Unsmiling. 'So I'm borrowing you for the day. Don't worry, the paperwork has just been filed and you are temporarily reassigned to this department. If you meet my exacting standards, I may offer you the reassignment on a permanent basis. If not, the search goes on. I am going to get the place sorted, or die in the attempt.'

No, not a toy shop thought Pemisegant, I have recycled, my physical body is gone and my mind has gone to heaven.

'A word of warning first. We have no time to "play" with the contents of this room. No matter how much you might want to, fiddling with the items, trying to get them to work whilst on duty, is strictly prohibited.'

'Yes, Ma'am.' Pemisegant's heart sunk, in the toy shop but not allowed to play with anything. Of course he knew if he started to fiddle with an interesting device, a whole afternoon could be swallowed up before he realised it. Also, just like any sketches he might have made upstairs, if he got something to work, the patent would belong to the Regiment. 'I understand, getting this project finished is the priority.'

'Weekends and evenings are another matter,' said a voice from behind them.

'Thank you Lieutenant Ryzinasant,' said the Commander. Her face looked like a bulldog chewing a wasp. 'Although, I would hope as the officer in charge of this building's security, you would display a more professional attitude.'

'It was a joke, Ma'am.' The Lieutenant's smile had not moved. 'To underline a serious point. I do spot checks on the contents of this room regularly. New measures to stop items going missing are now in place. However, my inventory is so out of date I've no way of knowing if something has been re-shelved in the wrong place, or become an evening or weekend project in the past. One which was never returned.'

'All right then. As you were Lieutenant. Subaltern, come with me to the office.'

'Yes, Ma'am.'

Pemisegant had gone from doing nothing for hours on end, to hours of heavy labour.

Much of the shelving was as it should be. Then every so often he would come across sections of complete chaos. Shelves piled high with a mixture of successful ideas, abandoned but still viable projects and whacked-out ideas which would never work, all sharing the same of shelf space. It all had to be taken down, cleaned and relabelled before an item was catalogued. Then it was returned to correct shining clean shelves, cleaned by three hard working Sprites.

Pemisegant's friend Althallant was a typical Mid-Trunk officer. He could sit quietly for hours at a time. However, when someone started talking to him, Althallant could carry a conversation. Not only did she never smile, Commander Yestarnsya rarely spoke and any attempt at conversation withered on the vine. Fortunately Lieutenant Ryzinasant was more talkative. He made regular checks on the Collection. This annoyed the Commander.

'If he is so keen on this archive,' she complained after one visit, 'why doesn't he apply for reposting here. His skills as a technologist are being wasted on security.'

'I don't know, Ma'am,' said Pemisegant, jumping on a rare conversational gambit. 'Perhaps he enjoys the surroundings,' he didn't like to say that their skills as technologists were also being wasted on this job.

'I don't think so, Subaltern. It's a warehouse, plenty of those in the Tree.'

'The SPS take all sorts,' said Pemisegant.

'Whatever makes you think he is with the SPS.'

'Security Officers for Regimental Headquarters are usually all SPS Officers, aren't they Ma'am?'

'Not in this case. R&D have just brought their security arrangements back in house. If you had been paying attention, you would have seen the Lieutenant was wearing a Green uniform, not Police brown one.'

'Then perhaps he is working on something during his downtime, and this is just killing time?'

'Then he needs to apply for a Private Development Licence,' she said, 'just as I successfully did last year.'

She had a PDL! Why the hell was she still working directly for the Regiment? With a PDL, she could go into business for herself, set up her own development company to create a product, or licencemeone like Tabbernant Then she would. have the capital for her next development.

'Yes, I know what you are thinking. So to answer my own question, going into business needs capital, Subaltern. Saving for that is why people end up working for the Regiment, other developers or Private Venturers like Pensioner Tabbernant.' The Commander had a dreamy look in her eye. 'Still not long now, and I will be ready to get rolling.' This was the most enthusiastic Pepisegant had seen the Commander.

'Rolling, Ma'am?'

'Yes, but until I have enough capital, I have to work for someone or something else.Which neither of us is doing at the moment. So less chatter, and back to work.'

Pemisegant was exhilarated. This had to have been the best day's work ever. He had learnt more in the afternoon than he had for weeks in his morning classes.

'Would you pop into my office before you go, Subaltern?' asked the Commander.

'Yes, Ma'am,' said an exhausted Pemisegant.

The office was an island of order in the sea of chaos in the warehouse. Although after their efforts, the tide was changing.

On a small shelf behind the desk sat a Kuffa percolator. There was very little else to personalise the office. Only the picture frame, with the picture turned to face the wall. Pemisegant was too polite to ask why.

'Thank you for your work this afternoon Subaltern,' said the stern style on the other side of the desk. 'I understand you have been assigned to the Patent Office for this Tour. I said earlier I have a vacancy in my department, and after your sterling effort this afternoon, I would like to offer you that posting.'

What, was she serious, this was much more fun than his normal job, of course he would take it.

'Yes Ma'am, I would be delighted to accept.'

'I knew you would. I took the liberty of filing the transfer papers this afternoon. Confirmation will be sent to you by 0700 tomorrow. In your inbox before you leave for college.'

She poured a mug of kuffa. 'Milk and sugar?'

'No thank you, Ma'am, I take it black.'

'There you go then. From tomorrow, one of your jobs will be making the Kuffa.'

A cheap bag of Kuffa beans was more expensive than four jars of Instaht, the hot, caffeinated and Kuffa flavoured beverage most people drunk. He had been introduced to the real thing and he had quickly learnt how to recognise quality Kuffa like this. He was definitely going to like working here.

'This posting will include regular trips to the Vehicular Prototypes Garage at location 07PE AJ1.'

'At Heartswood,' said Pemisegant. 'Isn't that in the middle of the Tree Ma'am?'

'That is correct. This modern habit of giving places names when they have perfectly good Post Codes is beyond me.'

Great green apples! She was smiling.

'We have a month long field trip during Septemp.'

'My Boot Camp month,' said Pemisigant glumly.

Every year all Tree-People under five had to attend two Boot-Camps. One in the Autumn, one in the Spring. Pemisegant would not be able to attend Boot-Camp and go on the field trip.

'Subaltern, there is no need for you to worry about any clashes. I have been reviewing your record. You have forty two days of actual combat experience under your belt this year alone. These days most Ensigns don't get any. You have more than proved your combat readiness. You realise that is why you are now a Subaltern? So you only need to complete one week a season with the Reserve.'

It was, Pemisegant reasoned, better to be born lucky than rich. A great job offer and news he didn't have to go to Boot Camp, all on the same day. He could kiss Commander Yestarnsya. No better not, don't want to jeopardise this new posting. 'Also, as you don't have drill practice, you can put in an extra afternoon on Trinitsday.'

'Yes, Ma'am. The extra pay will be very useful.'

'Ah, Subaltern Pemisegant. Found my peculator I see,' said Lieutenant Ryzinasant.

'Which would be of precious little use, if I did not buy the beans.'

'For which I thank you, Commander,' said Ryzinasant as he poured himself a mug. 'So, we all like it as it comes. Good. I never did understand why people adulterate their Kuffa.'

'Each to their own, Lieutenant. Imagine how boring it would be if everyone did have the same taste,' replied Commander Yestarnsya.

'That's true, Ma'am.'

It was now well into downtime and she was still being as formal as she had been whilst on duty. Oh well, some people were just like that. However, they usually had blonde hair. Great green apples, she was prickly, he wondered if she was the sort of person who disliked Empaths like Nevamarsya. Pemisegant also wondered what his girlfriend would make of his prickly new boss. He finished the Kuffa and put his mug and those of his superior officers in the cleaner.

'I'll see you both tomorrow,' he said as he was leaving, and just to keep his new boss happy, he turned and saluted. 'Ma'am, Sir.' Then left for his dorm with a song in his heart.

CHAPTER NINE

BEHIND CLOSED DOORS

Trinitsday, the third working day of the week. It did not seem like a working day to Nevamarsya. She had a single lecture, first thing in the morning. Then, as she did not participate in any of the traditional Trinitsday sporting activities and only had to attend drill practice one evening a month, the rest of the day was free. She could have just relaxed, but that didn't appeal. So she made her weekly visit to the Convent's awesome Library, which held a copy of every book ever published in the Tree. She had been granted unprecedented access by the educational resources of the Sisterhood as a reward for her bravry during the Virus Invasion. The singing lessons with Sister Matyfilsya, the Convent's Choir Mistress had started when Nevamarsya had been recovering from her final bruising encounter with the Virus Invader at the beginning of the year. After only a handful of lessons, her voice was unrecognisable. People now chose to hear her sing, instead of running away holding their bleeding ears.

It was a short trolleybus trip from College to Root Delta on the Western edge of the Hub. Behind the Delta Mall was the alleyway Nevamarsya was looking for. On one side were the loading bays of the shops of the Mall. On the other was a blank stone wall four stories high. Behind the wall stood the Great Cloister, the Central Basilica, the Chantry, the Chapter, the Great Library and of course the living quarters for the Tree-Nuns. Beyond them were all the workshops and farmland that supported the population of the Convent. Then came the Western Wall and the Abyss, where Root Delta turned through ninety degrees and began its long solitary plunge deep into the depth of the Earth. It was said that Root Delta was as deep below ground as the Tree was high above.

A non-descript wooden door halfway down an alleyway was the only way in or out of the Convent. The Tree-Nun on the other side of the small grilled panel was a familiar face. Sister Monijoasya stopped reciting the verse enquiring what business the caller had with the Sisterhood mid sentence and slid open the bolt on the door.

'And how are things in the Tree Without, Nevamarsya?' asked the gatekeeper.

'The same old same-old,' said Nevamarsya.

'I doubt it. Only the Tree Within is unchanging, the Tree Without is full of life,' replied Sister Monijoasya. Both Tree-Monks and Tree-Nuns refered to their homes and the lives they lived as "The Tree Within". 'Enjoy your lesson Nevamarsya.'

'Oh I shall Sister.'

Nevamarsya liked Sister Monijoasya, who was always friendly, unlike some of her sisters.

The bell for Midday Prayers interrupted her browsing in the Library. It summoned all who heard it to the Central Basilica.

After Prayers she followed the Sisters through the door into the Central Refectory, where she shared their plain lunchtime meal in silence.

Nevamarsya popped back to the library to have her books issued and then she made her way to the office of Sister Matyfilsya.

'I hope you are in good voice today, my child?' asked the Tree-Nun. Nevamarsya had no idea how old Sister Matyfilsya was. The elderly Tree-Nun had taught Aunt Kandy to sing two decades earlier, she must be ancient now.

'Yes Sister, a full stomach always helps.'

'In that case, we will start with breathing exercises.'

The lesson went well, and as far as Nevamarsya was concerned was over too quickly. She always left wanting more, but she still had much to do.

Sister Tregozasya, the Abbess' secretary sat at her desk in the antechamber to the Abbess' Office like a spider at the heart of its web.

'Can I help you my child?' asked the coldly efficient Tree-Nun.

'I hope so Sister,' replied Nevamarsya, who found this Tree-Nun disturbing because she was one of the few people she could not read. All Tree-Nuns appeared calm and emotionless but Nevamarsya could usually see behind the mask. Sister Tregozasya did not need the mask. She displayed no emotions what-so-ever. She was as cold as a slab of marble. Perhaps, thought Nevamarsya, it was best that she had chosen a life of religious seclusion.

'I would like to make an appointment to see the Abbess, Sister Tregozasya,' Nevamarsya asked politely.

'You realise she is very busy my Child?' Nevamarsya hated it when a Tree-Nun called her that, but at least she could imagine most of them as mothers. Not Sister Tregozasya, who was so cold. Nevamarsya could not imagine her being maternal.

'Yes sister. I was not expecting to see her today, which is why I asked for an appointment.'

'Very well, I will let the Abbess know you wish to speak with her. Good day.'

That was it. No chance to explain why she wanted to speak to Abbess Annaprysya. No indication of how long it would be before the audience was granted. Oh well, best not to push her luck.

As much as Nevamarsya enjoyed her weekly visits, she was glad glad to leave the precincts of the Convent. She could never be a Tree-Nun. It required a depth of faith and dedication to that faith she knew she would never possess.

A short walk away from the entrance to the Convent was the Atrium. The main feature of the Hub. How could anyone chose to turn their back on a wonder like this. Two hundred terraced decks forming a giant amphitheatre at the heart of the Hub.

The Hub reminded her of the Crown. Here the trunk split not into branches but Roots, as it was firmly below ground. The central area of parkland was as impressive as the Crown, but without its central lake. The Grand Central Channels rose up like pillars supporting the sky from a body of water beneath the floor of the Hub, which was fed by fresh water from the tips of the Roots.

Nevamarsya could have spent hours wandering through this wonderful space, lit by day-lighters larger than anything she had seen before. They brought the light of Mother Sun down to below the surface of Father Earth, emulating the brilliant summertime blue sky beyond the Tree. At night, when Mother Sun slept, electric streetlighters would illuminate the Hub. It was never truly dark in here. Business and pleasure took place in the shops, theatres, sports arenas and restaurants twenty four hours a day.

A trip on the Trolley-bus took her to the Alpha Mall on the other side of the Hub from the Convent. The place made Nevamarsya feel uncomfortable. In every shop Nevamarsya was surrounded by snooty Root Styles who she felt were looking down their noses at her. That was just the staff. No, stop that, she told herself sternly. They are just surprised by my unusual appearance.

Her scalp had recovered sufficiently to grow hair again. Unfortunately, it was completely white. Any attempt to dye it a more natural red made it fall out. It had taken weeks to grow into a shoulder length bob, but it was real. Nevamarsya didn't care how odd it looked. From today the hated wig was consigned to the dustbin.

'Are you sure you can afford to pay for those young lady?' asked the snooty assistant in a shoe shop where she was killing time. The hair salon she was looking for was too busy at the moment.

'Yes thank you.' Nevamarsya had no intention of buying anything here, no matter how pretty it might be. Anyway, these particular shoes weren't pretty, Nevamarsya was amazed at their impracticality. Stupidly high heels were the only item of female clothing she still disliked as passionately now as she had before she became female. These were four fractions [nearly five inches] high. Not that she would tell the shop assistant that. One hundred and eighty credits for the shoes, it was more than she had ever paid for anything in her short life.

'Would you be so kind as to prove that. This establishment is too busy for time-wasters.'

The shop was empty, but Nevamarsya politely handed her Indesn-Card over to be scanned.

'If you could place your thumb on the validator please,' continued the assistant, who obviously did not believe Nevamarsya.

To her surprise, the figure CR3,472.69 appeared on the display. There must be some mistake. She had saved CR472.69

from her wages with the Winter Squad, and that had been little more than pocket money. During the Winter, there had been nothing to spend her tiny salary on. All the normal bills had been paid for by the High Council. Nevamarsya was so flabbergasted she authorised the sale by accident. Now she would have to explain herself to her mother-to-be who kept a close eye on Nevamarsya's bank statements.

A flashing icon on her wrist-com caught Nevamarsya's attention. She had new e-mail, which she did not want to read in the shop. She would log into one of the Public-Access comboxes across the street. Maybe this e-mail would explain the anomaly.

On the plus side, buying the cursed footwear had rapidly changed the assistant's attitude from snottily superior to jollily helpful. On the negative side, she now owned an unwanted pair of expensive shoes.

Nevamarsya assumed the money in her credit balance had caused the change in attitude. By the standards of this shop, it really was a tiny credit balance. In truth the shop assistant was bathing in the glow of reflected glory. She would be able to brag for weeks about the young celebrity who had been her customer. Fame opened more doors than money alone ever could.

'Would the Subaltern be interested in a matching pair in grey?'

'No thank you, I just want these,' she replied. I really don't want these shoes either, Nevamarsya thought, but I'm not telling you that.

'Then would you like some help choosing an outfit to go with them.'

'No thank you. I already have something these shoes match perfectly.' Nevamarsya was telling the truth now, but she could not afford to spend anymore time here. She had to move on.

'Do call again,' said the shop assistant, as Nevamarsya reached the door.

Don't count on it, thought Nevamarsya as she put as much distance between herself and the shop as was politely possible.

Her final destination was in sight. First however, she made her way to the row of public access comboxes. Nevamarsya selected a booth, for added privacy. She connected her com-link to the workstation within, and through that into the tree-wide data network. Time to check that email. Nevamarsya read it again. There was only one person it could have come from. It read:

```
From:     Pensioner Tabernant 089/99 Islaw
To:       Subaltern 331/29 (Half) Fangkart
Subject:  About the MONEY. Spend It!!!
Body:     Dear Girlie,
              I know how much styles, even freshly minted
          ones like yourself love shopping. So here
          is a belated HolyDay gift. A little spending
          money for you, so you can have real fun in
          the shops of the Hub.
              Don't worry, I have checked it out with
          Shaz, she eventually said it was OK to give
          you it, but not to make a habit of it. I
          know you are too careful to spend it all at
          once, but do spend it. All of it. Otherwise
          I will be really disappointed.
                        Love,
                  Uncle Bernie.
```

She dialled his IndesnCode, waiting whilst the Guardhouse security system cleared her call. Eventually a familiar face appeared on the screen.

'Uncle Bernie, I can't accept all that money,' she said before the old anther could get a word in edgeways.

'Yes you can Girlie. Don't worry, I said I had cleared it with your Mother. Shaz wants you to get something nice with it.'

'Don't think I am not grateful, I am. But it is far too much.'

'No, given the price of things down there in some of those shops. Especially the one you just bought those shoes in, it is just right.'

'How do you know about them?' she asked.

'A marker on the cash. I want to know its been spent.'

'I'll have to have lessons from Lisha before I can walk in them,' said Nevamarsya.

'Or Shaz, she used to wear killer heals.' There was a disappointed tone in the old anther's voice. 'But she hasn't for a few years. No doubt she still remembers.'

Nevamarsya hated talking about clothes, she wanted to change the subject.

'So, you have access to the Comlink Network?'

'I've not been convicted yet Girlie,' said Tabbernant with a hurt tone.

'I'm sorry Uncle Bernie.'

'Well make good that apology by spending that money.' The usual twinkle had returned to Tabbernant's voice. 'But me no buts Girlie, I am serious about this. You four kids are like a family I never had. Besides, it is time some of that cash filtered back into the economy. Lisha has bought an antique pedal bike. Like the one she rode in the Canopy.'

It was apparent to her that just as Tabbernant was the only person who called her half-mother Shaz, the old anther was going to continue to call her Girlie, the nickname that had so irritated her before she had differentiated, for the rest of his life.

'So, I'm sure that shop can find you a nice dress that matches...' The connection abruptly cut-out. The line would not reconnect, so after three attempts she gave up.

'Right, better phone Mamny. Should have done it earlier,' she said to no-one in particular. She dialled Sharlensya's

IndesnCode but a stranger's face appeared on screen.

'I am sorry, but all connections to the Crown and beyond are temporarily offline for a complete system upgrade. On behalf of the Communications Regiment, I apologise for any inconvenience this causes.' The upper-trunk style repeated the script several times without mistake.

'You're not sorry at all, you can't be, you're a machine,' said Nevamarsya with a growing sense of annoyance.

The two adults she loved the most, her Half-Mother and Tabbernant were far away from her. Even Matriarchs had to do their week on Reserve, so Sharlensya was on a military exercise in the Canopy. Her favourite pensioner had been locked up by the Enquirers. To make matters worse, soon her boyfriend would be away for a month, up in the Trunk, on that silly field trip.

Lieutenant, distribute this Press Release. You're a scientist, you will give it more gravitas,' said Commander Dyscolnant.

That morning, a news story had appeared about the dangerous lack of flood preparations throughout the Tree. Commander Dyscolnant had been livid.

Yes you idiot, thought Kilkennsya, one you are deliberately ignoring. She read the Press Release with growing horror. It was playing down the previous day's water-logging of the far roots. Blaming it on over-sensitive sensors and stating the degree of water-logging was nowhere near as bad as had been originally believed. This was a load of old horse-feathers, if she put her name to this, she would be a laughing stock.

'Sir, I can't agree with any of this. It is all a tissue of lies.'

'You have to. Your friendly chat with that journalist has resulted in this "tissue of lies".' The Commander threw a copy of the morning's paper onto the desk. 'Something has to be done to counter it.'

'It had nothing to do with me, and I am not risking my scientific reputation on that fairy story.'

'That's it Lieutenant. You are refusing to undo the damage you caused. Consider yourself under suspension. Go home and think very seriously about your career in this Department.'

'Are you calling me a liar?' asked Kilkennsya.

'Yes, and a fool. Now go!'

'Yes Sir.' Kilkennsya was seething, but short of her punching Commander Dyscolnant, which would have earned her a genuine suspension, there was not a lot she could do.

Kilkennsya knew the real system logs would tell a story different from the one the Commander would tell. As soon as she was off the premises, fabricated data put in its place. Not only wasn't that good for the Tree, it would leave her with no evidence to defend herself in the inevitable disciplinary tribunal. So she spend the last ten minutes before she left downloading the latest data from the logs onto a memory stick prepared for this situation. Her problem was how to get the memory stick off the premises. The Commander would have her searched before she left the office complex. He would be a fool not to, well a bigger fool than usual, if that were possible. Her desk would be emptied and any paperwork destroyed. No doubt her locker in the staffroom would be searched. For once she blessed the enzyme deficiencies she suffered from. Nobody else in the office could open the jar of medicated tea she kept there without being violently sick. She slipped the memory stick into the jar, pushing it deep under the foul smelling dried leaves. Later that day she would return to the office to retrieve the medicine forgotten in her hasty departure.

CHAPTER TEN

GOOD HAIR DAY

'What can you do with my hair?' Nevamarsya asked Captain Euliyetsya of the Hairdressers Regiment. She was so pleased to have finally tracked her down, the big brassy Root Style who wore the most extravagant earings Nevamarsya had ever seen. Earings that clashed horribly with the Captain's uniform.

'Shave it all off and start again?' the stylist was not being rude, just being honest.

'But it has taken me weeks to get it to this length,' said Nevamarsya, 'I can't wait that long again.'

'There will be no waiting involved. It is a mistake to think that only time can reverse the effects of Shambling poisoning. The cuticles are obviously clean now. They just need nourishing and can be encouraged back to full health. Your scalp is ready for a series of herbal gel massages. After each dose I will let your hair grow back upto a half of a fraction, then repeat until the colour returns. After a final wash with of all things, very dilute Rohotel, it will be as if you never been poisoned. Your hair will be lush, long and stylish.'

'Thank you,' said Nevamarsya, running her hand through her ratty white hair.

'Although you could have had this treatment in any of the salons you visited in the past two weeks.'

'How did you know?' asked Nevamarsya.

143

'Its not as if you are hard to spot, dear,' said the older style. 'E-Wigs, even the good one you had, are obvious to a professional eye.'

'If I am going to have this done, I want it done by the best,' said Nevamarsya.

'You don't have to flannel me, young lady, I know why you wanted to find me.' Captain Euliyetsya was trying hard not to giggle.

'You do?' asked Nevamarsya, playing along with mock surprise.

'Yes, I do, you are trying to find Gaemlovant, aren't you?' asked Euliyetsya, the joking had stopped.

'He is the only person who can help Bernie.' There was a measure of panic in Nevamarsya's voice. 'And you are my last lead. All the others have dried up.'

'It's a shame I can't help you. As much as I would like to give you his address, I don't know it.'

'I have to find him. You were my last hope. You were at the academy together, one of his oldest friends.'

You did not need to be an Empath to see that Nevamarsya was disappointed. 'I know he is still alive somewhere. I get a HolyDay card from Gezz every year, but it never has a return address on it. I tried to trace him once, so I could send him a card in return,' said Euliyetsya, 'but even the Postal Regiment were baffled. His card just appeared in the system like magic, no evidence of it ever being posted. In the end, I just gave up.'

'He doesn't want to be found,' said Nevamarsya dejectedly.

'No dear, he doesn't. He is so completely hidden, it is as if he has become invisible. Only the Syndicate or the Tree-Monks can make an anther vanish that completely.'

'He is being very successful at hiding from the Syndicates. Also, he was able to send you a Holy Day Card each year. If he had become a Tree-Monk, then that would not have happened.'

There was a bang that made Nevamarsya jump in her seat. On the floor lay the remains of a bottle of what she assumed was an expensive shampoo.

'Curse my arthritic old fingers. Not as responsive as they used to be.' Already a Sprite was busy cleaning up the mess. 'Thank you, Sprite. Please fetch a new bottle of Xexia from the store cupboard when you have finished there, and use it to massage the clients scalp.'

'Yes, Ma'am,' said the Sprite.

'You know, that little one is the best Sprite I have had for years. It's such a shame I borrowed it from my cousin, up in the Trunk.'

'How long has she been asking for you to return it?' asked Nevamarsya, it was obvious that the Captain had changed the subject.

'About six months now,' Euliyetsya smiled. 'Of course, being a Trunk Sprite it will be tested on its return home. But it's been in the Roots for years. The Tree knows what it will look like when it sprouts'

Never play poker Captain, thought Nevamarsya, you have no subtly at all.

Each time Captain Euliyetsya shaved and massaged her scalp, Nevamarsya was temporarily as bald as Sprite IX702/14. However each time her hair returned, slightly longer, healthier than before. On the fifth treatment the colour and body had fully returned. This time she was shaved and her scalp was washed in a weak solution of Rohotel, the growth retardant.

'Don't worry dear, there is just enough Rohotel to shock the scalp without paralysing it. I know, ironic, isn't it?' As the stylist had promised, it set Nevamarsya's scalp alight as her hair began cascading long and red down her back. A final trim, shampoo and set was applied and she was put to sit under a large hair-dryer.

'The Sprite humbly requests that you lift your feet,' it asked in a high pitched voice as it was patiently sweeping the floor again. Nevamarsya felt deeply embarrassed. Since her arrival in the Roots, she had seen Sprites going about their business and she had just ignored them. Taken them for granted. The Tree would grind to a halt without them. When she had first sprouted, she had planned on doing so much to help the lot of Sprites, and she had done nothing.

Nevamarsya felt herself dropping to sleep as the masterpiece cooked under a hair-dryer. The sound of shouting woke Nevamarsya from her doze.

'Get out of my way you stupid little creature.' The voice was unmistakable, it belonged to Captain Samnundsya. She had been Nevamarsya and Serynazsya's nemesis for so long. Oh what a surprise, old witch was verbally abusing a Sprite.

'As I was saying, of course I recognise her. How could I forget the girl who cost my Branch a small fortune.'

Yes, it was definitely Captain Samnundsya, her snooty Root accent made the word "girl" sound more like "gell". 'I paid good money for the ugly bitch to go on that management course, and she let's herself get marooned up there, losing a Sprite in the process, which has increased the insurance premium.'

'I nearly didn't, Mamma. Not after all the changes from her rebirth and adoption.'

The other voice was familiar, but Nevamarsya couldn't quite place it, possibly because she had never heard anyone call Captain Samnundsya "Mamma".

'I'll admit that the nose job she got during the re-birthing is an improvement,' said Samnundsya, 'but why go to the trouble of getting rid of her piggy snout and wonky eye, if she is going to ruin it all by going native.'

'It suits her,' said the other style.

'You can't be serious girl.'

Of course, it was the obnoxious Subaltern Sofianesya. The Branch Captains shadow. Number one in the chorus of praise for the glorious leader. The concept of family had been alien to Nevamarsya when she had been a Sprite. Now she could see why Sofianesya acted the way she did. Explain, but not excuse.

'She looks stunning, Mamma,' said Sofianesya. 'Some Canopy Styles are really beautiful.'

'You have been spending far too much time with hick girls in that stupid flat. You should come home.'

Now that was odd, thought Nevamarsya, as she felt the wave of rebellion that emanated from Sofianesya. She never disagreed with the Captain in the Branch. Then Nevamarsya was washed away with the wave of horror emanating from the other style as Sofianesya realised what she had said. 'Well, um, she was never, erm, one of us. Was she?' asked the girl, desperately trying to paper over her mistake.

'True, but that is no excuse. What pig-girl has done is abandon the Pure-Stock and become a hick.' The two Root Styles dropped their unhealthily skinny frames onto the luxurious settee in the waiting area. They did not relax in the rich upholstery. They perched primly on the edge of the seat.

'I'm not surprised the liberal types are treating her like some sort of heroine, when in reality she has betrayed her heritage. Still, at least we don't have to put up with her any more.'

Nevamarsya had tried to keep her cool in the presence of that evil old witch, but it was no good.

'That's right, Serah will never have to suffer at your hands ever again,' said Nevamarsya, alight with indignant fury. 'And neither, thank the Spirit of the Tree will I.'

'Do I know you girl?' asked Samnundsya, 'I never forget a face.'

'Only if it belongs to a Sprite.'

'Don't be stupid girl, they don't have faces as such. Anyway, I asked you a question.'

'The last time you saw me, I looked just like that Sprite,' she indicated towards IX702/14, 'and you told me that you were far too busy to deal with a non-entity like me, because, and I quote, "wonderful, wonderful Autumn and Winter are coming and my exile will be temporarily lifted."'

'Great green apples, you were NM331/29?' The bigoted old style was almost lost for words. Almost. 'You were my missing Sprite?'

'Indeed I was. I am an officer now, Subaltern Nevamarsya 331/29, soon to be a member of Family Fangkart.'

'You're still uppity I see.' The towel had fallen from Nevamarsya's head, and her newly restored deep red tresses glowed like fire. 'Although once a hick, always a hick. Just because you are being adopted by a Fangkart and futher weakening that family's pattern, doesn't make you anything special. And how in the Tree's name are you a Subaltern at your age?'

There was no disputing the rank, as the emprintable fabric system embossed a small set of rank pips, somewhere visible, on everyone's off duty clothing.

Throughout this exchange, Sofianesya had been staring at Nevamarsya. 'It's her, the one who defeated the Virus,' she eventually said, in something akin to awe. 'You saved us. You saved us all.'

'And I proved you lot wrong, you pure-stock idiots, didn't I.'

'Well, I'm not staying here to be insulted.' Samnundsya had been interrupted, and it was obvious to Nevamarsya that she had not liked that. The Branch Captain stormed out of the salon without taking her coat.

Subaltern Sofianesya was slower leaving. Every so often she would stop and turn towards Nevamarsya, and look at her with a mixture of awe and bewilderment. Her eyebrows knotted together.

'Is it really that hard for you to take in?' Nevamarsya asked Sofianesya. 'That someone born from an ordinary Sprite-pod, and worked and grew up in the Canopy is equal to anyone from your precious Pure-Stock?'

'I have always been told, Canopy people are inferior all my life,' replied Sofianesya.

'Well, think about what you have been told. How much of it has been lies and propaganda?'

Outside Captain Samnundsya had lost patience with her daughter and walked back into the salon.

'Oh for goodness sake girl! What are you waiting for?' she demanded, almost dragging Sofianesya off the premises.

Nevamarsya felt elated, until she saw the stylist. 'Sorry, it looks as if I have just lost you two customers.'

'Don't worry about it dear, I have wanted to tell them to sling their hooks for months. I thought I had seen the last of them until Autumn,' she smiled broadly. 'As it looks as if I won't be seeing them ever again. You have done me a favour dear.' The older style was laughing. 'Now sit down here my dear. You're getting the works, not just the hair, your face, your skin and nails and anything else I can think of. Don't even think about paying for it.'

'But all I did was tell that dreadful old witch the truth. I wasn't fishing for freebies.'

'I know dear. Don't worry, next time you come here, when your fifteen minutes of fame are history, then you'll have to pay, just like everyone else. Today, it's on the house. Any way, you have been far more of a challenge than those two.

Pure-stocks are so boring, all of them tint their hair the same platinum blonde, all of them have it cut in the same style and all of them wear it up, even during their down-time. Dull as dish-water. To think, you are not just a strange little girl looking for someone old enough to be her grandad. I didn't realise I was working on the hair of a Heroine of the Tree.'

True to her word, Euliyetsya and Roemyohant went to town. Soon the clock on the wall was reading 1845, closing time for the salon.

'Although, I will give you a few words of advice dear,' said the older style, 'be a bit more guarded in future. How did you know me or Roemyohant over there isn't in a Syndicate member just waiting to take the little nugget you have just dug up to our superiors?'

'You aren't, are you?' Nevamarsya was horrified. How could she have been so stupid.

'Of course not, but you didn't know that, and still don't know if I am telling the truth.'

'But...' Nevamarsya was about to tell the hairdresser that she had empathic powers, then thought better of it.

'...Oh, I see what you mean.'

'The Syndicate have been looking for Gaemlovant for years. He really annoyed them back in the day. Also silence him and Tabbernant goes down and the Eltravator scheme with him. They will have redoubled their efforts recently, killing two avians with a single stone.'

'I'll be more careful from now on.'

'Right, you're done. Don't waste any more time, a Tree without Bernie would be a sadder place.

'Thank you, goodbye.' As Nevamarsya left the salon, it wasn't just her restored hair that was weighing heavily.

Yestarnsya now considered herself to be an army of one. Her long running feud with her brother had lasted for five years.

Half a lifetime of not speaking. Even their father's death had not healed the rift how could it, her brother had changed so much and refused to change back. He might as well be dead.

After her father's death, Yestarnsya's mother had withdrawn into the herself. Yestarnsya had thought it was her way of coping with her grief. It was something far worse. Dementia was incredibly rare amongst Tree People, but it struck her mother hard. Now Yestarnsya was regularly mistaken for her long dead grandmother by her only surviving parent, if she was recognised at all. She had built a wall around her emotions. Friends betray you and family breaks your heart. She was having none of it. All frivolities had been abandoned. She concentrated on work and work only because a job well done could not hurt you.

Ryzinasant was a nice person and she knew he found her as attractive as she found him. Sadly he was wasting his time if he thought anything would develop between them. She firmly believed there was now a wall as solid around her heart as the one at the Waterfalls of Heartswood.

Drip, drip, drip. The accumulation would never have begun, if it had not been for the Tree-quake, but once it started, nothing could stop it. Every second of every day the water was finding its own level. At first it had taken a whole day for enough water to accumulate on the piece of stone for gravity to have something to work with. Now gravity pulled another drop every second. As it did so, the cumulative effect of the drip became larger and the puddle beneath became deeper and deeper. Eventually a small hole was be created, breaking through the ancient blockage. With the flow of water, hydraulic pressure increased, flushing the pipe clean. The next time the Channel overflowed, the water would travel down an old disused pipe, instead of being diverted lower down the cascades. Nobody would notice that the great Waterfalls of Heartswood were a little less spectacular as some of its water had found a different route down through the Tree.

CHAPTER ELEVEN
SOFIANESYA'S CHOICE

As Nevamarsya walked through the glorious park at the base of the Atrium she felt like a million credits. Even seeing Samnundsya and Sofianesya again did not dent her spirits. They were having the mother of all arguments.

'If you go to speak with that creature, I am finished with you. You are no daughter of mine,' said Samnundsya.

'Well, you've never been much of a mother,' said Sofianesya.

'I did what I had to do, I did my duty according to the Code,' replied the older style.

'Always for the Code, never for me.' Sofianesya was close to tears.

'For you? You were a duty, an unavoidable one. Do you think I would have lumbered myself with a silly simpering fool like you, if I didn't have to?'

Sofianesya slapped her mother's face and then stormed away. The quarrel had reached its peak.

Couldn't have happened to a more deserving person, thought Nevamarsya. It would have been even better if Serynazsya had been here to witness the slap, but you couldn't have everything. She continued her stroll through the park, not really caring what that unpleasant pair did next.

Why can't you just leave me alone, I never want to see you again thought Nevamarsya a few minutes later when she spotted Sofianesya walking towards her. Nevamarsya really did not want to talk to her. Not now or ever again, thank you.

'Excuse me Miss,' said Sofianesya nervously. Nevamarsya just kept on walking, but it was no good, the other style had grabbed her attention.

'Oh, so it's "Miss" now, is it? It makes a change from "You there! Thingy!",' said Nevamarsya tartly.

'I'm sorry,' said the older girl.

'I don't want your apologies. Nothing you can say could possibly be of any interest to me.'

'Not even if I tell you that you are one hundred percent right. I am a Pure-stock idiot.'

She certainly looked the part. Despite being off duty she was wearing her long blonde hair tightly pinned up. In the same complex Pure-stock style she would wear with her uniform. Except there was something missing. Gone was the look of the ice cold arrogance. The crying had brought some colour to Sofianesya's cheeks.

Nevamarsya found it hard to keep the display of righteous indignation going. Sofianesya the fawning sycophant so richly deserved it. Sofianesya the penitent soul did not. Nevamarsya was almost knocked off her feet by the waves of genuine regret and remorse emanating from Sofianesya.

'Well,' she said, 'now you have admitted it, you can start to make amends.'

'In anyway I possibly can.'

Both styles were aware that Samnuandsya was glaring at them. However there was something mechanical about the old witch. Samnundsya was a picture of cold fury on the surface, but underneath there was nothing. Just like Sister Tregozasya, she was completely unreadable. Not that Nevamarsya cared, but she could tell that Sofianesya did.

'Would you like a kuffa?' she asked.

'Yes please, I know a charming café,' replied Sofianesya. 'It's not far, a few minutes walk.'

'You won't be welcome there anymore.' They heard her Mother saying in a cold and passionless voice.

It was a short and embarrassingly silent walk to the café. It did not look charming, Nevamarsya thought, deadly dull would be a more accurate description. They went inside and waited to be seated.

'We don't serve riff raff like her or those who associate with riff raff,' said the waitress.

In the background they could hear a familiar emotionless laugh.

'Oh, we'll have to go somewhere else then,' said Sofianesya, 'somewhere she won't be able to spy on me.'

'Just ignore her. Keep walking, there are other cafés here in the Atrium.' Nevamarsya was glad to get away from this awful place.

'That's the second time today I have been thrown out of somewhere because of her,' said Sofianesya.

'Welcome to the real world,' said Nevamarsya with a smile.

There was a short burst of shouting, then Sofianesya left the café and returned to Nevamarsya who was standing outside.

'I wish I had done that years ago,' the older style said.

'Done what?' Nevamarsya asked.

'Had the courage to stand up to her,' said Sofianesya, 'told her what I thought about her and her precious Pure-stock Code. I told the old witch I never want to see her again.'

'But she is your mother,' said Nevamarsya, slightly aghast.

'In name only. I know now why she has never shown me any love. She can't, she is an emotional vacuum. I was a pretty little blonde girl to parade in front of her friends. I was purely a business transaction.'

Nevamarsya didn't know what to say to this. Sharlensya was so demonstrative in her love and she returned that love by the bucket load. This explained why Sofianesya had always been more vocal than the other styles in Captain Samnundsya's shadow. The leading voice in a chorus of praise. She had been trying to get a maternal response from the old witch.

'I know, you find it hard to believe,' said the older girl.

'Yes. Actions speak louder than words,' said Nevamarsya. 'If you really have had a moment of enlightenment, prove it.'

'What do you mean?' asked Sofianesya, a note of trepidation in her voice.

'Let down your hair,' said Nevamarsya. 'Why do you think when you are off duty is called down-time? You'd never guess my Mother is a Mentor, would you?'

'Oh, I see.' Sofianesya began pulling pins and fasteners from her hair and let it fall to her waist.

'Now, drop the chin, look straight ahead; not down your nose, and for the Tree's sake, smile.'

'I beg your pardon,' Sofianesya said the usual icy disdain. Then she giggled. 'Smile, yes I can smile.'

'There you look so much prettier now you're not sucking a lemon.' They both started laughing. 'And if I may?' Nevamarsya fished a packet of wet wipes out of her purse. When the skin was clean, she pointed a short tubular device at Sofianesya's face. A beam of light scanned it and a fine spray followed.

'A little make-up never harmed anyone.'

'There, what do you think? I know it is my make-up program, not one designed for you, but it's a definite improvement?'

'I need a better look,' said Sofianesya, who walked over to a public emprinter. 'I'm no longer under a crushing burden. Not having to confrom to all those silly rules,' she laughed. 'You have heard me be called Fia, by someone who no longer has that right? You on the other hand do have that right.'

'Thanks Fia, you definitely have the right to call me Neva.'

Sofianesya was smiling a one million lumens smile that Annaprysya, who also lit up the room on the rare occasions when she allowed herself to smile.

'I've never dared do this in public either, in case it got back to my Mother,' said Sofianesya. Emprintable Fabric gave Tree-People the ability to change their outfit without having to take any clothes off. All public spaces were dotted with Emprinters, large metal framed mirrors with a card-reader and touchscreen keyboard built in.

'What's your outfit got to do with your Mother?' asked Nevamarsya, as the Brethinite spheres in the emprintable fabric Sofianesya was wearing rearranged themselves. Ankle length dress flowed around Sofianesya before settling into a pair of denim jeans and plaid shirt with loosely tied scarf and high-healed sandals similar to Nevamarsya's.

'Quote, Only tarts wear trousers, a demure style only wears a skirt, unquote,' the older girl said as she picked up the excess material and dropped it into a fabric recycler.

'Your downtime clothes should always be whatever you are comfortable with. You should only ever dress to please yourself, never to please others,' Nevamarsya said.

'Oh,' Sofianesya was obviously embarrased. 'I'm sorry. I didn't think.' Sofianesya was about to change again, not knowing if Nevamarsya was flattered or embarrassed.

'So, have they never heard of the Golden Rule?'

'Yes, but their stupid Code counters that by saying, "Do not backslide, or let any of your fellow Pure-stocks backslide. Friends help Friends to remain true to the Code at all times." I shall be free of that now.'

'That explains so much, its a charter to spy, bitch and backstab.'

'Isn't it just.' Both girls began laughing. 'I expect Mother to be mortified for weeks, until the harpies finally realise I am not one of them any more.'

'You didn't have a sudden revaluation today, did you Fia?' asked Nevamarsya, to change the subject from clothes. 'How long have you been planning your revolt?'

'I have been wavering for months Neva,' replied Sofianesya 'how did you know?'

'I suppose I'm very observant,' replied Nevamarsya cautiously, she did not know how Sofianesya responded given the growing hostility towards Empaths.

'Yes, you are very observant. You see at the Academy all the girls in my dorm believed in the Pure-stock ideal. We were introduced to the Code in sugar coated lessons. Everybody loves being told they are special. They gave me a way to maintain that specialness, I allowed myself to be swept along. The Pure-stock arranged for my adoption, which got me my job in our branch. It ran my life and I was happy to let it do so.'

'So what changed?' asked Nevamarsya.

'I started having doubts last year. I began feeling guilty about the way we had all treated Serynazsya. She came from the same pure-stock Sprite-pod as I had, but she just looked a little bit different, that's all. I started to think how could being so cruel, to someone who was so kind to everyone, be in anyway special. Soon I was questioning everything I had ever been taught.'

'Then, at the start of last Autumn I decided to try living independently for the first time. Because it was such an eleventh hour decision, there were no vacancies in any of the exclusively Pure-stock billets. So, thank the Tree, the Accommodation Board assigned me a place in a regular apartment block. For the first time I came in close contact with people from other parts of the Tree on a 24/7 basis.'

'A bit of an eye-opener, was it?' asked Nevamarsya

'I should say. I am sharing a flat with two Canopy styles and one from the Trunk.' Sofianesya took a deep breath. 'They were really friendly. I still had a bit of a snotty attitude when I first moved in, I didn't know any better. They could see I was trying to change, so they helped me. To get me involved in the multi-ethnic society here in the Hub of the Roots.'

'Good for them,' said Nevamarsya enthusiastically.

'But I couldn't loosen up very much. I was still working for my Mother, still being spied on by Friends in the Pure-stocks. So I started living a double life. At home I could relax, but as soon as I went out of doors, the mask went back on.'

'What did your flatmates think of that?'

'By that point, they had all met my Mother. They all loathed her. They could see the pressure I was under.'

'Was it getting harder to flit between the two lives?' asked Nevamarsya.

'You can't believe how glad I was to get home in the evenings, so I could relax a little.' They had stopped on a bridge over a small stream. Sofianesya seemed to be lost in the bubbling of the water as it passed under her.

'I planned on getting a new job a week before I was due to return to the Canopy with her. I was not bound by an Internal Exile, so I could have stayed down here whilst she was far away. I would have made a complete break from my past. It wasn't to be as her Internal Exile was lifted a year early. She said she was going to be running the business from the office in the Roots. That I would be working with her there. I was a coward, too afraid of her to make the final step whilst she was so close. After work she found ways to make sure I was always in her company. Tried to make me move back into the family home. I was close to giving up my tenancy of the room in the apartment. I was beginning to turn back into a robot.'

'Until today?' Nevamarsya asked.

'I had read the story of what you and the Winter Squad went through. I knew all about Subaltern Nevamarsya, but it was just a name. I never realised you were Serynazsya's missing Sprite. Seeing you in the flesh, seeing all you have achieved. Well, it was clinching proof that my mother and her kind were preaching madness. That if I didn't move now, I would end up as mad as them again.'

Nevamarsya ran her hand through her newly restored long red hair. Empaths read emotions, not the thoughts underlying them. A Empath could be fooled if a liar honestly believed their lies. However, there was something about the person staring sadly into the running water. She knew that Sofianesya was being completely honest and open with her.

'You're an Empath, aren't you?' asked Sofianesya from out of the blue.

'Er, um, er,' replied Nevamarsya. How was Sofianesya going to react.

'You must be, why else would I unburden myself to you Neva?' Sofianesya was smiling. 'Don't worry, I have no problems with Empaths. The old story that you are all in league and going to turn everyone into mindless slaves is just silly.'

'It's certainly gaining traction again,' said Nevamarsya, very relieved by Sofianesya's reaction.

'To tell the truth, I was thinking of seeing a Counsellor anyway. They're all Empaths.'

'Oh,' said Nevamarsya stupidly. 'I'm not a trained Counsellor. I wouldn't even call myself a novice.' That was the problem. She knew as an Empath she was broadcasting a field of calming reassurance and instinctlively probe, asking all the right questions, despite herself. Thank the Tree that when she finished her training, she would be able to control her gift, otherwise she would be driven mad by the weight of everyone else's problems. Until then, once again someone was un-burdening themselves to her and they felt so much better. Do I feel better? Nevamarsya thought. No, I do not. Now I feel responsible for keeping Subaltern Sofianesya 183/03 Zilfarayts on the road to redemption.

'It doesn't matter, I feel so much better already. Thank you.'

'So Fia, let's go and get that cup of kuffa.'

'Yes, let's.'

Now let me get this straight,' said the incredulous anther sitting behind the reception desk of Fangkart House. He had been counting the empty minutes until it was time to go home, when this nutter had appeared. 'You were Miss Serynazsya's Commanding Officer last year?'

'Yes,' replied Captain Samnundsya. 'She worked for me last day of the Spring/Summer Tour. She found a way of staying up in the Crown.'

'And now you expect us to pay you compensation for her actions?'

'That's right,' replied Samnundsya, 'she is one of you now, a Fangkart.'

'I will put this as politely as possible, shall I,' he said. 'Get stuffed.'

'I beg your pardon!' Captain Samnundsya bristled.

'This is Fangkart House, the headquarters of my Family. Miss Serynazsya is a cousin of mine. You hurt her and in doing so you hurt me.'

'She's gotten to you with her sob stories, hasn't she?' said the Captain rhetorically.

'I know who you are and what you did. Having now met you, I definitely believe her,' he saluted to signify this interview was now over. 'Ma'am.'

'Yes, well you're a young anther, and the biological adoption did a remarkable job on rebuilding her face, so she is now a pretty young style. Its obvious you fancy you're cousin, even though there is no chance she would fancy you. What with her being a dyke.'

'And now you insult her again, in her Family home,' he pressed a few buttons and the door of the office building swung open. 'So, will you leave quietly, or should I call security?'

'Oh, I'm leaving. There is more than one way to get redress.'

'Can you let me in Sargeant Darrylzant, I forgot my medicines?' Kilkennsya asked the nightwatch guard, so politely through the intercom.

'Be quick about it,' said the voice on the intercom. 'The Commander has suspended your security clearance.'

'I'll only be a few minutes.'

Each one of those minutes seemed to stretch for hours. Kilkennsya expected the Commander to make a surprise appearance and confiscate her precious data.

'Sorry you got suspended,' said Sargeant Darrylzant as she left the office.

'Don't say that too loud, or you will be joining me.'

'I know, but the buffoon is long gone,' he replied. 'Also, I won't take the datastick you are trying to smuggle out in that jar.'

'What datastick?' she asked with mock horror.

'Just because I am a nightwatch guard, doesn't mean I am stupid.' The door buzzed open and he saluted. 'He suspected you might have done something like this, and has been turning the place inside out.' The Sergeant opened the jar and took a long sniff. 'The Commander knows I have the same enzyme deficiency as you. I could have easily opened the jar for him, if he'd ordered me to.'

'Thanks Darrylzant, I owe you,' said Kilkennsya, who was also unaware of the guard's health problem.

'No worries Kilkennsya, I think he is an idiot too. Now, get out of here quickly.'

Nevamarsya and Sofianesya passed an open air kuffa bar by a small lake. A band was playing a pleasant tune. People at the tables were laughing and joking.

'How about here?' asked Nevamarsya.

'Why not,' replied Sofianesya, it's a pretty spot.'

'Surely this is too plebian for one so nobly born?'

'Some people might say so, but me, not any more.'

'Good evening ladies,' said a serving Sprite as the two styles sat down, 'how may I help you?'

'Two mugs of black kuffa, um, please Sprite,' replied Sofianesya.

She just said please to a Sprite and she is so elated, thought Nevamarsya. Obviously she has never done that before. She thinks not treating it like a machine is an achievement. Well, I suppose it is for her. It was a shame she assumed everyone took their Kuffa black.

'They look nice,' said the older style as another Sprite brought a tray of hot chocolates to another table. 'What are they?'

'The Sprite is proud to report that they are mugs of Cholayt Whips, the house speciality,' replied the Sprite serving them.

'Have one, they smell divine?' Nevamarsya asked.

'I couldn't, my diet,' said a horrified Sofianesya.

'What do you need to diet for?'

'It isn't done to be overweight.'

'In what way are you remotely overweight?' Nevamarsya asked. Sofianesya was so thin, she could dodge the jets of water in a shower and remain dry.

'You're right again. But I have always struggled to maintain the perfect appearance.'

'Tell me Fia, is it your definition of the perfect appearance or that Code again?'

'The Code of course. Oh, I see what you mean. To hell with the stupid diet,' she turned to the Sprite. 'Excuse me, I've changed my mind. Two of those please.'

'Certainly madame.'

'Thank you Sprite.'

Another first thought Nevamarsya. The two sat silently, drinking in the atmosphere as the day-lighters faded but never went completely dark. Street-lighters and coloured fairy-lights took their place. The drinks arrived and Sofianesya demolished hers with indecent haste.

'That was just awesome. I can see now why people make such a fuss over Cholayt,' said a breathless Sofianesya, with an ecstatic look on her face.

'You have had a silly grin on your face for the last five minutes,' said Nevamarsya eventually, 'anyone would think you have never tasted anything cholayt before?'

'I haven't, far too unhealthy.'

'Really?' No thought Nevamarsya, that can't be true.

'Yes, really.'

'Great green apples you Pure-stocks are dull.'

'But I'm not a Pure-stock anymore.'

'Say that again,' said Nevamarsya, 'and say it louder. Let the Tree hear you.'

'I am not a Pure-stock any more. I refuse to be blinkered by their prejudices or bound by their silly Code of Conduct ever again.'

A serious look crossed Sofianesya's face. 'I'm so sorry about the way I treated you before, when you were a sprite.'

'As I said, there is no point apologising to me. I took my chance, a chance you and your mother tried to deny me. Just think where the Tree would be if I hadn't.'

'I know that now.'

'There is a practical way you can make up for past misdeeds,' said Nevamarsya.

'How, I'm all ears.'

And not a lot else, she really was too thin.

'Good. When the sprites in my old branch have to be stored away again this Autumn, find a way to give them a chance.'

'How? I won't be working in that branch from now on?' asked Sofianesya.

'You are still a member of the Branch Management Regiment. If you put in a transfer request it won't take effect until the start of the next Tour. You mightn't be working with your Mother anymore, but your job will be Canopy related.'

'That's true, I suppose. Any new job this tour will send me up to the Canopy this tour, but not next. I hope to be in retraining by then.'

'So, make sure no sprite is cheated of its chance. Make it your business to guarantee that all the sprites from our old Branch get properly tested at the end of Summer.'

'I promise that. On my Word as an Officer.'

Nevamarsya wondered if the older style's word was as rock-solid dependable as her darling Pemisegant. His word as an Officer was unbreakable. Rats, now she was missing him again, and he was still in the Roots, she couldn't imagine how bad it would be when he was up in the Trunk.

'Great green apples Fia, is that really you?'

The questioner was a Upper-Trunk style whose hair was as dark as her skin. She walked towards Nevamarsya and

Sofianesya with a flowing motion, as if every bone in her body was made of rubber.

'Yes Kolah, it's me. Boring old Sofianesya.'

'Aren't you afraid mommy dearest will eat you up for daring to come into a place like this, and dressed like that?' asked the Canopy style who followed a few steps behind.

'No Petra, I am not. She can go to hell, as far as I am concerned.'

'Really?' said the first style.

'Yes Kolah, really.'

'So who's your friend?' they asked.

'I'm so sorry girls. Koolabasya 186/30 Sdoolk, Petrulksya 177/88 Grinlaff,' said Sofianesya, this is Nevamarsya 331/29 Half Fangkart.'

Nevamarsya stood up to shake the hands of the two styles. Still surprised by her formal introduction as Half Fangkart. She didn't think anyone did that any more. But it was the archaic sort of thing the Pure-stock would do. Sofianesya would not see anything unusual in the way she had introduce Nevamarsya.

'These are two of my flatmates. Espoidisya 164/79 Phone is no doubt out with her boyfriend.' Sofianesya was smiling again with a twinkle in her eye that she had not been allowed herself before.

'Have you come to a dance venue like this to dance Fia?' asked Petrulksya. 'Lots of handsome young anthers here tonight.'

'It's a good place to learn, Petra, wouldn't you say?'

'Yes, Fia, it is,' replied Koolabasya, 'but you will never dance in those clumpy old things.'

Koolabasya turned to Nevamarsya. 'If you will excuse us, we need to sort out Fia's footwear.'

By the time they returned a number of the tables had been moved off the dance floor, and the band had doubled in size. Sofianesya was now wearing suitable shoes for that dancefloor and a suitable dress with a hemline as abbreviated as her flatmates'.

Soon the bar would start serving alcohol. Nevamarsya realised she was now the youngest person there. It was time to be heading home.

'Look, I have to go now, it's almost Juvenile Curfew,' she said to Sofianesya.

'But you haven't touched your drink,' said Sofianesya.

'Maybe another time. You have it. You don't have to go, stay here, be raucous, have a good time for me. Well, maybe not the raucous bit, but enjoy yourself.'

'Thank you Neva. I'll do that. And please, keep in touch.'

'I will, just to monitor your progress. No backsliding, friends help friends you know,' Nevamarsya said with a wink.

'Don't worry Nevamarsya, we'll make sure of that,' said Sofianesya's flatmates, in unisons, unaware of what Nevamarsya and Sofianesya were lar.

'So long,' said Nevamarsya.

'Looking forward to it. Bye.'

'Hello, who is this?' asked Captain Samnundsya. Her comlink had been buzzing for ten minutes, and reluctantly, she had answered it. 'Whoever you are, you do realise it is still dawnsward.'

'I'm perfectly aware that it is only 0430, this could not wait,' said the voice on the other end of the link. 'This is vitally important for the good of the Pure-stock.'

'You realise that I am on parole at the moment, any wrong move and I will be exiled back up in the middle of nowhere.'

'If you do this for us, then friends will help a friend to stay in her home in the Roots permanently.'

All thoughts of sleep vanished, Samnundsya was fully alert.

'It is your duty to report the deserter Serynazsya. It is

obvious that she is being shielded by Matriarch-Elect Sharlensya 115/20 Fangkart. It is quite possible that the Matriarch-Elect helped Serynazsya to desert in the first place. You must include her and everyone she worked with last Autumn/Winter in your complaint.'

'May I ask why?' Samnundsya vaguely remembered Sharlensya from her days as a cadet. Despite all the efforts of the Mentors in the Pure-stock Academy, too many styles born from Sprite-pod "S" made no effort to maintain the Pure-stock's role as the natural rulers of the Tree. Some, like the traitor Sharlensya, even went as far as denying their heritage and becoming Hicks. However, that was no reason to include her in a complaint against Serynazsya.

'Quite simply, when Serynazsya is convicted of desertion and being absent without leave, her accomplices will become as guilty as her. The traitor Sharlensya will not be able to remain as Matriarch of the Family Fangkart. The only person who can fill that role is a true believer in the Pure-stock.'

'I understand. Of course I will report Serynazsya. First thing in the morning.'

'No, for maximum political embarrassment, you must wait until the traitor is sworn into office. She will find herself suspended on the same day.'

'Yes, of course.' Samnundsya was now starting to feel sleepy again. There was something about the voice on the other end of the comlink.

'Now sleep,' commanded the voice in a flat metalic tone. 'You will not remember this conversation, not even as a dream. You must will report Serynazsya for desertion. You will not do it straight away, but wait for day of her Mother's investiture. You will think it is all you're idea.' The voice was replaced by a low hum, and within seconds Samnundsya was fast asleep.

PART THREE
LAW

CHAPTER TWELVE

HORSE AND CART

'Great green Apples, Doc, you're early,' said schocked Commander Harpowlant, brushing the floor of his shop before he went for lunch. He wasn't expecting to see Keltonant for another week.

'I haven't come for a trim,' replied Keltonnant as he removed a white envelope from his jacket pocket. 'Here you are Harpo, your invitation to the big event. You're coming, aren't you?'

'Wouldn't miss it for the world Kelly.' An evil grin crossed the barber's face, 'you chosen your best man yet?'

'Well, Myghcomant if he is up to it.'

'So we can't expect much of a stag do then?' the barber sounded crestfallen.

'Which is no bad thing,' said Keltonnant, who was dreading that aspect or pair-bonding. 'I am twenty-six you know. Far too old for that sort of thing.'

'If you keep rejuvenating at your current rate, no-one will believe that.'

'Are you serious?' the Medic asked.

'As I ever am. Have you really not noticed how much thicker and darker your hair is. How much the lines have faded on your face?'

'I have been staring at this face in a mirror all my life, each time my first thought is "Yes, that's me".'

'Sit here and have a really good look' said the barber.

'I will Harpo, not that I'm expecting to notice any difference.' Commanders don't normally order Colonels around, but Keltonnant felt he had to obey.

'You've found an old photograph of me, and you are projecting it as the reflection in the mirror.'

'That I am not, Kelly,' said the barber with a note of awe in his voice. 'Something is working wonders on you. If you find it, bottle it. You'll make a mint.'

'Well, I can run some tests on myself.'

'You do that, find out how you have lost five years in just seven days.'

Keltonnant left the barber shop and headed back to work. He had a full list of patients that afternoon, so anything as trivial as his appearance would have to wait.

'This place is seriously lush Neva,' said Natalicsya as she wandered around her friend's new home.

' Nevamarsya replied.

'Does your mum really own all this?'

'No, silly. Fangkart House belongs to the Family Fangkart, which uses it for administration.' Nevamarsya explained. 'The suite the three of us are currently living in is the official residence of the Matriarch and her children.'

'Suite? Neva it covers one wing of the house. A suite is a few bedrooms and a shared living room, bathroom and kitchen.'

'Not my choice of words Lisha dear. It's the official description,' said Nevamarsya, in a hurt voice and making puppy-dog eyes emulating her friend. Natalicsya, with her large eyes in a small round face was the queen of sad and pleading innocence.

'Ok, I'll forgive you.'

'Oh thank you, PC Natalicsya.' Feeling the pride emanating from her friend, Nevamarsya had to ask. 'How is the training going anyway?'

'It's going. So many laws and regulations to remember. As well as learning how to deal with different people and different situations,' she laughed, 'I will be assigned to Admin in the Highways Division after Basic Training. I requested an Admin posting.'

'You won't be pounding the beat with Alth then?'

'No, but he does want to be an Enquirer.'

'Didn't your mother-to-be start in Enforcer Admin? She ended up an Enquirer.'

'I saw enough blood and guts last Winter to last a lifetime. I will be happy with my Administrative posting.'

'So,' said Nevamarsya, tactfully changing the subject, 'would you like to see the stable?'

'You've got horses? Really. I would love to see them.'

'Better take the lift up to the roof then.'

'How did you manage to get yourself suspended, Girl?' asked Kilkennsya's father.

'Not now Dad, I'm not in the mood.'

'But we are worried for you,' said her mother. 'In that job you were fractions away from all the important valves and pipes in the Tree. Real power, and now you look like you might lose it.'

'Only because the Idiot Boy is temporarily blighting the department,' said Kilkennsya.

'Are you surprised she got suspended, if that is her attitude towards superiors,' said her father.

'Well, it's the truth. We have been assigned a Trouble-shooter to iron out alleged problems in the way we do things.' Kilkennsya was sounding more exasperated with every word. 'All he has done is make things worse. It's not going to be long before he gets the boot, and I will be back at work.'

'So you say,' he said.

'So I know, Father. If Captain Xandropant had been in work, he would have overridden the fool.'

'What are you going to do with yourself dear?' asked her Mother.

'This is the Hub of the Roots Mam, there is plenty to do. I won't get bored.'

'Well don't go getting yourself into any more trouble,' said her Father.

'Don't worry Dad, there's no chance of that.'

The Tree was not solid wood. Within its body there were all sorts of open spaces. Just as a human body is home to millions of symbiotic bacteria, so the Tree's empty spaces have become home to many and various plants and animals. Many came from beyond the Tree for warmth and shelter. Many more have been created by the Tree from the same source material as the Tree-People. Once life had been breathed into them, they became independent living things. Over the years they matched the complexity of creatures that came into the Tree from the outside. The creatures that settled inside the Tree accepted that they would be manipulated by the Spirit of the Tree. Over the years the line between Tree made creatures and incomers blurred as the Tree became more adept at copying the incomers. Soon the only difference was Tree-made creatures multiplied asexually. Incomers reproduced sexually, requiring two parents.

The Spirit of the Tree knew that his soldiers had to get quickly and easily to different parts of the Tree. With so many different decks and stories within the Trunk, the ladders and elevators of the sapling soon became too slow. So he began to work on a beast of burden for his soldiers. There was already one creature used for transporting things in the Roots, horses. They had been one of the first outside creatures to wander into the Tree which were allowed to stay. The changes made to horses was one of the most radical. The Spirit of the Tree gave them an extra pair of limbs, large leathery wings that could lift horse and rider up into the air. He then gave the Tree people instructions on how to build carriages and wagons for use with horses. Common sense placed the stables for these winged horses at the highest point in the business or dwelling, in the Hub, that meant on the roof.

Soon the Tree People became over reliant on these wonderful creatures, and began drowning in an ocean of organic waste. So the Spirit began working with the inquisitive to find a better way of getting from A to B. Soon stables were replaced by garages as flying carriages were replaced by flying cars with anti-gravity engines. The number of horses dropped and soon owning one became a status symbol.

'They're beautiful,' said Natalicsya, walking into the stables.

'Aren't they just,' replied Nevamarsya.

Four horses were standing inside the enclosed paddock. All perfectly black from mane to hooves, glistened in the light. Their bright eyes followed the two girls as they approached. One walked up to Nevamarsya.

'Hello Dixie, oh you are a beautiful boy, aren't you,' said Nevamarsya as one of the horses walked towards her. 'Are you going to show off your full glory?'

On that cue, the horse opened his wings. Huge black leather constructs made up of hundreds feathers unfolded. A single beat created a powerful down draft as he folded his wings into a different position. The strength of the gust nearly knocked the unprepared Natalicsya off her feet.

'Look Lisha, he's got his wings in riding rest.

'Riding Rest?' asked Natalicsya

'Yes, they are as relaxed there as they would be fully folded.' Nevamarsya stroked the horse's long face. 'You have them like that when someone is riding you or you're hitched to a carriage, don't you Dixie?' she asked the horse.

The horse neighed softly in agreement.

'It's OK, stand down.' The horse fully retracted its wings as Nevamarsya fed it a lump of sugar. 'He's my favourite, the one I will be learning to ride.'

'You have to learn?' asked Natalicsya.

'Yes, the Matriarch, her heir and the spares have to be able to ride. It's tradition.'

'Lucky you, I would love to learn,' said Natalicsya with more than a hint of jealousy.'

'Not really, there is a lot of mucking out and brushing that goes with learning to ride.'

'That doesn't matter. Horses, riding and the freedom of the open air. I'd love it.'

'Good, Mam has said I could ask you if you would like one of the places in the class?'

'Would I? Oh thank you Neva,' Natalicsya replied with both question and answer. Then reality bit. 'Er, how much would it cost me?'

'Nothing, the Family Fangkart is paying. Not surprisingly Serah has asked Zofie to join the class.'

'Oh wow, when's the first lesson.'

'Not sure, Mam is still arranging everything.'

'So, plenty of time for me to go and make a pair of Jodhpurs then.'

'Nothing too fancy Lisha, I did mention the mucking out, didn't I?'

CHAPTER THIRTEEN
HIGHS AND LOWS

For the inhabitants of the Tree, the most important event in its history was the Graft. The merger of two plants when the first twenty eight Root Style Officers had taken up residence in the new composite plant. It brought all things feminine into the Tree. The twenty eight surviving male officers accepted the newcomers as their equals in their daily discussions. As the population of the Tree grew, it split equally between anthers and styles. The original survivors became the elders of the society. An Officer Corps was formed to take charge of the military part of Tree society, the Survivors Council took charge of everything else, eventually becoming the High Council. It maintained its original structure, twenty eight Patriarchs and twenty eight Matriarchs. The Tree Marshall and three Deputy Tree Marshalls were co-opted into the Council to represent the Officer Corps.

The title Family Matriarch has been traditionally passed down from mother to daughter. With Matriarch Symraltsya 079/15 Fangkart the title passed to her eldest female cousin, Sannarlsya. Sadly she died in the Great Treequake, before she could take office. As Sannarlsya's only daughter, Sharlensya now found herself in an anteroom to the Council Chamber, at the heart of the Council House the seat of government for the Tree. She was about to take an oath of office and become the eighth Matriarch Fangkart. Also the youngest Matriarch by a decade.

Sharlensya had spent more time in the company of Commander Sendarnsya than she would have liked, learning all about the operation of power. The Council might meet in the Chamber, but politics took place everywhere. Watching the other style had been an education for the professional teacher. The Matriarch and her Deputy were supposed to represent the feelings of the Family. It was perfectly obvious that Sendarnsya was out of control, using her position not for the good of the Family, but for the advancement of her own political alliance. Things were going to have to change.

Presiding Officer Reedsalsya was in charge of proceedings. She stood up and banged a ceremonial hammer on her desk. 'I call upon the Guild of Matriarchs to introduce their new member, the new Matriarch of the Family Fangkart.'

The first Matriarchs had banded together to form the Guild. As the oldest of the Matriarchs, Symraltsya had technically been the Guild's Chair-Officer. However, the old style who stood up, Matriarch Wraig had done the job for years.

'I call upon Sharlensya, being the daughter of Sannarlsya in turn the cousin of Symraltsya, who was the daughter of Scarletsya, who was the grandaughter of Sylpelksya, who was the sister of Soonlalsya, both the daughters of Sarflunsya the eldest daughter of Fangkart, being the Daughter Elect of her Family to take the Oath of Office and assume her role as the eighth Matriarch Fangkart.'

This was Sharlensya's cue to enter the Chamber. As she walked down the central aisle, she should have felt at home, the Chamber was laid out like a classroom. The Tree-Marshall sat at her large desk, like a teacher looking out onto her pupils. The Matriarchs, Patriarchs and Deputies sat in rows of desks facing the Tree-Marshall, Traditionalist on the right of the wide central, Radicals on the left and Neutrals at the back.

In the Council Chamber, on occasions such as today, the Matriarchs wore the sort of civilian dresses, with tightly laced corset and cumbersome hooped skirt, which had been fashionable in the Roots shortly before the Graft. She hoped she looked elegant as she approached the Tree-Marshall. She curtseyed politely, turned to the assembled Councillors and curtseyed again, then with her arms raised, making the Sign of the Tree, in a clear voice she said.

'I, Sharlensya, being the daughter of Sannarlsya in turn the cousin of Symraltsya, who was the daughter of Scarletsya, who was the grandaughter of Sylpelksya, who was the sister of Soonlalsya, both the daughters of Sarflunsya the eldest daughter of Fangkart, being the Daughter Elect of my Family, do hereby swear true allegiance to the Officer Corps and the High Council. I pledge to represent the wishes of my Family as the Eighth Matriarch Fangkart. I swear to honour the mandate of the Family Forum in this august body, without fear or favour. In the name of the Spirit of the Tree I pledge to uphold and maintain the Laws of the Tree of Life. May the Tree be my Judge,' she was so glad she had remembered the correct order of her predecessors and all the clauses of the Oath. Everyone else involved in this ceremony used crib-sheets, but etiquette decreed she had to know her part and say it without fault.

'The Daughter Elect has spoken, is there anyone present who would challenge her right to hold the office to which she has been elected by birth?' asked Matriarch Wraig. The old style waited for a minute before continuing. 'Having heard no objections to this election and having witnessed her swearing the Oath of Office, I call upon theTree Marshall to verify this appointment.'

Tree Marshall Pentwynsya stood and bowed at Sharlensya. Unable to return the bow, thanks to her corset, Sharlensya curtsied politely.

'I, Tree Marshall Pentwynsya hereby verify and appoint Sharlensya, Daughter Elect of the Family Fangkart as the Eighth Matriarch Fangkart.'

'I ask the Tree-Marshall's permission to take my place at my desk,' she said.

'Permision granted, Matriarch,' said the Tree-Marshall.

Sharlensya walked slowly back up the aisle towards the empty desk on the right hand side, in front of Matriarch Wraith and behind Matriarch Zilfarayts. She felt as if the room was spinning. Somehow she managed to get back to her desk and sit rather inelegantly.

As soon as she took her seat, the chamber erupted into applause.

Outside this chamber, people would still call her Sharlensya, Sharlee, and in the case of Tabbernant, Shaz in day to day conversation. Within this chamber she was the personification of her Family and would be addressed only by the name Fangkart.

'I call a twenty minute recess,' said the Presiding Officer, who must have seen Sharlensya's ungainly collapse. 'Dress Code Beta when the Council Resumes.'

Sharlensya felt so relieved.

'Got a fit of the vapours have you Fangkart?' asked Matriarch Wraig. 'You will soon get used to your stays.'

'I thought we only wore this get up for special occasions?'

'Indeed, but you are going to be here for a long time. There will be many special occasions in the years to come. So nice to see some young blood in this place. The fact you lead what is currently a Traditionalist Family is a bonus. I trust you will be sitting with your fellow Traditionalists and keeping those foolish Radicals at bay.'

'I'm afraid you have been misinformed,' said Sharlensya, 'I have been speaking to members of my Family, and they have mandated me to sit with the Radical Party.'

'Your predecessor never bothered listening to the mandate, nor her Deputy, why should you,' said the old Matriarch sharply. 'She believed a Matriarch's job is to lead from the front.'

'Then we definitely sit on different sides of the chamber.'

'Welcome Fangkart. If you are joining us Radicals, then you will have to get your desk moved to our side of the aisle,' said a middle-aged from the Upper Trunk. Sharlensya would have recognised her in normal clothes, now her name escaped her.

'Morning Matriarch Rust,' said the older style, 'How are you, this fine morning?'

'I'm fine thank you, Wraig,' replied the style, 'So good to see you in such rude health.'

'Thank you, my dear.'

Sharlensya could see that Matriarch Wraig had gone grey, well greyer than usual. 'I'm still not sure of all the protocols, so may I continue to ask you for advice Wraig?'

'This is your first day Fangkart, of course you will find it strange.' Some colour had returned to the old lady's face. 'Even though we have different politics, I will be delighted to help you in any way I can.'

Sharlensya helped Matriarch Wraig get up from her desk.

'Thank you for introducing me to the Council,' she said to the older style.

'It was my pleasure, I meant what I said about young blood. It will certainly make the debates in this place more interesting. I wish you well.' The older style left the chamber.

'Best to leave it for a few minutes, give the old dear time to get clear,' Matriarch Rust said. 'She is one of the nicer

Traditionalists. I dread the soon to dawn day her obnoxious daughter sits in her desk.'

I don't think she is as frail as she likes people to think,' said Sharlensya.

'Maybe not, but she is not the force of nature I remember when I first joined this august body.' There was silence for a few minutes. 'So, let's go and change into something emprintable for the rest of today's session, and breathing is a workable proposition.'

'How very much like a style, talking about clothes at such an important event,' said an attractive older anther.

'If you weren't such a Radical, I could almost think you believed that.' Matriarch Rust was laughing. 'Maybe you should try one of these corsets, then you would understand what we are talking about?'

'I think I voted for you at the last election?' Sharlensya asked the anther. 'When I still had a vote, I suppose I don't need one, now I am a Matriarch?'

'Right on both counts.' The group had left the chamber. 'Your spectacular move from Clan 1 to Clan 28 three years ago, from the heart of the Roots to the tip of the Canopy made you one of my constituents. Now you are my colleague. Matriarch Sharlensya.

'Thank you Patriarch Creavolant. It is nice to hear my proper name again.'

'We have been trying for years to get that silly law abolished, to be able to use our real names in there,' said Creavolant, 'but even some Radicals voted against it.'

'Just because I am a Rad doesn't mean I am going to rip every tradition up, Creaff.' Matriarch Rust said. 'And if you'd excuse us ladies, we weren't joking about being able to breath, move or sit comfortably. No wonder my ancestress was the first to ditch this sort of outfit.'

Throughout the morning, Sharlensya had looked up into the public galleries, watching how her daughters reacted.

'Well, what do you think?' she asked them as they entered the lobby of the Council House.

'One day I will be sitting down there,' said Serynazsya, 'looking as bored as you did. I wish you a long and healthy life.'

'Thank you dear,' she said to one daughter. 'What did you think Neva?'

'That you could roast chestnuts on Sendarnsya's anger. You really need to get rid of her.'

'Just think what it was like sitting next to her dear.' Sharlensya laughed.

'She was so angry because you voted to repeal a law nobody has enforced for thirty years,' said Nevamarsya. 'I can't see why.'

'Because it was there, continuity with the past I suppose,' said Sharlensya, glad to be back in Mentor Mode, familiar territory. 'The Statute of Separation was a silly idea, based on a groundless fear.'

'Why would the original styles think they would lose their identity, they were so obviously different to the original Anthers and nothing has changed since the Graft?' asked Nevamarsya.

'The original Anthers were in awe of all things feminine,' said Serynazsya, 'it being something new and interesting back then. They didn't want to lose it either, so they thought banning styles wearing trousers or anything masculine would be a good idea.'

'Well, that was part of the reason, nobody wanted unisex blandness.' their Mother continued, 'when that didn't appear, people began ignoring the Statute, then it got suspended by a Court Martial ruling. The Traditionalists have been trying to make in enforceable again for years. They were not expecting the Radicals to attempt to completely repeal it, which is why the Rads won the vote.'

'Good, I like being able to wear jeans,' said Serynazsya.

'When do you wear jeans? You're like Lisha, I've never seen her in trousers either,' said Nevamarsya.

'But I like have the option to wear them if I wanted.'

'Would Cousin Sendarnsya would have voted against? Not that it makes much difference.' asked Nevamarsya, moving the conversation back to politics.

'Oh yes, even though the Family was against the Statute, its just another example of how out of control she is,' added Serynazsya.

'You're right dear,' Sharlensya said her to her daughter. 'Don't worry, wheels are in motion.'

'Good afternoon, Matriarch Fangkart.'

'Uncle Kelly, you made it,' said Sharlensya.

'Of course we did, although we had to watch on the monitors in the Viewing Room.'

'So, can we still call you Sharlee, or are you above all that now?' asked Kanonypsya.

'Please do, Kandy. I need to remain grounded.' Sharlensya could see that her friend was more relaxed than she had been for weeks. 'It is nice to see you smiling again.'

'Thank you, Sharlee. Yes, we have sorted out our silly problem,' said Kanonypsya, as Keltonant put his arm around her.

'I'm glad to hear it,' said Sharlensya.

'It is said the Dining-Room in the Council House is the best restaurant in the Tree,' said Serynazsya. 'I'm looking forward to seeing if that is correct.'

'It is also the most exclusive in the Tree,' said Sharlensya as she slotted her IndesnCard into key reader on the door to the dining-room. She had been having nightmares about this for the past week. This was the point where she usually found herself standing back in a classroom full of unruly cadets after her card had been rejected. At least the clichéd nakedness never happened in her nightmares.

The door swung open and they were greeted by the Maitre D'.

'Good afternoon Matriarch and guests. It will be our pleasure to serve you. If you would follow the Sprite.'

The Dining-room was located in the dome above the debating chamber and the table they had been led to had a spectacular view of the Executive Centre. She could see Fangkart house, with a lilac and yellow pennant flying from a flagpole.

'I can see what you meant about keeping yourself grounded,' said Kanonypsya as she eased herself into a luxurious seat at the mahogony table. 'This is certainly an improvement on the stone floor and wooden benches of the refectory in the Convent.'

'At least the food they serve tastes nice,' said Nevamarsya, 'we have yet to see what it is like here.'

'True dear, plain food cooked well.' Kanonypsya laughed, 'I keep forgetting you have been there.'

'And continue to go there,' the girl replied.

'All part of life's rich tapestry.'

'Indeed dear. Now, let's see what is on the menu.

'**A**re you absolutely sure about this?' Sharlensya asked the Enforcer Sergeant who was standing at the door of the Dining-Room.

'I'm afraid so, Matriarch Fangkart.' The police officer doing the arresting looked more embarrassed than the person he was about to arrest. 'Obviously, we can't do anything here in the Council House, but if you would like to accompany me to the Station, then I am sure we can sort this out.'

'Thank you, Sergeant.'

Sharlensya had no doubt that this madness was all politically motivated. The warrant against Serynazsya named the entire Winter Squad as Serynazsya's accomplices, so until these ridiculous charges were dismissed by a Court Martial, she could not sit in Council.

'So Sendarnsya, you have to represent the family again.' At that moment Sharlensya could happily kill her Voting Deputy, who was barely concealing a smile.

'Yes, Matriarch,' said Sendarnsya.

'Do try not to look so happy about it. Despite this hitch, I'm Matriarch now, and I'm ordering you to follow the Family Mandate.'

'Of course I will, Matriarch,' was the polite reply.

Of course you won't, thought Sharlensya. You will continue to pursue your own political agenda. Enjoy the power while it lasts. It will speed your destruction.

She activated her comlink. 'Lieutenant Vordaunant, have you heard the news?'

'Yes Ma'am,' the chauffer replied.

'So, do I still have your services?' she asked.

'Certainly Matriarch. You can only get rid of me if you are impeached,' he replied.

'Oh good. Then can you bring the car round to the front of the Council House.'

'Certainly Ma'am.'

CHAPTER FOURTEEN
WITNESS FOR THE PROSECUTION

Serynazsya's Court Martial seemed to arrive in a flash The three charges she was facing related to her being Absent Without Leave during the previous Autumn and Winter.

The Pre-trial assessment had been a disaster. The Judge Advocate, Brigadier Denningant had insisted that the case be heard by a full Judicial Tribunal of the Courts Martial of the Officer Squad. Despite the fact that the Prosecution had a very flimsy case, built on circumstantial evidence and the testimony of Captain Samnundsya alone.

'I can't belive the old fool forced this one to court,' said Subaltern Bowlyxlant one of the court ushers to his colleague, as they prepared the Tribunal Chamber.

'Why should you worry, it pays the wages doesn't it?' asked his fellow usher, Subaltern Terndalant.

'But it is a waste of time. And it does not serve justice,' said Bowlyxlant.

'Subalterns Bowlyxlant and Terndalant, I can hear plenty of talking but I can't see much work being done.' Lieutenant Glennyxsya the Stipendiary Usher had entered the courtroom. She was responsible for its smooth running, so she wanted it ready in time for the day's business.

'Yes Ma'am. Sorry Ma'am,' the subalterns chorused as their boss's comlink chimed loudly.

'Well, chaps. It seems that old Denningant's gout is playing up,' said the Lieutenant. 'The case has been transferred to Colonel Rhojmapant. He has suspended proceedings until after lunch, whilst he reviews all the documents.'

'Which should take him ten minutes,' said Bowlyxlant.

'And that is why the case is not being adjourned until tomorrow, as would normally be the case with a Desertion trial.'

'That doesn't seem fair to me though,' said Terndalant.

'Never the less Subalterns, we have an extra few hours, so you two can study the existing case law on today's tribunal. Who knows, it might come up in your next lot of exams.'

Within the Tree, there were two types courts, the Courts Martial and Courts Civil. The most important are the Courts Martial, they deal with all criminal law and disciplinary matters. The Courts Civil dealt with property and contracts.

Cases in a Court Martial are presented by a Defence and a Prosecution Advocate. The system did not tolerate any form of time wasting. An advocate would lose control of the chamber if they spent too long between questions.

Once both sides had presented their case the Judge Advocate, the supreme authority in the court would come to a verdict. During a case, the Judge Advocate could also ask the witness questions to clarify matters. He or she would decide if evidence was admissable.

Yet more hours of hell. Why, Oh great Spirit of the Tree are you torturing your poor daughter so badly? How have I offended you? The mantra kept on spinning through Serynazsya's mind during the delay. Her advocate had told her the new Judge Advocate was likely to be far more sympathetic than the previous incumbent. He could hardly be less sympathetic than Brigadier Denningant, who had already convicted her. Serynazsya really didn't care. It was just extending the nightmare even further. It did not matter how sympathetic the new Judge Advocate presiding over the case was, the system was against her. She would be found guilty and as a result barred for life from the job she loved doing.

From her place in the Dock, against the back wall, Serynazsya could see most of the courtroom. The semi-circle with layers of tiered seating of the Public Gallery surrounded the Chamber. In front of the Gallery were the desks of the Ushers. On either side of the central arena were the Advocate's desks. Directly in front of the Dock was the Witness Stand halfway between each desk. The only person Serynazsya was not be able to see was the Judge Advocate who sat on a throne next to the ceremonial gong, on a dais, directly over Dock.

The Judge-Advocate struck the large gong signifying he was ready to begin.

'The Tribunal Chamber will rise,' said the Lieutenant in charge of this bleak odeon, 'for Judge Advocate, the learned Colonel Rhojmapant 079/63 of the Family Troobarq, who will hear all pleas for the Tree's Justice today.'

Serynazsya had no option but to remain standing, wearing a white sash with her best uniform. The mark of the Accused.

'Usher, which case is being considered by this tribunal?' asked Colonel Rhojmapant.

'Sir, this is Case 735-AN-185, the Officer Corps versus Subaltern Serynazsya 178/20 of the Family Fangkart,' Lieutenant Glennyxsya replied.

Serynazsya wondered why the Court still used the old-fashioned "of the Family whatever" naming system. Although, she thought, now was not the time to get lost in the minutiae of traditions. Things were about to start moving, and move at a hectic pace.

'Very well, the Tribunal is in session, the chamber may be seated.' Then he struck the ceremonial gong. 'Usher, read the Indictment for today's Tribunal,' ordered the Judge Advocate.

'Sir, this case is one of alleged Desertion and Dereliction of Duty. The Officer Corps accuses the defendant on three counts. Firstly, that on Fyfesday Bayta of Dixtemp, of the one hundred and eighty third year after the Graft, the then unassigned Ensign Serynazsya 178/20, did unlawfully absent herself from the Central Shuttle-port of the Crown. Secondly, that resulting from the first count, Ensign Serynazsya 178/20 did absent herself without leave for the whole of the following tour of duty from the educational establishment her lawful superiors had ordered her to attend. Thirdly, that without the permission of her lawful superior officer, did transfer herself from the Branch Management Regiment to the Nursing Regiment.'

'Subaltern Serynazsya 178/20 of the Family Fangkart,' said Colonel Rhojmapant, 'you have heard the charges. What plea do you wish to enter?'

Serynazsya was not being called as a witness today, so she only had to say a few words. She was more nervous than she had ever been in her life. Come on girl, she thought, straight back and strong voice, don't sound cowed by your surroundings.

'Sir, I wish to enter a plea of not guilty and call upon Captain Nestlansya 114/09 of the Family Fangkart to be my advocate.'

'The Tribunal notes your plea, and I hereby authorise your chosen advocate to speak in your defence.'

As if he was going to object. Why can't they just get on with it, Serynazsya asked herself. This was all theatre, the charges had been agreed upon in the pre-trial hearing.

Serynazsya knew her lines, in her head she had rehearsed everyone else's. Right up to her inevitable conviction.

Lieutenant Glennyxsya rose to her feet. 'Sir, the Officer Corps disputes this plea and calls upon Captain Soolnaysya 197/14 of the Family Reerkart to be its advocate.'

'Very well, I hereby authorise the Corp's chosen advocate to speak for the prosecution.' Then the Judge Avocate sounded his ceremonial gong again. 'May the search for truth and justice begin.'

Branch Captain Samnundsya 101/20 of the Family Zilfrayts had been feeling more than a little smug that morning. Her little revenge was all going so smoothly. Judge Advocate Denningant had agreed to hear the case against Serynazsya even though it was paper thin. It would terminally embarrass the political career of a dangerous radical and cause her to stand down as Matriarch of the Family Fangkarts. It was an act of genius.

She hadn't been overly concerned when Judge Advocate Denningant's health had failed him. The new Judge Advocate should be equally amenable. After all, he was from the Base of the Trunk, and the inhabitants of that part of the Tree had been subservient to the Roots for decades.

She had arrived in the courtroom early, to bag a prime seat in the row reserved for prosecution witnesses. She noted NM331/29, or whatever it was calling itself now, was the only person to arrive before her. Imagine letting riff-raff like that become an officer. What was the Tree coming to! Someone else to add to the list of people to deal with after today's triumph.

The preamble seemed to be taking forever. All the facts in the opening addresses had already been agreed upon in the pre-tribunal hearings. All they needed to do was call her to give here evidence, then convict that little cow.

'Calling Captain Samnundsya 101/20 of the Family Zilfrayts,' said the Stipendiary Usher.

At last, she thought, and now my chance to shine. Samnundsya got to her feet and marched smartly to the witness podium.

'I, Captain Samnundsya 101/20 of the Family Zilfrayts, swear on my word as a true and pure daughter of the Tree of Life to tell the truth, the whole truth and nothing but the truth.'

'Captain Samnundsya,' said the Judge-Advocate, 'that is not the proper oath, please repeat your swearing in using the correct one.'

Ouch, this Judge-Advocate might be more of a problem than I imagined, old Denningant would not have objected to the Pure-stock oath.

'I, Captain Samnundsya 101/20 of the Family Zilfrayts swear on my word as an Officer, to tell the truth, the whole truth and nothing but the truth.'

'Captain Samnundsya, would you please tell how you know the accused.' The prosecution advocate began the first of her questions immediately.

'I was her Commanding Officer last Summer, at Branch VK29 73FG. In the middle of the Spring/Summer Tour the previous year, I purchased the Syrup Production Licence, after the death of the previous Licencee. This was my first full tour in command of that dump. I took the opportunity to bring some freshly commissioned officers up with me, who would not object to the methods I wanted to introduce. Subaltern Serynazsya was one of that group unfortunately. She wasn't one of my first choices, or even my second. She was inflicted on me by the Corps. They had to find a posting for her some-where, I drew the short straw. She proved to be the worse of the group, a real no hoper.'

'I call for a rebuttal,' demanded the Defence Advocate. A rebuttal was a public declaration that the Judge Advocate would ignore that statement when he was deciding the case. 'The witness is here to report the facts of the events and not to make ad hominem attacks on the defendant.'

'Agreed,' said Colonel Rhojmapant. 'Captain Samnundsya, please stick to the facts.'

Ad hominem, what did that mean thought Samnundsya. And I am sticking to the facts, piggy was the worse of the new girls. Still, best to keep the Judge-Advocate sweet.

'I apologise, Sir,' said Captain Samnundsya as she bowed towards the dias before continuing. 'The fact was that Ensign Serynazsya refused to integrate with the rest of the squad. I had inherited a small group of the previous Commanding Officer's fellow hicks. They had long term contracts, so I couldn't get rid of them. They refuse to instigate a number of changes in the way the Branch was run. She fell-in with them. They encouraged the accused to use their unscientific and out-dated methods, not the new and superior methods of Drone Management developed in the Roots.'

Right, next question, something sensible this time.

'Why should this be? Surely a newly commissioned officer would want to impress her first Commanding Officer and fall in quickly to the C-O's way of doing things?' asked Captain Soolnaysya.

That's more like it, thought Samnundsya. Something I can get my teeth into.

'In my view Ensign Serynazsya was a hopeless romantic, she believes that drones have feelings and can be encouraged to be more efficient. This is, of course, ridiculous, drones are created to work and don't care about anything else.' All this was so obviously true, no had-nominame-thingies there. 'She thought I was cold and cruel, so naturally she would swallow the garbage she was being fed by the hicks.'

Samnundsya was beginning to enjoy herself again. 'Also Ensign Serynazsya's work was slap-dash and slovenly, so she fitted in well with the hicks. She was constantly saying she did not want to be a Branch Officer. She kept harping on about her impossible dream of training to be a nurse. If she had any talent in that department she would have been accepted by one of the Schools of Nursing. I dread to think what would happen to the patients if by some miracle she had been allowed to join that career. They would have been killed off by such an lazy nurse.'

'Again I call for a rebuttal,' said Captain Nestlansya. 'This is another attack on my client's character and has nothing to do with the events of 5B10/183.'

'Agreed, the Prosecution must encourage the witness to stick to the point,' Colonel Rhojmapant said wearily.

'Yes, Sir,' replied the Prosecuting Advocate, who turned to Captain Samnundsya, not wanting to lose control of the floor.

'The defendant was booked to take a Branch Management course during the last tour, was she not?'

'Yes, as she was never going so succeed in the nursing profession, I had arranged for her to be properly trained in the...'

'Captain Samnundsya,' Colonel Rhojmapant interrupted the witness, 'you have been warned about your constant unpleasant comments about the defendant. Stick to the facts or find yourself in contempt of this Tribunal.'

Oh do stop interrupting you silly anther, thought Captain Samnundsya, it's the truth, Serynazsya needed to be shown the folly of her ways. Captain Samnundsya continued with her prepared answer. 'As the girl's guardian, I only wanted what was best for her. She obviously could not see this, and was constantly insubordinate. This came to a head on the last day of the Summer tour. When she arrived at the shuttle port in the Crown she was in her usual unhelpful mood. She had lost a drone in transit. When I asked her to account for the missing drone, she exploded into a foul mouth tirade and stormed out of the building. Naturally I was concerned when she failed to report to the shuttle or the Training Centre she had been posted to. I found out that she claimed she was stranded in the Crown.'

'You reported her as being absent without leave?'

'I did indeed. That was all I could do.'

Captain Nestlansya did not wait for her colleague to sit at her desk. Each advocate took turns in asking four questions.

With no time wasting allowed, Captain Nestlansya began her series of questions.

'Records show that you did not report her until three weeks ago. Why was that, Captain Samnundsya?'

'At the time I believed that a Winter spent trapped in the back of beyond, cut off from civilisation was punishment enough. However, I recently began thinking that I could be guilty of dereliction of my duty of care if I continued to allow the accused to run wild.'

Duty of Care! I've got you on the run now you arrogant witch, thought Captain Nestlansya. You wouldn't know a duty of care if it slapped you in the face.

'Could it be that you knew you had put the defendant into an impossible situation on the day in question. You knew that if you made a fuss, your past record would be brought to light. You were trying to keep a low profile, were you not?'

'No, Captain, that is not the case.' Samnundsya turned to face Serynazsya. 'I have read the laughable work of fiction Subaltern Serynazsya has offered in her defence. She deliberately arranged to get herself stuck up in the Canopy. She is being supported in her wilful insubordination by a group of hopeless misfits. She needs to be shown the errors of her ways. My politics have nothing to do with this.'

Great green apples, she is bad-mouthing a group of genuine heroes. Not that I have time to deal with that now.

'So you deny that you lost your temper over the loss of a Sprite and ordered the defendant to return to the branch you commanded to find it?'

'Well naturally, I was concerned about the loss of a drone, they're not cheap you know. I may have chastised the defendant.'

'You did not order the defendant to return to Branch VK29 73FG, to recover the missing Sprite?

'I did not order her to leave the Shuttle Port. She left because she didn't want to travel down to the Roots. Though the Tree alone knows why.'

Oh you poor stupid creature. You really are going to regret saying that when I play my Ace.

The Defence Advocate sat down and consulted her notes. However, the Prosecution Advocate had not yet stood up.

When it was apparent that Captain Soolnaysya was not yet ready for her set of questions, Judge-Advocate Rhojmapant opened up his own line of questioning.

'I see from the notes on this case and your testimony today that you don't like the Canopy,' the Judge Advocate asked.

'No Sir, I hate it.'

I thought so. My notes for this case are shocking, he thought. No background information at all.

'Then tell me, Captain Samnundsya,' he continued, 'if you dislike the Canopy so much, why did you work up there?'

'I had no choice, Sir,' the witness replied.

'Really, why is that Captain?'

'I was placed under Internal Exile during the Summer.'

'And why is that, Captain?'

'As a punishment for my very minor involvement with the Sandampsya Coup. A recent re-evaluation of the facts by the High Council saw the lower ranking officers, who were only following orders and not a participating member of the Conspiracy granted a parole.'

As if I really needed to ask, thought the Colonel. I can see why you would want to keep quiet about it. Being involved in Treason, even obliquely does nothing to add to your credibility as a witness. But that's water down the Channel now. As much as I dislike this witness, I have to judge this case on the facts. So, I will give the Prosecuting Advocate a few more minutes to get her facts straight.

Of course, my particular brand of traditionalist politics are not in vogue at the moment, Captain Samnundsya thought to herself during this unexpected pause. This line of questioning from the Judge Advocate is unacceptable. If he knew his place, he would stop it immediately. He was playing to the Radicals in the media who would love to paint me as a reactionary firebrand. Just convict that bitch, don't do anything to tarnish my reputation.

The News Network were covering this trial. With one of the Heroes of the Winter Squad accused of desertion, of course it was going to be on every news bulletin on every public vid-channel. Captain Samnundsya stood in the witness stand looking smug and intrinsically stupid. The personification of the stereotype of the Pure-stock Style. Her needlessly verbose answers to simple questions had done more harm to her reputation than she could possibly imagine.

Captain Soolnaysya also wanted to move away from this line of questioning. She wanted to move away from this witness.

In fact, she wanted to move away from this case. Why had she ever agreed to work on it.

'At this time the Prosecution has no further questions for this witness.' Captain Soolnaysya desperately hoped the Judge-Advocate would not ask her opposite number if she wished to continue with the witness.

'Lieutenant Nestlansya, do you have any questions for the witness?'

Damn, the only real witness in this case is now discredited Nesta is going to tear her pieces.

'No Sir,' replied the Defence Advocate, 'the Defence has no further questions.'

'Very well, Captain Samnundsya, you may step down.'

Thank the Tree for that. The old harpy is off the hook of her own making. I bet Nesta has something up her sleeve. Normally she wouldn't let a golden opportunity float away.

'I, Commander Sharlensya 120/15, Eighth Matriarch of the Family Fangkart, swear on my word as an Officer, to tell the truth, the whole truth and nothing but the truth.' Her new official title sounded so pompous. If she had the choice, she would have sworn herself in as simple Sharlensya 120/15 Fangkart. She didn't have the choice, she represented her Family now.

Prosecution and Defence witnesses alternated. Sharlensya had been called as the first Defence Witness.

'Thank you Matriarch,' said the Judge-Advocate.

Sharlensya would normally never wish an attack of Gout on anyone, but old Brigadier Denningant's would have changed the facts to fit his pre-decided verdict. Major Rhojmapant would never do that.

Sharlensya bowed to the dias and took a deep breath. She

could see her daughter in the dock, looking like death warmed over. Right, a good performance now and I will be able to get my girl out from there.

'Matriarch, when did you first meet the accused?' asked Captain Nestlansya.

'On the first day of the Autumn/Winter Tour, last year. That would be 1C10/183.' Sharlensya coughed. 'Excuse me. That was three days after she was stranded up in the Canopy.'

'Not on or before that day?' asked the Defense Advocate.

'No, I was on seventy two hours compassionate leave. My Mother had just died in the Treequake, I was in mourning. Commander Tarprycsya and her husband Captain Treslelant had volunteered to stand in, and over the course of the next ten weeks acted as guardians.'

'You had no day to day contact with her?'

'My first responsiblity was to the class of Cadets I was mentoring. I had regular reports from the guardians, and came in contact with Serynazsya on a semi-regular basis, as technically I was responsible for all unaccompanied children.'

'And what was your initial thoughts on the accused?'

'I felt that she was a badly damaged individual. Prior to the biological adoption process, Serynazsya had a misformed nose and mismatched eye sockets. She had suffered months of bullying and abuse from her colleagues and superiors on the Branch Team she belonged to. Unfortunately, I did not realise how badly this had affected her. I am not a Counsellor, I missed a number of important signs a better qualified individual would have spotted immediately. I believed her anxiety and panic attacks were solely the result of the consequences of her missing her shuttle to the Roots. As a result she was obsessed with finding and possibly harming the Sprite she had misplaced.'

'Did you believe her story about being ordered to find the missing Sprite?' asked the Prosecuting Advocate.

'I could not do anything but accept it. The Sprite in question, NM331/29, had recently become Cadet Nevamar 331/29 and was one of my pupils. It confirmed everything that Serynazsya said.'

'Was there anyway that the Accused and the Cadet could have cooked the story up together?'

'Absolutely not, I made sure they had as little contact as possible. Serynazsya, was still issuing threats against the missing Sprite, I did not want her harming the Cadet it had become.'

'They have since formed a strong sibling bond, and you have adopted Serynazsya. Can you be sure their initial enmity was not an act?'

'Quite sure. The bond of love that now exists between the two girls was forged from the red hot hatred that existed in Serynazsya's pre-adoptive psyche.'

The Prosecuting Advocate sat down in her desk and stared at the Chamber's ceiling. After years of teaching, Sharlensya recognised that gesture. It was the sure fire sign that a bored pupil had lost all interest in a subject and was just giving up.

I'm going to get slaughtered here, thought Captain Soolnaysya. Old Denningant was supposed to shut down the mother, rule her an unfit witness during my first set of questions. Rhojmapant expects me to do the job properly, and I can't.

'You have since adopted Subaltern Serynazsya and have applied to adopt Subaltern Nevamarsya?'

'Yes, I found myself going through an accidental psuedo-pregnancy. The creature growing in my Uterine Chamber would cure most of Serynazsya's problems when it completed that stage in its life cycle and left my body. It was as if the Tree itself was watching over us, because the changes that were occurring in my body produced a serum that cured

Nevamarsya's own health problems. Such a rare combination of circumstances was too good to waste.'

'Isn't it true that the Accused became suicidal on the night of 3D11 last year?' Lieutenant Nestlansya asked as she began her latest round of questions.

'Yes, after a failed romantic gambit, Serynazsya became suicidal. I found her on the boating jetty of the Crown's Central Lake Beach.'

'Why was the accused in this state?'

Lieutenant Soolnaysya jumped to her feet. 'I call for a Rebutal. The witness has already stated she is not a Counsellor and has no psychiatric training.'

'I shall allow this chain of questions, Lieutenant,' said the Judge-Advocate. 'I want to see where this is going. I reserve the right to action your Rebutal.' Then turning to Sharlensya, 'you may Continue Matriarch Fangkart.'

'As has been pointed out, I am not a Counsellor,' Sharlensya continued. 'But even I began to see the reason for Serynazsya's deep depression.'

'That being?'

'The constant bullying from Captain Samnundsya and her staff during the previous Tour.'

'No further questions for this witness,' said Lieutenant Nestlansya.

'**M**atriarch Fangkart, this is all very interesting,' said the Prosecuting Advocate, starting her set of questions, 'but it has no bearing on the case at hand. That is Ensign Serynazsya deliberately chose to absented herself from the educational course she had been ordered to attend over the Autumn and Winter, flouting the authority of her Commanding Officer.'

Captain Soolnaysya could see that the witness was constantly glancing across the court to where Captain Samnundsya was sitting. Each time she did it, the witness appeared more angry than before. Maybe not all is lost, thought Captain Soolnaysya. If I get her angry enough to lose her rag, I will ask the Judge Advocate to disregard the Matriarch's evidence as flawed, the product of pure spite.

'A Commanding Officer who had given Serynazsya a series of orders on the day that contributed directly to her being marooned in the Canopy.'

'That is the defense that The accused is claiming. As you were not present on the day, your last statement was pure conjecture, was it not?'

'No, it is the truth, all the evidence heard today clearly reinforces the fact it is the truth.'

The ceremonial gong sounded again.

'Matriarch Fangkart,' said the Judge-Advocate, 'that is for me to decide.'

'Sorry, Sir,' said Sharlensya before continuing. 'I saw the state that Serynazsya was in during those dark days. There is no doubt in my mind who was responsible for her being a few steps from killing herself. I have also seen the progress Serynazsya has made since she became my daughter. When she was freed from the malignant influence of this person. It saddens me that this person is once again causing pain and confusion for my daughter.'

The Judge Advocate banged his gong. 'Matriarch Fangkart, I have read the notes and having heard your evidence today, which confirms everything in the notes, I conclude that there is no more you can add. You may step down as a witness.'

'Thank you, Sir.'

'The Tribunal is adjourned for thirty minutes.' The Judge Advocate rose from his seat and the courtroom emptied.

CHAPTER FIFTEEN
WITNESS FOR THE DEFENCE

The austere atmosphere of Tribunal Chamber Five did not intimidate Nevamarsya at all. She refused to let herself be overwhelmed by it.

The previous witness had been for the prosecution had been. The deck hand who had refused to let Serynazsya aboard the shuttle, had done more harm than good to the prosecution's case. Now it was Nevamarsya's turn. She felt buoyant.

Poor Serynazsya in the dock looks as miserable now as she was last Autumn, Nevamarsya thought. It was as if she was completely drained of life.

Nevamarsya did not find the appearance of Judge Advocate, Colonel Rhojmapant in his full dress uniform and purple sash of office impressive, it was merely over the top. Likewise the Defence and Prosecution Advocates looked overdressed in their full Dress Greens.

The white defendant's sash made Seryazsya's skin look even more pallid than usual. Oh curse Branch Captain Samnundsya for inflicting all this anguish on the girl.

'I, Subaltern Nevamarsya 331/29 swear on my word as an Officer to tell the truth, the whole truth and nothing but the truth.'

'Tell me Subaltern, how long have you known the Defendant?' asked the Prosecuting Advocate.

'Since before I became an Officer,' replied Nevamarsya.

'We are not interested in your time as a sprite, Subaltern. It is not relevant to the case. We are only interested in events since you became an Officer,' said the Prosecution Advocate.

'What a stupid thing to say. Permission to step down then,' she blurted out, instantly cursing her overconfidence and wishing she had not said anything.

'Young lady,' said the Judge Advocate, 'may I remind you of where you are, and the seriousness of the situation.'

'I am sorry, Sir,' she replied hoping that would be the end of the matter. No such luck.

'Now explain yourself?' ordered the Judge Advocate.

'Sir, Subaltern Serynazsya 178/20 Fangkart is accused of crimes said to have happened when I was still a Sprite.'

'Ah, I see.' The old anther smiled, 'I can see why you said what you said, but please remember where you are, and why you are here,' he then turned his attention to Prosecution Advocate. 'Captain Soolnaysya, I suggest that you do the same.'

With that, the Captain Soolnaysya returned to her desk, to check her notes. With the floor yielded, Captain Nestlansya, the Defence Advocate began asking questions.

'So, explain to the Tribunal the relationship between the Defendant and the Accuser.'

'Yes Ma'am, they hated each other.'

'Was the defendant regularly insubordinate?'

'No Ma'am, Subaltern Serynazsya always obeyed any order without question or complaint. She was always perfectly professional.'

'The record shows that the Defendant was constantly being disciplined by the Accuser.'

'Ma'am, Serynazsya was constantly being picked upon by Captain Samnundsya. Even the sprites could see that.'

The Prosecution Advocate finished checking her papers, stood and bowed.

'Captain Soolnaysya, you have the floor,' said the Judge Advocate. The Prosecution Advocate bowed to the Bench again. 'I request a formal rebuttal of the last comment.'

Now it was the Defence Advocate's turn to rise and bow.

'Captain Nestlansya, you wish to object?'

'Yes Sir, I do,' she picked up a folder. 'There are pages of evidence already accepted as valid and relevant by the prosecution, that reinforces the significance of Subaltern Nevamarsya's last statement.'

'Rebuttal denied. The last comment remains on the record.' The Judge Advocate looking mildly annoyed, decided to let the defence push forward their advantage. 'Captain Nestlansya, you have the Floor.'

'On the day in question, what was your relationship with the Defendant?'

'She was the officer assigned to transporting the phalanx of sprites I belonged to from our base in the Canopy down to the Shuttle-port in the Crown,' Nevamarsya replied.

'You did not make it down to the Shuttle-port.'

'I did, eventually.'

'But not with your phalanx?'

'No Ma'am, we were separated.' Nevamarsya hoped neither advocate would ask how and why she had been separated from the phalanx, it would seriously damage her testimony. This bothered Nevamarsya, as she had just sworn an oath to tell the whole truth. However, as Colonel Rhojmapant was deciding what was relevant or not, so much for the whole truth.

'Did you make an effort to catch up?'

'No Ma'am, by the time I was able to depart my base I was entering a sleep cycle.' Also technically true in as far as the question had been asked.

'That sleep cycle failed, didn't it?'

'Yes Ma'am, so I continued my journey.'

'I request a rebuttal,' said the Prosecution Advocate, rising from her desk.

'Continue, Captain Soolnaysya,' said the Judge Advocate from on high.

'Thank you, Sir,' said the Advocate, as she studied her notes. 'The travel arrangements of the Witness are irrelevant to this case. I request that my learned colleague should stop wasting this tribunal's time.'

'Captain Nestlansya,' asked Judge Advocate Rhojmapant, 'your colleague has a point. Subaltern Serynazsya is the defendant, please explain why her half-sister's movements are so vital to her defence?'

'Sir, we have already heard from Captain Samnundsya that she had no idea why the defendant left the shuttle-port and subsequently did not travel down to the Roots last Autumn. However, in a signed affidavit, the defendant says she was ordered to return to the branch to recover the Sprite NM331/29, who is now the young officer giving evidence. Subaltern Nevamarsya's testimony can confirm that the defendant left the Shuttle-port at the Crown in order to carry out those orders.'

'Very well, rebuttal denied, Captain Nestlansya. Continue.'

'Thank you, Sir.' The Advocate turned towards Captain Soolnaysya. 'I yield the floor.

'Tell the tribunal, Subaltern Nevamarsya, how you knew that anyone had been sent back to fetch you?'

'I saw Subaltern Serynazsya in an express shuttle-bus, heading back to the Crown.'

'If you were heading towards the Crown,' asked Captain Soolnaysya in a theatrically sarcastic tone, 'surely you would have bumped into each other along the way?'

'No Ma'am, I had taken a short-cut to the Trolley-bus station.'

'Indeed?' The Advocate's voice dripping with cynicism.

'Yes Ma'am, down a mail-tube, unpleasant but fast.'

'I find that hard to believe, how would a sprite have known about such a shortcut?'

'Because as a sprite I had been thrown down that tube many times.' Bitter memories popped into Nevamarsya's head. 'It is one of Branch Captain Samnundsya's favourite punishments, at the end of the working day, for what she called being an "Uppity Sprite". It was one way, so the return journey to the dorm was a long walk. By the time I or any other sprite returned to the dorm, the food dispenser would have been switched off and I, or whoever was being punished would go to bed hungry.'

'An entertaining story, but a story none the less.'

'It's the truth.'

'But nobody remembers things that happened to them when they were Sprites, our lives begin the day we are activated and become officers,' said Captain Soolnaysya.

'No Ma'am.' Nevamarsya could feel her temper growing. Careful now, don't want to blow my top.

'Yes, Subaltern.'

'No, we are taught to forget and most learn that lesson because they have no reason to hold onto the memory of a life now past. I chose to remember because I have reason to remember, and so I still know what the gnawing hunger of those sleepless nights is like.'

'I have nothing further to ask this witness, Sir,' said Captain Soolnaysya as she sat down.

'I have no further questions' said Lieutenant Nestlansya.' Nevamarsya was amazed at how glad she was to hear those words.

Serynazsya sat miserably in the dock. Why did it have to be beneath the Judge Advocate's dias. There was no way for her to know how he was reacting to what he heard. Captain Samnundsya had taken to the stand. The old witch had perjured herself left, right and centre. The Judge-Advocate had no way of knowing that. She was sure that even Nevamarsya's testimony, bless her heart, would not change Colonel Rhojmapant's mind.

'My colleague for the defence informs me that she has found a new witness to testify in this case. Sir, I have no further witnesses to call, so I have no objection to Subaltern Sofianesya 183/03 of the family Zilfarayts being called to give her evidence.'

Sofianesya? Sofianesya! Great green apples, I'm sunk now. What was Captain Nestlansya thinking, calling Samnundsya's daughter. Her number one toadying sycophant. Serynazsya wanted to cry, but there was no way she was going to let herself down like that. Not on a day like today.

'This is most irregular, I have no notes on this witness,' said Colonel Rhojmapant, 'but I have had no useful notes all day.'

'I apologise Sir,' said Captain Nestlansya. 'Notes were sent to Brigadier Denningant's Chambers yesterday, and should have been forwarded to you.'

'No doubt I will have the notes tonight, as I consider my verdict. You may proceed with the Witness.'

Serynazsya hadn't been paying attention to the people sitting in the courtroom, so had not known that her former superior officer was there.

'Subaltern Sofianesya 183/03 of the Family Zilfarayts, you are called to give evidence in this Tribunal. Please take your place on the Witness stand.'

Watching as the surprise witness took her place, Serynazsya could not help thinking this was a very different Sofianesya

Zilfrayts to the one she remembered. She marched with a happy smile on her face. In the past Sofianesya had always scurried wherever she went, usually a few paces behind her mother, never looking happy, only confused. Pure-stock styles all tried to remain stick thin, Sofianesya looked as if she had discovered the concept of pies and let nature take its course. She was definitely more curvacious. Nature had also been given free range with her hair, which was a dark blonde now, almost light brown. Definitely not the platinum yellow she used to sport. And was she really wearing a red and a black ribbon plaited through the rope of dark blonde hair running down her back? Only members of Origins Irrelevant, the Root Officers group fundamentally opposed to the Pure-Stock, did that. Was this going to be as big a disaster as Serynazsya had first feared.

'So Subaltern, can you please tell the Tribunal what you saw at the Crown Shuttle-port on Fyfesday Bayta of Dixtemp, 183?' asked Captain Nestlansya.

'On that day, we were busy packing up and evacuating our hafod at the end of the Syrup producing season.'

'Hafod?' asked the Judge Advocate, who had obviously never been up to the Canopy.

'Yes Sir, the industrial plant that is only used in Spring and Summer.'

This made Serynazsya smile. Hafod was a word used by people from the Canopy. In the past, Sofianesya would rather have had teeth extracted than describe her place of work in the summer in that way.

'Carry on Subaltern,' said the Judge Advocate.

'Thank you, Sir. As the Acting Executive Officer for that day, I was in constant contact with Captain Samnundsya. I reported to her that the last batch of Sprites had arrived at the shuttle-port, under the command of Ensign Serynazsya, as she was then. I also told her there were only forty nine Sprites present.'

'How many should there have been?' asked the Judge-Advocate.

'The phalanx should have had fifty Sprites, Sir.' Sofianesya looked across to Serynazsya. 'The poor girl was on the verge of tears. She knew that Captain Samnundsya would not be pleased.'

'So how did the Captain react?' asked Captain Nestlansya.

'She hit the roof. Sprites aren't cheap to replace. She stormed over to Serynazsya and ordered her to go back to the branch and look for the missing Sprite.'

'In evidence at this tribunal, the Captain has said she did not see Ensign Serynazsya after leaving the branch?'

'That is a blatant lie.'

Serynazsya expected the Prosecuting Advocate to jump to her feet, demanding a rebuttal. Instead she sat at her desk looking increasingly miserable.

'So you say that Captain Samnundsya knew exactly why the then Ensign Serynazsya was not on the shuttle that departed for the Roots that day, and why Ensign Serynazsya failed to attend the educational establishment that she had been posted to for the Winter?'

'Yes Ma'am.'

Serynazsya watched in amazement as Lieutenant Soolnaysya remained at her desk, sat with her head in her hands, utterly defeated.

'Oh shut up Fia, you are making a fool of yourself,' said Captain Samnundsya loudly from the gallery.

'Silence in court!' the Judge-Advocate said in a loud and authoritative voice as he sounded his ceremonial gong. 'Captain Samnundsya, you are sorely trying my patience. Lieutenant Soolnaysya, you have the floor.'

The Prosecuting Advocate got to her feet slowly, as her professionalism returned.

'Subaltern Sofianesya, is it true that you and your Mother, Captain Samnundsya are not on speaking terms, and had a very public falling out a number of weeks ago?'

'Yes Ma'am, that is true. We aren't talking and yes we did have an embarrassing quarrel in Central Hub Park recently.'

'And later that afternoon, you were seen with Subaltern Nevamarsya 331/29. It could be argued that you met to concoct your evidence to this tribunal. That speaking for the defence of Subaltern Serynazsya 178/20 is simply an act of defiance against your mother?'

'No Ma'am,' replied Sofianesya, 'that meeting took place before my Mother reported Subaltern Serynazsya. We went to drink Cholayt, not to read cha leaves.'

The sound of the gong from the Judge Advocate's dias quickly grabbed everyone's attention.

'I have listened to the evidence in this tribunal with growing incredulity.' General Rhojmapant said from the dias. 'That the Prosecution even thought that there was sufficient evidence to bring a case and that it was allowed to proceed to a Court Martial amazes me. The testimony I have just heard from Lieutenant Sofianesya has been the icing on the cake. I am therefore terminating this pointless tribunal now. Before it wastes any more valuable time. Subaltern Sofianesya, you may step down,' he had stood up and sounded the ceremonial gong again, summoning Lieutenant Glennyxsya to the Judges' Dias. She secured a blindfold around his eyes and lead him to the front of the dais, where Subaltern Bowlyxlant handed him a sword, which he held up with his right hand, then Subaltern Terndalant handed him a scales to hang from his left hand.

'I, General Rhojmapant 079/63 of the Family Troobarq, being the authorised Judge-Advocate in Case 735-AN-185, the

Officer Corps versus Subaltern Serynazsya 178/20 of the Family Fangkart hereby rule that the case be dismissed. The defendant has no case to answer and is to be completely exonerated. Subaltern Serynazsya, you may remove the white sash and you are free to leave this Court Martial with no stains on your record. This tribunal is dismissed.'

The gong sounded for a third time, the nightmare was over. Serynazsya could not describe the rush of emotions she was experiencing. It was beyond joy, it dwarfed happiness. Suddenly the darkness was sent scurrying away into the cold and unloved places from which it had emerged.

There was a commotion taking place in the gallery. Court officials and Enforcers were surrounding Captain Samnundsya. Arguing which had the right to hang her out to dry.

'Look mate, I don't care what your warrant says, she has committed perjury today, in my court, therefore as Stipendiary Usher, I get to arrest her,' said Lieutenant Glennyxsya loudly.

'This is a fully sworn arrest warrant, signed by my Regiment's Commander and countersigned by the Tree Marshall herself. This is my arrest, whether you like it or not,' the angry looking Enforcer replied.

Lieutenant Glennyxsya re-examined the document the enforcer was holding. 'Great green apples, that's the Tree Marshall's actual signature, not just a stamp. She's all your's my friend, that trumps anything I might have.'

The enforcer turned towards Captain Samnundsya.

'By the power vested in me by the Enforcer's Regiment and the Tree Marshall of the Tree of Life, I hereby arrest you, Captain Samnundsya 101/20 of the Family Zilfarayts on charges relating to the mistreatment of Sprites, falsification of Officer Training Testing Records, Illegal Sprite Storage, Wasting Police Regiments' Time, Perjury, Criminal Slander and Attempting to Pervert the Course of the Officer Corps'

Justice.' The officer stopped to take a breath. 'You do not have to say anything, as you have the right to silence. However, anything you do say will be taken down and may be used in evidence against you.'

'Oh don't be ridiculous,' replied Samnundsya. 'That is all a tissue of lies, I have done nothing wrong.'

'Please note, that you have the right to contact an Advocate, and have him or her present during any questioning.'

'Damn right I am going to get myself an Advocate,' she said, realising she would not be able to bluff her way out of this.

'OK, take her away boys.'

The Captain was marched away, into custody. Had that little piece of theatre been arranged for her benefit? Serynazsya didn't care. She looked up at Nevamarsya's beaming face. No, not just for her benefit, but Serynazsya knew that anyone who had suffered under that dreadful old witch Samnundsya would be happy today.

CHAPTER SIXTEEN
NEVER TO BE TOLD

It was Fyfesday morning, and the last working day of the week. More importantly for this group of Probationary Constables, after eight weeks it was the last day of their first term at Enforcers School. Next term they would be in work placements.

'I know you lot regard what you have been learning here as a waste of time,' said Sergeant Hipobrisya. 'As Probationary Constables, next term will be your first taste of real police work. For three weeks following the Boot Camp, you are to be sent to station houses throughout the Tree.'

'I don't know why you are so happy. After two weeks out in the Tree, out on the beat, during a cold and dark Dawnsward shift, you will be counting down the days to your return here for your second term. Every single Police Officer out on the beat in their first placement does. I know I did.'

None of the PC's in the room believed this for a second. The Sarge, out on the beat? Never. She was part of this School's fixtures and fittings.

'Although I dread to think how much you will have forgotten by the time you return from the placement.'

'So to today's assignment is practising the surveillance techniques you have been studying. I will split you into pairs. In the morning session one of you will try to evade the other, in the afternoon, you will swap. Do you understand?'

'Yes, Sergeant,' the PC's replied in unison.

Francelant had made sure that he had not been followed. He had sent the gymnasium's caretaker Sprite off on an errand.

At this time of year there would be nobody within three blocks. The entire district this gym was located in was known as Winter Gardens, although some also called it Hickville. It was the home of officers currently posted up in the Canopy. All he had to do was wait for the working day to end. Francelant would have beaten Natalicsya. He relaxed, he knew she would have been looking for a boy in civilian clothes, wandering around in style undress greens had been a master-stroke. Although in those boots it had been an uncomfortable master-stroke. He began changing out of the style uniform into his civilian clothes.

'Welcome to the World of itchy grey tights.'

The voice came from the other side of the room. Francelant's heart sank. She had caught him. He switched the emprinter into reverse.

'That's right, you're still on duty, you should stay in some sort of uniform, even if it isn't brown.'

'How did you find me, I thought I was being so clever?'

'You were. You do look very convincing dressed as a style, when you are standing still. The minute you start walking, it all falls apart. You walk like every other anther in a skirt. You left big fat "come find me" clues all over town.' Natalicsya was laughing. 'It was simply a matter of accessing the local security grid to narrow down the search to here.'

'Still doesn't explain how you knew to look for an anther in style's Undress Green?' asked Francelant dejectedly.

'I've thought there was something about you for weeks. I saw the Sarge requesition a new set of juvenile style Undress Green on Trinitsday and started to wonder why.'

'Oh. I couldn't do it. The QMS wouldn't have given me

what I needed. Even with my special dispensation.' The boy giggled, a very feminine giggle.

'Your non-regulation hair for the past week started making sense. The Sarge has said nothing about it, normally she would have been down like a ton of bricks on any young anther with hair that long. So when I couldn't find you as a him, so I thought, he's a herm and started looking for you as a her.'

'She helped me get minor details right on the disguise. he said. 'Sometimes being an active hermaphrodite has its uses.'

'So, you are a herm. Are you on the pills to keep you in your chosen gender?' Natalicsya asked.

'Until after adoption. Then I can have an operation to become an anther permanently.' Francelant replied.

'You remind me of a friend who used to say that before she differentiated,' she replied. 'It intrigued me, so I read all about Hermaphrodites. I've never actually spoken to one.'

'You mean Pezzi's girlfriend Nevamarsya. Its a different set of circumstances. With her, neither gender switched on and both were trying to. With me, both genders have switched on. I've always thought of myself as a boy. Its the way my brain is wired. The hermaphrodite thing is just getting in the way.'

'As it was for her. But she stopped be hermaphrodite the day she emerged as a style. You will always be both, even with the operaton. After a few years you could take another set of pills to reverse the operation and become a style.'

'Nah! I've seen enough of the horrors of being female today to put me right off flipping, forever,' said Francelant with iron certainty.

Nostrom was in a state of terror. No matter what she did, her overdue activation was making her look and sound increasingly feminine. Was that what had given her away. Even in an isolated hole like this they had found her. The young anther in disguise had sent her off on a wild goose chase, no doubt so he could search Nostrom's sleeping facility. Nostrom had not gone anywhere. Watching from the shadows she had seen the young style enforcer arrive, boasting about how easy it had been to find her. Nostrom knew she had to act quickly. Cause as much mayhem as possible, tie the two enforcers down in the pandemonium and then disappear again. There were so many people here in the Roots, looking to employ sprites with no questions asked, it could easily find a new job. I, she, no it was certain she knew the mistakes it had made, which had lead to its discovery. She would not make those mistakes again.

Natalicsya watched her friend as he emerged from the changing room dressed as a boy but looking like a girl. It would take at least a week for the breasts to shrink, waist to thicken and his hair return to a male rate of growth.

'You don't shave, do you?

'No, never needed to,' said Francelant. 'It's one thing about being an anther I don't like. At most, all I need to do is put a mild depilatory cream on once a week to control the fuzz.'

The gantry came crashing down, cutting the conversation short. Francelant's lighting fast reflexes saved them as he pushed Natalicsya and himself from the path of the falling metal.

'Ow. That was no accident,' said Natalicsya, spluttering in the dust and debris.

'No,' confirmed Francelant. 'There is someone up in the ceiling crawl space. If we go that way, we should catch them.'

Despite the shock, Francelant was already heading out of the room, giving Natalicsya hand signals to track the unseen perpetrator from the opposite direction. They doubled around the back of a heating duct, where a sprite was emerging.

'Gotcha!' said Francelant as someone climbed out of the grill.

'Sprite? Are you the caretaker for this building?' asked the surprised Natalicsya. The Sprite remained silent.

'I know you are, but my colleague here asked you a question Sprite, you must answer,' said Francelant.

'It must have been ordered to remain silent by someone with a higher rank than us.'

'Enough of this.' Natalicsya was starting to lose her temper. 'I am Probationary Constable in the Enforcers Regiment, which is equivalent to Ensign. However, everywhere else, my combat experience would be taken into account and I'd be a Subaltern and treated like an adult.'

'I know Lisha, but you have never made a fuss about it before. How does it change the price of protein?' Francelant asked.

'Because I'm not telling you, I'm telling this sprite. It now knows I have the authority to do this.'

She tapped the code into her com-link as she replied. A blue nimbus formed around the sprite.

'Sprite, I am instigating a Code Epsilon 392 Order that overrides all your previous orders. You will tell me why you sabotaged that gantry.'

'If you're going to kill me, do it quickly.' This was not the reply either of them had been expecting. What was worse, the Sprite sounded like a frightened little girl and not a sprite.

'What are you talking about?' Natalicsya was confused.

'He sent you, didn't he? I saw him trying to shoot the Tree Marshall and shooting the General instead. He sent you to find me. Now you are going to kill me, to keep me quiet.'

Natalicsya was dumbstruck. Did this sprite really know who the would-be assassin is.

'Sprite, tell me, who shot the General?'

'Inspector Dayvaiyant. He shot the General, I saw it, I have been hiding ever since,' the Sprite replied in the same definitely feminine childlike voice.

The Code Epsilon 392 induced trance should have held the sprite rigid. However it was now shaking violently, as if it were having a fit.

Oh great, she thought as she rapidly dismissed the Code Epsilon. Any attempt to use it on anything other than a sprite could be deadly. This creature was obviously more than it appeared to be.

'Control, this is PC Natalicsya. A code Sigma 41 situation has occurred at my location.'

'Copy that PC Natalicsya. Your location has been logged as the Nottingant Gymnasium in the Σ1 3ΣΓ However, I need clarification as to the nature of the situation,' said the unshakable Lieutenant on the Control Desk.

'An overhead gantry has collapsed in the main hall of the gymnasium.'

'Are there any casualties?'

'Yes, one sprite. we are going to need a paramedic team,' said Francelant

'Roger that PC Francelant.'

Francelant had been busy scanning the Sprite with a first aid kit he had found in the gymnasium's office.

'The sprite's condition seems to be unrelated to the Sigma 41.' The sensor was doing things he had never seen one do before. He transferred the file it generated in his comlink to the network. 'This data should be sent to the paramedics. I can't make head nor tail of it.'

'The paramedics are on their way, E.T.A. five minutes. Will the sprite last that long?' asked Saregent Hipobrisya, cutting into the conversation.

'Yes Ma'am. Its condition seems to have stabilised,' he quickly added another file to the one sent to the paramedics.

'I have sent you a copy of the statement the sprite made before it began its fit. Please forward it to CI Galeroysya.'

'Copy that,' replied the Sergeant, 'CI Galeroysya has been informed.'

Natalicsya's wrist comlink began chiming. It seemed to all be coming together.

'Lisha dear, are you OK.' Chief Inspector Galeroysya rarely phoned Natalicsya during the day. Why did she have to start now?

'Yes mum, I'm fine. A bit shocked. Francelant is securing the site and restraining our suspect.'

'Suspect? What the hell is going on?' There was an urgent beeping filling her office. Francelant's report must have just reached CI Galeroysya's comlink. 'Oh my word.' Natalicsya's half-mother swung back into professional mode.

'PC Natalicsya, PC Francelant, I will be there in two minutes. I'll have to see this with my own eyes. Call timed at 1826.'

Dayvaiyant's comconsole blinked to life. Damn it,he thought as he clambered out of his bed, why does this always go off when I am having a great dream. He had been doing a night shift that had stretched on well into the morning. He had been hoping for a good afternoon's sleep before starting another night shift.

The automated search facility had finally found something useful. The missing sprite had turned up. Hallelujah. One last loose end to tie up. Oh joy, it had been found comatose, so had not blabbed anything to anyone. It had been transferred to the medical unit at the Regimental Training Centre. Why was it being kept there, not at HQ. Oh, it had been apprehended by some PC's on a training exercise. Still that made getting to it and ending its life easier. So many things that could go wrong with the poor sick creature in an under equiped sickbay.

The siren blast woke the half-asleep anther.

'Inspector Dayvaiyant 271/26 Zilfrayts, you are to surrender immediately. Leave your apartment with your hands up. Please come quietly.' The voice coming through the comconsole speaker was undoubtedly that of Commissioner Lyndrevsya, his soon to be ex-boss. So, by the looks of things, the sprite had blabbed.

'Afternoon Guv. Is this some sort of joke? It's not funny you know,' he was trying to brazen it out with a "Who Ma'am, me Ma'am, I don't think so Ma'am." attitude

'Did I ever strike you as the sort of person who would carry out that sort of joke, Lieutenant?'

'No, Ma'am.'

'Good. I have here an arrest warrant signed by the Tree Marshall herself. She does not find people trying to kill her amusing. Can't say as I blame her.'

'I'm coming out. I'll be unarmed. Undressed even. I, of all people should know there is nowhere for a fugitive officer to hide in this sealed little world.'

He emerged into the daylight. Even as his eyes got used to the brightness, his professional eye summed up the situation. Overkill, plain and simple. Four suited and booted Enforcers in front of him, with weapons pointed at his head. Snipers on the roofs of all the surrounding buildings. Vehicles hovering overhead and parked as barricades to all pedestrian walkways. This was a circus. No doubt that bitch the Cocktail Waitress had arranged this. Oh why had he missed, this was embarrassing. At least the Guv had made sure they were all armed with nothing stronger than stun-rifles.

'The suspect will kneel with his hands on his head,' said the Commissioner over a loud hailer. He had no choice but to comply. He could see her now, walking towards him. 'You have the right to remain silent,' she said. 'If you surrender that right, everything you say will be transcribed and may be used by a prosecuting advocate against you in your Court Martial. You also have the right to be represented by an advocate. If you cannot afford one, then one will be appointed for you.'

As she finished, handcuffs were locked onto his wrists.

Commissioner Lyndrevsya watched Lieutenant Dayvaiyant staring back at herself and Chief Inspector Gaylroysya across an anonymous table in an anonymous interview room.

'This interview is timed at 2005 on Fyfesday Delta Sextemp, 184. Those present are Commissioner Lyndrevsya 104/51 Nott, Chief Inspector Galeroysya 146/68 Islaw-Rust, the suspect Lieutenant Dayvaiyant 271/26 Zilfrayts and his Advocate Lieutenant Philmitant 176/21 Wraig-Fangkart.'

'I make no excuses for what I did, I am an anther of principle. I did what I did because I believe in good governance and tradition. The current regime provides neither.'

'I am not interested in principles, I'm interested in facts' replied the Commissioner, 'besides, I've heard that sort of statement many times before.'

'My client has made a statement, that is all he is legally required to do,' said the anther sitting next to Dayvaiyant.

'Thank you Lieutenant Philmitant, but I am sure that your client has more to say.'

Indeed I do, thought Dayvaiyant. 'I helped you track down Sandampsya and her idiotic dinner party plotters. In doing so a great truth was revealed to me, that Anthers are on the whole superior to Styles. I quickly found like minded friends who could see the corrosive effect of a government dominated by styles was having on the Tree.'

'I planned on killing the four styles at the top of the Officer Corps. The four highest ranking Generals are anthers, there would be a male Tree Marshall again and he would have three male Deputies, one of whom would eventually replace him.'

'So why did you stop after shooting General Myghcomant?'

'Because I had not expected to miss, I only had three rounds left. It didn't matter if I shot the Cocktail Waitress with my next shot, one of the harpies would survive to replace her as Tree Marshall. Even with three male Deputies, the Tree's government would still be paralysed by years of dithering female misrule. I would not have altered anything.'

'Even with the three new male Deputy-Marshalls.'

'Even with three strong anther Deputy-Marshalls, there would still have been years of increasingly corrosive equality.'

'Lieutenant Dayvaiyant, kindly refrain from calling the Tree Marshall the Cocktail Waitress. She was a General in the Publicans Regiment. She owns several bars and was never a cocktail waitress. Also she has over two hundred days of combat experience to her credit. This includes breaking the seige of 33AG BB5.'

'She should have stuck to serving drinks and other female stuff. Not interfered in anther only bussiness, like War and Politics.'

'You don't think styles should order anthers?'

'Correct.'

'Am I to assume you despise taking orders from me?'

'You would be correct in that assumption. I don't know if I hate you for not being strong enough to live as an anther, or hate you for being a style who dared to try?'

'You know Lieutenant,' the Commissioner said, 'I have always thought you were many things, I never included stupid on that list. Until now.'

'History will prove me right. The Tree will suffer disaster after disaster, until anthers find their way back to the driver's seat.'

'This interview terminated at 2010. Take him away.'

One in two thousand Tree-People are Hermaphrodites, they possess working male and female organs. Most remain passive, happy to be one gender for life. However, some are active hermaphrodite and they can chose to change from male to female, or vice versa.

In her early life, Lyndrevsya had been Lyndrevant. Apart from an inability to grow a beard, nobody would have known he was hermaphrodite, he had appeared to be a perfectly normal anther. Until the day he had been attacked whilst on duty by an angry mob. As he recovered from the severe became more and more feminine and found he liked it that way. He had tried to continue living as an anther, to keep his family happy. Eventually he decided things had to change, so he completed the transition. Her family had been horrified. Her aged Father had taken it as a personal insult, her increasingly confused Mother could not cope with the change and her baby sister had been too young to understand and cut her off completely.

All this had been five years ago. She thought she had learnt to cope, but Lyndrevsya was suddenly aware of how much she missed her family, and how far away any hope of reconciliation with her sister now was.

The Commissioner left the room, not sure if she really believed the depth of arrogance and stupidity she had just witnessed.

She had been sure that she had been looking at a Tree-wide conspiracy by a group of hair-brained Pure-stock extremists. Now it looked like the act of a lone madman. Sexism had never really risen its ugly head in the Tree. In a world that lacks the words "man" and "woman", gender specific job titles like postman, fisherman or hangman are impossible. Every job was gender neutral, going to the best qualified person to do that job, whether male or female. It was universally accepted that there were only cosmetic difference between the two forms of adult Tree-People.

No, the Commissioner was not fooled, Dayvaiyant was not acting alone. He had been supplied with his methods and opportunity by someone with more brains than his fellow Misogynists. Somebody was welding all the malcontents, extremists and nutters into a Devil's Coalition. During the next Tree-Wide crisis, like last year's Treequake, the nutters would be encouraged to make their move. This would further disrupt the status quo. Out of the mayhem a third group would emerge, they would deal with the nutters they had secretly encouraged, gaining the support of the ordinary officers, and then with that support they would make an unstoppable grab for power.

PART FOUR
BUSINESS STUDIES

CHAPTER SEVENTEEN

DOWN IN THE DUMPS

It had been three weeks since Nevamarsya and her friends had been able to make any progress on clearing Tabbernant. She had tried to see Abbess Annaprysya, but the Tree-Nun had always been too busy to see her.

Would this be another Trinitsday afternoon with a singing lesson and no chance of seeing the Abbess? Would she end up considerably shortening her demure blue dress and go and have a glass of Cholayt or three with Sofianesya and her flatmates? Away from her Mother's poisonous influence, and with their help, Sofianesya was turning into a really nice person. All this was entertaining, but not very productive.

Nevamarsya rang the doorbell of the Convent and waited for the slat in the door to open.

'Did your exam go well this morning, Nevamarsya?' asked Sister Monijoasya.

'I don't know, I think I made a mess of some of the questions,' Nevamarsya replied.

'Well, if it is any comfort Nevamarsya, I used to find the braggarts who claimed they had aced an exam, had usually got something horribly wrong and failed. Those people who said they thought they had done it all wrong were usually the ones who passed with flying colours.'

'At least I only have to wait a few days for the results.'

'Well, best of luck. Oh yes, the Abbess wants to see you.'

'Thank you Sister. Do you know what the Abbess wants?'

'I have no idea Nevamarsya, I am just passing on the message.'

Nevamarsya walked through the tunnel like entrance and emerged into the covered walkway that surrounded four sides of a beautifully maintained lawn. This was the great Cloister, a single storey structure in front of the portico of the Great Basilica. Everyone had to walk around the Cloister in a clockwise direction. Walking on the grass was forbidden.

To Nevamarsya's surprise, the Abbess was sitting by a pillar on the inner wall of the Cloister waiting for her.

'You wish to see me Subaltern Nevamarsya?' asked the Abbess sternly.

'Yes, Abbess,' said Nevamarsya.

'Sit with me Neva, we have much to discuss,' said the Abbess, becoming less formal by the second.

'Thank you.'

'Don't worry, this is not your coronation.'

'Pardon?' asked a surprised Nevamarsya.

'This is traditionally where one Abbess passes on the office to her successor.'

Nevamarsya knew the code in the subtle variations in belt knots and veils which denoted rank within the Convent. Most Tree People assumed all Tree-Nuns dressed the same. However, everyone could recognise the Abbess, who wore a gabled hood called her crown. It looked as if she had a little roof under her veil.

The Abbess' secretary approached, and handed her Superior a folder.

'Thank you Sister Tregozasya. I shall be unreachable for the next hour.'

The other Tree-Nun departed as quietly as she arrived. As usual not leaving a blip on Nevamarsya's radar.

'This job affords so few opportunities to relax, one must take them when one can,' she said, turning back to Nevamarsya, smiling and visibly relaxing as she did so. 'So my child, I know you have been trying to see me. What is this all about?'

'I tried to make an appointment. I cannot just walk into the Convent and demand to see you.'

'I know Neva, but you have my undivided attention now.'

'Yes Abbess. It concerns Pensioner Tabbernant and a Commander Gaemlovant.'

'Why did you not say so, I would have made an effort to see you sooner.'

'Thank you, I did not think.' The formal speech pattern of the Convent was infectious. It could take hours to revert to normal outside.

'You were not to know. However, your task is of utmost importance.'

'Yes, I have to find Commander Gaemlovant. He can verify Pensioner Tabbernant's alibi and help clear him. Although Lieutenant Gaemlovant has vanished into thin air. My friends and I know he is still alive, but have no idea where. You are my only hope.'

'Yes, I do have information that will help in your search.'

'You know where Commander Gaemlovant is?' Nevamarsya was extatic.

'He has for a number of years been working for the Sisterhood. In return he has been granted the protection he requested.'

Oh do hurry up, thought Nevamarsya. Why do Tree-Nuns always have to be so long winded.

'Gaemlovant is the caretaker of the old Earth-Nuns Convent. It is within the Green Erratic, in Root Sigma.'

'Earth-Nuns?' asked Nevamarsya, she was so surprised, it was all she could think to say.

'Yes Neva, the old Order from the Roots which merged with the original Tree-Nuns and the Sun-Nuns of the Canopy.

The Crown Officers Residential Complex is built on the site of the Sun-Nuns' Convent.'

Nevamarsya felt so excited, a positive lead at last. 'Can you get in touch with him if he is on the property of your Convent?' she asked.

'I'm afraid there is no direct link. He establishes an untraceable ad hoc link when he needs to speak to me. You will have to find your own way of contacting him.' The Abbess smiled and then 'I am sure your clever young friend Pemisegant will find a way.'

'Thank you Abbess Annaprysya.'

'I believe you have a singing lesson now Nevamarsya,' said the Abbess as the formal face returned marking a return to full formality that marked the end of the conversation. 'We have kept Sister Matyfilsya waiting long enough.'

The lesson, bother. However Nevamarsya had waited this long for this information. It could wait a few more hours.

This is great news,' said Natalicsya. 'We now know where to find him.'

Nevamarsya was sitting in a public comconsole booth, speaking to her three friends.

'Careful Lisha, Neva is on an open channel,' said Pemisegant.

'Was on an open channel Pezzi,' said Althallant. 'When she phoned in, it activated one of your doohickies, we are also running through a few of my encryption algorithms. We have set up the sort of encryption and security on this video conference that would give the SPS nightmares.' Althallant had discovered a talent for identifying and solving logic puzzles when he was still a Cadet. This had developed into a fascination with codes and cyphers. He was now using that talent to stop anyone overhearing what the group was talking about.

'Then it is a good job for you they stopped monitoring this frequency when I retired,' said a wrinkly old anther who had just joined the conference. 'I still scan it though.'

'Who the hell are you?' asked Pemisegant.

'I, Subaltern Pemisegant, am Pensioner Jaxspriant 103/11 Laytening, I invented the secure video conferencing equipment you are using, years before you were born. Congratulations on getting it to work at efficiency levels I failed to reach.'

'Oh, back door access,' said Pemisegant.

'Blocked, young anther. I had to crack the extra encryption algorithms your friend is so proud of. I doubt any of my former colleagues would have bothered. The signal is supposed to look like random garbage on an obscure channel.'

'Pensioner Jaxspriant, it's an honour to meet you,' said Natalicsya.'

'And you too, Probationary Constable Natalicsya.' The old Anther smiled. 'I've been listening to your chat. I too have been looking for Gaemlovant for twenty five years. He owes me seventy five credits.'

'Alth, Pezzi, Lisha, how do we know he is the real deal?' asked Nevamarsya.

'Because this channel is genetically coded. Look at the log. that's the real Pensioner Jaxspriant,' replied Althallant.

'You'd better believe it, Subaltern Nevamarsya 331/29,' said Jaxspriant. 'Anyway, can't stay here chatting all day. You've got work to do. I don't believe for a second Bernie killed that old bastard Drwgdynant. Best of luck proving that.' The old anther's hologram faded from the conference.

'So after that interruption, back to my original point,' said Althallant. 'Do you realise how big the Erratic is, three miles long and two miles high. It's made of goodness knows what. Nobody knows how it got there. That's why it is called an Erratic.'

'Relax Alth, I have some toys in the Archive that will find him, and create a comlink as secure as this one. Wherever he is hiding.'

'If the dragon lady let's you play with them,' said Natalicsya, the only one of Pemisegant's friends who had met his new boss. She didn't like her.

'She suspects I am doing something during my overtime, but as long as I do enough proper work and speed up her precious audit, she turns a blind eye.'

'What if she catches you?' asked Althallant, ever the police-officer.

'She won't. She is far too busy working on her pet project in the lab in her apartment, to come back to the Archive after hours.'

'What about your rent-a-cop?' asked Natalicsya dismissively.

'Commander Ryzinasant is likewise too busy on his pet project. If the two of them would stop acting like children, they would see they are working on the same thing and get far more done by pooling their resources.'

'So, how long before we can go and talk to Gaemlovant?' asked Nevamarsya.

'Next week. On your day off Neva dear.'

'You have a habit of barging into my days off,' she said.

'I hope my signal will be completely invisible. However, just to be on the safe side I'll need a distraction. You fly down to the Erratic making yourself very visible. Whilst everyone is busy watching you, they won't notice any unusual comlink activity.'

A week later, Nevamarsya flew her car down the roadway the the stat-nav told her was the quickest way to the Blue Skull Arsenic Plant at the entrance to the Green Erratic.

All the fresh water that the Tree needed entered through the Roots. Along with the water they also pulled in tons of dissolved chemicals. A number of chemical extraction plants separated out useful substances whilst the water was purified.

Occasionally huge automated chemical tankers passed her, carrying the products of extraction plants to the hub and beyond. The huge automated tankers had exclusive use of the central section of the roadway. Automated systems prevented Nevamarsya from straying out of her lane.

After leaving the Hub, she had flown through the Kuffa plantations, before joining the express matrix to the tip. Her car had accelerated to its top speed of one hundred an eight miles and hour and she had settled down to the three hour journey. There were no daylighters for most of the road. Only the occasional glow of streetlighters at small industrial plants broke the monotony. Eventually, she noticed the diffuse glow, in the distance of a recharging station. Now would be a good time to take a break. She hit the automatic landing button and the car landed gracefully on the landing pad, then she used the caterpillar tracks on the landing gear to taxi into the forecourt.

'How can the sprites help you?' asked the leading member of a pack of four sprites.

'I need the battery recharged please.' replied Nevamarsya.

'The sprite is able to clean your windscreen, if you would like?' asked a second sprite, whilst the first attached the charging probe to the battery port.

'No thank you, but if you could test the cleaning fluid tank, I would be grateful.'

'Certainly Ma'am. The Sprite will do that.'

A similar forecourt was on the other side of a service tunnel which housed the station's shop. Each side had large spring loaded double doors folded back.

'Could you tell me what that is for?' she asked one of the sprites

'The Sprite is happy to help, ma'am. They are watertight bulkheads. This section of the Root is prone to flooding. All buildings have to have watertight seals on all doors and windows. Anything that cannot be taken indoors has to be stored under watertight canopies.'

Flooding, it hadn't occurred to Nevamarsya it would be a problem. It showed how far underground she now was.

What the hell was that car doing there, thought Lieutenant Evaperoant. This place was hardly a tourist magnet. Nobody came down this Root without good reason. He saw the same six regular customers each day. Never any new faces. He watched as a kid got out of the car and ambled towards his building.

'So, your driver decided to stay in the car. They do know this is the last public restroom for miles.'

'No, it's only me, but I do need to freshen up,' said the kid.

'Seriously, I haven't seen a car like that since I was an Ensign, and they definitely weren't driven by Ensigns back then, and certainly wouldn't be today.'

'Good job I'm not an Ensign then.'

'Come off it kid, I was not born yesterday, but you probably were. I will need the driver's IndesnCard to authorise the payment.'

'Oh for goodness sake,' said the kid, as she slid her card into the reader.

'Sorry about that Subaltern, but you do look mighty young.'

'That's because I am mighty young,' said Nevamarsya, 'but like everyone else, all my clothes have my rank clearly displayed on them. See,' she said pointing to the breast pocket of her blouse and a button with two white dots on a green background. 'The wearing of rank marking at all times was mandatory.'

'Great green apples, it's you.' Evaperoant read the name on the till display and was shocked. 'I suppose that's alright then.'

'I suppose it is. I'm looking for a place called the Blue Skull Arsenic Plant. The address is ΩΘ34 5TΠ, is that far?'

'About ten minutes drive, but why would you want to be going to that dump?'

'It's by the entrance to the Green Erratic. Supposed to be quite a site, if like me you have an interest in such things.'

'It's tunnels in rock, nothing more, nothing less. Hardly worth your time.' Evaperoant was amazed that anyone would be interested in that mined out pile of junk. 'And you don't need to go all the way down there. You're already standing next to it. The Erratic extends all the way up here, it's just down one of these side passages.'

'I'm hoping to have a peek inside the old Visitor Centre, next to the Arsenic Extraction plant.'

The workstation on the counter pinged, as the last cell of the car's battery finished charging.

'Please yourself. No doubt I will see you here when you get bored with the rock, which will be pretty damn quick,' he smiled at the kid. 'Your account has been charged with the cost of your refill, anything else you want before I close the sale?'

'No thanks, I'll be on my way.'

N evamarsya was not sure if the old creep in the charging station believed her spur of the moment excuse. She hated lying, but did not want to let any potential Syndicate member know where she was headed.

The stage of the journey seemed to drag. The solid green wall of the Erratic was spectacular when the roadway had first gently curved around it. Now it was as monotonous as the dull grey of the root wall.

'Unidentified air-car, you are entering the approaches to the Blue Skull Arsenic Extraction Plant. Please be advised that this facility extracts toxic products from root-water. In line with High Council rules and Officer Corps directives, I have to warn you that persons alighting here do so at their own risk.' The voice sounded as bored as Nevamarsya felt.

'I understand that,' said Nevamarsya over the radio. I only want to land at your car park and head to the old Visitor Centre next door.'

'Roger that unidentified air-car. Don't say you weren't warned.'

The car touched down in the car-park and Nevamarsya was met by a Base Trunk style. Suprisingly her long black hair was not tied into a plait down her back. She wore a lab coat on top of her uniform. A complicated mask over her face.

'Here, you had better put this on,' said the owner of the voice on the radio. This time with more interest, but not much.

'I'm Lieutenant Ilayanksya 461/09 Wadz, the Duty Chemist for this plant.'

'Pleased to meet you, I'm...'

'I know exactly who you are Subaltern, I have been ordered by the Major to take you to his office.' There was no hint of friendship in the other style's voice. Fortunately, there was no enmity either. 'And he wants to make this formal, I see you are in mufty, so I will take you via the changing room.

'No problem,' said Nevamarsya.

The two continued through the plant to an airlock. Once through it they both removed their masks.

'Won't I need more Emprintable Fabric?' Nevamarsya asked.

'No, you don't,' Lieutenant Ilayanksya replied.

With the expected buzz from the Emprinter, her clothes changed into an uniform, but not the one she was expecting.

Nevamarsya tugged at the hem of the short tunic dress of the informal uniform, usually worn by waitresses, barmaids and younger female shop workers whilst on duty, in a vain attempt to make it longer.

'Sorry about this. The old letch in charge sets dress code,' said Lieutenant Ilayanksya 'I can't change it. No need to put your hair into a ponytail, he likes styles to wear their hair down on duty. However, you will need a cap.'

'I see why you wear the lab coat. Can I borrow one?'

'You've got far better legs than I have, maybe it will distract the old fool a bit.'

'Thank you, but I still like to chose when and where I show them off.'

Finally a reaction form the other girl, who laughed out loud.

'What about the other staff, what do they think?'

'Since I arrived here it's just me, the major and the Winter Jumpers, aka Subalterns Bendertant and Queltodant.'

'I suppose they are thick and woolly.'

'Got it in one. As the only female down here, I have to put up with a lot of sexist crap.'

'I'd read about that.' Nevamarsya was amazed, 'I thought it was all made up. Surely the Major doesn't really think Anthers are superior to Styles?'

'In every way. He is one of a small minority, but sadly one that is growing. Added to that he is a real Root Supremacist. He's a bundle of joy to work for.'

They arrived at the Major's office, and Lieutenant Ilayanksya knocked politely on the door.

'Enter,' said the voice inside the office, as the door automatically swung open.

Before Nevamarsya even had a chance to sit down, Major Denfyopant was on the offensive.

'You are a very unwelcome visitor, and a possible source of additional expense to me,' he said as Nevamarsya was escorted into the office. 'Dismissed, Subaltern Ilayanksya. And take that bloody white thing off, you don't need it in here.'

The other style left before replying to the Major.

'I have to admit, it is nice to see an attractive girl down here, and one who isn't a dozy moonchild.'

Just because she has turned down your leery advances, doesn't make her a moonchild, thought Nevamarsya. If that were the case, I would be as gay as my half-sister and her girlfriend. So would any style with a pulse. Nevamarsya didn't think she had ever seen a fatter anther in her life. Every one of the excess square fractions oozed an oily body odour.

'Sir, I only wish to park my car here whilst I go on a trip to the Green Erratic. I have an interest in Geology.'

'You are not the only one Subaltern. Not the only one. However, it would have been nice if you had asked permission first.'

'Sorry, Sir. I should have thought,' said Nevamarsya, perhaps if she could get on his good side.

'These drones cost money to process, to protect them from Arsenic. Unfortunately, it ruins their immune system. The last thing I need now is to have them all put to sleep because of an outbreak of the 'flu'.

'Drones, Sir?'

'Yes, the sub tree-person drones not grown in officer pods. Little better than creatures.' The hatred for the Sprites, working in the plant, came shining through.

'Oh, the Sprites,' said Nevamarsya when the credit dropped.

'They aren't sprites, they will never be sprites, they can

never be officers because they are the product of inferior pods.'

'Sir.' Nevamarsya looked at the major. She wondered if like her old Branch Captain, his extremist views had earned him this unpalatable posting.

'You wouldn't understand, you are from the Canopy, they have no discipline up there. That will all change when the right thinking people come to power. Enjoy your commission Subaltern, when the revolution occurs, you will join the new lesser ranks. Only those bred to be officers will remain officers. When the new Tree-wide order will be established.'

'Permission to leave, sir?'

'Leave, and take your unwanted bacteria with you. I am ordering you not to return here without proper permission. Do I make myself clear Subaltern?'

'Perfectly, sir.'

'Dismissed.'

'Airlock, don't forget your mask,' said Lieutenant Ilayanksya as the two styles prepared to leave to the office building.

Through a window Nevamarsya could see the sprites that did all the hard and dangerous work here. Poor little souls. They were all wearing green overalls liberally dusted with deadly silver grey powder. It made Nevamarsya's heart bleed because she knew that they all had such a limited lifespan. At least Captain Samnundsya had not been as barkingly mad as Major Denfyopant. How dare he think like that. Each Sprite was born equal, each was entitled to be tested for potential officer training. Something had to be done about the Roots' twisted attitude.

The Lieutenant was waiting to escort her back to her car. Why the hurry, Nevamarsya had to remind her to let her change back into her civilian clothes.

'I hope we do meet again. In a more pleasant situation.' No response from the other style. Let's try another tack. 'How do you cope with that monster?' Nevamarsya asked.

'He's really gotten to you, hasn't he. Bit of a dinosaur, just like them his attitude will die out.'

'He is certainly big enough to be an unlimited supply of fresh protein. Fortunately the Tree has come up with something better.'

'I can't wait for the end of this tour. It's definitely been an experience I have learnt from. Although not one I care to repeat. My next posting will be far from here.'

At last, some reaction from the other style.

'Well, best of luck. So how do I get back to civilisation?'

'The tip-ward traffic have priority on this stretch of roadway. You will have to travel a couple of miles down this roadway to the next junction. Then you can do an U-Turn and head back up the Root.'

Nevamarsya closed the canopy on her car and waited for the auto take-off and stabilisation procedure to complete. She still had the facemask on.

'How the hell did you get through to this console. Nobody can get through to this console?' said Gaemlovant.

'One of the perks of working for the R&D Archive, Sir,' said Pemisegant.

'What's that supposed to mean, kid?' asked a surprised Gaemlovant. 'And how the hell can I hear you anyway. This console is a data only combox. No audio.'

'I managed to get a converter working here in the Archives. It uses the latency of the cloud to create a phased audio duplex wave.' Pemisegant was rather proud of his latest device, and he knew he had an appreciative audience. Gaelovant had be a bit of a nerd.

'You would need an Elsonic oscillator phased to a Trilateral field generator to do that.' There was a note of disbelief in Gaemlovant's voice. 'Which is not possible, there would be too much secondary loop interface.'

'It is possible, if you link in via a random tone modulator as well.'

'What's your name kid?'

'Pemisegant, Sir.'

'Ah. The one I heard so much about at the start of the year?' said Gaemlovant. 'Turning those auto-riveters into an anti-aircraft weapon was a stroke of genius.'

'Thank you, Sir.'

'Don't see why you went to the trouble to get to me though?'

'We had to find you. Only you can back up the alibi that Bernie has given the Enquirers. But you just vanished.' There was a touch of desperation in Pemisegant's voice.

'I'd heard that he'd got himself arrested. Wasn't really paying that much attention. What has the old fool gone and done now, kid?'

'The body of Captain Dyndrwgant was discovered four weeks ago and Tabbernant has been accused of his Murder!'

'That's ridiculous. He was with me and Myke the night that Dyndrwgant went missing. General Myghcomant will be able to back him up.'

'If he wakes from his coma before the end of the trial.'

'Oh, that explains a lot, kid.' In his hideaway Gaemlovant sat back in his chair and lit a cigarette, something nobody had done in the rest of the Tree for seventeen years. 'I have chosen to live under the radar for two decades. I watch but nobody can watch me.'

'Sir, we need you to return to the grid, to help clear Bernie's name.'

'I hid out here so the Syndicates would forget about me. If I dig Bernie out of the prickles, the Syndicates will be after me again.'

'Then your Sister can help you vanish again. Just as effectively as she did back in the day. Even more effectively this time, given her new job,' replied Pemisegant.

'So, that's how you found me.' Gaemlovant began laughing. 'Little Atheist Anny the head of the Convent. I warned her about messing around with the Convent's secrets, even if it was to help me. I said to her, if you know things that only a Tree-Nun should know you'll start thinking the way only a Tree-Nun should think. Next thing you know, you'll either be banging on their door shouting "Let me in!" or they'll come and get you. Either way, you'll never see the outside of that Convent ever again.'

'That's is hardly a laughing matter Sir.'

'She laughed at me. The members of Houses of Clergy have a different mindset and serve a different purpose from the rest of us. That's why the Spirit of the Tree likes to keep them seperate from us.'

'I didn't realise that,' said Pemisegant

'Neither did she.' There was a a pause then, changing the subject, the old anther said. 'You're so innocent, kid. How do you know your talking to the real deal, not talking to a Syndicate member? For that matter, how do I know you're the real deal?'

'Because this message is linked uniquely to our biological pattern. Go on, check me out. I know you can. Anyone else would just hear static. Also my girlfriend Nevamarsya has taken a trip down to the Green Erratic, to draw attention away from any unusual comlink activity. Just to be on the safe side.'

'Are you serious kid?'

'Perfectly, Sir. I said I worked in the archives of R&D.'

'No, I meant about your girlfriend?' Gaemlovant asked. And quit with the "Sir", kid. I'm hardly on duty, am I?'

'Suppose not, Gaemlovant.'

'That's better.' The old anther was being serious again. 'Do you know where she is now?'

'Her air-car left the Blue Skull Arsenic facility two minutes ago.'

'The Syndicate base, what the hell was she doing there?'

'It is on one of the main entrances to the Erratic. There's an old Visitor's Centre there.'

'Which is now one of the Syndicate's main Charline factories.'

'How do you know that?' Pemisegant asked.

'I know everything that is happening in this part of the Roots. It is a fair bet that once the Syndicate works out who she is they'll try to put the frighteners on her. Get in touch, tell her to land at the $\Omega\Theta 34\ 5T\Phi$ charging station. The dozy undercover copper there will help get your girlfriend out of trouble.'

Pemisegant could hear profuse swearing.

'Forget what I just said, I've got control of her car, I'll handle things from here on in.'

For some reason, Pemisegant did not find that thought at all comforting.

CHAPTER EIGHTEEN
FRIGHTENERS

At a junction, the air-car waited for an automated convoy of cargo carriers to pass by before turning onto the up-root roadway and engaging the autodrive mode allowing the traffic control system take the strain.

'Subaltern Nevamarsya 331/29, we strongly advice you to desist in your search for Captain Gaemlovant 175/44 Zilfarayts,' said a heavily disguised voice over the radio.

'Who is this?' asked Nevamarsya.

'Somebody who doesn't want that particular anther found for the next few weeks.'

'Syndicate? You must be.'

'Maybe, maybe not.'

'I won't give up you know. Uncle Bernie is depending on me.'

'Ha, Pensioner Tabbernant is as good as recycled,' said the voice.

'Are you threatening me?'

'Yes, girl, this is a threat and a promise. A threat to make you stop your interfering, a promise to leave you alone if you do.'

'I'm not going to stop you know.'

'I was afraid you were going to say something like that. You really shouldn't have been messing in the affairs of grown-ups child.' The voice coming through the comlink was distorted but its intent was clear. 'Your friend Tabbernant has annoyed people who should not be annoyed. He thought his box of stale secrets would protect him. His interfering has earned him his fate. You were foolish if you thought you could change anything.'

'I have to try.'

'Oh well, at least your death will be painless. Everyone will wonder how one so young got a driver's licence in the first place. People will blame you for the accident.'

The auto-pilot software had gone dead and she could not activate the manual controls. The air-car was now drifting dangerously into the freight lane. She could see a chemical tanker in her rear monitor. The blast from its bow wake shook the air-car as it passed. Nevamarsya tried to wrestle control back, but it was no good. Her car was now hovering in the middle of the freight lane. The next tanker would send her car crashing to the roadway and continue on its way as if nothing had happened.

That tanker's headlights were now visible. Nevamarsya knew she had just minutes to live.

'OK kid. I can give you just thirty seconds of control, before the Syndicate's system cut back in. Land this tub now. Get your skinny little bum to the Charging Station down the road.'

Nevamarsya realised that she was back in control and hit the emergency landing button. Her stomach lurched as the air car dropped down onto the deck. Well, at least it was all is one piece. The next tanker in the convoy rumbled over head. The canopy popped open and she threw herself from the vehicle.

Her military training clicking in immediately the first shot was fired. Somebody was returning a volley of covering fire from the recharging station. Nevamarsya weaved her way down the roadway and into the building.

'Can somebody please tell me what the hell is going on?' Nevamarsya heard the anther who ran the place asking as she ran through the door of the shop.

'The Syndicate is trying to kill me.'

'It explains why I get a message from nowhere that says, "Oi, Copper! Get your arse into gear!" then I hear gunfire.'

'Was that from a creepy sounding old guy?' asked Nevamarsya.

'That's right. Anyway, it looks as if we have been pinned down. The sprites are cowering in the workshop.'

The attackers must have seen Evaperoant through the window, as another volley of fire rang out.

'It's a good thing the Winter Jumpers couldn't hit a barn door at ten units,' said the exasperated anther. 'Even so, they have both normal exits covered.'

'So there is another exit to this place?'

'Yes kid. Fortunately those fools only know about two visible ones,' Evaperoant said. 'Oh well, I was about to blow this gig tonight. Might as well make an early exit.'

He pulled a rucksack from a cabinet by the till.

'And their boss, the Major?'

'He isn't the boss. He has the highest rank in the Officer Corps, but in the Syndicate its that bitch Ilayanksya who runs the Charline factory.'

'Charline factory?'

'Why do you think you have had such a warm welcome kid? You've obviously seen too much down here.'

A wave of fear crashed over Nevamarsya, followed by a rush of memories from all the combat she had experienced in her short life.

'Come on, Kid. Don't go freezing on me now. We need to get out of here.' Evaperoant was busy sliding a fridge away from a wall. 'I could do with a hand Subaltern.'

'Yes, Sir.' Nevamarsya helped with pulling at the fridge they quickly revealed a small hatchway.

'The problem is, once we leave, then the bad guys will know how we escaped, and come after us.' The hatch had opened and the anther was climbing down through it. 'After me.'

Nevamarsya didn't need to be told twice. The passage they entered was it by a luminescent rocks scattered all around them. Evaperoant pointed down a tunnel, 'we go down there for about half a mile and we will be back in the Root and we come back to your car. They won't expect that. Stay close, kid. You don't want to be lost in the tunnels of the Erratic.'

'Yes, Sir.'

'And lose the mask, the bad guys used it to get control of the car. Do you want them to use it again to track us?'

'No, Sir.' Well, thought Nevamarsya, that explains how I got into this predicament, after she dropped the mask there was a short burst of fire from Evaperoant's gun. Just to make doubly sure the mask was useless.

A raging torrent blocked Nevamarsya and Evaperoant's path. Somewhere further up the root, the wall was breached. This sort of thing happened regularly down here. In three weeks, the constantly growing root would repair itself and the water would be pumped out. The two fleeing officers could not wait three weeks for this to happen.

'So, now we can't go forward because of the torrent and we can't go back because of the Syndicate goons we are running from,' said Evaperoant. 'We're stuffed.'

'I think I have found something.' Nevamarsya said excitedly as she returned to the Erratic.

'I love your unbridled optimism, kid, but I think it is misplaced this time.'

'Thought so,' she said as she popped back into view.

The look of astonishment on Evaperoant's face as Nevamarsya vanished into solid rootwall and then reappeared was priceless.

'How in the Tree did you do that, kid? I have been living here for years, and even I have never managed that.' This was turning into one hell of an impossible day. Instead he was pulled through a doorway into a small entrance hall and up a short flight of stairs.

'I'll tell you later, but for now, we have to keep quiet, the goons are almost outside.'

'Where the hell have they gone?' asked Subaltern Bendertant.

'That old goat has lived down here for years, he might know something we don't,' said Subaltern Queltodant trying to be helpful. 'Maybe they are down a side root we don't know about?'

'I've lived here as long as he has, I know this place as well as he does. There are no places where they could have doubled back,' Subaltern Bendertant snapped back at his colleague.

'You didn't know about that hatch under the fridge, so you're hardly a font of knowledge.' Queltodant taunted.

'Shut it, will you.' Bendertant kicked the same section of wall the doorway their quarry had just passed through, but it did not open for him because it was gender-locked. 'We'd better go back and tell the boss, she is not going to be happy.'

In the stairs behind the door, Evaperoant could hear the retreating footsteps of the goons.

'So can you tell me now, what this place is?' he asked.

'It's an old abandoned Tree-Nun Hermitage. They used to use them a lot during the ninth and tenth decade. A bit of a fad, one sister would spend a week here, praying, singing and fasting as a way of earning penance for some sort of rule violation or other. Then they built the Priory of the Penitent Heart up in the Canopy and these places fell into disuse.'

'So you ain't a nun kid, how did you know about it?'

'I read up on the Sisterhood's history when I was staying in the Convent last Winter. They have the most amazing Library you know.'

'So that door is gender-locked?'

'That's right, and a couple more security devices added to that as well, so that only Tree-Nuns can enter.'

'I'll say it again, you ain't a Tree Nun, and neither am I.'

'But I've got this.' Nevamarsya showed the older officer the ring that Abbess Annaprysya had given her.

'You're Honoured Amongst the Laity. You really are full of surprises kid,' said Evaperoant. 'I have met three Honoured styles. None of them were ever this interesting.'

'I'm not the only interesting person here, am I?' Nevamarsya asked. Then to answer her own question. 'You haven't been moving like an older person, so how old are you? Certainly not a day over twenty one.'

'You're right kid, I just had my sixteenth Registration Day.'

'Also, there is no way I would have been able to get that door open if you are an anther.' Continued Nevamarsya. 'So I suspect you are an undercover Enquirer, and a style undercover Enquirer at that.'

'Indeed, two and a half years under very deep cover,' he laughed. 'So deep, I almost forgot who and what I really am.

But not quite,' said a voice that was definitely female

'So who are you?

'I am Inspector Cerysorsya 111/06 Riksbrant. I have been investigating the steady flow of narcotics from the Arsenic Plant.'

'I'm sorry if I ruined your operation,' said Nevamarsya, so much hard work wasted.

'Ruined my eye,' she laughed. 'The operation has finally borne fruit. I have just sent in my final report. That place will be raided within the next few hours. Those guys will have a great deal more than you to worry about.'

But until then, confusion to the enemy. Wouldn't you say.'

'Indeed, they won't know what hit them.'

Like a snake shedding its skin, the other person began removing the disguise she had been wearing for so long.

'It takes hours to apply this disguise,' she said, 'then at least a week to wear it in, so that it looks perfectly realistic. It will take at least day for my real face to recover.'

There had been something plastic about the wrinkles on Lieutenant Evaperoant's face. Inspector Cerysorsya's skin was naturally smooth and so much younger looking. However, her scalp looked as smooth and dead as a Sprite's. No, that was another layer of plastic. When it was removed Nevamarsya could see a crazy paving pattern of scars and burns on the smooth pate.

'You were very convincing,' said Nevamarsya, 'how do you do it?'

'I have a very particular talent,' she said. 'I can put my real personality to sleep and become a new person, so convincingly even my Mother wouldn't recognise me.'

'Of course being a revertive helps to maintain the illusion,' she said with a hint of regret. 'Be grateful you only lost your hair for a few weeks young lady. Mine will never return. Now, if you would excuse me for a few minutes.'

Nevamarsya left the room, as requested. After a few minutes a loud klaxons sounded throughout the root. Heavy rain outside the Tree was overwhelming the absorption system. The section of Root the Erratic was embedded in would be flooded for days.

'Damn, that is going to delay the raid,' Cerysorsya said. 'On the plus side, the bad guys will be as pinned down as we are.'

Inspector Cerysorsya emerged from the altar room wearing a female Enquirer's uniform with brown skirt and leather knee-length boots. Even with the long rope of plaited hair, which Nevamarsya knew was a wig, she still didn't look very feminine.

'We will be safe in here though,' said Nevamarsya as she engaged the vacuum seals around the hermitage's door.

'I hope so. This place hasn't been used for years, so I don't know how good those seals are.' Cerysorsya looked worried.

'Shouldn't be a problem, look at that wall, freshly painted. The Sisterhood know how to keep their house in order. The seals are good.'

'I hope you're right Nevamarsya.'

'It comes from being a Cadet with the Winter Squad. You learn to recognise good maintenance.'

'But it isn't the Sisterhood that maintains the seals there, dear ladies.' A third voice had joined the conversation, via the old comconsole. 'It was me.'

Cerysorsya raised her gun. 'Who are you, where are you and what are you doing here?'

'To answer your questions, I am Gaemlovant, and I believe one of you has been looking for me. I am deep within the Erratic, safe from the worse Winter or even Summer flooding, so you can put that gun away. Finally, I am here because I live here. Have done for twenty years. You will have to come to me.'

'Sir, I have to speak to you, about Pensioner Tabbernant.'

'That is the only reason I let you in here. I had a very illuminating chat with your boyfriend. Old Bernie did me a huge favour back in the day, time to pay it back. By the way, you are the first person in nearly two decades to come even this close to finding me. Like I said, I am further into the Erratic, you will have to come and find me if you want a longer chat.'

'Please, this is important. Can't you come to us.'

'I'm still not sure I can trust you. I have a few more sources to check out before I can let you in to my inner sanctum.'

The line went dead. No matter how many times Nevamarsya tried to resume the link, the device remained lifeless.

'So, we go to him,' said Cerysorsya. 'You know, kid, it's not just that old loon's security you managed to get around. Nobody has see past my disguise before, how did you manage it?'

'I recognised the e-wig.'

'Again, I've worn this for years, it is top of the range, nobody should know its an e-wig.'

'I had to wear one for a couple of weeks. It's fresh in my memory.'

'That's not all though is it?'

'I don't know why I realised it was a disguise, it must be part of this gift of Empathy everyone is telling me about.'

'An Empath, that figures. I was having difficulty reading you. Only another empath could block me.' The older style was looking at Nevamarsya in a curious way. 'Had much training?'

'A few months worth, now I'm studying to be a Counsellor.' An idea sprang into Nevamarsya's head. 'You mean I could use my gift to disguise myself that well?'

'Sure, with the right training. I can tell if anyone has spotted something wrong with my disguise then correct that mistake before it undermines it.'

A loud click and the creek of a seldom used door. 'I think we are being invited further into his realm,' said Nevamarsya.

'Will you come into my parlour, said the spider to the fly?' recited the older style.

'Oh don't. He can't be that bad.'

'Can't he. That old anther has been living down here, off the radar for two decades. That must have done something to him.'

Where was she? It had been several hours since anyone had heard from Nevamarsya. The section of the Roots she had last been spotted in was now flooded out. Why don't you call in Marcy dear, just let us know where you are?

Her half-mother was going frantic with worry. Sharlensya had thrown a Mingdynsya vase at Pemisegant. No doubt assuming correctly that another one of his brilliant schemes was going horribly wrong.

His comlink rang and his heart flew. Was that her at last?

'Subaltern Pemisegant, I presume.'

He recognised the face on the other side of the display, although he had never spoken to her.

'Yes, Abbess Annaprysya.'

'I have some good and some bad news for you.' The Tree Nun's face was as bland as beige wallpaper.

'You have, Abbess?' Why was he being called by the most senior Tree-Nun. What news could she possibly have for him.

'Our friend Subaltern Nevamarsya has been located. She is in the Third Hermitage of the Warm Stone.'

'Excuse me Abbess, but where is that?'

'It is down in the Green Erratic. She is accompanied by an Enquirer Lieutenant. It is my belief that she took refuge in there to avoid the attentions of the Syndicate members pursuing them.'

'Are they safe?' Pemisegant's heart was racing. Nevamarsya was still alive.

'Reasonably. It has been many years since anyone last visited that hermitage. We have no idea how sound it is structurally.'

For a few seconds the mask cracked and the Abbess looked as worried as everyone else.

'When I told her where to find Commander Gaemlovant, I did not expect the pair of you to dream up this crazy scheme.'

'We just wanted to talk to him. Things got complicated. She was only supposed to cause a minor distraction.'

I know my child, nothing remains simple. Which is why when I contact Commander Sharlensya, I wish you to remain of the line. I do not want her to be worried about the real reason her daughter went on this journey, but I am bound by my vows to always tell the truth.'

Had the Abbess really winked as she said the word truth? Indeed she had, although the look of serene calmness had returned to her face.

Pemisegant didn't think he had ever seen his former teacher and her other daughter so happy.

'You're sure she is safe Pezzi?' asked Serynazsya.

'They are perfectly safe, child,' replied the Abbess before Pemisegant could get a word in.

'If you can call getting caught in the crossfire between the Police and Syndicate drug runners safe,' said Sharlensya.

'The timing can only possibly be called unfortunate.

However, young Nevamarsya had the presence of mind to find somewhere safe. The Hermitage no longer serves its original purpose, however, there are still occasions when prayers need to be said down in the Roots. We can thank the Tree that the seals are still good on the doors.'

There was a general mumble of agreement over the comlink. The Tree-Nun's face vanished from the conference screen.'

Now then you little rat,' said Sharlensya, whose face had changed from an image of joy to one of extreme anger.

'What the hell is my Neva really doing down there. The truth now, I've always been able to tell when you are lying Pezzi. I don't have to be an empath for that.'

No you have not and yes you do, Pemisegant thought bleakly. Whenever you are upset I can get away with so much just by going for the extremely formal approach.

'I don't know what you're talking about, Ma'am.'

'So why did Neva take such a long trip to the middle of nowhere. Don't tell me she has developed a sudden interest in Geology. I don't believe it.'

'She has, Ma'am,'

'No boy,' Sharlensya spat the words out.

'Yes, Ma'am. I didn't believe it either.'

'I don't believe you. And I will refuse to believe any cock and bull story she will tell me after she gets home.'

Pemisegant decided he was glad he was on the other end of a comconsole line. Sharlensya had a face like a bulldog chewing a wasp. More angry than he had ever seen her before.

'She is grounded for a month, and don't even think of contacting my half-daughter. You are a bad influence.'

She cut the link, to Pemisegant huge relief. He had so much to do before the field trip he was going on with Commander Yestarnsya and Lieutenant Ryzinasant.

'Do you know why this Erratic is coloured green?' asked Cerysorsya, as they trudged down yet another corridor.

'It's something to do with its mineral content,' replied Nevamarsya absent mindedly.

'Clever girl. This rock formed around a disk of Copper and Tin.'

'But why would the roots have grown around that

'Because there is enough Tin and other metals in the mix to dilute it. As with the Arsenic from the Blue Skull, sometimes poisons are necessary for useful products.'

'Did you ever think of being a Mentor, instead of a copper? You are starting to sound like one of my Mam's history lessons.'

'Not really. I knew from when I was a Cadet that I wanted to be an Enquirer,' she laughed, 'But keeping on an educational vein, calling someone from the police a Copper was originally an insult. Because Copper is so poisonous.'

'Not a popular career choice.'

'No, you have to be willing to arrest your granny without question, if you catch her doing something illegal.'

'Is the fact Canopy people have coppery red hair the reason why some Root people dislike us? Our hair look like poison.'

'No, that's got nothing to do with it. Its because we have no full time home. Every year we descend on the Roots because the Canopy is uninhabitable. The blonde bombshells have to make room for us. They want our gratitude to be gushing. We are grateful, but it's measured because they show no gratitude for the work the Canopy and its officers do. They can't understand without us busting a gut during the light half of the year, none of us would survive the dark half.'

The surface they were walking on had changed. It was perfectly flat and metallic and was slightly warm to touch.

They had arrived at the heart of the Erratic.

They had both been hearing the scraping and snuffling for twenty minutes, and had been trying to ignore it.

'It's the rock trolls, they are coming to get us,' said Cerysorsya.

'Oh don't be ridiculous, they are a myth. Do you think I'm still a Sprite.'

'How else do you explain that then?'

Ahead of the pair was a monstrous shadow. Something with more arms than any creature could possibly need, and no trace of a head. attached to the oblong body. As the creature let out an ululating wail they both screamed. The discord echoed up and down the tunnels at the heart or the Erratic.

CHAPTER NINETEEN
INTO THE LABYRINTH

So this is where you have gotten yourself. Oh, you are a silly little thing. Come to Uncle Gezz.' The shadow loped off down a tunnel, towards the voice. Whatever was casting it was chittering happily. 'Yes dear boy, you are a long way from home. That'll teach you to go wandering off.'

'I shoshee, Ungle Yesh,' something said in a very squeaky voice.

'And you two can come along as well. I know you are down there. Neither of us will bite,' said the first voice.

'U fwends, Ungle Yesh?' asked the high pitched voice.

'Yes little one,' he said calmly, 'but what were you doing down here anyway. Your designated care-giver will be having a fit.'

Nevamarsya recognised the voice, so interrupting the conversation between the anther and that thing she asked, 'Commander Gaemlovant, is that you?'

'Girl, nobody has called me Commander for two decades, but I do admit to being Gaemlovant.' There was the sound of more laughter. 'Come on, I'll take you to my farm. I am sure that you are both tired, I have made up a pair of beds, you can get a good meal; a chance to freshen up and a night's sleep.

They followed Gaemlovant into a huge cavern. It should have pitch black, but its walls glowed with natural luminescence, making the entire structure as bright as day.

'The light in here is natural,' said Gaemlovant, 'it seems to be effected by the Daylighter Field, on when it is powering them, off when the Field is absent and the Daylighters are dark.'

The lower slopes of the eastern wall was separated into five terraces. A variety of crops planted on the first three terraces and the upper terraces given over to pasture, home to grazing animals.

The slope behind the terraces was covered with a forest of large bushes and Nevamarsya could see pigs snuffling amongst them. Also four huge creatures, with long necks and longer tails.

'They can't be,' Nevamarsya said.

'They are you know. The only surviving Dinosaurs anywhere in the Tree.' Gaemlovant voice was edged with unashamed pride.

She also spotted at least twenty of the white furry creatures, pillows with arms, like the small creature currently wrapped around the old anther. The only difference being the other creatures were at least three times taller than any of the Tree People. The bottom pair of limbs were used for walking on, using the limbs on the other three sides as arms. However they seemed to have no concept of up and down, so which ever set of limbs was at the bottom when they wanted to walk, became legs.

'They were primitive hunter gathers when I first arrived here, close to extinction,' said Gaemlovant

'What are they?' asked Nevamarsya.

'They are your non-existent Rock Trolls,' said Cerysorsya.

'They're so clean and white. Not like the mud and gore encrusted creatures of the stories.'

'That is because they're in their natural habitat. The monstrosities of legend are the trolls who have wandered out of the Erratic and gone mad in the Roots.'

'They certainly don't look like primitive hunter-gathers now,' said Cerysorsya.

'Clever buggers,' he pointed towards a small garden. 'That was my original farm. I thought they were just blindly mimicking me when they set up their first farm. They were copying, they'd been watching me and learning from my mistakes. Soon their farms were larger and far more productive than mine. What amazed me was that they had learnt Treelish from listening to me, and soon came to me asking questions. To be honest, they have taught me as much as I have learnt from them.'

The group had made its way to the bottom of the cavern and entered a tunnel. This was not a natural structure, and soon opened out into a monastic cloister. This was obviously the old convent of the Daughters of Father Earth, the so called Earth-Nuns.

'This has been my home for two decades. In the early days I saw it as my prison. But since I met the Trolls, teaching and learning from them, my life has been so happy. This isn't my prison, it is my playground.'

Nevamarsya and Cerysorsya looked at each other. Was he mad? How could a solitary existence, surrounded by alien creatures possibly be happy. He pointed at a door. 'I have set up some quarters for you in there. I have a stand alone emprinter here. It will clean and repair your clothing. Its memory is full of my clothes, so you won't be able to change your outfits.'

'Not to worry, I keep a copy of my wardrobe on a memory stick,' said Nevamarsya. 'Will the emprinter read it?'

'I should imagine so,' said the old anther.

Nevamarsya plugged the memory stick in. The machine hummed as a selection of outfits flashed across its mirror.

'Is there anything I could wear on there, without looking like mutton dressed as lamb?' asked Cerysorsya.

'I am sure I could find something for you, my friend,' replied Nevamarsya, not sure what real and vat grown sheep meat had to do with borrowing her clothes?

'Anyway,' their host continued, 'I am sure that you would both like to freshen up before dinner. And the spa pool is through there. I recommend you have a dip before you turn in, it's wonderfully relaxing.'

They were left alone in the simply furnished room.

'Dinner, I would rather have a few hours sleep,' said Cerysorsya.

'OK. I'll take first watch whilst you sleep for a few hours, then we swap. Make sure that our friend doesn't do anything whilst we sleep?'

'So you don't trust him either. Do you Nevamarsya? Very wise.'

'You said it. He has been down here alone for all those years. I don't think he is even remotely sane. The Tree knows what he might do.' Nevamarsya replied. As much as she wanted to like the old anther, she would rather be safe than sorry.

'Oh for goodness sake,' said a voice over the intercom, 'I am not crazy, and I am not going to do anything to harm you.'

'You are still spying on us,' said Cerysorsya.

'You don't trust me. I am not sure if I entirely trust you yet.' The reply was perfectly logical.

'Have you got a video feed on this room? Have a good look as young Nevamarsya here gets changed.'

'No, I was once an officer you know. I have still the honour and the principles.'

'Really?' asked a sceptical Nevamarsya.

'Yes Subaltern Nevamarsya 331/29, Cadet member of the Family Fangkart.'

'Very well then. Sir.' Nevamarsya saluted as she spoke.

'Dinner is in one hour.'

*T**he bronze Roman coin was old and of little value tarnished to such an extent that the brick-maker hadn't really cared when he had lost it in his workshop. By accident it had been baked into a clay brick, one of a batch due for shipment to Gaul. The brick had been bought by the Imperial Army and ended up travelling further north. It was part of a consignment being used to build a fort to police the rebellious Silures in the west of Britannia.*

When the Romans abandoned the West, the fort eventually fell into ruin and the brick, with the coin still inside it, ended up in the waters of the estuary. Copper and tin salts from the coin dyed the once red brick green and the tides and currents knocked the sharp edges from it. Soon all that remained was a small pebble with a metal heart, nestling amongst the seaweed.

In the Middle Ages, the local farmers harvested the seaweed to fertilise their land, which is how the pebble ended up in the field. Over the years the pebble sunk deeper underground. Farmland became parkland, which in turn became an expensive suburb on the edge of Penarth.

The Apple tree had been planted near the pebble. As the tree grew, its roots wrapped around the pebble. After more than a century the roots totally surrounded and absorbed the pebble. Other stones were absorbed into the tree in this way, but they were local stone and none were as large nor so universally green.

O n Arbouron, nobody knew how or why the rock had been incorporated into the biomechanical citadel that was the Tree. All they did know was its unique green colour made it sacred to the Daughters of Father Earth and they built their Convent within it. Mining within what they called the Warm Stone had been forbidden. However, when the three competing female religious orders amalgamated, forming the Sacred Sisterhood of the Style, the newly created Tree-Nuns moved to their new convent in the Hub.

A fter a delicious meal Cerysorsya waited half an hour before visiting the Spa Pool with Nevamarsya. She was surprised to find a small crescent shaped lake in a sub-chamber below the ruined convent. The ceiling was covered with the same glowing crystals that illuminated the convent. They were starting to dim as the day waned. The floor of the chamber and pool was a green veined marble. Every few hundred yards steps were cut into the banks of the pool.

'I must be mad for doing this,' said Cerysorsya. She was wearing an identical floral swimming costume as Nevamarsya, which hung baggily on her.

'Swimming in this water or wearing a copy of my cozzy?'

'Both.'

'Well, when I learnt to swim last Autumn, I still thought I was going to be a boy. I wore a pair of baggy trunks and a t-shirt. I still feel strange in this sort of swimsuit.'

'Maybe that's what I should be wearing, kid.'

'You don't have to continue calling me Kid, my friends call Neva. Is that ok with you?'

'Of course and thank you, Neva. Please call me Cerys.'

Cerysorsya could hardly object to being on familiar terms with Nevamarsya, she was borrowing her clothes.

'Here goes nothing,' she said and winked at Nevamarsya

before they dunked their heads under.

'Wow!' said Cerysorsya when she came up for breath. 'That was just amazing.'

'Gaemlovant should bottle this stuff. He'd make a fortune.'

'R&D would spend years analysing this water before I could get a licence to sell it. Tests I would have to pay for. It would be at least a decade before I made any return on the investment. And then the Sisterhood would confiscate it all. Just like their predecessors confiscated the luxury resort complex that was going to be here. They however had no interest in rejuvenating spa pools and luxury health treatments. They turned what had been constructed into a convent with no frills.' Gaemlovant had appeared like magic on the banks of the spa pool, in a baggy pair of Bermuda shorts and a shirt that looked like an explosion in a paint factory.

Speak of the devil Cerysorsya thought.

'He's right Neva, the Tree-Nuns own this rock and everything in it,' said Cerysorsya.

'No, not even little Annie could help me with that one,' continued Gaemlovant.

'Who?' asked Cerysorsya.

'I thought everyone knew.' said Gaemlovant.

'Knew what?' she replied.

'Gaemlovant here is Abbess Annaprysya's older brother. He calls her Annie.' Nevamarsya could see confusion in her new friend's face. She had assumed Cerysorsya knew about the relationship between their host and the Abbess.

'But she's Root, he's Trunk.'

'So were Neva's great-uncle and her late grandmother.' There was a twinkle in the old anther's eye, it reminded Nevamarsya of Tabbernant, and the reason she was here in the first place.

'So, you will help Tabbernant?'

'I said I would, didn't I? I just have to wait for Annie to get her end in order,' he had a distant look on his face. 'I really don't want to leave here. It's my home now.' He smiled, 'but she can make me vanish again, back down here after the shit-storm has blown over.'

'As effectively as the vanishing act just then,' said Nevamarsya, 'he appears to have melted into the wall.'

'He knows all the nooks and crannies.' The older style yawned. I don't know about you, but having taken the dip he recommended, I'm ready for bed.'

CHAPTER TWENTY
FAMILY FEUD

Why had Major Harlaynsya, of all people, called her in for this meeting. The call had come at lunchtime on another wasted day that seemed to drag on forever. Despite being on suspension, Kilkennsya arrived at her place of work a few hours later in formal uniform. Security had waved her through the lobby and into the executive lift. Excellent thought Kilkennsya, I must be getting reinstated if I'm getting a welcome like this. Kilkennsya imagined the Major wasn't happy with what was happening in the department. Were things starting to go in the right direction.

An Enforcer was sitting at the Major's desk. Not just any Enforcer. Commissioner Lyndrevsya 104/51 Nott, the head of the Special Protection Service. Great green apples, Kilkennsya thought, what had she done to come to the attention of such an important person.

'You are Lieutenant Kilkennsya 207/19 Sdoolk?' asked the Commissioner.

'Yes, Ma'am.'

'You look surprised to see me.'

'I was expecting this to be a disciplinary meeting with Major Harlaynsya from Personnel Resources,' said Kilkennsya, 'I was hoping to get reinstated when she finds out about the criminal negligence in this department. The criminal negligence I refused to let Commander Dyscolnant cover up. So he suspended me.'

'I'm sorry, I arranged this meeting for other reasons,' said the Enquirer. 'Your name appeared on my radar at a priority level in three separate areas. That normally only happens to someone in serious trouble.'

'But Ma'am,' said a now worried Kilkennsya, 'I haven't done anything to get into your bad books.'

'That is true, which makes you unusual. The first Priority Level appearance concerns the Death of Subaltern Symzbarsya 290/73 Formil?'

'Oh! So you aren't interested in my evidence?' continued Kilkennsya. Finding the truth about her friend's death was important, but it was not as important as dangerous truths being ignored at work. Kilkennsya felt deflated. 'Am I ever going to get people to see the facts?'

'The failings at the Hydrology Department of the Central Command and Control is the reason for the Second Priority Level appearance. I will come to that later.'

'Symona, I thought that was a closed case.' She had not believed the official explanation from the Enquirers.

'That is what I want people to think, for the moment. I would ask you not to mention this part of our meeting to anyone.'

'OK.' This is strange thought Kilkennsya, but I have no choice but to agree. 'What is said today will remain secret, Ma'am.'

'I'm afraid I need a little bit more formality than that,' said the Commissioner. 'Do I have your word as an Officer.'

'Yes Ma'am, I give my word as an Officer that I will not disclose this discussion to a living soul.'

'Thank you Lieutenant.' Commissioner Lyndrevsya opened the first of three files in front of her. 'So you were a friend of the late Subaltern?'

'Yes, Ma'am. We were cadets and commissioned together.

We should have been promoted to Lieutenant on the same day. Off duty we were the best of friends. More like sisters I would say, both Hyposalemic. She'd cheer me up when I was poorly and vice versa.'

'Yet you are a Canopy style, and your friend will be remembered as a radical Pure-stock extremist,' said the Commissioner.

'That's so wrong. Poor Symona didn't give a stuff about where you came from. It was who you were that mattered.'

'Which is what everyone who ever knew her has told me,' said the Commissioner. 'This makes no sense. Unless she underwent a recent radicalisation. A sudden conversion to the cause.'

'I saw her the day she died. She was the same old Symona I always knew.'

'Are you sure about this?'

'Very sure Commissioner. She hated the Pure-stock and their silly Code.'

'As I suspected. The evidence is now pointing towards her being coerced and then sacrificed. She did not willingly work on the establishment of a new Pure-stock Style Sprite-pod.'

'I can believe that. Oh poor, poor Symona.' Kilkennsya could see that the older style meant business. 'So, you are going to try to clear Symona's name?'

'I will do more than try, but for that I need evidence,' said Commissioner Lyndrevsya. 'The innocent should never be left to carry the blame for the guilty.'

'She tried to send me a message before she died.' Kilkennsya wanted to be as helpful as possible. 'Here it is, Ma'am. I can't make head nor tail of it. I'm afraid it has been scrambled.'

'Her mother, boyfriend and two other friends received similar messages. They too were all scrambled. With not enough in the combined messages for my experts to unscramble.'

'Do you think this will help, Ma'am?' asked Kilkennsya.

'It can't harm, can it?' replied the older style. 'If you will excuse me.'

Kilkennsya watched as the Commissioner phoned one of her colleagues. The voice of a studious anther played over the comconsole's speakers.

'Jakx, I have another piece for our puzzle,' Commissioner Lyndrevsya said. 'I'm uploading it now.'

'Any good?' asked Kilkennsya, feeling a little out of the loop.

'Yes,' replied the anther, 'this is excellent. I should now have enough material to play with. Having strands from six of the seven recipients is good. Finding the seventh strand would be even better.' There was something about his voice, something old, Kilkennsya thought.

'Of course, I can now forget any hope of finding an unscrambled copy of this message. Or a copy that is more coherent.'

'Can't you refer back to the comconsole the message was sent from?' asked Kilkennsya.

'I can tell by the way this message was scrambled that the comconsole it was written on was surgically wiped whilst the message was being sent. It's a miracle anyone received it at all,' explained Jacx 'As it is, each recipient has got a different piece of garbage.'

'You want to mix it all together and distil the full message from that?' asked Kilkennsya.

'In theory.' There was a slight delay as the hologram screen fizzed back to life. Kilkennsya could see she had been speaking to a very old anther, wearing pyjamas with no rank symbols.

He's a pensioner. The Tree preserve us. Why is Commissioner Lyndrevsya, who has access to the Police Service's arsenal of high-tech gadgets turning to someone retired for assistance.

'Because he is still the best,' the older style said. 'I can tell by the way your face exploded that you have realised Jakx is no longer part of the Police Service.'

The Commissioner looked at her notes again. 'Which brings us to another Priority List appearance.' The Commissioner closed one file and opened another. 'Jakx is retired, one of my resident Hydrologist is about to do the same.'

'So you want me to join your team of techies, Ma'am?'

'Yes Lieutenant, but we call them Analysts. After I had taken your witness statement, I was going to interview for a job in my department as an Analyst.'

'May I ask why the SPS would even need a Hydrologist as an Analyst?' Kilkennsya was intrigued.

'Protecting the Tree-Marshall and the High Council from assassination is our headline job. But we also deal with the security at a number of high profile locations, including all departments of the Secretariat. This means we deal with the sort of crimes that are beyond the remit of the normal Police Regiments. The SPS has expert analysts in many fields. Permanently transferred from other regiments.'

'Why me, Ma'am?'

'I did a search of the Personnel database, looking for someone with the required qualifications and suitable personality. Your name was at the top of that list. I must say you have impressed me today. The way you interacted with Jack, you'll fit in well with the other Analysts.'

'So, I have passed the interview, Ma'am.'

'Yes, you have, Lieutenant.' The Commissioner opened a different file in front of her. 'Its not just your department. The way the whole of the Secretariat's Water Management Directorate has been running is starting to concern me. Your suspension from duty earned you your third appearance on my Priority list. I can't help but suspect the thinking of a department that would suspend someone for doing their job well. It looks like your expertise whilst the SPS investigates Water Management's short-comings will be invaluable.'

'There is a lot that is not quite right. I will be able to quote chapter and verse. Working for you to clean up the mess would be a pleasure.'

'So, I would like to formally request for you to be seconded to the Special Protection Service of the Enquirers Regiment for an initial period of three months, with the option of a permanent transfer. Is that agreeable to you?'

'Yes, Ma'am,' said Kilkensya, saluting.

'Good, the request has been sent. 'Thank you Analyst Sergeant? Report to the SPS HQ at 0900 tomorrow. Wearing a brown uniform.' The Commissioner slid a small box across the table and Kilkennsya picked it up.

'You are dismissed Sergeant.'

Kilkennsya stood up, saluted and left the room, then ran home.

The Police Service is an important part of the Officer Corps, however, it existed outside the Officer Corps' normal chain of command, with brown uniforms and its own Rank Structure. This separation allowed investigations to go forward without the guilty using normal rank to stop the investigation.

'You're home then love?' asked her mother. 'Did it go well?'

'I'll tell you in a minute Mam.'

'OK dear.'

She walked into her room and locked the door behind her. The emprinter in the corner switched itself on. Kilkennsya removed her Lieutenant's pin. The cluster of three silver leaves fitted perfectly into the unlocked section of the box. She snapped the lid shut. There was a small hiss as her old pin was sealed and the partition containing the Sergeant's pin sprung open. Nervously she attached the new pin to her uniform. The box was called a Promotion Box, because the electronics within usually sent a message confirming an Officer's new rank when used, today it just confirmed the change in her existing rank's title. For Killkensya, it felt like a promotion.

She heard a buzz and watched in the emprinter's mirrored surface as her uniform changed from military green to police brown.

'Great Green Apples Girl,' said her father, 'where did you get that uniform?'

'Yes love, that's a real Copper's uniform,' said her mother, 'Impersonating a Police Officer is a crime you know.'

'But only a member of one of the Police Regiments has access to these brown uniforms. Which means, I've joined the Police.'

'Don't be daft Girl,' said her dad with a snort. 'You, a Copper?'

'Yes, I'm now an Analyst Sergeant with the Special Protection Service, so technically I'm a Copper.'

'What, you mean you can arrest somebody?' asked her Mother.

'No Mam, I would have to do an eight week Basic Police Procedure course before I could do that. In reality I am still a glorified researcher.'

'Thank the Tree for that.'

'Don't worry Mam, all of Dad's dodgy deals have always been on the right side of the law.

Infuriatingly twee. That was the only thing Popisedsya could of as she watched the programme on the preset entertainment channel. Did Rolinalant and his cronies really enjoy this sort of rubbish. She switched off the televiewer. Another hour before the Family Meeting, so she took a book-reader out of her bag and settled down to read.

All in all it had been a pleasant afternoon off. Grandad Rex had called a family forum meeting, but there was nothing on the agenda that warranted one.

Soon she would be back in her new billet. It was comfortable, but a bit too functional for her liking. It was a good job it would never be home. She had recently followed Tabbernant's advice and put a deposit on a small unit in the Crown, which was already worth far more than she had paid for it.

She decided to go for a walk and was half way up the stairs leading out of the Farm's residential unit when she spotted a friendly face coming in the opposite direction.

'Aunty Mae,' she said, embracing the other style.

'Poppy dear,' Peripalsya replied. 'Aren't you going in the wrong direction?'

'I was going to get some fresh air before this meeting.'

'Is he being his usual poisonous self?' Peripalsya asked.

'I have no idea, I arrived an hour ago, and haven't seen him.' They were referring to Cousin Rolinalant. 'They are having problems draining field seven.'

'I told that fool to get better ducting, but did he listen? Of course not.'

'I don't think it is a problem with the farm's infrastructure. Grandad Rex says Rolly has been cursing the Hydrology Department for months.'

Popisedsya had noticed that a lot of the water courses in this part of the Trunk, that were usually bone dry at this time of year, still had a good level of water in them.

'Well, it takes a fool to spot a fool. The Lord of Darkness would fit in well with that shower.'

It looked to Popisedsya that Aunt Mae was agreeing with

Rolinalant, not that she would ever admit to that.

'Do you know why Grandad Rex has called this meeting?' asked Popisedsya.

'Nope, I am as in the dark as you are dear.'

'Either up or down ladies,' said the familiar voice of Pensioner Remixerant.

'Grandad Rex,' said Popisedsya. 'Did you find what you wanted at the Heartswood?. He had been very secretive about his reasons for travelling to the regional capital.

'I did indeed, Little Flower,' said the old anther, 'be prepared for a pleasant surprise.

And he was gone, leaving the two confused styles in his wake.

The Conference Room in the farm was full of members of the the Family Siylm originally from this and other local farms.

A few officers from Heartswood had made the same journey as Popisedsya to be here.

Pensioner Remixerant, in his formal business suit, with a red sash denoting he was the Thread Moderator, stood up on a dais and banged a ceremonial bamboo staff onto the floor.

'Cousins,' he said a loud but clear voice, 'I would like to draw this meeting to order.'

The room quietened down immediately. It had split into two factions. A small group of twelve anthers, who were loyal to Rolinalant sat in the front two rows. The majority, who had no time for the anther or his cronies, sat in the remaining five rows.

'I apologise for bringing you here at such short notice,' continued Remixerant 'and not supplying an agenda for this meeting. As you all must know, our bodies are designed to last exactly forty two years from the day we cease to be Sprites and become Officers. If we do not die in defence of the Tree or from some noxious disease before hand, we will pass away peacefully in our sleep on our Deathday. It is inescapable. I know that I am rapidly approaching that day.'

Everyone in the room knew this, so the audience sat respectfully listening to every word the old anther said.

'So, I have decided to draw up a Living Will. With my end so clearly marked out, I have decided not to wait until that day. Everyone I love will receive their inheritance now.'

'I have spent the day in the Archives of the Officer Corps Local Headquarters checking these facts. What I say now is without challenge the truth. On 4D10/171 Sprite PS100/97 was born. A year later on 1A11/172, Sprite RN109/31 arrived in the Tree. PS100/97 worked here for seven years before activating and becoming the style officer now called Popisedsya. RN109/31 spent just two years working on the farm, before becoming the anther officer Rolinalant. Both these officers were adopted by children of mine, becoming my grandchildren. Custom and practice only counts the number of years since activation for age, so Rolinant is considered the older grand-child. However, in matters of inheritance, the law states that the date of birth as a Sprite takes precedence. Therefore my Grandaughter Popisedsya has always been my oldest grandchild and my heir.'

'This means that as of 1200 today, when Judge-Advocate Zudokuosya 156/59 Alstratz ratified my Living Will and granted an immediate Deed of Probate, she has been the legal owner of this farm and owns my shares in a number of associated agri-busisesses.'

The room erupted. Those Officers loyal to Rolinalant roared their disapproval. The majority of Officers, were cheering and congratulating Popisedsya.

Again the ceremonial staff banged against the floor. However, Popisedsya was not listening. She was still in a state of shock. She responded to the congratulations as best she could. Was she going mad, or could she smell food.

'Will the family please come to order. I have a further announcement to make.'

'This is a disgrace,' said Rolinalant, I will challenge this all the way to the High Council itself.'

'I am afraid, grandson of mine,' replied Remixerant, 'that you will achieve nothing from that. I doubt if you will find a Judge-Advocate anywhere in the Tree who will hear your case.'

'In that case, I resign my position as farm manager with immediate effect.'

'Very well, put it down on paper, sign it and leave it on my desk.'

Popisedsya knew this was unnecessary, as all existing contracts of employment had been terminated when she inherited the farm. She wondered if Rolinalant knew.

There was a load scraping of chairs as Rolinalant and his cronies stood up and left the room.

'Try running this place without me and my friends,' the anther said to her. 'I'm having nothing to do with you, cousin or not.'

'So you won't be staying for the meal I have ordered. Pity, the caters have been busy all afternoon,' said Remixerant, who had finished listing who now owned what and had walked over to Popisedsya.

'Caters, what caters?' asked Rolinalant.

'Just goes to show how observant you are Rolly,' said Aunty Mae, holding a paper plate with dimsum sitting on it.

Once Rolinalant and crew had left the room, everything became quiet and ordered again.

'The Law states that anyone subject to a Living Will cannot hold the office of Thread Moderator, so we must now chose my successor.'

'Surely it will have to wait until the formal Election Cycle?' asked Cousin Lynnwinsya, the only remaining pro-Rolinalant officer in the room.

'Whoever is elected tonight will only be a caretaker until that Election Cycle,' replied Remixerant.

'In that case, I nominate Cousin Popisedsya,' said Aunty Mae, with half a dozen cousins quick to second the nomination.

'Are there any more nominations?' asked Grandad Rex.

'I wouldn't normally vote for Rolly, said a voice at the back of the hall, 'sorry Poppy, but we must be seen to be doing things correctly, So I nominate Cousin Rolinalant for the post.'

'You are not so foolish after all, Cousin Mellingant,' said Remixerant. 'Does anyone second it?'

To no one's surprise Cousin Lynnwinsya, raised her arm.

The electronic voting system quickly confirmed Popisedsya's landslide victory.

'These are also yours now, Popisedsya,' Remixerant said as he handed her the staff the sash of office. Also a Promotion Box. 'Congratulations, Commander Popisedsya.'

'But I have only been a Lieutenant for three months.'

'And what has that got to do with the price of protein, cousin,' said Aunty Mae.

Taking the staff in her right hand she announced in a voice that was close to breaking. 'I think this is a good time to declare this meeting closed.' The ceremonial staff rapped the floor three times as she signified the end of the meeting. 'With the formal business complete, let's eat.'

Remixerant could see his granddaughter looking like an overawed child. The enormity of the situation had not yet sunk in.

'I'm sorry to have dropped that on you, Little Flower,' he said. 'But I did tell you to expect a pleasant surprise.'

'Granddad Rex, that is more than a pleasant surprise.'

'You mean a very pleasant surprise,' he said.

'I take it you had to move quickly, to stop Rolinalant challenging what you were doing?'

'Yes, if he had found out, and put in an objection, then my friend Zudokuosya would have had to have gone through a full Probate Hearing. As it was, the Living Will appeared to be unchallenged.'

'Is there any way that Rolinalant can have it overturned?' asked Popisedsya, 'is all this really all mine now?'

'No and Yes Little Flower,' said the anther enigmatically. He was in a melancholy mood. He loved his grand-children equally, including Rolinalant. He wept for the mean spirited person his grandson had become and he knew now it was too late for him to change. 'No, he cannot overturn my Living Will, not after it was publicly read. Judge-Advocate Zudokuosya ratified it. And yes, this is all yours now.'

'And the funds to restore it to its former glory?'

'Indeed. The dividends from the shares will more than cover it. The insurance would pay out if we were to lose the entire production run, but the whole farm would have to be flooded for that to happen.'

'Why do we have that insurance?'

'Better safe than sorry, Little Flower.'

CHAPTER TWENTY ONE
WONDERLAND

The room was filled with an ear shattering shriek which could wake the unrecycled dead. There was no way Nevamarsya, in the other bed, would remain sleeping after that.

'I'm terribly sorry Neva,' Cerysorsya said.

'Where's the fire?' asked a drowsy Nevamarsya.

'Nowhere, I just had a shock. A huge shock,' replied the older style.

Instead of a bald and badly scarred scalp that Cerysorsya had been keeping hidden under an e-wig for years, she now sported an anther-like headful of fine red hair.

'That's just impossible,' she said as she ran her hands over the hair. 'I've been bald for years. I would need a complete scalp graft of material grown in a grafting pod. Which isn't possible, scalps can't be regrown. Even if they could, I'd have to wait months before I get this sort of growth. This cannot be happening.'

'I would love to know exactly what is in that water too,' said Nevamarsya. I've had an acid burn on my arm all my life. It's completely gone.' She got out of bed. 'The only person with answers is the mad old fool.'

'Neva, don't be rude to our host,' said Cerysorsya sharply.

'You've changed your tune Cerys.'

'Its called good manners young one.'

'I'm sorry, you're right,' Nevamarsya replied, now fully awake.

'On the other hand, he is a mad old fool,' said the older style. 'Who I'm sure can supply some answers.'

They found a note but were unable to decipher the scrawled message. It took them another half an hour to locate Gaemlovant, as he walked back to the ruins. He had already been up for hours, tending to the farm animals, now he was going to cook his guests breakfast.

'Overalls are provided, if you would like to help out ladies,' said Gaemlovant, 'there's always something to do on a farm. Didn't you see the note?'

'Were you taught to write by the same Mentor who taught my Grandfather?' asked Cerysorsya.

'Could have been, could very well have been,' replied Gaemlovant. 'Why do you ask?'

'Because his handwriting was diabolical too.'

'Oh,' said a crestfallen Gaemlovant. 'I appear to have fallen out of the practice of writing legibly.'

'Good job we aren't asking for any written answers,' said Cerysorsya.

Nevamarsya could see the Enquirer was back in business mode. She found that strangely comforting.

'Certainly Cerys.' Then realising his mistake, 'I may call you Cerys?'

The old anther's social skills were rusty. He should have waited for permission to move from the long formal names to shorter familiar names.

'Do I have the choice?' replied Cerysorsya coldly.

'Of course you do. I was being dreadfully presumptuous.' The old anther sounded suitably guilt ridden. 'I apologise completely.'

'Call me what you like, as long as it isn't "Saucy"'.

'An academy nick-name, I presume?' he asked.

'Yes, and one which never seems to go away.'

'Enough about me,' said Cerysorsya. 'Maybe then some answers with our breakfast?'

That was an excellent meal, thank you Gaemlovant,' said Nevamarsya after tucking into bacon, sausage, fried eggs and beans. 'As was the one last night. I haven't seen any protein vats. Would I regret asking about the meat.'

'It depends how squeamish you are, and please call me Gezz.'

'Bernie insists on eating fresh caught pysgod, and when I visit the Convent, I end up eating what the Tree-nuns do.'

'Yes Neva dear, this is all natural meat.'

'Oh, I see why people rave about it. But I would hate to think of animals wasting their lives, just to feed me.'

'How can it be a waste, if that life would never have started without a farmer like me?'

'I suppose so Gezz.'

'Enough philosophy already. What's happening to me?' asked Cerysorsya. 'My badly burned scalp is no longer badly burned. But that is chicken feed compared to what is happening to the rest of me.'

'The rest of you?' Nevamarsya was confused.

'Yes, I would have difficulty passing as an old anther now. I actually needed a B cup bra this morning. I can understand why the pool is repairing my scalp, something in the water that is good for the skin. The rest is serious genetic manipulation.'

'This place is rebuilding you, just as it rebuilt me,' said Gaemlovant. 'When I first arrived here, I had a misshaped spine and one arm was longer than the other.'

There was no sign of that now. Gaemlovant looked so normal it was hard to believe what he was saying.

'You're seriously telling me that I am being rebuilt from the chromosomes up?'

'Yes, the old Earth-Nuns and Earth-Monks could not abide physical imperfection. When the Orders merged, that is one dogma that got ditched.'

'That's amazing. Thank you Gaemlovant and thank you Earth-nuns. I've always hated being revertive and wished I was a normal Style again.'

'I'm glad your pleased,' said Nevamarsya, 'but just like Cerys, I need to know how long do you think it will be before the roots are clear for travelling?'

'I can see you're in a hurry to get back young Neva,' said Gaemlovant. 'However, it's going to be at least another day before the water levels outside the Erratic are low enough for us to leave for the Hub.'

'I've never known so many flooding incidents this late in the year,' Cerysorsya said. 'If it keeps up like this, the Hub will flood again.'

'Nah, not after the last one, nearly four decades ago,' said Gaemlovant.

'That was the one that got the Sisterhood all messed up, wasn't it?' asked Nevamarsya.

'No Neva. The Book of Song went missing in the flood before that, back in the Spring of 120, when all the snow melted,' the old anther replied. 'The flood of 149 followed two incredibly hot dry summers, people got complacent.'

'Were you there?'

'I'm not that old, kid.'

'And people say I have no sense of humour.'

'If you thought that was funny, they're right,' he took a sip of Kuffa. 'Anyone who was there would have either been a child, or still a sprite. My parent's generations made sure such a flood never happened again. Today the flood is mere history. Are we still vigilant in our preparations?'

'That is currently not our concern,' said Cerysorsya. 'We

need to get back to the Hub as quickly as possible.'

'I don't have any submersible vehicles here. We will have to wait until the waters subside. Also, Cerys can't leave.'

'What do you mean?' asked a shocked Cerysorsya.

'I said you are being rebuilt by the Erratic. You cannot leave until it has finished. You're going to be stuck here, with me for at least a year.'

'But its my duty to return. My case, I have to see that through to a successful conclusion! Then there's my career damn it.' Nevamarsya thought she sounded less convincing on the second point.

'Do you, they can carry out the raid without you. Watch it on the comconsole over there.' Gaemlovant pointed vaguely in the right direction. 'Your colleagues will find all the evidence you collected, and some I left them.'

'And the next case?' she asked.

'Don't worry, my dear. Once my sister explains you are on extended sick-leave, everything will be sorted.'

'I wish I had your faith love.'

After breakfast, he had returned to tending to the animals on the upper terrace. The two styles had gone to help him. They had taken a picnic lunch, but by mid afternoon, Nevamarsya was building up a huge appetite. She watched the way Cerysorsya and Gaemlovant were getting on. You didn't have to be an Empath to read the signs, so she volunteered to return to base to cook the evening meal.

The kitchen was well equiped, their host was obviously someone who loved cooking. In fact the whole place was the home of someone who loved life. How could someone who had lived off the grid for so many years live so well? He should be a hermit, living with barely the clothes on his back.

To her surprise, she heard a comconsole chiming as she was tidying the kitchen. Strange, she thought.

She followed her ears and found the noise was coming from a machine in the study. A text message was on the screen. It read "Neva, look in the drawer beneath the monitor."

Inside the drawer was a disc that Nevamarsya quickly popped into the nearest comconsole. A familiar face appeared on the screen.

'My dear Nevamarsya,' said Abbess Annaprysya. 'If you are watching this then you have found my big brother's little hide-away.'

'Yes, thank you,' said Nevamarsya, although no-one could hear her.

'You were correct when you said that only a Tree-Nun could vanish so completely. Or arrange for someone to vanish so completely. When Gaemlovant came to me, saying he needed to vanish, I knew how to keep him safe.' A pained look crossed her face. 'I never wanted to join the Sisterhood, it is so ironic I now lead it. Only a Tree-Nun should have been considered for the job of caretaker of the Erratic site. I sacrificed my life in the Tree Without for him. I altered the records so that the Novice Mistress would come for me. When I was no longer a nosy outsider, I had more access to the Order's secrets than ever before. I arranged for an outsider, and an Anther outsider at that, get the job. By taking my vows, the Sisterhood gave him protection, with unlimited and untraceable access to whatever he needed to be complete invisibile.'

Your new job is not in the slightest way ironic, though Nevamarsya. Neither is your remarkable rise through the ranks prior to that. So much for sacrifice. You have never been an ordinary Tree Nun and have had absolute power in the Tree Within for years.

'The Sisterhood still has many secrets. Once my Brother has testified in Tabbernant's defence, those secrets will close around him, and he will vanish again. I promised him he would be safe for life. Safe he shall be.'

The puff of smoke from the disc tray as it slid open exposing a destroyed data disc.

'Sacred Sisterhood of the Paranoid would be a better name for the female House of Clergy,' she said to no one in particular. 'So, where does he keep his tomato puree. This Lasagne isn't going to cook itself?'

'This whole place is awesome, I can see why you love it down here,' said Cerysorsya. It was the evening of the fifth day Nevamarsya and Cerysorsya had been staying at the Erratic, but it seemed like they had been there forever.

Before eating, the three headed for the warm blue waters of the Spa Pool. Cerysorsya's swimsuit no longer hung baggily and she needed a cap to cover her shoulder length hair.

'There is a but coming here. I know there is,' said Gaemlovant.

'Yes, first thing tomorrow you return to civilisation.'

'Yes, that is inevitable,' he said.

'But there is more. I'm so glad I will remain here. It would have been my duty to arrest the anther I have fallen in love with,' said Cerysorsya dejectedly 'or watch someone else do it'.

'That was a but I didn't see coming.' The old anther was taken aback.

'You two have been using your pet names for each other for a couple of days now,' said Nevamarsya. 'Was I the only person to notice?'

'We have?' asked the anther. 'Yes, I suppose we have,' he laughed. 'But there is no need to worry, Annie will get me off the hook.'

'I don't think she will be able let you wriggle out of this one Gozo.'

'We shall see,' he said.

'Of course she will, she told me so,' said Nevamarsya.

'So you found the disc,' said Gaemlovant. Then turning to Cerysorsya he asked, 'so do you want me to ask Annie to make you permanently vanish too? You'll become part of our family, I'm sure she could arrange it.'

'Great, because I have another duty now. A duty of care to this place,' said Cerysorsya. 'Neva came here looking for your assistance. She want you to help your old friend Tabbernant. Leaving means your place will be unattended. Someone has to remain here until you return. It can't be Neva, she is too young to be left on her own. It has to be me.'

'And you can't leave here until you are fully fit,' said Nevamarsya. 'You know, I never did believe in love at first sight. It took a while for things to click with me and my darling Pezzi. You two have convinced me.'

'So you have been reading me again, damn your good for someone untrained. I thought I was putting up better barriers.'

'Of course you have. You have been so obvious, even to a non-empath. And Gezz over there, has been laughing all day.'

'What's all this, stylish intuition?' asked Gaemlovant, who had not been paying attention.

'You could call it that. 'I'll grab some food and leave you two lovers to sort things out.' Nevamarsya had climbed out of the water and had grabbed a towel.

CHAPTER TWENTY TWO

MEETINGS AND MEANINGS

Abbess Annaprysya sat serenely at her desk, a cup of cha cooling in front of her. Freshly laundered habit, extra starch in her wimple. Nevamarsya suspected she wanted to make a good impression on her long lost brother.

This was not the almost comfortable Parlour Nevamarsya usually saw the Abbess in. This was her main office.

Behind the desk was a large representation of the Tree in delicate protein glass.

Nevamarsya suspected there was good reason for this meeting taking place here, instead of in the friendlier surroundings of the Parlour. This was going to be an uncomfortable meeting.

'Nevamarsya, my child,' said the Abbess, 'so nice to see you returned safe and well.'

The Abbess stood up and began walking towards the door. 'I wished to see you before I met my brother.'

'Yes Abbess Annaprysya.'

'You really are a foolish child sometimes,' said the Tree-Nun, with the full force of her authority. 'Your actions, though well intentioned, were extremely foolhardy.'

'I am sorry Abbess, things spiralled out of control,' said a shamefaced Nevamarsya.

'As young Pemisegant told me when I spoke to him a few days ago. An intelligent young anther, but with no common sense. I expected better of you.'

'Sorry, Abbess,' Nevamarsya replied meekly.

'This room is known as the Abbesses' Court. However, I leave the punishment to your Mother-to-be, who you have badly frightened.

'My designated care giver,' said Nevamarsya absent-mindedly.

'I beg your pardon?'

'Something your Brother said.'

'Oh,' she replied, none the wiser. 'Now, shall we go and speak with him.'

'Great green apples, it really is you?' aksed Gaemlovant as Abbess Annaprysya with young Nevamarsya in tow, arrived at the Abbess' Parlour, where he had been waiting patiently.

'The years have been kinder to both of us than we deserve Gezz dear,' she said as she greeted her older brother with obvious affection.

'Indeed they have Annie,' Gaemlovant replied. He took a hanky from his pocket to blow his nose. Abbess Annaprysya watched as he carefully folded it before dropping it in the bin. How many years had it been since she had last seen any of her brother's idiosyncracies?

'So, you will testify for Tabbernant?' she asked.

'How could I not. I know exactly where Bernie was the night somebody nailed Drwgdynant,' he replied with certainty.

'And you can prove it?' she asked. 'After so many years.'

'Of course. However, I will need you to corroborate my story.'

'Surely that will not be necessary.' The Abbess had been dreading this, she knew what was going to come next.

'A good Prosecution Advocate will be out to discredit everything I say. If you testify as well, they will have to believe me.'

'I'm afraid that is not possible. Neither I, nor any of my Sisters can testify at a Court Martial.'

'In the Tree's name, why not?' asked her brother.

'Because we are supposed to be above such mundane matters.'

'Then it's a good job it's not going to get that far, especially if you come with me to the Police Station,' said Gaemlovant, pleading to his kid sister.

'I cannot do that either.'

She saw Gaemlovant reaction but remained unmoved. Even when a look of disgust crossed Nevamarsya's face, Abbess Annaprysya sat like a statue.

'All that danger and discomfort is going to come to nothing,' Nevamarsya said.

'You old hypocrite.' Gaemlovant had gone bright red with anger. 'So much for your holy order, if it will not raise a finger to stop an old man being punished for a crime he did not commit.'

'You are overlooking one fundamental point. The very fact that I can summon the police here, to hear your evidence is corroboration in itself. The Rules of the Order forbid direct interference. They say nothing of indirect suggestion and manipulation.'

'That depends entirely on the Copper dealing with the case. We just have to hope that old Myghcomant recovers in time to give evidence,' said Gaemlovant. 'He will corroborate everything I say. He was there at the time.'

Nevamarsya began crying. She seemed to be doing that a lot in this room. Remembering how ill the General had been a few days earlier.

'Dry your eyes dear. The General woke shortly after you left the Hub. He is off the critical list,' said Abbess Annaprysya reassuringly.

'He is?' A light broke behind Nevamarsya's eyes.

'But he is still recovering from his injuries. It will be a long term process. He might be to ill to testify.'

'I can't see that stopping him,' said Nevamarsya. 'He is one of the few people who can call Tabbernant "Uncle Bernie" with it being one hundred percent accurate.'

'There is that my child.' The Abbess returned her attention to Gaemlovant. 'You will remain here whilst you are in the Hub. I shall summon the police. This is the safest place you can be. If there is a Court Martial, the Syndicates will do their best to stop you testifying.'

'Haven't you forgotten I'm an anther.'

'For a while, dear brother, you will have to pretend to be my one of my Sisters.'

'Even in a wimple, I would still look like a bloke.'

'You obviously haven't met Sister Andtrozsya, great green apples she's butch.'

'How am I going to make a believable witness statement, if I am locked up in here, pretending to be a Tree-nun?'

The Abbess looked at her brother. 'I could always get you going, couldn't I, Gaemlovant?'

'What?' he asked, ever so slightly confused.

'Of course you don't have to pretend to be a Tree-Nun. You are the the Sisterhood's long serving employee. It is only right and proper that we should offer you hospitality when you are visiting the Hub.'

'No questions?' Gaemlovant asked.

'Who is there to ask them, Brother dear?' asked Abbess Annaprysya rhetorically.

'So will you arrange for an Enquirer and Pensioner Tabbernant's solicitor to visit me here?'

'Also the Enquirers from the Drugs Squad dealing with the Charline Factory down at the Arsenic Plant,' she said, her brother could be really slow at times. 'I can arrange for you to speak to someone about that as well.'

'OK, Annie. I'll stay here for as long as necessary. I am however anxious to get back to my farm.'

'I think you will find it is the Sisterhood's Farm, but yes, I see your point. Affairs of the heart, who would have thought it.'

'You can't help it, can you Annie, you have to wind me up.'

'Why break the habit of a lifetime?' The Abbess smiled. 'I have seen her bio-data, you want me to make her disappear as well.'

'She had to stay below. That Spa-Pool is magic.'

'Which is highly addictive. I only hope you finish your business here before the withdrawal symptoms kick in.'

'That water is not addictive Annie,' said Gaemlovant.

'Tell me that again after the cramps and the cold sweats.'

'Goodness,' said Nevamarsya, 'will I get those?'

'No, my child, you were not exposed to the active ingredient in the water for long enough.'

'That's a relief.'

'Your friend Cerysorsya on the other hand, she will become as hooked as my brother is within a month.'

'There is nothing addictive about that water,' he repeated.

'Yes there is, you won't admit it. Anyway, regarding your new friend. Yes, I can make her vanish when you disappear in a few weeks time. I'm Abbess now, that makes things so much easier. Although the challenge of getting into the system Sister Stefyopsya set up would be fun.'

Everyone laughed, and then like flipping a switch, Abbess Annaprysya's mood changed. She had to go back to being the Abbess. Stiff and as starchy as her wimple.

'There are of course rules you have to obey during your stay. First you must refrain from calling me Annie. A Tree-

Nun abandons the Informal Name she used in the Tree Without. Only using the name Our Lord gave us the day we were born.'

'Very well, Abbess Annaprysya. Although to be perfectly honest, I never liked Annie much.'

'The second rule I have to impose is you can not see me again during the duration of your stay here.'

'Isn't that a bit harsh?' asked Nevamarsya.

'Harsh but fair. Many Tree-Nuns would dearly love to see family members again. Today I have been granted a privilege denied to them. I shall have to do some penance.'

'Of course, I wasn't thinking.'

'Now, my child, it is time you went home. Your mother is waiting for you in the next room.'

The atmosphere in the car was frosty. Hang on, this was the car she had abandoned in the Roots a week ago.

'It is a good job all government vehicles have a fast return switch fitted,' said Sharlensya. 'And don't think I will be letting you drive this for a while.'

The vehicle landed on the roof of Fangkart House and mother and daughter climbed out.

'You could have been killed Nevamarsya. Life is not a game. The Syndicates don't play let's pretend.'

'Syndicates? What have they got to do with it?'

'Don't try to act the innocent young lady.' They had entered the upper porch. 'That story about your sudden interest in Geology doesn't wash with me.'

'Oh.'

'You chose one hell of a time to remember you are still a child. I thought you were cleverer than that.'

The insult cut to the quick. Nevamarsya knew she was in real trouble.

'You are grounded young lady. Also you may not contact that fool Pemisegant until I see fit. He knows he is persona non grata and will not be welcome here until I say so. Do I make myself clear.' Nevamarsya did not reply. 'I said, do I make myself clear?'

'Yes Ma'am.'

'Good, now go to your room.'

PART FIVE
DRAMA

CHAPTER TWENTY THREE
ARRIVALS AND DEPARTURES

'What do you mean by that?' asked a flustered Commander Yestarnsya.

'Exactly what I said. This is the Honeymoon Suite, booked for a honeymoon and booked by you,' said the pompous Subaltern who was showing them to their cabin.

'Oh don't be ridiculous, why would I book a honeymoon suite?' asked Commander Yestarnsya, angrily snapping back at the Subaltern.

'You'd better get your son over there to explain it, or even your new husband?'

'Lieutenant Ryzinasant is not my husband, and Subaltern Pemisegant is not my son,' she said in a very bad temper. 'I booked the two cabins my party require last month. One with two single beds for the anthers and a single room for myself. Both down on the Economy Decks.'

The fun and games had started a few minutes earlier, when Pemisegant and his two superior officers had boarded the shuttle that would take them from the Hub to Location 01AA A01, aka the Heartswood, the main population centre in the Trunk. The plan had been to take one of the express shuttles to the Crown, which broke the journey with a single stop in the Trunk at Heartswood, on its way to the Canopy. Instead, they found themselves on a regular shuttle that stopped a dozen times en route. It would take an extra day and a half to get them to their destination.

Being escorted to the Honeymoon Suite was the icing on the three tier Wedding Cake.

'Madam, here is your booking. You clearly requested the Honeymoon Suite plus one extra cabin for the lad over there. You are therefore now standing in the Honeymoon Suite.' The Subaltern from the Purser's Department was exuding smugness whilst appearing to be calmly efficient. Pemisegant disliked someone just a few years older than himself calling him "lad". He was however, desperately trying not to laugh. He knew it would be wise to quickly put some distance between himself and his angry superior officer before she exploded.

'And exactly where do you think you're going, Subaltern?' Commander Yestarnsya asked.

'Sorry, Ma'am,' he saluted. 'Permission to go to check our equipment is all aboard, Ma'am.'

'Very well. Off you go Subaltern, at least somebody is doing their job properly.'

Pemisegant saluted and left the gaudy cabin as fast as his feet would carry him.

'I think,' said Lieutenant Ryzinasant, who had been checking the paperwork 'you will find this booking you are referring to is in the name of a Lieutenant Yeffarnsya 136/30 Laftbrant. Made for her Daughter and new Son-in-Law, plus a room for their half-daughter. I think you had better run along, and hope the Happy Couple have not arrived at our cabins. Imagine how disappointed they would be to find bunk beds.'

The Subaltern was no longer calm and smugly superior. 'If you would excuse me, Ma'am, Sir,' he said as he slowly edged away.

'That's right, run as soon as you think no-one can see you,' said Ryzinasant as soon as the anther had left the Honeymoon

Suite. 'If you had been doing your job, instead of being so pompous, you'd know the Happy Couple don't come aboard until Station 3, this evening.'

A few minutes later, the two officers were standing outside the correct cabins, located a few decks down and definitely more utilitarian. Ryzinasant realised it was one of the rare moments where Commander Yestarnsya felt she needed to talk.

'Thank you, Lieutenant. I didn't handle that very well, did I?' she said.

'Not a problem, Ma'am. That Purser needed taking down a peg or two,' he said.

'But there are ways of doing it. I shouldn't have lost my temper, it was so unprofessional,' she said, and I shouldn't be admitting it to a subordinate, she thought, even one as understanding as Ryzinasant.

'If I may make a suggestion, Ma'am.'

'Go ahead Lieutenant.' Please don't spoil it, she thought. Don't say anything that breaches protocol.

'I would use the extended journey time to get some extra sleep. I certainly will, so I am better prepared for my security inspection at the facility at the Heartswood.'

'Yes, I think we could all do with a rest day tomorrow.'

He smiled as she visibly relaxed. She still looked as exhausted as he felt, but at least she was smiling now. He had not planned on making his inspection at the same time as the Commander and Subaltern Pemisegant. But that infuriating style had insisted, as it would save money. The inspection would have taken two weeks work if he had done it solo. Why did he find spending a whole month with her so exciting.

'Permission to go and find Pemisigant and guide him to the correct deck.'

'Granted. Good idea Lieutenant,' he heard her saying absentmindedly as she walked into her cabin.

Pemisegant opened his eyes. Daylight was filtering through the curtains. He was so glad he had been assigned a billet with a window. Not that he had really cared in the early dawnsward when he had arrived at the hostel. When the rented automated cargo-van had been loaded with the team's equipment, there had been room for one passenger. The Commander had ridden on ahead. He and Lieutenant Ryzinasant had walked from the dock to the hostel. Four miles of badly lit service tunnels.

He got out of bed and threw back the curtains. He had seen it in photographs, but this was the first time for him to see the majesty of the Great Cascades of Heartswood.

'Awesome,' he said to himself as the full majesty hit him. The word awesome was over-used and had lost its power in most respects, but these cascades, safely behind a wall of laminated mineral and protein glass twenty units thick was truly awesome. 'Now that is something worth waking up to.'

Heartswood had been engineered to form a pressure valve for the Grand Central Channels as the Tree had grown. Without them, the weight of water in the channels would crush the reinforced hulls of the shuttles which traversed them. Similar valves existed, but the Heartswood was the oldest, the largest and by far the prettiest of them all.

This was where the Research and Development Regiment had chosen to build the Large Vehicular Prototype Store. Anything too large to fit into the archive down in the Regimental Headquarters in the Roots ended up here at the LPVS. All sorts of prototypes for boats, aircrafts and ground vehicles gathered dust in the LVPS.

Whilst Pemisegant was marvelling at this fusion of nature and and engineering, his comlink chimed.

'Ah Subaltern, I'm glad you're up.' It was Commander Yestarnsya. Pemisegant couldn't tell if she was being ironic or not. She was so difficult to read. He doubted even Nevamarsya would be able crack that ice cold exterior.

'Yes Ma'am,' he replied.

'Good, I need you to report to the Collection A.S.A.P.'

Great green apples, thought Pemisegant, she's keen. Silly me, its Commander Yestarnsya, of course she is keen. 'Ma'am, I haven't had any breakfast yet.'

'There is a perfectly serviceable cafeteria in the same block as the Collection. You can have your breakfast there. However, the delay in getting here means we have a day's work to catch up on. Work first, breakfast later.' The screen went blank.

'Yes Ma'am.' Of course it does, it is in the same block as this hostel.' But his commanding officer was long gone.

The Hostel was on a square at the base of the wall of protein glass that separated the Cascades from the community that had grown up in this part of the Trunk. At the centre of the square was a Rotunda where the population worshipped on Sunday at Temple Parade. A number of civic buildings, such as the Regional Command and Control Centre and Officer Corps Regional HQ were located around the edges of the Square. The streets that lead off from it quickly became a maze of deep ravines between the different blocks. These ravines were anything up to twenty decks high, each deck having a row of windows that looked across to a matching row of windows. At regular intervals were the entrances to the blocks, each one boasted a café, restaurant or bar in addition to the lifts and stairwells up and down.

Pemisegant didn't have time to explore the maze of ravines. With a fresh boiler suit, he made his way to the Collection.

An anonymous single storey bulding gave no indication of the size of the LPVS's collection. It served as an entrance to the caverns below, following the pattern of the Archive in the Regimental Headquarters, on a grander scale, if that were possible.

'Morning Subaltern.' It was the ever cheerful Lieutenant Ryzinasant.

'Has nobody ever worried about this place being flooded out?' asked Pemisegant.

'From where, Subaltern?' asked Commander Yestarnsya. 'The composite glass separating the entrance to these hangars, and the rest of this district from the cascades is nearly seventy units thick at its living base. The whole wall is a single unit from a shelf in the base-wood five mile below the cascades to its upper limit a mile above their start. Over the years it has continued to grow at the rate of one seventy-second of a fraction a year. In fact it was allowed to grow for a decade before the first overflow water from the Grand Central Channel was allowed down the cascades. The Tree itself would have to fall before that wall would leak. I grew up here, I know what I am talking about. We Mid-Trunk Officers are all rightly proud of the indestructible wall.'

Pemisegant had often wondered about this. Commander Yestarnsya's red hair and pale skin marked her out as being from the Canopy. However, her facial features, especially her eyes were definitely Mid-Trunk.

'Yes Subaltern, I was a Sprite here and I spent my childhood here. The Tree only knows why I have the appearance of someone from the Canopy.'

'Which just goes to show how stupid categorising people by regional appearance can be,' said a deep but still obviously female voice in the shadows. 'I'm also Mid-Trunk, but you wouldn't think it, if you saw me.'

The voice made Pemisegant jump. He had no idea that there was another person in the room with them. He instantly pulled himself together and saluted the Lieutenant's pips of the person the voice belonged to.

'Subaltern Pemisegant 150/48,' said Commander Yestarnsya, 'this is Lieutenant Wrendigsya 144/60 Nott-Alzstraat. She is the curator of the LVPS. We will be working with her on this audit.'

'The Bond has been broken for four years now, Ma'am. My name has reverted to its original form. I want no reminder of that waster I was pair-bonded with.'

Pemisegant saluted and then had his hand shaken by the biggest hand he had ever seen.

There were people of all shapes and sizes in the Tree, big and small. There was nothing small about Lieutenant Wrendigsya, but it all looked so natural. Large but not fat, well rounded and not obese. She could not possibly be Mid-Trunk, not with skin like chocolate and a voice like honey.

'I suspect it is because we live in Heartswood, a crossing point for the whole Tree, that all the many misfits around here end up in Family Nott.'

'Oh, I see,' said Pemisegant.

'So, Subaltern Pemisegant, I'm Lieutenant Wrendigsya. I'm nominally in charge of this joint. Off duty I answer to the name Wren. You have my full permission to use that when we are away from this dump. What do you call yourself? Pemmy, Pemmo or what?

'Its Pezzi actually ma'am.'

'Well Pezzi, I bet my niece, Commander Yestarnsya here is skipping breakfast again.'

Her niece? Pemisegant didn't think his boss had any surviving family. She certainly acted as if she were all alone in the Tree.

'Lieutenant Wrendigsya, we are behind in our schedule, we don't have time.'

'It is my belief that nobody should ever skip breakfast. Its the most important meal of the day,' Lieutenant Wrendigsya said. 'Even if it is a bowl of rice porridge and salty chocolate syrup in these parts. You can't get a decent fry-up for love nor money.'

'Argh, rice porridge. The salty chocolate syrup doesn't sound too bad, but rice porridge.' Even thinking about it had put a brake on his enthusiasm for breakfast.

'Around here, before breakfast, nothing is formal. After breakfast, we work through to the evening, respecting Estar's precocious protocol, isn't that right dear?'

'Thank you Lieutenant, we will have to agree to disagree,' Commander Yestarnsya replied.

'Although, we don't have time for a lunch hour,' said the Commander. 'I suggest a twenty minute lunch break at 1330.'

'Twenty minutes,' Lieutenant Wrendigsya was horrified. 'I haven't had a twenty minute lunch break for two decades. I'm not starting now.'

'I'm sorry, Lieutenant. I insist,' the Commander said icily.

'You might formally outrank me, but you don't outrank General Lilpingant. He set up the protocols for this facility, which state the Executive Officer defines the hours of business. As X.O. of this facility, I get to set the daily time-table,' said Wrendigsya loudly, 'and you have to respect that. We have an hour off for lunch at 1300.'

'Oh very well then,' said Commander Yestarnsya, with a resigned sigh. 'Let's go eat.'

During breakfast the two styles did the best they could to avoid avoid each other.

'This is another layer of fun to add to this already fun assignment,' Pemisegant said to Lieutenant Ryzinasant.

'Isn't it just, Pezzi my boy,' said the older anther.

'This porridge is horrible. How am I supposed to get a full morning's work done on this?' Pemizegant drizzled a spoonful of porridge back into his bowl.

'Leave it. Go and get a plate of steamed dumplings. They are full of bacon and egg,' said the Lieutenant as he popped another one into his mouth. 'But keep your spoon, unless you know how to use chopsticks.'

'Yes sir,' said the boy as he headed towards the counter.

'You only have five minutes to eat those, Subaltern' said the Commander when Pemisegant returned to the table with a bowl of dumplings.

'Yes Ma'am,' he replied, narrowly avoiding tipping his bowl as he saluted.

'Sir, why can't I find any knives or forks?' he asked as he sat back down.

'This is the Mid-Trunk Pezzi, bringing weapons to the dinner table is considered bad form here.'

Pemisegant considered this for a few minutes, as he ate the delicious savouries. The Commander had already returned to the Collection, and would no doubt be expecting him to quickly follow.

'I didn't think she had any family?' Pemisegant asked Lieutenant Ryzinasant.

'She doesn't,' replied Lieutenant Wrendigsya from the other table. 'My late brother-in-law could be very pigheaded. His daughter has inherited that trait and rejected my attempt to rebuilt a bridge between us. As far as I am concerned, she is just my superior officer.'

Why hadn't that crazy old besom retired? She must be touching thirty five by now, thought Commander Yestarnsya. I could put a more amenable person into her post. I suppose she will be bitching about me to my brother at the first opportunity.

'Great green apples, doesn't she ever loosen up?' asked Lieutenant Ryzinasant, as the clock ticked past 1800, ending another eventful day.

'She is driven, Sir,' replied Pemisegant.

'To the point of madness. You know, she might as well be a Tree-Nun and lock herself up in the Convent. I don't think she knows how to have fun.'

'How dare you!' neither anther had realised Commander Yestarnsya had still been in earshot, they had both assumed she had returned to the Hostel for the night. 'What right do you have to judge me and the way I live my life,' she looked like she was about to explode. 'No right, no right at all.'

'Ma'am.' Lieutenant Ryzinasant was taken aback by this sudden outburst.

'Don't say anything more. I am considering whether or not to report you.'

'Report him, Ma'am?' asked Pemisegant.

'Keep out of this boy, this is between the grown-ups.'

Pemisegant had not realised he had said anything. At the moment, the big ugly barracks he called home was a more attractive place to be.

Then turning her fury back to Lieutenant Ryzinasant, 'Are you one of these new radicals who think styles are inferior to anthers, is that it. Do you resent being commanded by a female?'

'No Ma'am. I find that suggestion far more offensive than anything I might have said. I demand an apology.'

There was an embarrassing stand off. Pemisegant watched as his superiors glowered at each other.

'Very well, I apologise for suggesting you are a Misogynist.'

'Thank you,' replied Ryzinasant. 'I also apologise for any inadvertant offence.' The two continued glowering at each other.

'Thank you Lieutenant, goodnight.' With that, she stormed out of the LPVS, back to her room in the hostel.

'Well, I didn't expect that,' said Lieutenant Ryzinasant. 'Thought she had already gone home.'

'I'm afraid you pushed all the wrong buttons there Sir,' said Pemisegant, again immediately regretting saying anything. He didn't want to make the Lieutenant as mad with him as the Commander was with the Lieutenant.

'Perhaps I should do something?'

'I wouldn't advise it, Sir. Not tonight anyway,' suggested Pemisegant. 'Let her calm down a bit.'

'You have an old head on a young body, Pezzi.'

'Not too old. I still know how to have fun,' replied Pemisegant, trying to lighten the atmosphere, 'you still up for a game of Bar Billiards or two tonight Rycky?'

'Of course Pezzi.' Ryzinasant smiled, 'this time I am going to beat you.'

'Yeah, right.'

'Like I said, an old head on young shoulders. I used to think I was the youngest person in the Tree who still played the game.'

'Nonsense, there is a table in the common room at home, it is always busy.' Pemisegant laughed 'Bar Billiards, Darts, Dominoes and Pool. All the retro games are really popular at the moment.'

She knew Lieutenant Ryzinasant was watching her, just pretending to be looking at the clock on the wall. She had been in a state all day. She had gone too far yesterday. She seemed to be losing her temper a lot recently. Ever since Ryzinasant had entered her life, messing with her well ordered emotions. What was he doing to her?

'Time for us to clock off,' she said, finding herself smiling.

'Thank you Ma'am. It's been a long day.'

'Yes Lieutenant. I have to apologise for the way I reacted yesterday. It was rude and unprofessional.'

'No worries Ma'am. I shouldn't have said what I did. It was also unprofessional,' Lieutenant Ryzinasant replied graciously. 'My informal name is Rycky, by the way.'

How do I deal with this overture, she thought. This anther infuriated her at times, he also fascinated her. However, he was a colleague and she had always believed in keeping working relationships formal. But that smile, oh Mother Sun that smile. 'And you might as well call me Estar, now we're off duty,' she found herself saying. Accepting it and enjoying the full opera she concluded. That was the only way to deal with the overture.

'Thank you, Estar,' he replied.

'Rycky.' No, you are not a "Rycky" she thought, you're a "Rich", because you have such a rich singing voice, thought Yestarnsya. A rich voice and smoldering good looks, you can sing to me anytime. She realised she was grinning, oh for goodness sake, pull yourself together, one side of her personality was telling her, whilst another side complained loudly that it didn't want to pull itself together.

'Have you decided where you are going for your meal tonight?' she asked. 'I know you are planning on eating out?'

'Not yet, Estar,' replied Ryzinasant. 'I thought I would take a stroll through the town, to see what takes my fancy,' he replied.

'Do you mind if I join you. I don't fancy eating alone tonight and having a local to guide you can never be a bad thing,' Yestarnsya found herself saying.

'Of course you can,' he said, with a dazzling smile. 'No talking shop though,' Ryzinasant said with a grin. 'Down time is down time.'

'OK Rycky, I do know how to relax,' she found herself saying.

Pemisegant was exhausted by the time he returned to his billet that evening. Almost too tired to write his daily email to Nevamarsya. The message had to be written and sent through a third party. Aunt Sharlee had not yet forgiven him. However, Pemisegant thought, there was something far more romantic about reading a letter than a simple face to face video call. As he typed he realised how much he was missing his girlfriend. Exactly two weeks until he returned to the Roots, with no knowing if Aunt Sharlee had forgiven him enough to let him see Nevamarsya.

He had left his front door slightly ajar, so heard the approaching voices in the corridor beyond. It was probably the Commander and the Lieutenant back from wherever they had disappeared on one of their evening trip.

'Thank you Rycky, it was another very entertaining evening,' said Yestarnsya.

'Yes Estar, it was fun wasn't it?'

'Although I do feel guilty leaving young Pezzi with so many solo night shifts,' said Yestarnsya. She actually did sound guilty.

'When you set up the rota, he didn't object because you gave him the following morning as downtime to compensate.' Ryzinasant said. 'And you need the breaks, there's more to life than work.'

'I suppose you are right,' she said. She had become very work orientated. 'Yes, this evenings has been fun.'

'Exactly,' said Ryzinasant.

Pemisegant knew that the Lieutenant must be smiling. On the journey up here he had said he wanted to make the boss have some fun for a change. 'After today, Pezzi is probably sound asleep and will enjoy his lie-in tomorrow.'

'If he knows what's good for him. So, I'll see you first thing in the morning then,' Ryzinasant continued.

'Yes, back to work,' said Yestarnsya.

On the security camera Pemisegant saw the Commander awkwardly offering her hand to be shaken. Oh come on Ricky, he thought take the next step, kiss her hand instead of shaking it.

'How about going for another meal tomorrow night?'

'Oh, yes, of course. I look forward to it,' she said as Lieutenant Ryzinasant opened the door of his quarters. She was speaking in a soft absent minded voice Pemisegant had never heard before. 'Hello, are you alright Pezzi?' she asked as she pushed the door of his quarters open.

Oh great green apples, I thought I had closed that door, Pemisegant thought. He decided to pretend being asleep in his chair. He was half way there already. Once he surrendered to his tiredness, pretence rapidly became reality. Even so, he could not fail to notice she was calling him Pezzi now.

'You should be in bed now, my boy.' There was definitely something different about the tone. It wasn't the usual hectoring, it had a definite friendly feel to it.

'Yes mum,' he said. There was no difficulty in sounding genuinely groggy. Letting one vowel slip to another.

'Off you go, and turn your light off. You might have the morning off tomorrow, but you won't appreciate it if you don't get a good nights sleep.'

'Thanks mum,' he said again as he climbed into the bed.

'I'll lock the door on my way out.'

'Thanks mum,' he repeated absentmindedly and was fast asleep within a minute.

H ad young Pemisegant called her mum? It wasn't the first time. It had been light hearted on that occasion, she had not been pleased. Tonight it was accidental, so she would play along with it for a while, a little harmless fun. Although Yestarnsya was surprised by how much she liked it. Had her mother experienced the same thrill when she had been called mum by Yestarnsya and her brother?

Once again, the young anther had reminded her of her parents. This time she was thinking about her mother, a serious minded style from whom Yestarnsya had inherited her stoicism. Her mother must have been the age she was now when she had pair bonded and started her family. First adopting Yestarnsya's older brother, then a few years later herself. She realised how much she missed both her parents and began to cry. Huge wracking sobs shook her entire body. The feeling of loneliness was all engulfing.

She felt a comforting arm around her shoulder. It was her Aunt, the style she had blocked from her life for so many years.

'I'm sorry Aunty Wren, so sorry,' she said like a penitent child.

'It's alright dear. I understand entirely. I tried locking myself away from everybody, when I found out my husband was being unfaithful.'

'I remember, you tried to become a novice Tree-Nun,' said Yestarnsya.

'That's right. But they knew I was running from something. They told me to return to my old life and stop trying to use their life to get away from my troubles.'

'I can't imagine you as a Tree-Nun, Aunty Wren. You're too full of life.'

'And I can't imagine you as one either, my dear.'

'You heard that outburst yesterday as well?' Yestarnsya began laughing as she asked the question.

'That's more like it. You know, your mother would hate to see you so miserable.' Wrendigsya smiled. 'Your father as well.'

'I know Aunty Wren,' she looked at the other style, always so happy. 'You managed to mend your life. Can you help me to mend mine?'

'Of course I can dear girl. But I think you have someone close at hand who would do a better job,' said the older style sagely.

'We're just friends Aunty,' replied Yestarnsya. Tonight had proved that she and Ryzinasant were more than colleagues. 'Good friends.'

'Well, that's a start,' replied Wrendigsya, 'a very good start.'

Commander Yestarnsya watched her young trainee working his way through the row of cars he had been assigned to audit.

Since arriving at the Heartswood, not only had they caught up with the delay caused by their late arrival, thanks to young Pemisegant, they were actually ahead of schedule. The boy continued to reminded her of her late Father. It had been from him she had inherited her curiosity about how things worked and she had followed him into the R&D Regiment. Just like Pemisegant he had an impulsive streak, but her Father had never displayed the recklessness of her young assistant. No, she thought, it must have been the impulsiveness that lead to him pair-bond with a style half his age. Whoever eventually adopted Pemisegant would have a wonderful son. She felt slightly envious of this unknown stranger.

'Have you had your lunch yet Son?' She asked absent mindedly.

'Not yet, mum,' he looked up from his bench. 'Once I have finished recalibrating this sensor, I'll go get something.'

'That can wait. You're on a late shift again tonight, and won't have a chance to grab a snack whilst you are here on your own.' She pointed towards the exit. 'You had better go and get a good meal now.'

'O.K. Mum, I'm on my way.'

That's odd, thought Pemisegant as he left the LPVS. Normally the boss would have exploded at any sort of familiarity.

Was she softening a bit. Was there a person under that frightening exterior after all.

His wrist-com pinged. A message from Nevamarsya. It was a bit garbled. He hit the dial button on the screen and was instantly connected to her.

'Pezzi, I'm so glad to see your face,' said Nevamarsya. Pemisegant didn't think he had ever seen her looking so happy. There was an edge though, her voice quavering. 'It's Uncle Bernie. He's been freed at last.'

Nevamarsya's voice was becoming even more quivery. 'Oh Pegs. All that hassle we went through, but it was worth it, he has been completely exonerated.'

That was it, tears were trickling down Nevamarsya's face. She looks so young. Don't be stupid Pezzi she is young, so are you, he thought. Aunt Sharlee is right, what we did was stupid.

The connection had been cut. He must still be persona non grata. Aunt Sharlensya had let him get the good news from his girlfriend, and only the good news.

'That's great news Pezzi,' said Yestarnsya. 'I couldn't help over-hearing. I've known Uncle Bernie all my life. He was a great friend of my father. Aunty Wren had an enormous crush on him.'

'I did not!' said the older style.

'You did too,' replied her neice.

The Commander shared Nevamarsya's look of shocked exhaustion and jubilation, seasoned with the inquisitive. 'She said, all the hassle you went through? When you have the time, you will have to explain.'

'I, um, had better, um get my lunch.' Pemisegant was beginning to be a bit freaked out by the Commander. She definitely wasn't herself.

'Take an extra hour, you're in shock and obviously need it.'

'But the audit, Ma'am,' he said

Pemisegant felt an arm on his shoulder.

'We are ahead of ourselves, so it can wait an extra hour. Go and get yourself calmed down.'

To Pemisegant's horror, he began crying. The Commander handed him a hanky, and he blew his nose.

'See. You're in no fit state at the moment.'

'Thank you,' he said, and headed off for his lunch. It wasn't just the good news that was causing his shock. This was not a face of Commander Yestarnsya he was used to seeing.

CHAPTER TWENTY FOUR
SONS AND LOVERS

The Heartswood could be a nightmare labyrinth for the unwary. Popisedsya had invited him for lunch her favourite restaurant close to her new billet. So Pemisegant made sure he had downloaded the most up to date maps from the Statistical Navigation Network to his Stat-Nav device, that it was fully charged with a good connection to that network. Even so, it was a confusing journey.

'Pezzi, you found the place then?' she asked as he walked into the restaurant.

'Yes, I'm more concerned about getting back to the hostel in Central Square.'

'Oh, there is no need to worry about that. Getting to the middle of the Tree is easy, make sure the streets get narrower.'

Strange, she was wearing a pair of Officer Corps uniform bib and braces dungarees, people around here called them overalls. Only farmers wore them. Surely a warehouse admin officer would wear a normal uniform on duty. Not that Pemisegant really cared, she was smiling, which meant she was happy again.

'So how have you been?' he asked politely.

'I have been very well, thank you Pezzi,' she embraced him, kissing both cheeks. 'It is so nice to see you. What brings you to the Heartswood?'

'My current posting. It's with the Archives Department of the Research and Development Regiment. I am assisting in a stock-take of the Large Vehicular Prototypes Collection.'

'The Bangers and Mash,' said Popisedsya with a giggle.

'I've never heard it called that before,' Pemisegant replied, but it did make a better title than LVPS.

'A little bit of local colour,' she said. 'I don't suppose you've heard my news?' asked Popisedsya.

'I didn't think working as an administrator in a Rice Warehouse counted as news. I thought your branch of your Family owned a farm around here? Why aren't working on that during the Summer?' asked Pemisegant, tactfully as ever, as he loaded something crispy onto his chopsticks, not noticing the shiney new rank pips.

'Yes and no. My Grandfather, Pensioner Remixerant 078/23 Siylm owned a rice farm two decks down from here. The day to day running was the responsibility of my cousin, Commander Rolinalant 123/72 Siylm, and he had no vacancies this Tour.'

I've obviously said something wrong, thought Pemisegant, he could see Popisedsya's face dropping.

'Oh, I see,' he replied.

'And then at a meeting of the local Thread of the Family Forum my Grandfather announced the terms of his Living Will. He has given the farm to me.'

Pemisegant was at a loss for words.

'I know, crazy isn't it?' continued Popisedsya.

'How did your cousin react to the news? I take it he was as shocked as you were?' Pemisegant asked, having finally gotten his head into gear.

'Extremely badly, he and his cronies marched out of the Thread Meeting and off the farm.' Popisedsya was laughing. 'You wouldn't fancy transferring to the Agricultural Regiment, I need all the help I can get at the moment?'

Was that Pemisegant over there. What on Arbouron was he doing here? Oh yes, he had the morning off and was meeting a former colleague from the Winter Squad for lunch.

'Commander Yestarnsya?' The boy had just spotted her.

'Just Yestarnsya, whilst you're off duty you know.' However, before she could answer, the boy was speaking again.

'Sorry, automatic respect for the uniform,' Pemisegant said apologising. 'It's just I wasn't expecting to find you here. It's a bit of the beaten track.'

'Oh, where are my manners.' Pemisegant stood up and pointed towards his friend. 'Mum, this is Commander Popisedsya 100/97 Siylm. We worked together in the Winter Squad.' and then turning towards his superior officer. 'Poppy, this Commander Yestarnsya 170/54 Nott, my commanding officer.'

'A pleasure to meet you Commander Yestarnsya,' said Popisedsya.

Yestarnsya knew the other style thought she was from the Canopy, as she was shaking her hand. The traditional off duty greeting from up there.

'And a thousand blessings upon meeting you,' said Yestarnsya as she bowed, the traditional Mid Trunk greeting. 'This restaurant was an old haunt of mine. I haven't been back for years.' She was smiling wickedly. 'I'm booking a table for tomorrow night.'

Was he imagining things, thought Pemisegant, or was the boss embarrassed to be here?

'I'm not late am I?' Pemisegant asked.

'No Pezzi, I'm taking back some time owed to me. I finished an hour early. Although I'm glad I found you. I'm going to the Cinema tonight. I'll have to switch my comlink off.'

Taking time off during the working day and going to the cinema in the evening. Was this really his boss? Yes, it was and Pemisegant approved of the changes.

'Yes Mum. You and dad have fun. If there's a problem, Aunty Wren will be on duty until 1800.'

'Kindly refrain from referring to myself and the Lieutenant as "Mum and Dad", Subaltern,' she said to him. A little formality returning to her voice. 'So much for respect for the uniform.'

'Yes Mum, sorry Mum.'

'Oh, I give up,' replied Yestransya, all the formality had vanished from, her voice. 'Make sure you are in bed by 2230 dear. We have a long day ahead of us tomorrow.'

'Don't worry Mum, I intend to.'

'I'm your Mother, it's my job to worry, Son,' she smiled at him, 'two can play that game. And yes, I am going out with Rycky again.'

'As if I didn't know,' said Pemisegant.

'OK. We shall see you tomorrow.'

Yestarnsya hugged him and gave him a peck on the cheek. He could see her heading for the door, with a song in her heart and a spring in her heel.

Great green apples, what is wrong with me, Yestarnsya thought as she left the restaurant. This little joke is starting to get out of hand. Had she really called herself young Pemisegant's mother, and hugged him in public. That sort of demonstrative display of affection just was not like her. Or was it. She had been surprised at how easily she had taken to being in charge of that boy's life, not just on duty, but off as well. And he was such a typical anther, he was glad when an older and wiser style took him in hand. She supposed it was because they were in such close contact everyday whilst here at Heartswood. On their return to the Roots they would go their separate ways, her back to her apartment, him back to the barracks.

Now there was a horrible thought, going back to a loveless Barracks for Unadopted Children. No doubt similar to where she had spent six terrible months prior to being introduced to her parents. What a strange system they had here in the Tree. In a year from now Pemisegant would have to go through the adoption process. She knew now, she would be the style who gave him that most precious of gifts, making her his real Mother.

'So,' Popisedsya asked once Yestarnsya had left, 'how long before she really is your mother? Twelve months?'

'I don't know what you mean Poppy, it's just a joke,' he looked at his friend, was she being serious?

'Oh come off it Pezzi that was no joke. Those were the actions of a really fussy mother and an embarassed son, not a Commanding Officer having a few light minutes with a young subordinate.'

'Do you think so?' Pemisegant really hadn't considered the question of family. Nevamarsya and Natalicsya had both landed on their feet, finding parents immediately.

'Yes Pezzi, I do. You're so grown-up and yet still a child inside. The way you called that style "mum". You don't realise it, but you mean it. And did you see how her face lit up when you did call her "mum". That's the real thing.

He looked at his friend, 'Anyway I'm still too young to be actively looking for parents.'

'Not really. The sooner the better.' Popisedsya picked up the last piece of vat grown chicken with her chopsticks waving it as she spoke. 'Is she pair-bonded, is there a potential father in the equation?'

'My potential adoption is not on the horizon at the moment. However, the way she and Rycky, that's Lieutenant Ryzinasant by the way, have hit it off during this trip, I wouldn't be at all surprised if they are tieing the knot.'

'If I were a friend of either of your two superiors, should I be considering buying a new hat?'

'Poppy, what's that got to do with headwear?'

'Didn't you know, if she's not one of the bondsmaids, a style always wears a hat, usually a new one, at a pair-bondings.'

'No, I didn't. Any reason why?'

'Don't ask me, I was rubbish at History,' said Popisedsya fishing in her purse for her IndesnCard. 'Thank you for a pleasant lunch.'

'No, thank you,' he said putting his card on the table.

'We must do this again,' said Popisedsya.

'Yes, its been great,' he replied, realising he had no idea what to do next. Saluting would be wrong and a handshake too formal. To his surprise Popisedsya hugged him. Twice in five minutes. But this was different, it was just for show. It didn't have the emotion of the hug his mother-to-be had given him. Stop it, the Commander is not my mother-to-be.

'I'll ring you next week, to arrange something. Just before you head back down to the roots.' And with that he was left watching his friend head for the exit.

Pemisegant quickly found his way back to the centre of the Tree. Popisedsya had been right about at least one thing, it was easier to get back than to get out. She was completely wide of the mark about Commander Yestarnsya. The day he had first met her, he had known there was not an ounce of maternal feeling in her. Except things were different now. Since the start of this trip she had changed. During the first week of this posting, when he had driven a splinter into his finger, her efforts to extract it had been purely functional and delayed by the paperwork she had been doing. A few days ago, when he had cut himself on a loose floor panel on a catamaran, her first aid had been embarrassingly melodramatic in his opinion. She had become far more demonstrative since the day Tabbernant had been released.

Also he began to realise that his actions in work over the past few weeks had been more than just trying to impress a difficult boss. He now realised that he wanted her to be proud of him.

Still everything would change again when they got back to the Roots. He would move back into his dorm room, the one he shared with Althallant, Francelant and Olmskirant. Oh Tree preserve him, did he really have to go back. Sharing with his best friend Althallant wasn't too bad, but the other two just wound him up. He missed the room he had up in the Canopy. On the same corridor as Aunty Sharlee, her daughters and the other cadets, it had been more like a family home. The Barracks was so loveless.

Damn, what was Mum doing over there, wasn't she supposed to be getting ready to go out with Ryzinasant. The cinema wasn't it. A musical set in the tenth decade, when people had worn funny clothes and the Tree had been so much simpler.

Speaking of funny clothes, Pemisegant knew his friend Natalicsya would have something to say about what Mum was wearing. A lose fitting brown tunic and jeans. Was that make-up, she must obviously be out of practice.

'Pemisegant, I think we need to talk,' Yestarnsya said.

'We do?' he replied disarmingly.

'Yes, Son, we do,' she said. 'You know, all those weeks ago, I was only looking for an assistant. Someone to work with. I wasn't looking for someone to care for. Someone to be responsible for. I thought my chance to be a mother was passed. Soon you are going to need a gift only a mother can give. Will you let me give you that gift? Will you let me be your mother?'

Pemisegant looked at the style who had just asked him the most important question of his young life. Then he spotted the Enforcer standing to one side witnessing this little chat. Yestarnsya was serious.

'Oh Mum, I thought you would never ask,' he replied. Where had that come from. Pemisegant didn't know. At that point he didn't care. 'Of course you are my Mother. And I will make you proud as your Son.'

'So Ma'am, that exchange has been recorded and sent to the Family Affairs Bureau, to document any formal application you make. Congratulations to the pair of you,' the Enforcer said. 'Now, if you will excuse me, I will leave you two to celebrate.' With that he was on his way.

'Some celebration,' said Pemisegant, 'I've got a late shift at Banger's and Mash.'

'Oh, forget that tonight. We're all going out to celebrate,' said Yestarnsya.

'Are you feeling alright, Mum?' he asked his new mother-to-be.

'Of course I am Pezzi. Don't knock it, it may not happen again. But tonight is a night off for everyone.' Then Yestarnsya asked 'Bangers and Mash?'

'It's what my friend Popisedsya called the LVPS.'

She started to laugh. 'Oh Pezzi, I love you, you make me happy.'

'I love you to Mum,' he said. And it was for real. No longer a joke to help make a boring job more bearable. She was his mother-to-be and he was now part of a family.

Only five more days left in the Heartswood. Yestarnsya looked at the great cascades, safe behind an impenetrable wall of Protein and Mineral Glass. Spotlights illuminating the water as it fell like liquid jewels.

She used to keep her heart locked away behind walls as impenetrable. So much had changed over the past few weeks. She had forged an unbreakable parental bond with Pemisegant, and tonight with Ryzinasant, everything had changed.

A few weeks ago, sensible and dull Yestarnsya would not

have gone out for the evening with Ryzinasant. She would not have gone dancing with him into the small hours of the Dawnsward. She would not have been dancing in a dress like this. Great green apples, a few weeks ago she had been so very boring.

Their first night out had been an education.

'Why don't we give this one a try?' Ryzinasant asked, at the entrance to one restaurants in the maze of streets in Heartswood. 'Can't you smell the delicious spices?'

'Exactly, all those horrid mouth burning compounds that make it impossible to taste anything.'

They were walking past a restaurant that specialised in the cuisine of the Lower-Trunk.

'You have obliviously never had a well prepared meal from my home region, have you Estar?' he asked rhetorically. 'Yes, there is the fire, but if you can't taste the other ingredients, then what is the point of the spices.'

'Well then, show me what a good Curry should be like.'

'Well the first lesson,' he said with a smile 'is "Curry" is a word you will never hear in the Lower-Trunk.'

She had really enjoyed the experience. She had discovered so many subtle flavours and aromas she had never encountered before. Having such a knowledgeable and entertaining teacher made all the difference.

A few nights later, she had repaid the favour by teaching him to use chopsticks, Mid-Trunk style. She was certain he deliberately dropped the sticks, as an excuse to get her to hold his hands as she placed the sticks back into place.

So it continued, with the pair going out more often, until it had become a nightly occurrence. The time they stayed out had also increased. After a pleasant meal tonight, Yestarnsya and Ryzinasant had walked past a small group of people waiting outside a doorway. The group all wore fur trimmed velvet clothing, fake tails and a cat masks.

'Good gracious! Exclaimed Yestarnsya 'A KatKitKlub. I haven't seen a nightclub like this for years. I don't think I have been in one since I was an Ensign.'

'Don't tell me that by-the-book Yestarnsya used to indulge in under-age clubbing?'

'Yes Rich, I was a bit of a rebel before it all went wrong. I was never asked to show proof of age once. I suspect it was because I'm so tall,' she smiled, 'My very straight laced mother would've had kittens, if I had been caught.'

'Was that a joke?' asked Ryzinasant with mock sincerity.

'It was indeed,' she replied, keeping a strait face.

This sort of nightclub came and went out of fashion on a regular basis. Yestarnsya remembered the tail end of their previous burst of popularity, when clubs were closing on a daily basis. Those that remained open turned a blind eye to the age of their customers in their desperation to remain open.

'Sorry folks, there's a problem,' a style said to the group as she arrived at the entrance. 'I got my schedule wrong, and Dezsh won't come here without me.' The style's uniform and disappointed expression told the rest of the story.

'OK Lexza, maybe next time,' said one of the styles. Once Lexza was out of sight, she turned to Yestarnsya. 'Excuse me, would you like these two spare tickets?'

'Sorry Ma'am, Sir,' one of the club's bouncers said to Yestarnsya and Ryzinasant, 'if you want to come in, you have to follow the club's dress code.'

'Oh don't worry Chigo,' the style said to the bouncer, 'they can borrow the outfits Lexza and Dezsh were going to wear. I'm Kalzonisya, by the way. This is my husband Revwixlant and these are our friends Tiannamsya and Bernaddant.'

'Hello, I'm Yestarnsya, don't worry, I still have an old Kit-Kat Dress. This is Ryzinasant, he will have to borrow something.'

'Pleased to meet you. We're with the Museums Division of the Historians Regiment.'

'Ryzinasant and I are from the Archives Section of R&D.' The doors of the club had opened.

'Do they sell KatKit masks here?' Yestarnsya asked Tiannamsya.

'Yes, there's a small membership fee on your first visit, the cost of the masks can be added to that,' said the style. 'Emprinting booths just inside the foyer, see you on the dancefloor.'

'You're not serious Estar, are you?'

'Yes Ricky, very serious. I fancy a dance, don't you?'

'Well Ezzia, are you ready?' Ryzinasant had asked as he waited outside the changing booth.

'Yes Rich, how to I look?' she replied with her own question.

'That's amazing Ezzia,' said Ryzinasant, blown away by the transformation.

She wore a low cut and short yellow velvet dress trimmed with saffron fur and a tail. The top of her face behind a golden cat mask.

'Good. Because I'm feeling amazing. At least five years younger,' she took a few minutes to inspect Ryzinasant's new outfit.

'You're looking very smart,' she said.

'No I'm not Estar, I always look ridiculous in velvet. In this dark blue velvet jumpsuit, with tail and cat mask, doubly so.'

'You can be really boring sometimes, Rich,' she laughed.

'Who are you, and what have you done to the real Yestarnsya?'

'I'm here. The avatar I wore for too long is back in its box, for good.'

Then at the end of the evening it happened. The DJ had put a couple of slow songs on a digiplayer as she started to pack away her old fashioned music platter equipment she had been using.

'I love you so much Rich. I think I always have.'

'Well Ezzia I know I have always loved you.'

So they kissed. Not the chased peck as a sign of friendship and thanks for a pleasant evening. A proper kiss, on the dancefloor. Its effect had been like a bolt of electricity passing between them.

The water was still cascading down through Heartswood, behind its impenetrable wall, as it always had and always would.

Now it was impossible for her to put her heart back behind its impenetrable barrier, not that she had wanted to. Which is why, when she had returned to her room she had changed into her sensible pyjamas. Then she switched on the emprinter and they turnedt into a negligee that was silky and short. She switched off the emprinter, its screen becoming simply a full length mirror again, in which she examined herself.

Here goes nothing she thought, as she knocked gently on the knocked connecting door between her room and his. The final step. After all, they were using romantic names for each other.

'Rich,' she asked softly, 'can I come in?'

The lock on the door clicked open. She looked back at the bed in the room. I won't be sleeping in that again.

Only Three days left in the Trunk. Pemisegant would be sad to leave. He knew he would never get tired of seeing the water cascading.

The comlink chimed.

'Pemisegant,' he said as he answered the call.

'Pezzi, we need you back at the collection. Something's happened.' Was that terror Pemisegant could hear in his half-mother's voice.

'On my way, Mum.'

'Pezzi dear, you'd better bring your Wellingants with you.'

'OK Mum, I'll be right there.' Wonderful, he thought. My first afternoon off this week, and I get called back into the office. Mum sounds really spooked. She's there with Ricky and Aunty Wren why did they need me.

'And Pezzi, remember to keep it formal at work. There's a good boy,' she said as she cut the line.

As he left his room in the hostel, he grinned the sort of grin that only an adolescent boy could. Pemisegant knew that although he had seen her emerge from her room for the past two mornings, a gossipy sprite had told him that her bed had been undisturbed. It did look as if he would be getting a father as well.

'Well then, Subaltern, what do you make of this,' said Lieutenant Ryzinasant as Pemisegant entered the room.

'Great green apples,' said Pemisegant as he saluted his superior officer. 'Sir.'

The whole of the upper floor of the LVPC was covered in brown water which was rushing down to the lower floors, wherever it could. The water was flowing, like a fountain, through a large crack in a wall, just below the ceiling, so roughly at street level outside the building. Any further inundation was caught in a large tub drained by an electric pump.

'Indeed Subaltern, indeed.'

'Where did all this water come from?' Pemisegant asked his superior.

'Your guess is as good as mine.' The Lieutenant was busy mopping up the dirty water. 'Its not from the great cascade. That is for certain. As they say around here, the Tree would have to fall over before that wall cracked.'

Pemisegant turned around and saw a face he had not seen for weeks. His Commanding Officer had a face like thunder. Neither he nor Ryzinasant said anything, they just reached for mops.

Ryzinasant could see, as his young colleague sluicing up the water, the youngster was totally oblivious to everything but the mess. At this rate, he would clean it up single handedly in a morning. The sprites that Lieutenant Wrendigsya was requisitioning would be surplus to demand. Then he noticed Commander Yestarnsya was crying. She was in a mess, all her usual bluff and bluster washed away.

'Ezzie, what's the matter?' asked Ryzinasant.

'You mentioned the wall cracking Rich. Why do you think myself and everyone around here make so much about the strength of the Wall? Its because we are all secretly terrified that it will crack one day,' she had gone completely white. 'This sort of unexplained flooding plays on that fear.'

Ryzinasant put his arm around her and handed her a hanky. 'I'm sorry my love.'

She sniffed. 'Look at me being so silly, the Tree would fall before the Wall breaks,' she said like a sacred mantra, one she was having difficulty believing.

'Of course it would,' he said in a reassuring voice. 'That Wall is the backbone of the Tree.'

With that a smile returned to her face and she kissed Ryzinasant's cheek.

'Thank you, Rich.'

'For what?' he asked.

'Just for being here. For being you. I couldn't imagine my life without you now.'

'Are Maintenance or Hydrology looking for the leak?' he heard Pemisegant ask, from the other side of the room. The boy had his back to them, emptying yet another bucket down the big sink.

'They are both looking into it, son,' said Yestarnsya.

'Thank you, Ma'am. It shouldn't be long before they know?'

'It's something the authorities will investigate as a matter of urgency Subaltern,' replied Lieutenant Ryzinasant. 'This sort of leak could be connected to something serious elsewhere in the Trunk.'

'I hope not, Ricky,' Yestarnsya said. 'Although nobody has worked out the full extent of the damage done by the Tree-quake last Dixtemp. The whole trunk moved for the first time in decades.'

Then Pemisegant realised how relaxed his new half-mother was, even using his informal name. It looked as if the old Ice Maiden was now permanently thawed.

'Pezzi,' she said, 'have you heard when the sprites we ordered will arrive?'

'About ten minutes, Ma'am,' he replied, not yet responding to the change in tone.

'I know what I said, but I think we can forget about formalities today. You are as wet and grubby as I am.'

The words went over Pemisegant's head. He was too busy watching Lieutenant Ryzinasant.

'Mum, I think Dad has something to say to you?'

'Ezzie,' said Ryzinasant, who was kneeling on the floor in dirty water, looking mildly ridiculous. 'I've loved you since the day we met. In the past month we have become very close. Do you love me as much as I love you? Will you pair-bond with me, my darling?

'Of course I will Rich,' she replied with a silly grin plastered on her face. Although what else would she say.

Ryzinasant slipped a silver ring with a perfect turquoise stone onto her finger then stood up. 'This was my grandmother's engagement ring. Do you like it.'

'Oh Rich, it's beautiful,' she said and kissed him.

A group of giggling sprites ruined the perfect moment.

'Well, I'm blowed,' Wrendigsya said, 'I go off to get some sprites to clean this place up, and I miss all the good stuff.'

Yestarnsya looked up from her fiance straight into the glowering face of her aunt. This just made the moment all the more perfect. To be surrounded by the people she loved most in the entire Tree.

'Don't worry Aunty Wren, there is the bonding ceremony to plan. You're my nearest female relative after my Mum. She won't be able to do it, so you're the one who has to arrange it.'

'Such a shame about your Mam, but that said, a Bonding Ceremony to plan, loving it already,' said Wrendigsya, whose face was now beaming.

'Although,' Yestarnsya continued, 'the milliners won't be run off their feet. I have lost touch with so many friends.'

'Well dear, this is the perfect time to get back in touch.' Wrendigsya always seemed to know the right thing to say.

'And there is someone else who would love to buy a new hat for the occasion, isn't there?' asked Aunty Wren.

'Yes there is. I'm sure my Sister would love to come,' Yestarnsya replied. 'Would you make overtures, I wouldn't know where to begin,' said Yestarnsya. 'Also I don't think she would reply if I tried to contact her.'

'And I can bring along my rent-a-crowd Mum,' said Pemisegant helpfully.

'Thanks Son,' she said. Oh bless him, so totally unaware of the nuances of the situation.

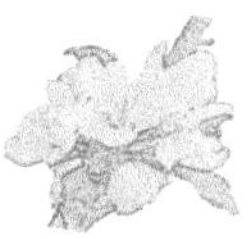

CHAPTER TWENTY FIVE

SEARCH AND RESCUE

Like all farms in the Trunk the, Popisedsya's inheritance had thirteen wedge shaped fields surrounding the main farm house, like a sliced pizza.

The porch, garden and the garage for the farm's cars and agricultural vehicles were the only things above ground. Stairs led from the porch to an airlocked entrance hall. Although only the tractors now remained in the garage, as Rolinalant and his cronies had taken all their cars.

As you went around the fields, you went from fallow to newly planted to mature and finally harvested rice. By growing several different varieties of Rice the farm would be in production all year round. Field Eight had just been harvested, with the last bag of rice dispatched to the Heartswood.

It was only because she had been in a probationary period in her previous posting she was even here now. There were plenty of family members who wanted to return to the farm. Sadly, they had to serve notice with their current postings, so they were unable to help bring this harvest in. Aunt Mae was able to send people from her farm for a few days, but Popisedsya's Granddad Max, and a dozen Sprites had done the bulk of the work. They were all totally exhausted.

Even after the return of family members, Popisedsya knew she would still have to go to Heartswood to recruit three more staff to fill the gap. She would also have to buy herself a car. Relying on taxis had worked when she had been an occasional visitor to the farm. As its owner it was completely impracticable. However, she could allow herself a few quiet days on the farm to recuperate, she had forgotten how tiring these harvests could be. In just under four weeks, Field Nine would be ready for harvesting. During that time all the other fields would need attention.

Rain in the Trunk was computer controlled irrigation falling from hidden vents up amongst the daylighters. The sound of thunder would be alien to everyone who lived in the Tree, so Popisedsya could not recognize the low rumbling she heard as the farm's transporters took off with their cargo.

'Little Flower, are you alright?' asked Grandad Rex.

'Yes, I'm fine. I have no idea what that was, but I'm fine.'

At that point the water began falling in torrents.

'What the hell are Hydrology playing at? Nobody has ordered an irrigation burst,' said Remixerant. Water was falling not just on farms but throughout the deck. 'This is like the rain beyond the Tree I saw in my youth.'

'I hope our drains will cope with this. Do you know when Rolly last had them cleaned?' Popisedsya asked.

'About a month ago, I think. I have had very little to do with the day to day running of the Farm for years.'

She worried about the old anther. This is not how he should be spending the last year of his life, she thought.

'I am more concerned about the seals on our front door,' said Remixerant. 'We live under the fields, any water the drains cannot cope with will find its way down into the house.'

'The seals should be good, as long as this water does not rise to higher than the middle of the door.'

'Are you sure about that Poppy?' asked the old anther.

'No, it is a general rule of thumb,' she replied. The water continued to flow for hours, and soon the farm was under water. Even the garden was flooded, leaving the porch and the garage as the only pieces of dry ground for miles around. The seals on the door would not be a problem.

The house was not designed to be surrounded by so much water. Slowly but surely, it began to perculate into the living quarters back up through the drains. First the Sprite Barracks at the base had to be abandoned, then the bedrooms on the second layer. Soon the kitchen and living rooms on the top layer began filling with dirty brown water. Popisedsya regretfully came to the decision that as soon as the farm's cargo transporters returned, they would use them to escape the flood.

'Is that Commander Popisedsya?' asked an unknown anther at the end of the comlink.

'Speaking,' she replied tersely.

'I have some bad news, I'm afraid,' he said.

'Well get on with it, I'm waiting for my transports to return.'

'I'm afraid that is the bad news, Ma'am,' he paused ominously. 'The Transport Regiment have decided, given the weather conditions, to put a ban on all vehicles leaving the Heartswood for the next twelve hours.'

'Excuse me?' asked Popisedsya quietly and extremely politely. Everyone who knew her would say this was not a good sign.

'I'm afraid we cannot allow your transporters to return to your farm. Ma'am.'

'Excuse me?' she repeated, in a quieter voice, with more menace.

'You will have to wait for your vehicles to return.'

'Do you have any idea how difficult that makes my situation, Subaltern.'

'Its only for a few hours, Ma'am. You'll just have to wait,' he cut the link.

'Don't you walk away from me, get back here,' Popisedsya screamed at the screen. Then she took a deep breath and began meditating. The anther had been right, it was only a few hours, and it wasn't as if the water level could rise any further.

There was a loud rumbling. Popisedsya had learned to dread the sound of distant thunder. All around her, water began streaming from the sky again. Calmly she switched her link to the emergency channel. She knew in a few hours the porch would be inundated.

'Emergency! Emergency! This is Commander Popisedsya 100/97 Siylm calling from Rice Farm 10AB EF7. We require immediate assistance to evacuate this facility. I repeat, we require immediate assistance to evacuate this facility.'

L ast day at Heartswood. That evening the three would be travelling back down to the Roots. For the return journey they would be travelling together, in a family suite. No mistake this time.

'I'm concerned about my friend Popisedsya,' said Pemisegant. 'She was supposed to be coming up to Heartswood this afternoon to say goodbye.'

'Perhaps she is too busy dear,' said his Half-Mother. 'Didn't you say she has just inherited some property here in the Trunk?'

'Yes Mum, a big semi-automated Rice Farm, a few decks down.'

'Well, with all the flooding down there yesterday, she probably doesn't have time for social niceties.'

'Flooding, what flooding?' Pemisegant rarely watched the news or kept up with current affairs.

'Apparently an overflow tunnels from the rainmaker equipment has ruptured,' she disappeared into a side office for a few minutes, leaving Pemisegant to digest this information.

'Like that flood we had here a few days ago,' she continued when she returned to the room, 'Treequake related. They say that Hydrology is in melt-down. The only staff member who warned about this happening had been suspended for spreading malicious rumours, whilst the rest did nothing to stop these floods occurring.'

'Great green apples. Poppy could be in trouble!' said Pemisegant. 'No wonder I can't get a reply on the comlink.'

'There's no need to jump to conclusions Pezzi.'

He supposed she must be right. Never the less, it was the top of the hour. No harm in having the radio news on, find out what was happening.

'...gency! Emergency! This is Commander Popisedsya 100/97 Siylm calling from Rice Farm 10AB EF7. We require immediate assistance to evacuate this facility. I repeat, we need immediate assistance to evacuate this facility...'

Pemisegant had just turned the radio on.

'...That was the sound of the owner of one of the affected rice farms,' said the newsreader. 'The authorities have not heard from her for the past two hours. Sergeant Dockdixant, of the Green#1 Enforcer station, said that the remaining staff of the farm were still alive, as the Regional Command and Control Centre had launched a surveillance drone and had spotted them on the roof of the farm's Tractor Garage, which is now the largest flat dry area for miles around.'

'In other news,' continued the newsreader, 'more arrests are likely after the publication of another anonymous dossier...'

Pemisegant swithched off the radio. The room filled with an embarrassed silence.

'Why isn't anyone trying to help them?' asked Pemisegant.

'Because they can't Pezzi,' replied Lieutenant Ryzinasant. 'The entrance to that deck is flooded, nothing can get in or out.'

'We could,' said Commander Yestarnsya, 'we have the Velsonnant/Karapansya semi-submersible prototype here. That should be able to get through, it's rated for travel in the Central Channel.'

'If it's so good, why is it stuck in the non viable section of Bangers and Mash?' asked Lieutenant Wrendigsya. 'Are you sure its safe enough?'

'The development company went bust before they could go to the next stage of production, 'said Lieutenant Ryzinasant. 'It always amazed me that nobody ever snapped up the patent on that vehicle and took it into production.'

'They went bust because it was a terrible design,' said Lieutenant Wrendigsya. 'Too many functions crammed into too small a vehicle.'

'By the time the company folded, better vehicles doing the same job were already in production. That dinosaur never stood a chance,' said Lieutenant Yestarnsya.

'Mum, Dad, Aunty Wren, my friend is in danger, we have a way to help her, and all we are doing is discussing patent history.'

'I'm sorry, but that thing needs two qualified drivers, one at the wheel and the other to navigate because it predates the Stat-Nav-Net, only Wren here has a licence.'

'Seriously,' asked a flabbergasted Pemisegant, 'neither of you has ever learnt to drive.'

'Why should we, we live in the Hub of the Roots, with it's excellent public transport network.'

'But neither of you were born there?' Pemisegant just could not believe what he was hearing.

'True, but we were too young to learn when we were living in the Trunk.'

'Well its a good job I have a valid licence,' he said placing his IndesnCard on a reader. 'So, we have the two drivers.'

'How, you're only nine months old?' asked Wrendigsya.

'Everyone who was a cadet with the Winter Squad is taught to drive, it's vital for the Squad's functioning. Of course, most of them don't have forty two days combat experience, so have to wait until they are five years to get a full Drivers Licence.'

'They still have to pass the compotency test to get that licence,' said Yestarnsya.

'Like that was ever going to be a problem?'

'Right then Pezzi, if you're so smug, you can be my navigator in that monster,' said Wrendigsya. 'If we get the boss to agree?'

'OK then people, let's get going,' said Commander Yestarnsya, once again displaying her businesslike authority.

'Thanks mum.'

The Velsonnant/Karapansya Semi-submersible vehicle had been designed for underwater search and rescue work.

Theoretically it could fly to the location of the accident, convert to a subaquatic vehicle to find the damaged submarine, evacuate it and take any casualties to hospital. There was no doubt it worked, but it was too big and too slow to be an effective flying emergency vehicle. Also it was too small to be an effective underwater emergency vehicle.

'So, pre-take-off checks are complete,' said Wrendigsya, 'are we all aboard?'

Pemisegant was sitting next to her in the cock-pit. Yestarnsya and Ryzinasant were sitting in the paramedics seats in the hold, which was easily large enough to accommodate the two officers and twenty sprites from Popisedsya's farm.

'The roof door of the Collection building is open,' said Pemisegant, 'we can leave when you are ready.'

'OK, engaging anti-grav now,' said Wrendigsya joining the local traffic matrix.

The great teardrop shaped vehicle floated upwards through the space created by opening the Collection sliding roof.

'Unidentified vehicle, please note all traffic has been grounded until further notice,' said a voice over the comlink.

'Copy that Command and Control. This is a prototype rescue vehicle. Heading for the farm at 10AB EF7.'

'Unidentified vehicle, your transponder is not working. We have no way of confirming that. Until we receive a ping from your transponder, you are ordered to land.'

'Crap,' said Pemisegant under his breath. He got out of his seat and began unscrewing the housing of the Transponder control. 'Has anyone got a battery pack?' he asked.

'In the hold, Pezzi,' said Wrendigsya. 'Sorry, there isn't usually a need for the Transponder to be on, so it is stored away.'

'I'm bringing it up now.' Yestarnsya had unstrapped herself and was carrying the heavy battery pack up to the front of the vehicle.

'Thanks Mum,' he said, taking the heavy battery from her.

'I don't think I will ever tire of hearing that Pezzi,' she said as she helped him drop the antiquated battery pack into place.

'There we go, the transponder should be running now.'

'VK001 Alpha,' said the style at Command and Control. 'We have received your vehicle's data. It appears it is one of the few not affected by the ban on traffic. You are cleared to make your way to the farm at 10AB EF7. May the Tree bless you,' she said, 'and you manage to get to the people trapped there whilst they are still alive.'

'Thank you C and C,' said Wrendigsya 'VK001 Alpha, out.'

'**G**et out of my way, you pathetic little anther,' said Sergeant Kilkennsya as she returned to her old desk. Despite the late hour, the building was full of life. In her old office, were the eight familiar faces of her former colleagues who had been dragged from their beds. Unfortunately that also included Commander Dyscolnant, who was now barring her way.

'I'll get security to have you removed,' he said petulantly. 'You are under suspension. You have no clearance, you shouldn't even be in the building.' The Commander was unused to having his authority undermined

'I restored her clearance,' said the old anther who had arrived in the Office with Kilkennsya. 'Are you questioning my decision?'

'No, Captain Xandropant, Sir.'

'Not that I need the Captain's permission. Or hadn't you noticed?' said an annoyed Kilkennsya. She could see the Commander's day was about to go from bad to worse.

'But aren't you too ill to return to work, Sir?' Commander Dyscolnant asked, totally ignoring Kilkennsya.

'No, I was beginning a phased return to work tomorrow. It looks as if I will have to start it a few hours early.' Captain Xandropant eased himself back into his control desk.

'Very well, Sir,' Commander Dyscolnant said as he saluted. 'It's time for the Regimental Song anyway.'

He went over to a console in the wall and Music began filling the building.

'Belay that racket,' shouted the Captain and the speakers fell silent.

'But Sir, the Regimental Song instils group cohesion and is good for morale,' said the Commander, sounding like a whining child.

'Indeed, but if you must play it, get a decent recording, not one with that dreadful background screech.'

Kilkennsya was amazed, someone else can hear it. Her other former colleagues had said she was imagining the background noise.

She watched Commander Dyscolnant just standing there uselessly. But what else could he do, he was a PR officer, and not a very good one. He was just glued to the spot, emanating waves of weapons grade stupidity.

'Commander Dyscolnant, go make yourself useful,' said the Captain. 'The Instaht is still in the third locker in the Staff Room?'

'Er, yes Sir, but I...' Dyscolnant replied.

'Good, it's going to be a long night, we will all need a cup, go and make it, there's a good fellow,' orderd the Captain before the Commander could finish his objection.

'Oh, great green apples!' Finally Commander Dyscolnant noticed Kilkennsya's brand new brown uniform.

'Yes Commander, I have transferred to the Enquirers, as a trainee Analyst for the Special Protection Service.

'So, you'll be getting your petty revenge, arresting me on some trumped up charge, are you?'

'You have to do a six week Basic Police Procedures Course before you can arrest anyone. So, despite the colour of my uniform, I'm still a technician. Although your incompetence is responsible for this mess. As soon as we have this crisis sorted, one of my new colleagues will no doubt be along to do the honours.'

'So what are you doing here,' Dyscolnant asked, 'if you're a copper now?'

'The Captain asked if I could come in to help with this crisis. As it will aid an ongoing investigation, my new superiors were more than happy to oblige.'

There was a sound of sniggering coming from one of the desks.

'That's enough of that. We are in too much trouble for anyone to be amused about anything,' said the Captain. There was no doubt now that old anther was back in control. 'Sergeant Kilkennsya, you have five minutes to update your data, then I want some suggestions on how to solve this mess.'

'Yes, Sir,' she said, already busily studying the statistics. 'Aquatic landing achieved, switching to diving mode now.' Lieutenant Wrendigsya said as the vehicle landed gently on the lake where the trans-sectional tunnel used to be.

'Hydrology reports the next two levels are completely flooded out, Ma'am,' said Pemisegant who was relaying navigation data to Wrendigsya. 'Fortunately the drainage is better on the level of Popisedsya's farm. As long as no more water escapes from the irrigation reservoirs higher up the Trunk, the roof of her farm's out building will be higher than the flood level.'

'Estimated time of arrival at your friend's farm Subaltern?' asked Lieutenant Wrendigsya.

'0120 Hours tomorrow, Ma'am. That ETA is based on current reports from the sonar. If we have to bypass any tall structure, it could be up to three hours later in the dawnsward.'

'I'm down in the engine chamber now with Lieutenant Ryzinasant,' Commander Yestarnsya said over the intercom. 'We are attempting to engage the backup engines.'

'Ma'am,' said Lieutenant Wrendigsya, 'much as I would

appreciate the boost to our speed, I think we should keep the backups in reserve. We might need them later.'

'Copy that, Lieutenant. We will run a systems check only.'

Pemisegant didn't hold out much hope for the backup engines ever working, whatever his mother-to-be said. They were experimental engines back when this vessel had been built, and little had been done to maintain them in the intervening years.

'Precious little work going on down there,' said Lieutenant Wrendigsya, once the comlink had gone dead. 'Those two will be over each other like a rash.'

'Aunty Wren!' said an exasperated Pemisegant, 'really, at a time like this.'

'Wouldn't you and your lovely girlfriend, if it were just the two of you, isolated for hours on end with nothing to do?' asked Lieutenant Wrendigsya with a wicked glint in her eyes.

'How am I supposed to keep a straight face when I see them next?' he replied.

'The way you have every morning this week.' Wrendigsya said as she laughed. 'So, back to business. Keep your eyes open on the sonar, Subaltern. Switch the sensors to full gain. Its pitch black out there, and anything could have been washed into this water.'

'Yes Ma'am.'

Kilkennsya was pleased with how smoothly things were running now, although it had been a hectic night. She had spotted Pensioner Tabbernant at one point in the night, but she had no idea what one of the Heroes of the Winter Squad had been doing here when the new drainage protocols were being uploaded to the system. There was nothing for the exhausted technicians to do but wait for the new protocols to take effect.

'Why don't you go home Sir,' she said to her former nemesis, 'there is nothing you can do here now.'

'To wait for one of your new colleagues to try and arrest me,' replied Commander Dyscolnant. 'They won't get very far, I've been working under direct orders from the Tree Marshall herself. She sent me a message, thanking me for the work I had done. It also warned me about saboteurs like you.'

'Can I see that message, please?' Kilkennsya asked.

'No!' he replied childishly

. 'Oh for goodness sake. I can't arrest you, but I can do this,' she placed her IndesnCard on the comconsole and activated her Warrant. 'Now, show me.'

'Great Green Apples, that is a terrible fake,' she said. It was so blatantly obvious that the message was a forgery.

'What you mean, that is completely genuine,' said a shocked Commander Dyscolnant with unshakable certainty it was genuine.

'The idiot's right you know,' said Subaltern Armadahsya, 'that is a perfectly genuine message from the Tree Marshall.'

'Subaltern, you do not refer to your superior officer as an idiot whilst on duty,' Kilkensya said sternly. 'Even if he is one.'

'Yes, Ma'am. Sorry Ma'am,' said the embarrassed girl as she left the office.

Kilkennsya had a suspicion she knew what was going on here. That Subaltern had been one of Dyscolnant's biggest cheerleaders. Now she was calling him an idiot, to his face.

'Sergeant Darrylzant, can you come to Commander Dyscolnant's office please,' she transmitted over the PA system. If he can also see the same faults in the message that Armadahsya can not, I might be onto something. Especially as Captain Xandropant had heard the background noise on the background of the recording of the Regimental Song, which had arrived in the same digital envelope as the fake message from the Tree Marshal. Things were beginning to add up.

'Sergeant, do you know why the Captain was on sick-leave?'

'He had a polyp removed from his Thyroid Gland. Why do you ask?'

'So he now has the same enzyme deficieny as us?'

'I suppose so. Ah! I see where you are coming from.'

Kilkennsya busily typed a number into the comconsole.

'Great Tree protect us, look at that metadata,' she said as the screen was filled with an old anther's face. 'Jax, I've got something for you, in relation to the Puzzle. But I would watch it through an Omega Filter if I were you.'

Popisedsya was trying to get some sleep. The roof of the tractor garage was not a very good place to do this.

'Commander Popisedsya 100/97 Siylm, can you hear me Commander?' asked a voice over the radio.

Was she dreaming, Popisedsya could have sworn she had just heard Pemisegant's voice on the comlink. It had been dead for twenty-four hours. She wasn't really sure why Grandad Rex had insisted on bringing it up onto the roof with them. Surely additional food for the two of them, and the seventeen surviving sprites, would have been a better choice.

'Repeat, Commander Popisedsya 100/97 Siylm, can you hear me?'

'Pezzi is that you?' an amazed Popisedsya asked.

'Yes Poppy. We are currently twenty five minutes away from your location.'

'Oh thank you Pezzi, I was beginning to lose hope,' she said.'

'We'd be there sooner Poppy, but the conditions are too unstable for us to fly and this old crate can't travel on the surface of water, so we are making our way under it. Naturally this is unpredictable, which is slowing our progress.'

'Pezzi, your amazing,' said Popisedsya.

'Don't just thank me, I couldn't have done it without my family.' Pemisegant voice was full of pride.

'Your family? No, tell me when you get here.' So many questions and no time to ask them. What she had said in the Singing Frog must have proven to be spot on. Good for Pezzi.

'OK, Pemisegant out,' and the comlink fell silent again.

'Did you hear that, Grandad Rex?'

'Indeed I did Little Flower. Your impetuous young friend is riding to the rescue,' he replied.

There was another crack of thunder, that could mean only one thing.

'Let us hope, he arrives in time.'

'So what in the Tree's name is happening out there now?' asked Commander Yestarnsya.

'I suspect another inundation, Ma'am,' said Pemisegant. 'Hydrology are trying to drain the two levels above. Some of the overflow is heading our way.'

'How long before we arrive at your friend's farm?'

'ETA twenty minutes. Ma'am,' replied Lieutenant Wrendigsya. 'That is at maximum speed in these conditions.'

The rain had stopped as rapidly as it had started. Dawn was breaking, as the daylighters began to light up the sky.

Channelling the first light of Mother Sun as it hit the outside of the Tree. Popisedsya could just about make out a dark shape rising out of the water. To large to be a pysgod or any of the bizarre giant crustaceans that lived in the Central Channels and had been washed into the level by the flood water. Never the less, she drew her revolver, just to be on the safe side. Overnight she had lost a sprite to one of those creatures. She didn't want to lose any more.

A silver grey teardrop broke the surface next to her unlikely place of safety. A hatch on the top of the craft opened. Great Tree be praised, it was Pemisegant, he had come with his family to rescue what remained of hers. Standing next to him was the style she had met in the Singing Frog, what seemed like several lifetimes ago.

'Sorry we're late Poppy,' said her young friend.

'Better late than never Pezzi,' she replied. Then more formally she addressed the style, feeling as if all her HolyDays had come at once. 'Commander Yestarnsya, permission to come aboard.'

'Granted, Commander Popisedsya. That must be your grandfather, Pensioner Remixerant.'

'Indeed it is, Commander Yestarnsya. Do I also have your permission to come aboard and bring the sprites?' he asked.

'Indeed you do, Sir.'

With the formalities over, they all clambered aboard. An unpleasant gurgling noise, which increased its intensity with every passing minute, filled the air.

'I'm afraid we have to dive immediately Ma'am,' said Pemisegant, 'I have just received a report from Hydrology. Now you are safe, this level will have to be completely flooded before any of the other levels can be drained. We're hearing the sound of water pouring into this level.'

'But why?' asked Popisedsya. She could see from the hatch that her rooftop refuge was now completely submerged.

'This level is forming an air-lock Ma'am,' she could see that Pemisegant was back on duty. Well, they were not safe yet, there was still the return journey.

'Thank you Subaltern,' she turned to the other style in the cabin. 'Commander Yestarnsya, do you have some dry clothes I could change into?'

'Yes Commander Popisedsya, if you would like to follow me. Pensioner Remixerant, if you would go with Lieutenant Ryzinasant he has dry clothes for you.'

'Thank you Commander,' the old anther bowed politely as he replied.

'I'm afraid they will be undress greens,' said Lieutenant Ryzinasant.

'Oh well, its not as if I've never worn them before,' said the old man with a twinkle. 'Like meeting an old friend for a chat.'

'You see Little Flower, why I was right to take out that insurance against flooding,' said Grandad Rex smugly. It had been half an hour since they had be picked up. He and Popisedsya were in the galley, making themselves mugs of Instaht.

'Will they pay out, or will those crooks, who have quite happily been taking your premiums for years, will declare it an Act of the Spirit and refuse.' Popisedsya had no time for Insurance Companies, regarding them as little better than the Syndicates.

'They will have to. The High Council will force their hand. With twenty percent of the Tree's rice harvest lost, food prices are going to rise. Nobody likes paying more than they have to for food.'

'And how much legalised theft will I have to pay out?'

'You mean policy excess. I am not sure, it is in the policy documentation. Fortunately, that is stored in the bank at the Heartswood.'

'Yes, no-one else makes you pay twice for the same service?'

'But it keeps the premiums low, Little Flower, by reducing excessive false claims.'

'Rubbish. You don't buy a chair at a reduced price, and then pay the furniture shop for the first few minutes you use the chair to increase the working life of the chair. I would rather pay a fair premium and get all my money, when I make a fair claim.'

'I see your point. But it is a system that works.'

'Yes, for the benefit of the insurers.'

'Oh, not that old rant again Poppy,' said Pemisegant, who had just walked into the galley.

'You too have heard it many times, young Pezzi?' asked Remixerant.

'Yes, once a week, last Autumn and Winter.'

'I do not worry about the excesses and soon neither will you. The annual dividend from the shares the Farm holds in all of the leading three insurance companies, will chase your worries away.'

Pemisegant could not help laughing. Nor could Popisedsya.

She hugged the old anther. 'You old rogue. I love you so much.'

CHAPTER TWENTY SIX
HOME AND AWAY

Twenty minutes after entering the flooded transit shaft on their way back to Heartswood, there was a loud bang.

'Commander Yestarnsya Ma'am, we are losing power on main thrusters,' said a worried Lieutenant Wrendigsya over the comlink.

'Damn it...' was the reply from the Commander before the Comlink went dead.

'All three cylinders have died, Ma'am,' said Pemisegant 'and the internal comlink is recalibrating itself.'

'Subaltern, get down to the engines, see if you can find out what the problem is,' said Commander Popisedsya. 'I'll take your place in Navigation.'

'Yes Ma'am.'

He rushed down the length of the rescue vehicle. At the engine his two superiors were covered in engine fuel.

'Why ever did I let you persuade me into coming on this joy-ride?' asked Commander Yestarnsya? 'This heap of horse-feathers has thrown a hissy fit over the fuel in tank three,' she was pointing at the main engine block.

Maybe because you are loving every second of it, thought Pemisegant. The wild-haired amazon in dirty overalls was so far away from the well turned out pin and paper perfect Commander Yestarnsya he had first met.

'Report to the pilot that the engine will be back on line at reduced power in five minutes,' said Lieutenant Ryzinasant. 'Cylinder One is completely shot. Cylinder Two will be back up to eighty percent once it's cleaned and Cylinder Three can run at max. So she will only have sixty percent of normal power for the rest of the trip.'

'What about the boosters, Ma'am?' asked Pemisegant.

'What about them, our initial estimate of their utility was overly generous,' Commander Yestarnsya glumly replied.

'You mean it was a guess?'

'I'll pretend I didn't hear that, Subaltern,' she replied.

'I see you have been relieved as Navigator by Commander Popisedsya. In that case, once you've delivered that message, get some overalls on, and get back down here,' ordered Lieutenant Ryzinasant. 'You can help us work on the boosters. If we get them running, we may have an extra twenty percent power.'

It had all been going too well. Pemisegant had started to think that it was plain sailing back to Heartswood. Now they were likely to be flushed into the Central Channels at the next junction. Fortunately the crate could survive the pressure within that waterway. With so much extra traffic in the Central Channels, they would be picked up within an hour.

'Yes Sir,' he saluted the Lieutenant and returned to the cockpit.

Rescue Craft VK001 Alpha, do you copy?' asked the voice over the comlink. 'Repeat, this is Officer Corps One, do you copy?'

'Copy that, Officer Corps One,' replied Wrendigsya.

Officer Corps One was the call sign used exclusively by the vessel the Tree-Marshall was travelling in.

'VK001 Alpha, we are going to take you aboard, prepare to surrender control.'

'Copy that,' replied Wrendigsya, opening command channel four for you. You should be receiving our handshake code now.'

'Roger that, VK001 Alpha, you will be stowed in berth A3. You will be met by an Officer of the Watch and escorted to the Tree-Marshall's office. Officer Squad One, out!'

The internal comlink squawked back to life.

'Thank the Tree for that,' said Commander Yestarnsya down at the engines. There was almost a hint of disappointment in her voice. 'We don't have to worry about the manoeuvring thrusters to dock with Officer Corps One. They'll just suck us in with a grav-beam.'

'Yes, Ma'am,' replied Lieutenant Wrendigsya. 'As there is nothing more that we can do, permission to go and scrub up smart for the Tree-Marshall.'

'Roger to that Lieutenant. You, Commander Popisedsya and I will have first shout with the limited fascilities aboard.'

'That means we anthers will have thirty seconds each, as the styles will be in there for ages,' said Granddad Max.

'I heard that, old anther.' Popisedsya said, 'berthing this tub with Officer Corps One, will take at least two hours.'

'Exactly, leaving us anthers thirty seconds to get ready.'

Just under two hours and a half later, the hatch on VK000 finally opened, and the passengers and crew disembarked. The sprites lined up behind the officers. Everyone looked exhausted, but their uniforms were all parade ground perfect.

A style in overalls approached them.

'Good Morning, I am Subaltern Ralkzotsya, Third Assistant Officer of the Watch. Welcome aboard Officer Corps One.'

'Ralkzotsya? Lisha's Ralkzotsya? I thought you're a musician.'

'You must be Pemisegant,' the Subaltern replied, 'Yes, one and the same. Lisha's told me all about you. Normally I work as a pianist. However, in this crisis, I volunteered for emergency aid work. The Tree-Marshall and everyone aboard this vessel are off to Heartswood to help in the reconstruction of the flooded areas.'

'I see,' said Yestarnsya. 'So it was fortuitous this vessel was passing.'

'Not really, we have been following your effort with great interest. Lisha will be so pleased you are aboard.'

'She's here?' asked Pemisegant.

'Yes, all the Winter Squad have signed up for the relief effort. Adults and juveniles. Now that you and Commander Popisedsya are aboard we have a full house of Squaddies.'

'What, even General Myghcomant?' asked Pemisegant.

'Sure, the General is aboard, but he is stuck doing office work. He's an old sweety, isn't he?'

Pemisegant had never heard anyone describe his former boss like that before. He just didn't know what to say, so stayed silent.

As they progressed through the vessel, the group began to feel over-dressed, everyone was in work clothes.

'Here we are, the Tree-Marshall's Office. If you could wait here whilst I let them know.'

Nevamarsya stood in the Tree-Marshall's office waiting for the door to open and her darling Pemisegant to walk in.

She knew that the Tree-Marshall would want to talk to him and his new family first. She hated it, knowing how long the Tree-Marshall could spin out a ceremony, but she would have to wait.

'Well done to you,' said Tree-Marshall Pentwynsya, once the passenger and crew of the VK001 Alpha entered the room.

'I am impressed by your bravery, taking an old experimental vehicle on a mercy mission that could so easily have failed as spectacularly as it succeeded.'

'Thank you Ma'am,' said the striking style at the lead of the group. Was that the same Commander Yestarnsya, she had briefly met weeks previously when she had simply been Pemisegant's new boss? Half-Mother, she didn't seem like the same style.

'All the credit must go to my Half-Son here,' she said.

Yes, that was Pemisegant's new Half-Mother, which meant the younger of the two anthers was his future Father. It wasn't fair, he would have a beautiful Mother and a handsome Father when he was eventually adopted. Her Half-Mother was beautiful but remained steadfastly single, despite the best efforts of Captain Campbelant.

'Impetuous as ever, young Pemisegant,' she heard her mother-to-be saying.

'Yes Ma'am, sorry Ma'am,' the boy replied.

Nevamarsya cringed slightly. What was her Half-Mother going to say to her boyfriend. Was she still cross with him.

'Don't apologise. You have nothing to apologise for. All is forgiven, I suppose you will want to spend some time with my Half-Daughter after we have finished here.'

'Yes Ma'am.'

'I thought so.'

Nevamarsya stared at her mother. Oh thank you, she thought.

'Sometimes being impetuous is the only way to be.'

The look on Pemisegant's face was priceless. Nevamarsya wanted to laugh when her boyfriend realised old Tabbernant was in the room.

'Bernie, what are you doing here?' Pemisegant asked.

'Same as everyone else Pezzi my boy, helping with the

relief operation.' The old anther smiled. 'Anyway, I don't think Penny here has finished.'

'Thank you Pensioner Tabbernant.' The Tree Marshall turned to Granddad Max and Popisedsya. 'I am so sorry that you have lost so much in this crisis. Needless to say, the whole Officer Corps is mobilised to get your property, plus all the other damaged farms restored and back into production as quickly as possible.'

'Thank you Ma'am,' said Popisedsya, saluting.

'So, I will let you get some rest before we arrive at the Heartswood. I take it you will be joining in the relief effort?'

'Yes Ma'am?' they replied.

Pemisegant wanted to speak to Nevamarsya, but old Tabbernant was standing in the way.

'Pensioner Tabbernant, Sir,' he saluted the older anther.

'Hell boy, when was the last time you saluted me?'

'I'm in the Tree Marshall's Office, I'm doing things by the book,' the boy replied.

'To hell with the book. It never got me anywhere, did it Penny.'

'No Bernie, you were always a reckless spirit.'

Pemisegant felt his knees shake. He was in the presence of the most powerful person in the Tree, and Bernie was casually calling her Penny.

'Your solution to the crisis was ingenious Bernie,' she said to the old anther.

'The water had to go somewhere. Diverting it into that Fistula was the most logical thing to do.'

'Your name will be mud with your investors though, flooding one of the Eltravator shafts.'

'My name is always mud Penny, it's only the depth that varies.'

Pemisegant thought Tabbernant was taking this far too lightly.

'So Bernie, what aren't you telling us?' he asked.

'What's that supposed to mean, eh Pezzi?'

'Well, if you had to abandon that shaft, it would mean reboring its opposite shaft,' said Pemisegant, 'which would be a massive expense, larger than even you could bare.'

'You're not wrong son. Fortunately, the engineers were able to seal everything up, create a link between the flooded fistula and the Central Channels, then build special housing for the shaft, to keep it dry now that it is permanently surrounded by water,' said the old anther, then turning to the Tree-Marshall, 'pick your jaw off the floor Penny, it's making the place look untidy.'

'There has been talking about extending the Hydropone for decades. Nobody has ever agreed to having their home habitat flooded, even if they would gain hectares of valuable farmland.' The Tree-Marshall was amazed at Tabbernant's audacity.

'Well, now, nobody gets flooded out. And I get a shed load of prime real estate,' He winked at Pemisegant.

'How much more pain are you going to inflict on the Syndicates then?' asked a familiar voice. Dear sweet Tree thank you, thought Pemisegant when he saw his girlfriend.

'Four weeks in jail, accused of a crime they committed and an attempt on your life. I think another two dossiers should do it Girlie,' replied the old anther. 'Well, that's enough jaw flapping from me for one day. I need some shut-eye, and so do Pezzi and his friends.'

'My family and friends, Bernie.'

'And there was me thinking I had all the luck,' said the old anther with his usual twinkle.

Pemisegant had been sleeping on his feet. When Nevamarsya hugged and kissed him, he was wide awake again.

'You can't believe how glad I am to see you Pegs,' she said, using the special name that only she called him.

'The same here Marcy,' he replied using her special name.

'You must be Nevamarsya?' It was his future Mum, come to collect him no doubt.

'That's right Yestarnsya, she replied. 'He calls my mother-to-be Aunt Sharlee, 'how may I address you?'

'My Informal Name is Estar, but you can call me whatever you like dear,' Yestarnsya was smiling. 'Whatever you like.'

'Thank you, Aunt Estar. I'm Neva.'

Pemisegant could see the glow in his mother-to-be's eyes. Eyes as tired as his.

'So Son, time for bed,' said a familiar voice. There was no compromise in Yestarnsya's voice, 'Young Neva will still be here tomorrow.' Pemisegant could not argue, he was so tired.

'Are you sure about this Jakx?' asked Commissioner Lyndrevsya. 'It just seems like too much of a coincidence?'

'Sometimes in the end it all comes down to luck,' said the old anther. He was busy plugging an isolated storage device into a comconsole on the Commissioner's desk. 'When Kelsha confronted her former boss, she found a fake message from the Tree Marshall. She's a clever girl, she recognised the meta-data of the message. Knew it came from the same comconsole as the one Subaltern Symbzamsya tried to send her message from. She knew it was the key to unlock that message.'

'Are you telling me that you now know what was in the message,' she said, 'I had reluctantly consigned it to the junk pile?'

'Well, it's far from junk. It was an archive containing five separate files. Number One is a short file that explains the other files.

'Number Two is a dump of the memory unit attached to the comconsole. Chapter and verse on Sylvkohsya's conspiracy. She must have spent years setting this up.

'Number Three is the missing security video from the day young Symbzamsya was forced to make a cutting from the old Sprite-pod "S". It must have taken chutzpah to do that, when she knew her life was in danger.

'Which brings me to Number Four and Number Five. Four is a memory dump, in an ingenious proprietary file format I have only seen twice before. To be used in conjunction with Number Five, the location of a tissue sample that could be used to grow a brand new recently sprouted body, one to hold those memories encoded in Number Four and carry on her life from where it left off.'

The old anther had finished plugging the memory unit in.

'And here it all is,' said the Commissioner. 'Such a shame four and five are never going to be used. Full body cloning is illegal.'

This was going to be good. Tonight all the fruit cake extremist groups are going to rise up in rebellion. Then the specially orchestrated flooding of Hickville will add to the chaos. The Cocktail Waitress and the High Council will collapse under the pressure. I will ride to power at the head of an organisation that will become known as the Daughters of the Sun. The group's members all think they elected me to be their Supreme Leader.

The plebs will be too busy turning on the extremists. They will see the Daughters of the Sun as their salvation and beg them to form a stable new government. Well, they have no choice I have the Psycho-Modulator. The plebs will do anything I tell them, and thanks to my carefully orchestrated campaign against Empaths, there will be nobody to notice there is no free will any more. With the destruction of the Sacred Sisterhood and the Grand Order and the nationalisation of their wealth, my grab for power will be complete. The plebs will never realise their salvation is really their damnation. Neither will the Daughters of the Sun, they won't realise they are as much my slaves as the Plebs. I will be more than a Tree-Marshall. I will be a goddess.

Chief Inspector Sylvkohsya heard someone enter the room. There wasn't supposed to be anyone else in the building.

'I thought I ordered that I was not to be disturbed.'

'You did. But there is nobody to obey that order,' said a voice. 'You're not going to be in a position to give orders ever again.'

'Commissioner Lyndrevsya, to what do I owe this honour?'

'I've come to arrest you. I have a copy of your plans. A list of all the lunatic groups who were about to rise up in revolt.'

Damn it, why haven't my guards stopped her, Sylvkohsya thought, angry at her minion's failure. Still in a few minutes, she won't remember what she came here to arrest me for.

'I have no idea what you are talking about?'

'Oh drop the act. Your magic box of tricks won't work on me. I'm not nearly as open to suggestion as some of the people you have used it on. Years ago I was given an artificial block to the empathic field generated by a Psycho-Modulator.'

'Psycho-Modulators? If there were any left, they would be safely under lock and key in the R&D Regiment's Archive.'

'I was so annoyed when R&D decided to fill the vacancy for Head of Security at their Regimental HQ with one of their own officers. However, it turned out to be a blessing. Your successor at R&D, Lieutenant Ryzinasant reported the missing Psycho-Modulator prototype within hours of taking over. One of the first things his security audit turned up.

'When we unscrambled Subaltern Symbzamsya final message everything fell into place. We know everything about your megalomaniacal plan. It would be a lot easier if you just admitted it. Daughters of the Sun. Honestly, where did you trawl that stupid name from.'

'It was then she realised all was lost. Only her most loyal lieutenants knew the organisation's true name,' said Lyndrevsya to her sister. 'I suppose her cast iron certainty the thing that really got to me. So completely unbending.'

They had agreed to meet up in a neutral location. The press conference after the arrest of Sylvkohsya had nearly derailed this meeting.

'Like the way Dad was so certain about you remaining as an anther. Well, I can see now he was wrong. You are so much happier as a style,' said Yestarnsya, who had recognised a perfect opportunity to move the conversation on. 'I'm sorry I treated you so badly, Sister of Mine.'

'Do you know how many years I have been waiting to hear you to say that. It's a bit of an anticlimax now. But I still accept your apology. I also apologise for the way I have behaved towards you.'

The two sisters hugged.

'So, your getting married. When do I get to meet him?'

'How do you know I'm pair-bonding with an anther. I might be a moonchild and marrying another style.' Yestarnsya frowned, 'you haven't been using your position to spy on me, have you?'

'No Estar dear. I would never do that.'

'There I go, speaking without engaging my brain. Sorry Lyndrevsya.'

'It's OK, most people think I am all seeing,' she laughed and the awkward moment passed. 'And please, call me Lilly, it's my Familiar Name now.'

'Thank you. I didn't know how you would react to Lynno?'

'Nobody has called me that for years,' replied Lyndrevsya. 'We had good times when we were younger, didn't we Estah?'

'Yes Lilly, we did.' Yestarnsya had a tear running down her cheek. 'We can again, starting with my Pair-bonding with Ryzinasant. He's in a similar line of work as you. He's the security chief at R&D's Regimental HQ.'

'Ricky, your marrying Ricky. He's gorgeous.'

'Are you jealous Lilly?'

'Enough about me. I want all the details about you and Ricky.'

CHAPTER TWENTY SEVEN
HUSBAND AND WIFE

Natalicsya had recommended her to the lady getting married, so Nostromsya had been signed out of her usual accademy for a week, to take part in a pair-bonding ceremony. Nostromsya didn't know who was getting married. Who needed the services of a newly differentiated style to play the role of the Wide Eyed Innocent in the Bonding Ceremony. She didn't really care either, and had only volunteering to get away from Roots Academy Gamma 5. Away from her Mentor, who had made her new life such a misery.

The time spent in hiding, as a sprite down in the Roots, had delayed her activation. So had the wait before she could to give evidence against Lieutenant Dayvaiyant. People only saw the cosmetic effect on her hair and eyes, so she had strawberry blond hair and turquoise eyes. Internally, she suffered from dyslexia and was slightly autistic.

Commander Sharlensya, the temporary mentor, had set up a classsroom. Nostromsya and the four other girls attending pair-bondings in the Crown that week were not missing out on their education. It had been so different from the lessons she was used to. Commander Sharlensya had not mocked, she helped Nostromsya cope with her problems so much, she did not want to go back to her normal academy.

'Please Ma'am,' she asked Sharlensya after the end of that mornings lessons. 'Can I please go to your academy when we return to the Roots?'

'Sorry, little one, I don't teach in the Roots. I have another job there. I only mentor in the Canopy in the Winter now.'

'But I don't understand Mathematics with my normal mentor.' She didn't understand many things with her usual mentor. 'He thinks I'm stupid because I can't read properly.'

The tears started, so Sharlensya wrapped her arms around the weeping child.

'Have you never been tested for Dyslexia?'

'No Ma'am, my Mentor says that it does not exist, nor Dyspraxia and Dyscalclia, he says they are just an excuse for thick kids like me.'

'Nostromsya, you are not thick. How dare he say so.'

'Thick and Female, the two worse things in the Tree, is what he regularly says.'

'What is his name?'

'Lieutenant Jochfinant 101/55 Floam.'

Sharlensya knew all about the imfamous Doctor Jock.

'How the hell did you end up in a dump like Roots Academy Gamma 5?' she asked,

'It was the only place left when I finally activated,' the youngster replied.

'Who told you that?' asked Sharlensya who was becoming increasingly angry.

'The style officer with blonde hair in a funny bun. She said I should be grateful after all the lies I had told about Lieutenant Dayvaiyant. But I didn't lie.'

That was it, the final straw.

'Right, there is someone I want you to talk to, dear, right now.'

She quickly shepherded the girl out of the makeshift classroom and into a small office. She phoned a friend from the Comconsole.

'Sharlee, nice to see you. Enjoying yourself on the way to that pair-bonding?' asked the Anther at the other end of the link.

'Yes thank you, Rafe,' she said.

'You don't look very happy,' Rafe said. 'Anything wrong up there?'

'Not up here Rafe, its down there the problem lies. You remember our last conversation, in the Council House?'

'Yes, your first day on the High Council Education Committee,' he said whistfully. 'The day you became my boss, Matriarch.'

'That's the one,' she said to her old boss. She brought Nostromsya into the field of the comlinkcam. 'I want you to listen to this.'

'OK.' Rafevivant recognised the child immediately. 'Hello Nostromsya. I've been trying to speak with you for a number of weeks now.'

'Norah dear, this is Captain Rafevivant, I want you to give him your name and IndesnCode. Then tell him exactly what you told me about your Mentor.'

'But my Mentor said I was never to speak to that anther. That he would kill me if I did.'

'Your Mentor threatened you?' asked a horrified Sharlensya.

'Yes, he said 'Nostromsya 251/07, if I ever find out you have spoken to Captain Rafevivant or any of his mob, I would not live to see another day.'

'Do you believe him?' aked Captain Rafevivant.

'Yes Sir,' the child answered and she started telling the two adults about everything she had seen during her time at Roots Academy Gamma 5.

'Nostromsya, this all checks out. Thank you. When you return to your Academy you will have a new Mentor and things will change,' said the Captain.

Sharlensya had switched back into uniform whilst the child had been talking. She saluted signifying she was no longer acting as Matriarch but was once again in the normal chain of command.

'Commander Sharlensya,' the Captain said as he saluted in response. 'I understand you have duties elsewhere this Tour which prevent you taking over at that Academy full time but you could be part of the staff on a part time basis?'

'Yes Sir,' Sharlensya replied, 'I can arrange that. Also I suggest the pupils be relocated.'

'I would like to Commander, but I have nowhere else to put the twenty eight kids at that academy.'

'Sir, the Red Wing at Fangkart House is currently not in use. Within the precincts of that building, my word is law. I'm going to order its staff to do everything in their power to assist you set up Red Wing as an Academy. Moving the cadet quarters there immediately is possible. It would take a week before anyone could begin mentoring them there. I don't think a weeks holiday would do them any harm.'

'Seriously, you have the power to do that?'

'Yes Rafe, she is a Matriarch, even if she is currently pretending she's still an ordinary Mentor. So yes, she does have the power. And she has a rich old friend with the cash to foot the bills.' Tabbernant had walked into the office. 'Sorry to barge in, but Pastor Rumsfelant wants to speak to that little one about her role in the up-coming ceremony. Couldn't help overhearing everything. I've also got a pretty good horsewhip for that so-called Mentor.'

'Absolutely bloody brilliant, well not the horsewhip bit. I've been waiting for years for an opportunity like this. I'd better set the wheels in motion. Thank you Sharlee, and you to Bernie.'

'We heard all that Mammy,' said Serynazsya. The two sisters

had followed Tabbernant.

'You realise if you are serious about starting a new academy, you won't be able to Mentor for the Winter Squad. You'll have to stay down in the Roots until it is properly established.'

'Good job I have already drawn up plans for a proper academy in the Crown for Canopy born officers, instead of shipping them down to third rate dumps in the Roots. Fangkart House is the new Academy's temporary home. Onwards and upwards.'

'The day has finally dawned,' Kanonypsya said. 'I can't really believe it. Today I finally pair-bond with my beloved.'

'You're so excited,' said Nevamarsya. As Primary Bondsmaid she was responsible for making sure the Bride was fully prepared for the ceremony.

'I am dear. For eight years this day was a dream stolen from me by the Great Ignorance, and then buried by my own stupidity for a further twelve miserable years.'

Kanonypsya's last night as a single style had been a restless one. Now she faced one last worry, wondering what dreadful outfit the girls had found for her. By tradition, the Bride arrived at Sacred Salon to be dressed in her nuptial finery wearing her oldest, tattiest most disreputable clothes, whose patterns had deteriorated so badly, not even the magic of emprintable fabric could restore them. The problem was, she didn't have any old clothes. During her two decades in the Convent, she had accessed the communal clothing store and the outfit had never varied, it had always been a Tree-Nun's Habit. So Nevamarsya and Natalicsya had raided their respective half-mother's wardrobes to find something for her to wear. Until the half-mothers had found out, and forbid Natalicsya from choosing, on the grounds that she could not put together an awful outfit, even if her life depended on it. All her choices still looked fabulous.

During a singing lesson Nevamarsya remembered the store room of clothes abandoned by styles upon joining the Sisterhood. It had been her wardrobe during her stay at the Convent that Spring. She was once again handed the key to the storeroom and told to help herself. Nevamarsya was glad her friend Natalicsya was not with her, as she was certain some of the outfits in that room whould give the other girl nightmares for weeks.

'Ready, Aunty Kandy?' asked Nevamarsya.

'As I'll ever be,' she replied to the girl. 'Great green apples, that's your grandmother's camera?'

'Yes, I've taken up photography. Mammy was so pleased. Everyone uses digicams on their comlinks these days.'

So, thought Kanonypsya, with any luck the photographs of me in this dreadful outfit will be blurred, shakey and unusable.

'Oh well, on with the Motley,' she said with a resigned air. And it was a motley collection of garments. She picked up one item 'Neva dear, this bra is like the Roots Rangers, no cups and very little support.'

'It's only temporary. Once you're in the Salon, you will be pampered and preened by experts, and you will emerge wearing that gorgeous dress.

'You won't look so bad yourself, I know you like lilac.'

'I like wearing corsets,' she replied.

'You know, when I first met you, that was something I never thought I would hear you say,' said Kanonypsya, fighting a fit of the giggle.

'I know, I was an idiot back then.'

'But, seriously Neva? A fully boned and laced corset?' asked the astonished older style.

'Yes Aunty Kandy. I can get my waist down to eighteen fractions.'

'And you can still breath?' Kanonypsya was flabbergasted.

'Oh yes. Lisha gets so jealous.'

'I had to wear one under my habit. The Tree knows why? Those tunics hide any natural curves, so augmenting them seemed so pointless.'

'Its armour, Aunt Kandy. The corsetry protect your heart, liver, stomach and any of the other major soft items in that part of the body. Also, your corset would have had a prayer embroidered into it. Didn't you know that?'

'Really, no I didn't. Even after two decades, there is still a lot about my former life I never knew or really understood. Just goes to show I should never have been a Tree-Nun in the first place. The truly devoted know it all inside...' Kanonypsya didn't finish the sentence. The emprinter had cycled again and something awful in the mirror had grabbed her attention. 'No, I am not wearing this, not even if it is only temporary.'

She was wearing a bib and braces dungarees with red and white stripes. It was accompanied with a red blouse and stripy head scarf.

'I'm supposed to look dowdy, not like a clown.'

Click went the camera.

'Relax, I just packed that as a joke. I wanted to see your face, and photograph it.'

'Oh, thank you very much,' she said as the emprinter cycled for a final time.

As Kanonypsya and Nevamarsya approached the Sacred Salon, they were greeted by the other members of the Bride's Party.

Natalicsya, Sharlensya and young Nostromsya. The entrance to the building was barred by Commander Mevagissya an Offeiriad Priestess ready to perform the first section of the Pair Bonding Ceremony. She would be jointly officiating at the main ceremony later that day with Colonel Rumsfelant.

'Sisters, we are gathered her to prepare for the Ceremony of Pair Bonding' she said in a sonorous voice. 'Who in this party is to be our Bride?'

'Blessed Lady, I Kanonypsya of the Family Rust wish to enter this sacred portal to prepare for my Pair Bonding to Keltonnant of the Family Fangkart.'

'Tell me, Kanonypsya of the Family Rust, do you come here of your own free will?'

'I do,' she replied solemnly.

'Do you love the son of the Tree you wish to pair-bond with?'

'With all my Heart and Soul.'

'Who is your protector in this venture?'

'Sharlensya of the Family Fangkart, niece of my beloved.'

The Offeiriad turned to Sharlensya.

'Sharlensya of the Family Fangkart, do you swear upon your honour to guard Kanonypsya of the Family Rust and guarantee her safe arrival at the Temple.'

'Blessed Lady, I, Sharlensya of the Family Fangkart swear upon my honour to guard Kanonypsya of the Family Rust and guarantee her safe arrival at the Temple.'

Turning back to Kanonypsya, the Offeiriad asked, 'Who assists you in this happiest of days?'

'Blessed Lady, my Bondsmaids are Nevamarsya, Cadet Member of Family Fangkart, daughter-to-be of my Guard of Honour. Also Natalicsya, Cadet Member of the Family Rust, friend of Guard of Honour, Bondsmaid and myself. Finally Nostromsya, a wide-eyed innocent.'

'Bondsmaids, I entreat you to serve your mistress well.'

'Thank you Blessed Lady,' replied the three girls.

'Now, let us prepare for the feast.'

The doors of the building swung open and the six styles entered. When they emerged an hour later, in their finery, they were barely recognisable from the scruffy rabble that had entered.

The Offeiriad Priestess led the way, in her full ceremonial robes, carrying her golden sceptre, the symbol of her authority. Then came Kanonypsya, in the beautiful white wedding dress she had first seen as a cadet three decades earlier. Then came Nostromsya, holding the train of the dress, slightly over-awed by the event. Either side of her were Nevamarsya and Natalicsya carrying censers filling the air with the sweet smell of burning incense. All three girls were wearing pretty lilac dresses, the older two, like the Bride, were laced in as tightly as they could bear.

Finally came Sharlensya, the honour guard dressed in the dove grey version of the ultra formal dress uniform, worn at all Sunday Temple Parades, but today only by herself and most of the members of the Groom's party. Her hair looped and piled onto her head. At her waist hung a Bastard Sword, which earned its name not because of its length, but because it had the words "get lost creep" elegantly engraved along the length of its wicked sharp blade. Anyone who knew the mild mannered school teacher would be surprised that such a radical reformist could be at home carrying such a weapon. But only if they forgot that they lived a martial society.

Each of the five fully grown styles in the procession were carrying items that could be used as very pretty and utterly deadly weapons. Censers could be used as flails, sceptre as a bludgeon and of course Sharlensya's bastard sword. Not forgetting that as part of their daily devotions, Tree-Nuns practiced a form of Tai Chi with the daggers they carried on their belts. So if threatened Kanonypsya could and quite happily would fillet anyone who tried to stop her wedding with her ivory and silver filigree handled daggers she was wearing in her garters.

Keltonnant woke with a head like an angry bear. Had it really been necessary to drink so much oal the night before? Or wear the orange suit with arrow and the ball and chain attached to his right leg. He spent all night carrying the ball.

His hangover was made bearable only by the knowledge that everyone else in the lodge would be suffering to an equal degree.

The breakfast gong sounded. Did it have to be so loud, and four groggy anthers made their way down to the kitchen.

Dawn was breaking in the world beyond the Tree, so the daylighters were beginning to glow and the Crown was filled with a grey light. Almost as grey as the skin of the Groom's party.

'Tuck in Kelly, your last meal as a free anther,' said Tabbernant.

'A state you have only ever known, old friend.'

'Miaow, saucer of milk for table number two,' said the old anther. 'Not through want of trying, you know. I have been days away from this wedding breakfast on several occasions.'

'Sorry old friend. Call it pre-nuptual nerves.'

'No offence taken,' he spotted his nephew at the table. 'Morning Myke, how are you?'

'Passable,' Myghcomant replied. 'You know, even if I wasn't still on those damn pain-killers, I would still be the only sober person in this room.'

'Somebody has to keep their wits about them. Guard of Honour and all that,' said Tabbernant.

The General laughed.

'Look who has just surfaced. Top of the morning to you young Pezzi.' Myghcomant greeted the new arrival.

'And the rest of the day to yourself, Sir,' whispered Pemisegant hoarsely, whilst silently cursing the older anther for talking so loudly.

'Pezzi. You're awake?' said Tabbernant.

'Yes, and from this day forward I am exclusively a cha drinker,' he replied.

'That won't last my boy,' said the General with a chuckle.

After breakfast, they all returned to their rooms in the lodge and dressed wedding day outfits. Serving Officers in their grey uniforms and Pensioner Tabbernant in a grey morning suit with top hat.

On their return to the main hall, where they were greeted by Brigadier Rumsfelant, in his full regalia as Offeiriad Priest.

'Morning Lads,' he said trying to sound casual, as he spoke the lines of a script as old as the Tree itself.

'Morning Pastor,' they chorused, all instantly regretting it.

'Right, which one of you is getting spliced?' asked the Pastor.

'As if you didn't know,' said Tabbernant rebelliously.

'It's in the script Bernie,' Rumsfelant hissed under his breath.

'Pastor, I, Keltonnant of the Family Fangkart' said a very nervous Groom. Though there could be no mistake, his uniform as white as his bride's dress.

'So, do you love her?' continued the Pastor.

'Yes,' said Keltonnant 'I love Kanonypsya of the Family Rust more than life itself.'

'Are you sure, it's not to late to do a runner.'

Which was Myghcomant's cue to remove half his sword from its sheath.

'Put that away son, you could have someone's eye out with that,' said Pastor Rumsfelant. He hated this part of the ceremony, the faux joviality in his opinion had no place in a religious service.

The sword returned to its resting place.

'Right, so you're here to make sure he gets to the Temple on time. So who are your assistants?'

'Here Pastor,' said Althallant and Pemisegant.

'Tree protect the Groom from his friends,' said Rumsfelant, turning to Tabbernant. 'And are you the Ancient Wise One?'

'Charming,' said Tabbernant.

'Bernie, please, I've got to stick to this stupid script. And so will you!'

'Yes, I am the Ancient Wise One,' and Tabbernant bowed with an exaggerated flourish.

'Right lads, we have a wedding to go to.'

The Bride's party approached the Temple from one side, the Groom's party from the other. Unlike the styles, with their pretty pseudo-weapons, all the anthers were carrying shorts swords and parrying daggers.

'Brother's and Sisters, we are entering a place of Peace. Please leave all weapons here,' said the Offeiriad Guardian of the Temple.

The Guardian's assistants gathered all real and potential weapons from everyone before allowing the Bride with her Wide Eyed Innocent and the Groom with his Ancient Wise One entered the Temple. The merged party formed the inner circle. The rest of the happy couple's family and friends arranged themselves in concentric rings around the Temple and began singing the first hymn.

'Who come to pair bond?' asked Pastor Mevagissya.

'I, Kanonypsya of the Family Rust.'

'And I, Keltonnant of the Family Fangkart.'

'I ask now, are there any with valid objections to this couple bonding for life?' asked Rumsfelant.

'If so, speak now or forever hold your piece?' asked Mevagissya.

'We can't they're peace bonded with the Offeiriad,' whispered Tabbernant.

When no serious objections were heard, the couple turned to face each other.

'I, Kanonypsya take you to be my pair-bond for life.'

'I, Keltonnant take you to be my pair-bond for life.'

Mevagissya took a silken rope and tied it around one of the happy couples wrists. Rumsfelant took a fine gold chain and did likewise to the other pair of wrists.

'We now call upon the Prime Bondsmaid to sing the Song of Supplication. Asking the Spirit of the Tree to bless this union.'

Nevamarsya had been practising this for weeks with Sister Matyfilsya. As she approached the most acoustically perfect place in the Crown, Nevamarsya could feel a wave of dread emanating from those who remembered her old singing voice. Boy, were they in for a surprise.

Far below, in a side chapel in the Convent's Central Basilica, eight Tree-Nuns began singing the acappella accompaniment to Nevamarsya's song. It travelled through the Tree-Nuns' network and blended perfectly with Nevamarsya's pitch perfect performance in the Temple. For the penultimate verse, the deep Bass male voice of the Spirit of the Tree joined into the mix. Then there was silence and Nevamarsya sang the final verse alone. She was so relieved when she finished, and was quite overwhelmed by the cheering and clapping and waves of support from the congregation.

'Prime Bondsmaker,' intoned the two Offeriad once the temple had calmed down, 'the Couple have bonded themselves with love and respect, far stronger than rope or chain. That bond has been blessed by our Lord, the Spirit of the Tree. Sever these false ties and place the Bonding Rings on their fingers, so they can start their new lives as equal partners in a truly unbreakable union.

Pemisegant picked up a pair of ceremonial scissors and cut the silk and gold with one cut. Replaced the scissors and after giving the couple their rings returned to his place outside the Temple.

'What the Spirit Tree has brought together, let no one put asunder,' the Offeiriad said in unison. 'You may kiss.'

Young Nostromsya had watched the ceremonial goings on with delight. Now she was enjoying the party afterwards. Although there was something missing.

'Nostromsya dear, there are some people looking for you,' said Sharlensya.

'For me, who could possibly be looking for me?' Then she spotted the couple. She had never seen them out of uniform before, but it was definitely Captain Raddconsya and her husband Captain Jomlirdant.

'We were so worried about you Nostromsya,' said Raddconsya. 'When you failed to turn up for Officer Training I was so upset.'

'Yes,' said Jomlirdant, 'she nearly took off down to the Roots to look for you personally.'

'But I'm safe now,' she said happily.

'If you had come to see us dear, instead of haring of to points unknown, you would have been safer for longer.' There was a slight scolding tone in Raddconsya's voice. This didn't stop her from gathering the child up and giving her a hug. 'Don't ever frighten us like that again young lady.'

'No Mum, I won't.' Where had that come from.

'I have been speaking to Commander Sharlensya. She has been telling us about the terrible time you have had at that Academy. How alone you have been. We'll make sure you are never alone again.'

Nostromsya was suddenly overwhelmed by how much she had missed these two adults. Her mother and father.

S ideways in space and time, an old man was carrying a baby towards a fine looking apple-tree. Harold Spenser was taking his new granddaughter, Isabella, to see his tree for the first time.

'You and your blessed Tree,' said his daughter Maria 'I sometimes think you love it like one of your children.'

'Maybe not such a bad thing. Its gorgeous, I hope young Izzy will love it as much as I do already,' her partner Frances said.

'Welcome to the family, Frances,' said Harold Fraser. 'If that doesn't make you one of us, nothing does.'

At that moment baby Isabella touched the the Tree her namesake ancestor had planted and began giggling.

On a world called Arbouron, the facet of the life force of the Apple Tree was so pleased he started singing. Everyone in the Tree on Arbouron heard the song, but sideways in time, for the first time, Harold Spenser in his garden outside Penarth heard it. His wife Esme told him she heard the tree singing all the time. Until now he had dismissed this, she had been a Hippy in her youth and still believed all sorts of nonsense. Not today. Today he heard the deep baritone and his normally cynical heart was filled with happiness. Throughout the multiple Universes, for today at least, life was good.

Explanatory Notes

Ranks and Regiments

The people who live in the Tree know their primary function is to defend the Tree. As the tree grew, it had become more complex. and the inhabitants had other jobs, to do when the Tree is not in danger. The military nature of society was arranged so the inhabitants can be mobilised at the drop of a hat. Everyone is an Officer and all professions belong to one of the thirty Regiments. Everyone has a rank and wears a uninform at work when they are officially on duty. Practically though, the ranks are now simply positions on the pay scale.

Juveniles have two ranks, Cadet and Ensign. As they are the legal responsibility of their parents, their wages are little more than pocket money. Adults have ten ranks, from lowly Subaltern to all powerful Tree Marshall. Thirty Five years old is the standard retirement age for all officers. An officer who reaches that age gains the rank of Pensioner.

Ranks	(Pay grade: Title)
J1:	Officer Cadet
J2:	Ensign
O1:	Subaltern
O2:	Lieutenant
O3:	Commander
O4:	Captain
O5:	Major
O6:	Colonel
O7:	Brigadier
O8:	General
O9:	Vice Marshal
O10:	Tree Marshall of the Tree of Life
P1:	Pensioner

NAMES

Inhabitants of the Tree start life as sprites, identified by an unique IndesnCode. On becoming a Cadet they gain a Root-name. This consists of two elements. The first element begins with the first letter of the IndesnCode, which corresponds with the Sprite-pod they grew in and is four letters long. The second element is three letters long, the first being the other letter in their IndesnCode. For example SN became the root-name Serynaz.

Root-names cannot be used by two officers at the same time. This is to guarentee that there is never any confusion about who did what and when.
Pure-Stock Style officers from the Roots all emerged from Sprite-pod S and all have names starting with S. Likewise, Pure-Stock Anther officers from the Roots have names starting with D as they are all products of Sprite-pod D.

When a Cadet becomes either Style or Anther the Root-name gains a gender suffix creating their Formal-Name. The suffix is either A-N-T for an Anther or S-Y-A for a Style. For Anthers the stress in pronouncing the Formal-Name is on the first element of the Root-Name, for Styles, the emphasis is on the second element and the suffix is usually pronounced She-ya.

When adopted, a juvenile officer gains a Family-name to add to their Formal Name. In many cases this Family-name is also used by officer children who have been legally accepted for adoption, but who have not gone through the process.

Pair-bonded officers may add their partner's Family-name to their own with a hyphen.

When on duty, an officer is formally refered to by Rank, Formal-Name and IndesnCode and Family or by Rank and Formal-name and Family-name. For instance Commander Sharlensya 120/15 Fangkart or Commander Sharlensya.

When off-duty, an officer is formally refered to by Root-name and suffix only. Officers may be addressed by an Informal name by family and friends. However, addressing someone with an Informal name without permission is very bad manners.

Finally, romantically attached officers use Romantic names to refer to one another which can only be used by the individuals in question.

Formal-Names and how to pronounce them (Stress on the BLOCK CAPITALS)

Althallant	-	ALTH all ant
Annaprysya	-	annar PRYEE shah
Campbelant	-	CAM bell ant
Crysgoxant	-	CREAZ gocks ant
Gaemlovant	-	GAYM loaf ant
Galeroysya	-	gayl ROY shah
Hanazofsya	-	harroz OFF seeyah
Jaxspriant	-	JAKS pree eeant
Kanonypsya	-	kanon IPP shah
Kilkennsya	-	kill KEN seeyah
Myghcomant	-	MY comm ant
Natalicsya	-	nattal EESH shah
Nevamarsya	-	nayvah MAR-sheeyah
Pemisigant	-	PEMMIZ agg ant
Popisedsya	-	popee SED shah
Remixerant	-	REEM ickzer ant
Rollinant	-	ROWL een ant
Rumsfelant	-	RWMS fell ant
Samnundsya	-	sam NOOND shah
Serynazsya	-	sair INNARR see-yah
Sharlensya	-	shar LENN see-yah
Untrugyant	-	UN trewgy ant
Tabbernant	-	TABB air nant
Voynvarant	-	VOYN var ant
Voynvalsya	-	voyn VAL shah
Xandropant	-	ZHAND rope ant
Roseteesya	-	rose TEA shah
Yestarnsya	-	yes TARNS shah

DATES AND TIME

The year in the Tree is split into thirteen months of twenty eight days. This leaves one day left over, which is regarded as a HolyDay celebrated at the start of each new year, on the Winter Solstice. For administrative purposes the year is split into two Tours of Duty, Light Half (Quadtemp to Noftemp) and Dark Half (Dixtemp to Rydtemp). For religious purposes the year is divided into the four Solar Seasons of Spring, Summer, Autumn (or Fall in the Canopy) and Winter, which are tied to the Solstices and Equinox.

As the year is actually 365.25 days long, every fourth year has an extra HolyDay called the LeapDay.

The thirteen months plus HolyDay are:

Iantemp	22nd December - 18th January
Bystemp	19th January - 15th February
Rydtemp	16th February - 15th March
Quadtemp	16th March - 12th April
Pentemp	13th April - 11th May
Hextemp	12th May - 7th June
Septemp	8th June - 5th July
Octemp	6th July - 2nd August
Noftemp	3rd August - 30th August
Dixtemp	31st August - 27th September
Elfsemp	28th September - 24th September
Colsemp	25th October - 22nd November
Trisksemp.	23rd November - 20th December
HolyDay	21st December

Each month is sub divided into four week:

Alfa	Bayta	Camma	Delta

Each Week is subdivided into seven days:

Monesday	Duosday	Trenitsday (Trenzday)
Fursday	Fyfesday	Saxurthsday (Saturday)
Sunday		

The date can either be written using the full names of the day, week and month in question, for example Fursday Camma of Bystemp of year 184 After the Graft.
It can also be represented by an alpha-numeric code, so the same day could be expressed as 4-C-02/184.
The HolyDay is either written as HolyDay of Year 184 After the Graft or 0-H-0/184
Leap days are refered to as LeapDay of 184 or 0-L-0/184

Each day is divided into twenty-four hours, each hour consisting of sixty minutes. Time is written hour-number eg 2359, 1418 or 0630

Each day is also divided into four six hour watches?
Dawnwards (midnight to 0559)
Morning (0600 to 1159)
Afternoon (1200 to 1759
Evening/Night (1800-2359)

WEIGHTS AND MEASURES

When all officers were identical, they all wore the same sized shoes, one Unit long. This was the basis of Identrical Measurements with Units subdivided into ten fractions.
All weights in the Tree are measured in Pounds and Ounces. A Pound is based on the weight of one square unit of water. An Ounce is one twentieth of a Pound. The volume of one square Unit is a Pint, which is sub-divided into twenty Fluid Ounces.
The arrival of individuality meant that an officer's foot was no longer a standard length. The uniform height of sprites formed the base of Metriccant Measures used by scientists and engineers. A Metron is divided into one hundred Centrons. A Centron is subdivided into ten millimetrons. Weights are measured in Kilograms and Grams. Volumes in Litrons.

ACKNOWLEDGEMENTS

Is it really four years since I first started writing about the existential apple tree and all its inhabitants? Yes, and over two years since the rest of the World was introduced to Arbouron, with the publication of Winter Squad.

First of all, I would not have been able to write at all without the support of my family. My Mother, Patricia Rees has read this story almost as many times as I have. My Sisters, Janet Guy and Carolyn Davies, their husbands Andy and Gary and my neice Martha Patricia Davies and nephews William Rhys Davies, James Doherty and James Guy.

Thanks are extended to Lynda Carter and Timothy Farr who also proof-read the manuscript and asked the questions that needed to be answered to aid the flow of the narrative.

I would also like to thank my other colleagues at Treorchy Library, past and present.

I know that this is not as comprehensive a list as I would like. If I have missed you out, I apologise, but thank you none the less.

John Campbell Rees,
29th February, 2016.

9 780957 644465